CATALYST

CATALYST

—

PHILIP CORNFORD

BANTAM BOOKS

NEW YORK • TORONTO • LONDON • SYDNEY • AUCKLAND

CATALYST

A Bantam Book / August 1991

Library of Congress Cataloging-in-Publication Data

Cornford, Philip.
    Catalyst / Philip Cornford.
      p. cm.
    ISBN 0-553-07122-X (hardcover)
    I. Title.
    PR9619.3.C587C38   1991
    823—dc20   90-24116
                                   CIP

Bantam Books are published by Bantam Books, a division
of Bantam Doubleday Dell Publishing Group, Inc. Its
trademark, consisting of the words "Bantam Books" and
the portrayal of a rooster, is Registered in U.S. Patent and
Trademark Office and in other countries. Marca Regis-
trada. Bantam Books, 666 Fifth Avenue, New York, New
York 10103.

PRINTED IN THE UNITED STATES OF AMERICA

BVG   0 9 8 7 6 5 4 3 2 1

To all who question

PART I

—

MOSCOW

1.

"You're the first," Control said.

He could not see his companion's face, just the outline of his body. There was no moon, no stars. The forest loomed hard against them, its shadows as impenetrable as any physical barrier. It was a lonely place for a farewell.

"They told me," Gerald replied. Now that the moment had come, he was extraordinarily calm.

They never lied; it was a great honor to be trusted, to be accepted as part of them. They told you the hard truth, believing in you.

"Are you afraid?" Control asked, not in anxiety but out of sympathy and curiosity. They were brothers, these two. Not by blood but by choice, of a brotherhood. They did not know each other except by false names, Control and Gerald; yet there was no sense of falsity in this farewell. They had met only once before, shortly after Gerald's arrival in Moscow; everything was painstakingly planned to ensure they would leave no trace of coming together. They were absolute strangers and yet they understood each other as well as human beings can.

"Yes. But I can do it," Gerald replied, in a voice younger and stronger than his years. They had taught him how to overcome frailty. They had shown him how to be unafraid. His gratitude was overwhelming.

3

"Tell me," Control asked. "What were you before?"

He knew. In fact, they knew everything that could be known about Gerald. In the long preparation that had led to this parting, Gerald had surrendered all his secrets, and in so doing he had lost all his fears. But asking was part of the ritual.

"A nuclear physicist," Gerald said, laughing softly in the dark.

Control gravely embraced him and went away, leaving him alone in the night, in the midst of the forest.

Gerald walked down the road. If the guards had been alerted they would come quickly, sure of their strength, arrogant with authority long unchallenged. The only weapon Gerald carried was zipped inside a weatherproof bag, but he made no move to prepare it. If he was discovered, he would not fight. Success depended entirely on his remaining undetected. If he was seen, his mission became impossible to accomplish, and so did escape. Killing a few soldiers would only be a waste of lives.

If they found him he would kill himself.

He wished it would snow so that once more he would feel the flakes brushing softly against his face. To feel clean and at peace was a great gift, seldom given.

His clothes were bulky and heavy and long hours of training had not made him accustomed to the discomfort, particularly the boots. He stopped frequently to rest. After half an hour, he saw lights ahead and left the road and went into the forest, sinking to his knees in the snow. It was hard going, but he made it to the thirty-meter-wide swath of clear ground that followed the fence and served as a patrolway and, in summer, a firebreak.

Gerald took off his gloves and unzipped the weapons bag and took out a rocket launcher. It was a Soviet-made RPG7; the meter-long firing tube and its two pistol grips and trigger mechanism were painted white. Only the raised NSP-2 night sight was its original black. Gerald removed the protective caps from the launch tube and the rear blowpipe. He took out two high-explosive antitank missiles and screwed in their rocket motors. He loaded one missile into the launcher and laid the second on top of the weapons bag, ready for instant use. Several times, he practiced sighting the weapon. Loaded, the RPG7 weighed 9.25 kilos, too heavy to hold in readiness for long periods, so he rested the nose of the projectile on the weapons bag.

He heard voices, the steady hum of the car engines idling. The gates opened and the headlight beams of the lead car pierced the night, illuminating the forest.

Gerald removed the mitten from his right hand and reached inside his white camouflage smock to find the electrical switch that was wired into his clothing. It fitted snugly into the palm of his hand. It was a cheap plastic connector: all that was required to activate it was a quick thrust, flicking the switch from right to left. He had taped down the switch so that it could not be activated accidentally if it was pressed against his body. He would remove the tape only if he heard soldiers approaching.

In training they called the switch "the button," an insignificant word, simple and straightforward yet full of import. They were clever men, who had infused Gerald with their strength and commitment, and for this he was thankful beyond a measure ordinary human beings would never understand.

Gerald blinked against the hard glare. He lifted the RPG7, aiming at the gate. His heart was pumping and he felt a rush of blood to his brain; he took a deep breath to ease the pressure and then he was conscious only of what he saw through the night sight, which washed out the dark so that it was like looking through a faint mist. A car came out of the gate, a black Volga, the lead escort car, moving slowly, cautious of the ice on the road. Then into the sight slid the smooth black lines of a Zil—one of the big, sleek limousines reserved for the leaders of the Soviet Union—low to the ground and heavy. It was illuminated by the lights of the second escort Volga that was following behind.

Gerald picked up the rear door through the sight and traversed with it for one second, then two, his arms trembling with the strain, pulling back hard to steady the RPG7 and letting go his breath when his brain counted to three. He pulled the trigger and screamed into the night, losing the sound in the crack of the explosion that launched the missile, emptying his lungs and his brain in one shriek, a wild cry from deep inside, because in that moment he knew he had done it, and for the first time in his life he was truly free.

Ten meters out from the RPG7, the rocket motor ignited and spat out four stabilizer fins which held the missile in a low trajectory as it flew over the snow at three hundred meters a second. Its maximum effective range on a moving target was three hundred meters. Gerald fired from seventy meters. The 85mm hollow-charge warhead hit the Zil a fraction of a second after Gerald pulled the trigger. It was capable of penetrating 320mm of tank armor, and the projectile went through the armor plating of the Zil so easily it did not detonate until it was only centimeters from the man sitting alone in the rear seat. The detonation wave traveled at seven thousand meters a second, exploding the charge in the missile stem, melting the copper in the warhead, and ejecting it at tremendous pressure through the tapering hollow nose cone as molten copper and superheated gas.

The effect was devastating. More than six hundred pellets of molten copper shredded flesh, plastic, leather, and even metal beyond recognition. White-hot copper pierced the gasoline tank, igniting the fumes and engulfing the Zil in flames.

Gerald felt no exultation. The cry that had issued from him had not been one of triumph, but of release.

He fired the second missile into the burning Zil.

This time, instead of a rush of hot air, Gerald felt a soft sting on his cheek.

It had begun to snow.

2.

The city fell behind with dramatic suddenness. The big black Chaika limousine broke out of the encircling girdle of high-rise workers' apartments onto the plain, which was flat and vast. It was always a relief to leave the drabness of the outer suburbs behind. Even the softening mantle of snow could not completely overcome the geometric ugliness of the buildings. They were all alike and crowded close together, and yet each building seemed isolated in its desolation. All showed the scars of unfinished promises; it had been decreed by those who would never live in them that they were good enough. Klimenti Amalrik was glad that he was privileged enough to escape this judgment.

From the plain, the buildings seemed welded into a solid escarpment of brick and concrete and glass, sullen and threatening against the gray sky. The windows looked down with the cold, dead stare of glazed eyes; they would have to drive many kilometers to escape their maimed scrutiny. The snowplows had pushed up icy ramparts alongside the Minskaya Chausse, giving the impression of an eight-lane canal dug into the plain. There had been a light fall of snow just before dawn, but the snowbanks were still hard packed and blackened with the slick of gasoline fumes.

"What did they tell you?" Nikishov asked.

"I'm to go with you to Usovo," Klimenti said.

7

"That's all?"

"Yes."

Nikishov fell silent again. Klimenti stared out at the landscape, aware of his companion's unease, sharing it. The Chaika sped across the plain at 120 kilometers per hour. Being a heavy car, it rode easily. It was warm and comfortable in the back seat. They were lulled by the drone of the engine, the hiss of the heaters, the hum of the tires, and the muted crackle of the two-way radio. Yet Nikishov's expression was brooding and his gestures were nervous and fretful. He tugged at his bottom lip, drummed his fingers on his knee.

After giving it considerable thought, Nikishov said, "That's all they told me too."

Keeping his hands below the level of the front seat, Nikishov pointed to the driver and gave an almost imperceptible shake of his head. The gesture surprised Klimenti. The Chaika was one of the outward manifestations of Nikishov's rank, and Klimenti had assumed that the driver was a handpicked bodyguard. Yet Nikishov's gesture was unmistakably a warning.

Why had they been summoned to Usovo?

Their destination was a village thirty kilometers southwest of the city, in forest land watered by tributaries of the Moskva River. The Tsar's aristocrats had built their extravagant dachas along the river banks. The dachas had been acquired by the inheritors of the revolution, the autocrats, and Usovo and the villages around had become favored as weekend resorts by those who ruled the Soviet Union. Lenin, Trotsky, Stalin, Khrushchev, Molotov, Mikoyan, Kosygin, Gromyko, Brezhnev, and Andropov had all spent their weekends at Usovo. In spring and summer, the months of rebirth, Stalin had moved there for weeks at a time, but the soft, warm days and long twilights spent walking with the tang of fresh-bled pine resin in his nostrils had not eased his torment, or that of the people he ruled.

Lesser men among the *vlasti* also had dachas in the area, but none of those minor officials would warrant the level of secrecy that concealed the purpose of this journey. This was extraordinary, even within the considerable experience of Klimenti and Nikishov. A summons from the Politburo was a compliment of the highest order, a testimony to their importance and value to the Soviet State. Any service the Politburo ordered would be of the greatest merit. It was a singular distinction. Satisfactorily concluded, Klimenti thought, it would accelerate his career.

Unsatisfactorily concluded, it would destroy it.

The landscape was broken occasionally by scattered *izbas*, the wooden houses of commune workers who had each been given one-eighth of an acre of land to farm, a concession to private enterprise forced by the failure of the collectives to feed the city. They were unpainted, scoured by many winters, and gave the appearance of being derelict. Yet they squatted behind broken picket fences with an air of individuality, breathing smoke from their fuel stoves, and Klimenti sensed in them an attitude of defiance, as if they had made conscious decisions to fall apart rather than change. He felt there were eyes peering out in watchful silence.

Even from the security of the speeding car it was possible to feel the inertness of the land. In the clear breaks between the falls of trees, the snow ran unchecked all the way into the sky, or so it seemed, because it was impossible to define a horizon, where the dishwater gloom of the sky began. The sun was shrouded by a cloud cover twenty-thousand-feet thick and it gave a frowning light. It made the land somber.

And silent, Klimenti thought. Silent with the suffering and secrets of winters beyond counting. He stared out at the landscape, feeling its weight, and worried about the secrets that lay waiting for them among the naked birch trees of Usovo.

A convoy of camouflaged Ural 3750 ten-wheeled trucks came rushing down the highway toward them, buffeting the Chaika as they passed. Soldiers sat huddled beneath tarpaulin covers, their AK-47 assault rifles between their knees. They wore field-camouflaged combat jackets and, despite the cold, helmets. Klimenti counted twenty trucks. Four hundred men. Three rifle companies and command and support units, the vanguard of a battalion. They were going into Moscow and driving much faster than an army convoy would normally travel.

Klimenti became aware for the first time that, apart from the convoy, the highway was empty. The Minskaya was the principal road between Moscow and Minsk and it normally carried heavy traffic, especially big transport trucks; yet, ahead and behind, no other vehicle intruded into his vision.

"They've put up roadblocks," he said.

The driver was watching him in the rearview mirror; his eyes were a pale, washed-out blue and intelligent—they gauged him with cool detachment, the eyes of a professional. After a moment, the driver unhurriedly switched his attention back to the road. He showed no concern or embarrassment at being caught out.

Nikishov said, "I want to use the radio."

The driver did not react. He held the steering wheel with both hands, staring hard ahead.

Nikishov flushed. He snapped, "Did you hear me?"

"I'm sorry, sir," the driver said, "but my orders are to maintain listening discipline. No transmissions are permitted"—he paused for emphasis—"sir."

The driver did not turn, perhaps to save Nikishov embarrassment. It certainly was not because of fear. His voice was calm and he spoke with deliberation and politely. He was perhaps not so sure of himself, but he was very sure of the authority on which he acted.

"On whose orders?" Nikishov was unable to disguise his anger.

"Lieutenant General Viktor Pavlovich Radchenko"—and again the calculated emphasis—"sir."

There was a cadence in the way the driver gave the name, a drumroll of pride. This time he inclined his head to stare at Nikishov. He was perhaps thirty, broad-cheeked and fair, a Slav. His regard was steady. Any nervousness he had felt had been overwhelmed by that tattoo of rank and names. It was not surprising. Lieutenant General Viktor Pavlovich Radchenko was the commander of the KGB's Ninth Directorate, the Guards' Directorate which protected the Politburo and high Communist Party officials and their families. They were the only men permitted to carry weapons into the Kremlin or in the presence of the *nachalstvo*, the bosses. They were an elite within an elite. In all the Soviet Union no men were more thoroughly vetted, trained, indoctrinated. They answered only to Radchenko. And Radchenko answered only to the Politburo.

The driver held out his KGB pass. The cover bore the embossed insignia of the service, the Sword and Shield. Inside were a color photograph, name, rank, serial number, and date of issue. It was signed by the Chairman of the KGB, confirmation of the great responsibility and power that lay invested in the pass.

In the precise, clipped words in which officers were taught to repeat orders, the driver said, "I am Major Anatoli Kharkov. I have been instructed by Lieutenant General Radchenko to take you to Usovo. That's all I know, sir."

He was telling them he would not answer questions. Nikishov paled with anger. He was a KGB major general, and on another occasion Klimenti, his junior in rank, would have felt sympathy for him. But on this journey there was no room for such emotion.

"Major!" Klimenti kept his voice soft, knowing it would be unexpected.

Kharkov switched his pale, clear eyes to the rearview mirror. "Comrade Colonel?"

"Turn up the radio."

It was an order, quietly given but in a tone that expected to be obeyed. Klimenti had a scar running from the right side of his mouth down across his chin and under it. It was an old wound, and when he first saw the colonel, Kharkov had wondered how it had been inflicted. Staring into Klimenti's unblinking eyes, Kharkov knew he was dealing with someone who would accept his authority only within the strict confines of Radchenko's orders. Beyond that, beware!

"Yes, sir," he said and reached forward and turned up the volume. Nikishov stared out the window. He should not have left it to Klimenti to redress the major's arrogance. But Klimenti had been too quick, counterstriking instinctively, as swift and as dangerous as a wolf. A fighter.

The radio traffic was continuous and cryptic, full of terse code names and unit numbers that Klimenti did not recognize. However, they seemed to mean something to Nikishov, who leaned forward, listening intently.

"Mobilization orders," Nikishov said. "The convoy we passed are reinforcements for the Moscow Garrison."

The major's eyes flashed up into the rearview mirror again. They were using a Ninth Directorate code and he was surprised that Nikishov could read it. So was Klimenti.

Nikishov said, "They've doubled the Kremlin guard and sealed off Red Square."

Major Kharkov stared ahead, frowning in disapproval.

"KGB troops are being posted outside all foreign embassies. All foreign personnel have been ordered to remain within their embassies or apartments."

Nikishov sat upright and stared at Klimenti in alarm.

"*Spetsnaz* units"—the name was a hiss of shock—"are guarding all government buildings."

"*Spetsnaz!*" Klimenti exclaimed.

"Yes, *Spetsnaz.*"

In the front seat, Major Kharkov stiffened. The Spetsnaz units did not belong to the KGB but to the GRU, the Chief Intelligence Directorate of the Soviet General Staff. They were a force of thirty thousand highly trained specialists and commandos who had spearheaded the Soviet interventions in Czechoslovakia, Poland, and Afghanistan. They were assault and counterinsurgency troops, not security forces.

"The KGB has taken over all television and radio stations and all communications. Telephone or telex messages out of Moscow are not permitted. All incoming messages have been stopped."

Major Kharkov had pushed the Chaika up to 140 kilometers per hour. They sped out of the open plain and into the forest.

"All incoming road traffic is being halted within a hundred-kilometer radius of Moscow. No traffic is permitted to leave the city. Airports and train stations have been closed."

"Vnukovo 11?" Klimenti asked. Vnukovo 11 airport was reserved for the Politburo and top Party and government leaders. If they were leaving Moscow, it would have to be operating.

"It's under guard," Nikishov said.

Moscow, the fourth largest city in the world, had been totally sealed off. Its five airports, ten international train stations, and thirteen transnational highways were closed. But most of its eight million inhabitants, at work and at home, would not yet be aware of it. There had been no pronouncements on radio or television. The capital of the Soviet Union was a closed city, and only a very few very powerful men knew why.

"Antisocial elements are being detained for questioning."

Nikishov took out an elegant Italian gold cigarette case and a matching gold Dunhill lighter. They had been a gift from the Chairman of the KGB on his promotion to major general. With exaggerated care he extracted a British Players and lit it. His hands were shaking with excitement.

Klimenti said bleakly, "The last time they sealed off Moscow an army lieutenant tried to kill Comrade Brezhnev."

That was January 2, 1969. A long time ago. This was the age of Mikhail Sergeyevich Gorbachev, a very different Soviet Union.

Nikishov nodded gravely. "He was a Jew, of course. And insane."

"Totally," Klimenti said dryly, unable to suppress the sarcasm. Nikishov gave him a sharp, cautioning glance.

They fell silent, contemplating all the fearful possibilities. They were impaled by their ignorance, which threatened them. Klimenti, who knew the power of knowledge and understood better than most why the State so jealously guarded information, had never before felt so helpless because of his lack of it.

"We'll soon know," Nikishov said lamely. "Well, something anyway."

The radio continued with a flood of coded messages, but Nikishov no longer bothered to translate them. "Unit orders," he said. They sat apart, each man locked inside himself with his thoughts and fears as the Chaika plunged along the black highway between the ramparts of snow. Their journey to Usovo had taken on new and fearful implications, yet neither of them was ready to discuss it. The silence of the land had reached inside the Chaika.

"Checkpoint, sir."

Ahead, the blue Volga cars of the Militia stood out. A barrier had been erected across the two-lane paved road that led off the highway to Usovo. The signpost had been covered by a tarpaulin. The Militiamen in their gray greatcoats and fur caps stamped their knee-high cavalry boots and beat their gloved hands together to keep up the circulation.

"Turn off the radio," Nikishov ordered. KGB radio traffic was not for the ears of the police. But it was not necessary. The Militia officer saw the "MOC" registration plates of the KGB and waved them through.

They began passing NO STOPPING signs which were posted every kilometer. On both sides of the road they could see villas, some masked by trees, others hidden behind high wooden fences. Single-lane access roads branched off to the dachas. All were marked with promiment NO ENTRY signs. As they passed through the village of Zhukovka, Militia cars were parked outside "Khrushchev's store," which had been built by the now-discredited former leader in the Fifties, and was stocked with imported foods and wines without which a weekend at the dacha would not be so pleasant. The Militiamen were taking advantage of the situation to stock up on luxuries unavailable to the general populace.

The forest grew thicker. A five-man KGB ski patrol, AK-47s strapped across their chests, ghosted through the trees in white winter-camouflage smocks. Here, the curious were not only discouraged but forbidden.

They came to another roadblock, manned by troops of the KGB Chief Border Guards Directorate. They had an air of professional confidence and alertness that marked all well-trained soldiers. Most of them were veterans from the barren wastes of the Sino-Soviet border— where most of the 350,000-strong force was posted—who had been rewarded with transfers to more pleasant duty in cosmopolitan Moscow. Their names had obviously been radioed from Moscow, because a major checked their KGB passes against a clipboard list.

"Orders are all radios are to be turned off, sir," the Border Guards major said.

An ambulance came slowly down the road. If there were injured to move, they would have used medi-evac helicopters, and done it long ago. An ambulance driven without urgency could only mean corpses.

"Whose dacha does this road lead to?" Nikishov asked. He, too, had understood the significance of the ambulance.

"I don't know, sir," the major said, and they believed him.

They drove deeper into the forest.

"Comrade Gorbachev has a dacha at Usovo," Nikishov said, voicing the name and the fear that was in all their minds.

"Somewhere around here," Klimenti said.

But it couldn't be Gorbachev. It was unthinkable!

A grotesque figure stood barring their way, one hand upraised, the other holding a machine pistol. They had come around a corner and on it so suddenly they were all shocked. It was an officer wearing a white camouflage smock and dark green snow goggles and a balaclava—a faceless, inhuman threat. Their journey was over.

Layer by layer—first the Militia and then the KGB border troops—they had penetrated the protective armor around the Politburo. With each passing moment Klimenti had felt he was moving into a shrinking universe, the density increasing as they moved toward its center, assuming a weight that threatened to crush them. It was like a voyage to the center of the earth. And now they had reached the fiery mystery of its core.

They had entered into the control of Radchenko's men, the Praetorian Guards, and the difference was immediately apparent. The soldiers did not stand out in the open but lay in concealment in scrapes dug in the snow, watching with lifeless snow-goggled gaze. Four sprinted across the road to take up positions by the Chaika, assault rifles at the ready. No orders had been necessary. More nightmare visages stared down from behind a 12.7mm-caliber machine gun and a B-10 recoilless rifle mounted on an eight-wheeled BTR-60P armored personnel carrier, which blocked the road and the view beyond.

"Will you step out, please?"

The Guards lieutenant's lips were the only flesh that was visible inside his mask and they opened and closed on the words with the impersonal detachment of a marionette.

Klimenti, Nikishov, and Kharkov all wore greatcoats but after the warmth of the car the cold was a shock. Two Guards began to search inside the Chaika. A third slid beneath the car, inspecting the chassis. No orders had been necessary.

"Are you armed?" The marionette lips moved. The words came out flat and impersonal.

"Yes," Kharkov said. He opened his greatcoat and the lieutenant removed a 9mm Makarov pistol from a side holster.

"No," Nikishov said, but the lieutenant searched him anyway and then Klimenti. He checked the photographs on their KGB passes against their faces. He, too, had their names on a checkboard list.

"Thank you, General," the lieutenant said and saluted. It was the first recognition of rank that had been permitted. Klimenti was impressed by their professionalism.

None of them asked the lieutenant what it was all about. They knew they would not get an answer.

Major Kharkov drove the Chaika away to be parked. The lieutenant led Klimenti and Nikishov over to a mobile canteen, which served them hot tea. A group of Guards stood a respectful distance away, drinking tea and eating with the intense concentration of men whose training has involved deprivation. Klimenti watched them with a feeling of loss, remembering how it had been once, before sophistry, refinement, and cynicism had eroded the wonderful, powerful rawness of young manhood, and replaced it . . . with what?

Nikishov said scornfully, "Radchenko's clones!"

He stared broodingly at the silent forest, as if he expected an enemy to lurk there. Finally he turned and, with a directness that surprised Klimenti, said, "It feels as if Iosif Vissarionovich has reached out from the grave."

Stalin!

"It's not possible," Klimenti said.

But they all knew it was. It had happened in 1964 to Khrushchev, another reformer who had tried to keep Stalin buried, and in Czechoslovakia in 1968, when Dubcek had foolishly decided it was time to give the people a taste of freedom. The Stalinists had struck. Iosif Vissarionovich had reached out from the grave! And the events of 1964 and 1968 were nothing compared to the revolutions that had seen the ruling Communist parties humiliated and thrown out of office in East Germany, Poland, Czechoslovakia, Hungary, Bulgaria, and Romania since Gorbachev had taken over. And now the Soviet republics were in revolt.

Was it Gorbachev's turn?

"With Stalin anything is possible," Nikishov said. "They've broken up his empire. All this shouting about freedom, about taking power away from the Party, has wakened him. He's coming to crush them."

Lieutenant General Radchenko honored them by coming to get them personally. His service greatcoat flapped around the ankles of his highly polished cavalry boots, emphasizing his stockiness. Radchenko did not so much walk as thrust his way forward, arms pumping by his sides; it conveyed an immediate sense of purpose and energy. He essayed what Russians respected most of all—strength.

"Welcome to *la dachavita*," he said with a sardonic smile, surprising them with his humor.

They saw the wreckage of the Zil the moment they walked past the BTR personnel carrier. It lay overturned and burned out. Areas had been taped off to keep people from walking over them. Perhaps fifty men, most of them in uniform, were searching and measuring.

"Who was it, General?" Nikishov asked, his voice unnaturally stiff to hide his anxiety.

"Comrade Dmitri Mikhailovich Lysenko." Radchenko's voice was hoarse and graveled.

Klimenti felt the tension go out of his chest in a long hiss that became steam on his lips. He had really begun to believe it was Gorbachev.

"Lysenko!" Nikishov was so relieved he almost smiled.

"The assassins. Did they get them?" Klimenti asked.

"No," Radchenko said bleakly.

"They got away?" Nikishov said in disbelief.

"No," Radchenko said, the word as sharp as a pistol shot.

They stared at him, puzzled.

"There was only one," Radchenko said. "At least, that's what we believe. There was one set of tracks coming in. None going out."

"Then they must have got him," Nikishov said.

Radchenko pointed into the forest. "Over there."

"An antitank missile?" Klimenti asked as they walked.

"Almost certainly," Radchenko said.

"There'll be a launcher," Nikishov said.

"Normally." Radchenko's reticence was becoming unbearable.

About seventy meters from the road there was a small rise thickly sown with birch and pine trees. Natural clefts formed where the first January blizzard of the year had blown snow against the trees. The snow waves rolled over the rise, except for an area that was torn up. A big hole seemed to have been dug in the snow and around it there was what appeared to be discolored mud. But that was not possible. The earth lay under two meters of snow and was frozen solid at this time of the year. They stopped at the marker tapes and were able to recognize the stain.

"Blood," Klimenti said. A huge amount of it.

"So there is a body?" Nikishov said impatiently.

"No," Radchenko said. "There's no body."

"For God's sake," Nikishov exclaimed. "Tell us."

"The assassin self-destructed," Radchenko said tonelessly. "There's no body because he blew himself to . . . oblivion."

They stared at Radchenko and then at the discolored snow, seeing it with new eyes but still unable to believe it.

"Nothing," Nikishov said in a hollow voice.

"There *has* to be something," Klimenti protested. "There's always something."

Radchenko pointed to the snow. "That's it. That's all there is."

A huge force had converted an entire human being into mucus, liquefying flesh and bone and blood, spraying it into the snow; it had atomized cloth and leather and metal and plastic. But the slick it left was no longer the color of flesh or blood. It had frozen and was now black and shiny. Nikishov picked up a small piece of congealed human mush. It was brittle and it snapped between his fingers.

"Why," Nikishov said, awe overpowering revulsion, "it's just like toffee."

3.

A t the time of his death, Dmitri Mikhailovich Lysenko was aged seventy-eight and hardly known to the 260 million people he had helped rule for so long. Lysenko had come of age under Stalin and knew it was best to be as inconspicuous as possible. He had never been part of the public face of the Politburo. He had been a worker ant within the Communist Party, a faithful functionary who had progressed by diligence, obedience, ability, and the harrowing process of survival to join the Party's most powerful clique, the Central Organs Department of the Central Committee. The Central Organs Department administered the affairs of the Politburo and controlled all promotions and appointments within the Communist Party; it was both the servant of the Politburo and its kingmaker, and it exercised its power behind closed doors.

In this inner sanctum, Lysenko had been both feared and respected. He had helped the Party's chief ideologist, Mikhail Suslov, get the support within the Central Committee to overthrow Khrushchev in 1964. A grateful Brezhnev, recognizing his conservatism, made Lysenko his numbers man, whose job it was to vet promotions to the Central Committee and Politburo, to make sure the Old Guard were in ascendancy. But Brezhnev was long dead and the Old Guard had been undermined by Gorbachev's appointees. Lysenko, the most powerful of Brezhnev's surviving cronies, had become the focal point of

19

reactionary opposition to Gorbachev's policies of *glasnost* and *perestroika*, which gave citizens hitherto unknown access to the government as the price of economic reform and pragmatism.

It was hardly a reason for assassination, Klimenti thought.

Or was it?

Lieutenant General Radchenko said, "There wasn't much left in the Zil either. Just enough for a State funeral."

Two tractors with front-end scoops were digging up the snow around the blast hole and loading it into trucks. A tank recovery vehicle lifted the wreck onto a low-loader.

Klimenti and Nikishov walked back with Radchenko to the mobile canteen. A truck loaded with snow drove slowly past. They were taking it away to thaw it out, to see what they could find.

"*Chi,*" Radchenko ordered and the canteen sergeant glowed with pride at being recognized as an Afghansty, one of the veterans who had fought the fierce Mujahedin in the Hindu Kush.

Radchenko drank his tea slowly, relishing the hot liquid. He had the patient, expressionless face of a peasant, sculpted by centuries of repression. Into such a face you could read what you wished: brutishness, ignorance, cruelty—or compassion, understanding, and kindness. It was a face that was putty in your imagination. Watching its immobility, Klimenti knew better than to start kneading; he, too, was a country lad.

Nikishov said, "General, I understand I need your permission to use a radio."

"You do," Radchenko said. "And you've got it."

"Thank you," Nikishov said stiffly, unable to disguise the antipathy between them.

Watching him go, Radchenko said, "You don't have a lot to say, Colonel."

"I'm waiting, Comrade General."

"For what, Colonel?"

"To find out why you brought us here."

Radchenko buried his heavy head deep inside his collar. "You're wrong. Getting you out here wasn't my idea at all."

His officer's cap was pulled low on his brow and his dark eyes shone like polished coal. He does it deliberately, Klimenti thought. This cat-and-mouse with subordinates. Testing, troubling, seeking always to find weakness. He waited, watching the men at work, determined not to be provoked into further questions, not to play the general's game.

Finally, Radchenko grunted. He said, "It was Comrade Poluchkin."

General Grigori Poluchkin was one of the six Deputy Chairmen of the KGB. One of his specific responsibilities was the security of the Politburo and Central Committee. In this respect he was Radchenko's immediate superior in the chain of command that led through Poluchkin to the Chairman of the KGB to President Gorbachev himself. All three—Radchenko, Poluchkin, and the Chairman—were Gorbachev's appointees.

Klimenti said, "With all respect, this is for policemen, forensic experts. There's work here for scientists and pathologists and technicians. But not for me."

"Perhaps," Radchenko said, "but the Deputy Chairman says you know as much about terrorists as anyone in the Soviet Union."

Klimenti said nothing. It was his turn to bury his head deep inside his greatcoat collar and wait.

Radchenko said, "After all, you trained them. In East Berlin."

All of them so young. So full of passion and ideals. So willing to kill. Some of them were also ready to die.

"It was some time ago," Klimenti said, remembering their eyes.

Radchenko did an uncharacteristic thing. He sighed. He was tired of the sparring and it was a considerable compliment. He said, "I need to know what I'm up against."

"The assassin died alone," Klimenti said. "But he did not act alone."

"Why not one man acting by himself? A loner? A madman? A psychotic with a grudge? Why must it be a plot?" Radchenko wanted to believe he was right. If it was one man acting alone, everything would be so much simpler.

Klimenti said, "In that case, we'd be sitting in an interrogation room right now listening to the idiot babbling his head off. A man like that wants you to know *he* did it. He wants the whole world to know. Even if he was determined to kill himself, the last thing he'd do is blast all evidence of his identity into a hole in the ground. It'd rob him of his glory."

Radchenko's face was wreathed in a stoicism bred into his stock. It was a face that hid behind itself, a face that waited in ambush. Only his eyes were alive, small and quick. Klimenti felt in him the animal instinct to sense fear. Sniffing it out, he would strike unerringly, without hesitation.

Well, Klimenti thought. I, too, know how to wait.

Once again, it was Radchenko who broke the strained silence. "We're dealing with fanatics. Madmen. Obviously."

"No, General," Klimenti said softly. "He may have been a fanatic but he certainly was not a madman." Remembering those faces, he said quietly, "He was a martyr."

Those they sought most of all. In two years in East Berlin they had found only three who were suitable for preparation. Two men and a woman, and she had been the best of them. Klimenti had never been able to be sure which was the stronger in them, love of their cause or hatred of the enemy. The emotions were so painfully and exquisitely intermingled he was sure they did not know themselves and, for reasons he had never been able to identify, this troubled him.

"A martyr!" Radchenko frowned. The word, with all its religious mysticism and fervor, worried him. In Afghanistan, the Mujahedin had seen themselves as martyrs dying in a jihad, a Moslem holy war. Such a death was a passage to paradise, and Radchenko had been more than happy to oblige them. He did not like such emotive words being applied in the shadow of Lysenko's dacha to a man who had struck at the Politburo, whom he was sworn to defend.

"You think he believed in paradise, Colonel? Fucking houris by streams flowing with wine and milk and honey? On a couch hollowed out of a single pearl? In a tent inlaid with amethysts and sapphires and rubies?"

His words were rancid, the coarseness deliberate. He felt the need to shake Klimenti's calmness.

"Your contempt is undeserved, General," Klimenti said coldly, ready to fight for what he knew and respected. "He did what he set out to do, against difficult odds. He was cool enough and good enough to kill Lysenko, despite all the protection, all the guards you put around him. And when he'd done it, he was committed enough to obliterate himself. To destroy any evidence that could allow us to identify him or his group."

He spoke with deliberation, stabbing the words into Radchenko's heavy face. Yet he felt no satisfaction in seeing a flush beneath the peasant mask.

"We'd have welcomed him in Berlin, General," Klimenti said, and it was the truth. "He'd have been one of our best."

No subordinate had ever dared to contradict Radchenko in such withering terms. Yet, despite his anger, Radchenko knew that the Deputy Chairman had sent the right man.

Klimenti said in a matter-of-fact way, "It's impossible to guard against an assassin who is prepared to die. It takes a lot of time and money and access to rare skills to produce someone who is prepared to self-destruct. So we can accept that the group he belonged to is well organized and equipped. It is capable of intense psychological conditioning and extremely detailed planning."

Nikishov came trudging back with a tall man in an expensively cut British overcoat and a Russian fur hat who moved with a limp, the legacy of a leg wound from a German artillery shell. He was Academician Alexander Morozov from the Serbsky Institute for Pathology and he was accompanied by several of his staff. Morozov was in his late sixties. He was wealthy, was allowed abroad, and had kept in good enough health to enjoy a successful retirement. But he shunned any thought of giving up his work and no one had so far had the courage to suggest it.

The Academician halted before Radchenko, towering over the chunky soldier. His staff stopped several steps behind. Morozov made no attempt to introduce them. It was not arrogance or bad manners. He was so involved in the problems of the moment it just did not occur to him.

"Is that you, Klimenti?" he demanded, peering closer.

"Yes, sir, Comrade Academician. It is I, Klimenti Sergeyevich."

"Well, hello, nephew," Morozov shouted as he stepped forward and embraced Klimenti, kissing him on both cheeks to the amazement of all assembled. Klimenti blushed but he was nonetheless flattered by the warmth of Morozov's greeting.

Morozov's eyes gleamed on either side of a huge, bony nose. He waved his arms in the direction of the blast hole. "Do you gentlemen have any idea of just how difficult it is to destroy the human body?" he shouted. Morozov was partly deaf, the result of shell blast. "Do you have any notion? Why, it's almost impossible, as hundreds of foul murderers have discovered to their dismay."

He stared at each of them in turn, as if they were students at one of his famous lectures. "They've used acid, lime, fire. They've hacked them up and fed them to the wild beasts and the fishes. But always something turns up to accuse and condemn them. A set of teeth in the bottom of the acid bath. Charred skeletons in the furnaces at Dachau. A half-eaten skull in a wolf's lair. An arm in a shark's belly."

He waved his arms. "Why, it's absolutely miraculous how the frail human body denies its own destruction. Absolutely wonderful, I tell you. Those car bombs in Beirut blow up half a city block. But they always find something of the bomber. A head in an open field half a mile away, hurled there by the explosion. A hand, complete with fingerprints. A boot with a human foot still in it."

He beamed around at them. No one, not even Radchenko, would have presumed to have interrupted.

"Why, there's always something!"

The Academician swung around, scything his arm like a saber, so that his staff had to stumble out of the way or get knocked down. He pointed dramatically to the knoll.

"But over there, gentlemen, there is *nothing*. Just some frozen glug. I tell you, that hole in the ground represents one of the greatest challenges of my career. Probably the greatest."

Klimenti was so affected by the old man's great pleasure that he laughed. To everyone's surprise and considerable relief, Morozov laughed with him.

"Academician," Radchenko asked, frowning, "will it be possible for you to tell us something about the assassin?"

Morozov pursed his lips. His brow creased. For a moment, Klimenti thought he was going to tell Radchenko he must be crazy.

Morozov said, "If you look hard enough, there's *always* something. If necessary, we will examine the whole area, the whole damn forest, with a microscope. I'll dig up every bit of damn snow between here and Moscow if I have to. But I'll find something."

Morozov had already forgotten them. He strode off, head down, like a great bear, his staff trotting to keep up.

Klimenti said, "He once stood up to Beria."

Radchenko walked with them to the Chaika, where Major Kharkov waited. Nikishov said, "You think it's the Americans?"

"I suspect everyone," Radchenko growled.

"Of course," Nikishov said with distaste.

Radchenko stared at the tall and elegant major general with brooding malevolence. Nikishov represented the dandy, well-connected officer he loathed. Well, Afghanistan and the savage Pathans had sorted the fops out; they had left their aristocratic testicles withering on thorn bushes all over the Hindu Kush, and Radchenko thought that was how it should be.

"Tell me," Radchenko said harshly. "Why would *anyone* want to kill an old has-been like Lysenko?"

The brutal description of the dead Politburo member and the anger behind it shocked Nikishov.

"Indeed," he said dryly, and slipped into the car.

Radchenko checked Klimenti as he was about to follow Nikishov. He said, "Why'd they pull you out of Berlin?"

In his eyes, Klimenti sensed cunning as well as intelligence, and the former was a lot more dangerous. He wondered why Radchenko wanted to know. "You could ask the Deputy Chairman," he said. "But I can assure you, General, he won't tell you."

Klimenti got into the warm car. Radchenko was already stalking away, stamping down the snow with powerful strides, as short and as stout as a penguin.

Nikishov said with disdain, "At the officer academy they called him Radchenko the Terrible."

"But never to his face," Klimenti said quietly. "Not then. And especially not now."

In the rearview mirror Major Kharkov grinned.

4.

On the drive back, Nikishov watched Klimenti covertly, slipping him sly glances that increasingly became full of impatient curiosity. Finally he could no longer stand the suspense.

"So Academician Morozov is your uncle?"

"Not really. My wife's uncle. But they claim me as one of their own, mostly because of our daughter. They're a strongly knit family."

Even now, after all these years, it still hurt. Klimenti still spoke of his wife as if she were alive.

Nikishov rode a few more kilometers in silence, considering this. He came from a family that had long been entrenched among the new aristocrats who had replaced the *ancien régime*, and he was well versed in the intricate web of blood and marriage connections of this self-perpetuating elite.

Nikishov said in a tone of some hurt, "You know, Klimenti, I never knew. You never speak of it."

"No," Klimenti said. "I never speak of it."

They were stopped at roadblocks on the Moscow Circular Road and the Kamer-Kollezhsky Rampart, the outer two of the five ring roads that girdled the city. They drove past vehicles, mostly trucks, that were backed up for kilometers along the M1. Major Kharkov inquired what instructions were being given to the waiting drivers.

"To go home. Back to their depots and factories."

"And they wait?"

The Militia officer said sullenly, "They're used to waiting."

As Kharkov drove along the line of trucks, a beefy driver hung out of his cabin, waving his arms.

"Hey, *tovarishch*, what's going on?" he shouted boldly.

No answer came from the Chaika. The truck driver made a two-fingered gesture, eloquent in every language in the world. Other truck drivers smoked and played cards and chess. Some of them drank vodka, but only a few: Gorbachev's campaign against drunkenness on the job had dispatched many offenders to hard labor sentences amid much media fanfare, and they were well warned.

They kept their ears cocked to their radios, awaiting some official explanation. Since *glasnost*, Gorbachev had shown himself to be the first Soviet leader who was not afraid of the truth; people had become accustomed to getting news quickly and, so it turned out, accurately. In the vacuum they seized on rumor and conjecture for comfort.

"The Americans have invaded Panama again."

"In that case they'd tell us."

"Before it even happened!"

But even this wisecrack got none of the usual laughs.

"It's the goddamn Armenians again."

"Then the tanks'd be in Azerbaijan."

"They're in Moscow, so the problem's here."

"Let's face it. It's Patchy Gorbachev. He's gone too far, too quickly. Those bastards have been waiting a long time to get him."

"Yeah. It had to happen."

"Just as well, too. If it wasn't for the Party, where'd we be?"

"All this crap about a multiparty system. Who needs them?"

"What's wrong with a bit of freedom, dick-brain?"

"What freedom? To starve! To be humiliated! When the Party was in control, at least we fed ourselves. We didn't have to beg from the Germans. *The Germans!* We beat the bastards, not so long ago either, and now we're swallowing their charity. I don't know about you, comrades, but I'm choking."

They argued. It was a day full of uncertainties and anxieties, and the men who could resolve their fears were silent.

The traffic thickened as the Chaika sped down Kutuzov Prospekt, one of the twelve-lane jugular veins of the city. Normally, its great width accommodated the traffic with comfort. But two armored personnel carriers had taken up positions opposite the Arch of Triumph, commemorating the victory in the Great Patriotic War, and they were caught in a slab of trolley cars, buses, trucks, official Volgas, and privately owned Zhigulis, the little Russian-built Fiats. It was forbidden for private motorists to sound car horns in the city; Klimenti, who had spent four years in New York and Washington, where the slightest traffic interruption brought immediate pandemonium, was struck by the passivity and quietude of the scene.

"They're Russian," the Militia officer had said at the roadblock, rubbing it in. "Always full of hope."

All along Kutuzov, KGB Guards were posted outside clusters of modern, eight-story buildings which contained the apartments of high-ranking Party and government officials. The heaviest concentration was outside No. 26, where a number of Politburo members lived, along with the Brezhnev and Andropov families. They crossed the Moskva River. Halfway down Kalinin Prospekt, four APCs and a company of soldiers were stationed outside Communications House, Moscow's biggest telephone exchange.

A block-long queue had formed outside the New Arbat supermarket. Muscovites were showing their first reaction to any alarm. They were stockpiling food.

Red Square was sealed off. The Kremlin's towers and soaring spires and golden cupolas had always aroused in Klimenti a deep feeling of "Russianness"; nothing else in the great metropolis conveyed so eloquently a sense of almost mystical power and secretiveness, and finding it so utterly isolated gave it a sense of brooding menace. Klimenti wondered who now ruled within its turreted walls.

More APCs were parked outside No. 2 Dzerzhinsky Square, the headquarters of the KGB, and the eight-story slate-gray office building opposite, which was the headquarters of the Secretariat of the Central Committee. Apart from the customary hammer and sickle emblem cast in stone, neither building bore any legend to identify its function. They were anonymous, yet in a crisis these two buildings were more important than even the Kremlin, for inside them was vested the full power of the men who ruled the Soviet Union; without these two vital organs they would be defenseless and without authority. Gorbachev had an office on the fifth floor of the Secretariat. The Politburo met there once a week, on Thursdays. It was possible that the Politburo was meeting inside at that very moment.

If the Politburo was still in Moscow. Indeed, if the Politburo was still the Politburo.

Major Kharkov dropped them at the rear entrance to the nine-story office block German prisoners of war had built as an extension to No. 2. Their work had incorporated Lubyanka Prison into the KGB building, melting the two together in a deadly harmony. The Lubyanka was the most notorious and feared building in Moscow, probably in all the Soviet Union, yet outwardly it looked like another office block. Only huge steel gates, two stories high and fifteen meters across, gave any indication of its true function.

The major in charge of security checked that they had no weapons and issued them passes, which they conspicuously displayed on their lapels. Armed guards were posted along the corridors and at all elevator and stair entrances. A sergeant escorted them to the third floor. A small man came scurrying toward them, carrying a bulging leather satchel. He was Major General Tarabrin, commander of the Yevsekzia, the Jewish Department. Tarabrin's uniform had been beautifully tailored by one of those whom he so severely suppressed. Yet nothing could disguise the truth—no man had ever looked more like a clerk.

"It's terrible," Tarabrin wailed, loud enough to ensure that his distress had been witnessed. "It's absolutely terrible."

The sergeant led them down the corridor. The silence was stifling; no sounds, not even the subdued clatter of typewriters or the ringing of telephones, came from behind the closed doors. Their feet trod noiselessly on the heavy carpet. Klimenti had a feeling that they were being pursued. He realized it was the eyes of the guards, following them as they went. Nikishov looked around with interest; it was his ambition to occupy one of these offices someday.

A fire door led them into the old building. They had entered the KGB's inner sanctum. Here were the offices of the Chairman, his six Deputies and their workhorse, the KGB Secretariat. It had been the headquarters of the All-Russian Insurance Company before it was commandeered by Chekists who had good reason to appreciate its nearness to the Lubyanka, which was originally a Tsarist prison where many of them had once been incarcerated. The Cheka inquisitors had taken up instruments of persuasion still warm from the grasp of the

Tsarist torturers. The hundreds of thousands of unfortunates who had made the fearful walk across the courtyard to vanish inside the prison included three former Chairmen of the KGB and Lavrenti Pavlovich Beria, who had come menacingly close to succeeding Stalin.

On a day such as this, it was something to think about.

General Poluchkin awaited them in his suite of offices. A grenade had exploded in the Deputy Chairman's face during the street fighting in Stalingrad and had carved out part of his left cheek and mangled his nose. The surgery, which had been carried out without anesthetic in a makeshift operating theater set up in a cellar, was interrupted when the orderlies had to fight off a German patrol that burst into the floor above. Poluchkin had taken up his tommy gun and joined the fighters. Only his courage had pulled him through and it had not deserted him since. Poluchkin, at seventy-five, had probably risen as far as he would go; he lacked the political astuteness to become Chairman or be appointed a Deputy in the Defense Ministry. He hoped one day to become a Candidate Member of the Central Committee, and that was the limit of his ambition. But no man within the KGB carried a greater weight of respect than this veteran political commissar.

"Relax please, gentlemen," Poluchkin said, indicating chairs and offering them cigarettes. He, too, had a gold cigarette case and gold lighter, a gift from the Chairman. The cigarettes were French Gauloises. Klimenti, who did not smoke, politely refused.

"Too strong, sir," Nikishov said and Poluchkin chuckled. It was, Klimenti realized, just the answer he had hoped to hear and he found himself marveling at Nikishov's adroitness.

"That's the pleasure of them," Poluchkin said and lit one with a flourish, sucking the smoke deep into his lungs to prove the point. He had a strong, husky voice that rasped from the damage he had done, and was continuing to do, to his throat. The grenade had damaged his left eye. Close up, dilated and distorted by the thick lens, the eye looked grotesque, a living Cyclops, veined and red. It must have made reading very painful.

Poluchkin said ponderously, "You're here, gentlemen, because on the express instructions of Comrade Gorbachev I have been appointed, by the Chairman, to personally take charge of the investigation into the assassination of Comrade Lysenko."

Gorbachev was still in charge! Once again Klimenti was surprised at the relief he felt.

Poluchkin opened a file and took out a photostat. "This is why you are here," he said.

The photostat was a copy of a typewritten note. It read:

Lysenko was chosen to die because he was an evil man, an advocate of aggression and confrontation. He opposed nuclear disarmament and worked to sabotage those who seek it.

An American who is equally guilty of the same contempt for the desire of all the peoples of the world to live in peace and without the terror of nuclear annihilation has also been chosen to die.

Those who by their crippling distrust and mutual malevolence would condemn the world and all living things to destruction will know that they will be the first to die. Lysenko and the American are their vanguard.

This is our promise.

It is better that a few evil men die so that all the innocents may live.

Vigilantes for Peace.

"Disarmament!" Nikishov exclaimed. "They want nuclear disarmament?"

"So it seems."

Nikishov was outraged. "Vigilantes for Peace! What hypocrisy. It's totally irrational. We're not dealing with fanatics. We're dealing with maniacs."

"Colonel?"

Klimenti read the note a second time. He, too, found it hard to believe. Had he been wrong in so bluntly contradicting Radchenko, whose opinion was now echoed by Nikishov?

Klimenti said, "Only an irrational person would believe that you can achieve nuclear disarmament by killing Comrade Lysenko."

"But could irrational people prepare and execute the plan to kill Comrade Lysenko?"

"No, sir," Klimenti said

"It's the *glavni vrag!*" Nikishov said. The principal adversary. The Americans. "Comrade Gorbachev and President Bush might have declared an end to the Cold War, but the CIA wasn't listening."

"Perhaps," Poluchkin said gravely, but Klimenti got the impression he was glad Nikishov believed it was the Central Intelligence Agency, the old enemy. For him, the Cold War would never end and he was sure that the same attitude ruled at the CIA headquarters in Langley, Virginia. Poluchkin found this reassuring.

Encouraged, Nikishov said, "All this talk about disarmament is nonsense. A red herring to put us off the track."

"I think we may accept that as *one* working hypothesis," Poluchkin said. He was a prudent man.

Nikishov snorted in indignation. "The Vigilantes for Peace! Why, it's straight out of Hollywood. Pure Rambo."

Klimenti said quietly, "Excuse me, Comrade General, but it seems to me that the Americans have the least reason of all for killing Comrade Lysenko."

Nikishov regarded him with frosty amazement.

Poluchkin said coldly, "Why is that, Colonel?" He, too, did not approve.

Klimenti said, "The Americans saw Comrade Lysenko as an advocate of Soviet nuclear supremacy. They were able to use him as propaganda to justify their own missile program. While they could portray him as the wolf at their door, Lysenko was of greater use to them alive than dead."

Poluchkin took off his glasses to polish them. Without them, his wounded eye became normal. He limped to the high-arched windows that looked down over Dzerzhinsky Square. He was the son of a Bolshevik who was swallowed by the Lubyanka in the Great Purge of 1937. His mother had been sent to Siberia for refusing to denounce her husband and never returned. He did not know what had happened to his brothers and sisters, whether they too had perished or survived. He was saved by the fact that he had been in the Komsomol, the Communist youth league, and had been considered unpolluted by his parents' heresy. He had been raised in a State home, along with other "Stalin orphans." He had suffered for his country. But when you measured his personal suffering against what had happened in the past, before the Revolution and since—and what could come again in the future, to millions—it was nothing. Absolutely nothing!

Finally, Poluchkin turned to face them. "They promised to kill an American. Let's see if they do it."

5.

Darkness had already fallen when all State television and radio stations announced Lysenko's death in U.S.S.R.-wide broadcasts at 4 P.M., Moscow time. On television the news readers wore black armbands. They showed a black-bordered portrait of Lysenko bedecked with decorative sashes and medals. They all carried exactly the same report:

> Comrade D. M. Lysenko, a member of the Politburo of the Soviet Union, was killed early today in a car accident while returning to Moscow. The car overturned on icy roads and burst into flames. Comrade Lysenko, seventy-eight, was killed instantly along with the driver and a security guard. At a special meeting of the Politburo, President Gorbachev praised the self-sacrificing example Comrade Lysenko set in a lifetime of work dedicated to the security and welfare of the Soviet Union and its citizens. The Politburo sent a message of condolence to Comrade Lysenko's family.

There was no mention of the roadblocks and troop mobilizations. But to those in Moscow who had witnessed the disturbing events of the morning, the announcement of Lysenko's death was all the explanation that was needed. They quickly connected the two events and were comforted; they were accustomed to official paranoia and they put their earlier anxieties behind them. They were even glad it had been a nonentity like Lysenko, someone they didn't care two hoots about. They were especially glad that their fears of a Kremlin coup had proved groundless, not because Gorbachev had won some degree of popularity—he had made as many enemies as friends—but because ever since Khrushchev and his cronies had dragged Beria to the basement of the Lubyanka and shot him, they had become accustomed to an orderly progression of leadership. Even Khrushchev had been allowed to die in bed, and he had been succeeded by a procession of old men dying peacefully in office. The people feared the return to the murderous old days and all the misery and suffering that had gone with them.

Within an hour of the broadcast, at least twenty million bureaucrats across the Soviet Union were wearing black armbands. Most of them had never heard of Lysenko, but they knew intimately how to exploit the system he had helped create.

"Are we jamming foreign broadcasts?" Klimenti asked.

"It's not necessary," Nikishov said. "They're running the official Tass release."

So the assassins had made no announcements to the Western media, which was unusual for terrorists.

At 4:30 P.M., Klimenti was summoned back to Poluchkin's office, where the Deputy Chairman handed him a message written in his own hand in large block letters. It read: "SUSPECT AMERICAN INVOLVEMENT IN LYSENKO ASSASSINATION. ACTIVATE SQUIRREL IMMEDIATELY."

Poluchkin said, "I want you to code it and send it."

Klimenti carefully reread the message to gain time. It was to a KGB colonel whose cover role was Second Secretary at the Soviet Embassy in Washington. His real job, however, was with Special Service 11, which ran foreign agents and for which Klimenti also worked. The colonel was Klimenti's line of communication to Squirrel.

"If we send it, General, it puts Squirrel at risk. Every contact is dangerous. Even dead drops. He doesn't like it unless it's absolutely necessary."

Poluchkin frowned. He was not accustomed to arguments. "Rest assured it's absolutely necessary. We need to know if the Americans are involved. For obvious reasons we need to know quickly, and Squirrel is our best-placed source."

"He won't take orders, sir. We can ask him but we can't tell him what to do."

This reminder of Squirrel's independence irritated Poluchkin. He said, "I'm well aware of Squirrel's sensitivities, Colonel."

But it wasn't sensitivity, and they both knew it. Klimenti felt he could not let the point pass unchallenged. Too much was at stake. "For him, it's survival. He won't risk exposing himself by seeking information, probing where he shouldn't. He takes it as it comes to him. That's why he's lasted so long."

"All these years and he still doesn't trust us?"

"He's American. Why should he?"

Poluchkin growled, "You sound like you approve, Colonel."

"No, sir, I don't approve. Not from our point of view. It weakens the hold we have over him. But if I was Squirrel, if I was taking the risks, it's what I'd do."

Yes, Poluchkin thought, I believe he would. Klimenti, he considered, was disciplined, careful, intelligent, perhaps even clever. A professional. But he also had a dangerous independence of spirit. Poluchkin admired these qualities. As a Deputy Chairman of the KGB, however, he prized obedience over brilliance. He had seen several outstanding individualists, men who could not be constrained by the system, and none of them had survived.

Poluchkin was one of the few men in the world who knew that Squirrel existed. He belonged to an even more select group who knew Squirrel's identity. This numbered Klimenti, Poluchkin, the Chairman, his predecessors, and three former Deputy Chairmen who had been promoted into other ministries and who at various stages of their careers had held Poluchkin's responsibilities. Even the Special Service 11 colonel in Washington, who operated Squirrel's dead-letter drops, had no idea who he was. He was strictly forbidden to attempt any personal contact.

It irritated Poluchkin intensely that of this select number, Klimenti was the only one who was indispensable.

"You recruited him. You're the only person who's ever met him," Poluchkin growled. "We don't approve. For eleven years we haven't approved. Yet he still refuses to deal with anyone but you."

"He distrusts organizations," Klimenti said.

"Obviously he trusts you," Poluchkin said sourly, stroking his wounded eye. "Otherwise you'd still be in East Berlin."

Normally, Klimenti worked from the headquarters of the First Chief Directorate, which controlled all the KGB's external activities from a crescent-shaped ten-story building on the Moscow Circular Road on the outskirts of the city. Poluchkin, however, had ordered that Klimenti and Nikishov were to work under his direct command. The office set aside for their Operations Room was soundproofed. Several desks had been moved in, along with chairs and electric typewriters and a secretary from Poluchkin's own office. Technicians were installing telephones. Klimenti sensed immediately its former function: an interrogation room. A video camera, set high in one corner, had enabled the psychologists, psychiatrists, doctors, and senior officers to monitor interrogations without the distress of getting splattered with urine and excrement and blood, or smelling the nauseating odor of human fear.

Nikishov had his desk set up already. Everything was neatly arranged, papers here, pens there, order everywhere.

"There's no guard, no shredder, no safe," Nikishov complained. He detested disorder of any kind. Within an hour, a security sergeant took up his post at the door, a shredder was delivered, and a safe was installed. Beneath his stiff superciliousness, Nikishov was a power-house of discipline and energy, a natural organizer.

Klimenti put down on paper the assessment he had given both Radchenko and Poluchkin. The secretary from Poluchkin's office, Marietta Pronin, was a handsome woman in her early thirties who had a top security clearance, so he gave her the document to type.

As so often happens in the midst of frenetic activity, there came a lull in which there was absolutely nothing for Klimenti to do. After the tension and excitement of the long day, he felt tired and depressed. He sat it out with the stillness of a man who has done a lot of waiting in difficult circumstances. He sat at his desk with almost hypnotic inertia, turning inward. He thought about Squirrel and how it was to be alone and vulnerable, and it made him lonely for his daughter, Nadya, who was so like her mother in moods and temperament and features, the way she moved, the way she talked. Sometimes, watching her, Nadya broke his heart. Klimenti had not had any contact with Nadya for several weeks. She was beautiful and headstrong, living her own life, too busy to sense his loneliness. He loved her too much and was too proud to protest.

Sometimes, his dead wife and living daughter fused into the same person, opening old wounds.

Watching Klimenti, Marietta Pronin thought she had never seen a human being capable of such immobility. The Deputy Chairman had instructed her to keep a particular watch on the colonel with the scar that sometimes gave his face a twist of bitterness. Marietta Pronin wondered how he had received it.

Nikishov bustled in. He showed Klimenti an arrest warrant that had been signed by Poluchkin. Klimenti had never participated in an arrest before and when he started to protest that his attendance was unnecessary, Nikishov curtly cut him short. "It's orders." He was unusually tense.

Academician Morozov telephoned while they were getting into their greatcoats.

"Nephew, we've found some hair."

"Hair!"

"Do I have to repeat myself? Four human hairs. They were in the snow we melted down. I told you, it's damn near impossible to destroy the human body."

He was very excited.

"Well, Academician, congratulations. But I have to tell you that you're supposed to report all forensic evidence to Lieutenant General Radchenko. Not to me."

"Of course, of course," Morozov said irritably. "I know the procedures. But I thought you'd like to know."

Morozov hung up and Klimenti realized that he had wounded him by his lack of interest. The Academician was a great man, a man of history, but he was also old: it was not often these days he found something to excite him and make him feel young again. And Klimenti had doused him in the ice water of his detachment.

"Hair!" Nikishov exclaimed disdainfully. How could human hair help them?

"Four hairs to be exact," Klimenti said, wanting to defend the old man.

"It's scalps I'm after," Nikishov said and strode out.

Two Volga taxis from the KGB garages awaited them. They did not use black Volgas with the telltale MOC registration plates on operations such as this. A strong young man in leather jacket and jeans and heavy boots stood by one of the taxis, his face mostly hidden by a scarf and fur hat. He stepped forward and saluted. It was Radchenko's aide, Major Kharkov.

"Sir, I've been seconded to act as liaison officer."

"On whose orders?" Nikishov snapped.

"Lieutenant General Radchenko. Sir."

Klimenti was sure he saw a flicker of a smile hovering around Kharkov's lips. He was young, arrogant, and too confident; too proud of himself and his unit and particularly his commander. But it was the way of young men, and Klimenti remembered that there was a time when he had been much the same.

They drove southwest along Komsomol Prospekt inside the great curve of the Moskva River, where it doubles back on itself like a snake. The river was frozen. The bridge lights and the street lamps of the embankment faintly illuminated the snow deep below.

They were heading into one of the city's most sought-after residential areas, the Lenin Hills. You needed *blat*, a lot of influence and privilege, to get an apartment here. As they passed the great dome of the New Moscow Circus, Klimenti asked, "Who is he?"

"His name's Navachine. He's from the Upravleniye Delami."

Nikishov made a sour face. The Administration of Affairs was an entire department charged with providing every luxury imaginable for the Politburo, Party, and Central Committee leaders and their families. It stocked their larders with foreign foods and wines, their wardrobes with designer fashions from Paris and Rome and London and New York, their apartments with furniture and utensils from Scandinavia and West Germany; it supplied them with valets, cooks, butlers, gardeners, housemaids. It ran the special closed stores at which only those eligible for the "Kremlin ration" were permitted to shop.

They, more than even the KGB, knew all about the private foibles and pleasures of the inheritors of the revolution.

"When did he start working for the Americans?" Klimenti asked.

Nikishov was a thorn in the side of every American in the Soviet Union, their deadliest foe. He was head of the First Department of the Second Chief Directorate, which spied on and harassed Americans inside the Soviet Union. Nikishov used blandishment, threats, bribery, and blackmail to recruit agents among American embassy personnel, journalists, businessmen, even tourists. His most spectacular sex trap had snared two American Marine guards in 1986. With their assistance, Nikishov's men had been able to enter the United States Embassy and get inside the top-secret Communications Programs Unit on the ninth floor. There they not only bugged the crypto machines but tapped into the main power source, thus enabling the KGB to read both sides— plain language and coded—of American signals. One immediate result had been the identification, arrest, and execution of twenty-five Soviet citizens who spied for the Americans. For two years now, the Americans had been running a ring of spies inside the Ministry of Defense, unaware that each recruit was one of Nikishov's own men, a brilliant disinformation coup.

Nikishov said, "We got onto him only three weeks ago."

He carefully tapped a cigarette out of his gold case and lit it with his Dunhill. The flare of light and shadow elongated his handsome face.

"Lysenko closed his dacha down for the winter. He was old; he preferred to stay indoors in Moscow. But on Thursday he ordered it prepared to receive a number of weekend guests. The only people who knew about his plans were his family, his personal staff, his guests, his bodyguards. And the people at the Upravleniye Delami."

His tiredness was gone; this was the merciless face of Nikishov the hunter.

"Navachine supervised the arrangements," he said.

And told the Americans. Klimenti should have been told earlier, before he prepared his assessment. Instead he had been allowed to go ahead, totally ignorant of this vital evidence.

"Why wasn't I told?" He did his best to control his voice, but Nikishov sensed his anger.

Nikishov said, "The Deputy Chairman didn't want to influence your judgment. He wanted pure analysis."

The English cigarette glowed brightly. The only thing Russian about Nikishov was the flesh he moved in. And his soul. The rest of him belonged to his tailor and was French, Italian, British, American. Even the soap he washed with, the cologne he used. Yet he would be deeply offended if you called him bourgeois.

"He comes from a good family," Nikishov said and his voice had a hint of sadness at Navachine's class betrayal.

Nikishov's men were waiting outside the apartment block. Three were dressed in the uniforms of Militia officers. The Politburo members who had survived the midnight snatches of Stalin's era had moved quickly to make it illegal for the KGB to make arrests. The KGB could now only recommend action to the MVD, which controlled the Militia. But there were ways around every law, and Militia uniforms were easy to come by.

Kharkov accompanied the arresting officers. In ten minutes they returned with Navachine. His hands were manacled behind his back and already his body seemed gaunt, his face haggard.

Kharkov said, "We told his wife that if she raises a stink, she'll lose the apartment. I don't think she'll give us any trouble."

Nikishov sent the other cars back to the Lubyanka. He ordered the driver to detour around the Palace of Young Pioneers and along the Berezhkovskaya Embankment, which skirted around the river.

Ahead, Klimenti could see the two towering chimneys of an electric power station pumping gray smoke into the blackness and, beyond, bright and bold in the night sky, the illuminated red star on top of the spire of the Ukraine Hotel. They turned over the Kalinin Bridge and pulled up outside the hotel, which was a tribute to wastefulness and bad taste and a time when the men who had betrayed the revolution were desperate to mask their failures in grandeur, to disguise the poverty within. Apart from a Militiaman standing guard in the warmth of the hotel lobby, there was no one in sight. The floor show ended at eleven o'clock and the restaurant shut half an hour later.

A lot of foreign dignitaries and officials lived in the apartment blocks across from the hotel; the Soviet government discouraged national enclaves and had instead created an international one, for few Soviet citizens ventured past the men in Militia uniforms who guarded these buildings. They were, in fact, KGB men and they noted the names, addresses, and business of everyone who came and went. It was ostensibly for the protection of the foreigners, but everyone, particularly the Muscovites, understood better.

A figure, heavily muffled against the cold, got out of a parked Volga taxi and came down the pavement.

"Not yet, sir," he reported.

"Thank you," Nikishov said and pointed a gloved hand at the exhaust fumes rising from the surveillance car. They were running the engine to keep the heaters going. "Why don't you switch on flashing lights and sirens as well?"

The agent trotted back to the surveillance car. The exhaust fumes stopped.

"Who is it?" Klimenti asked for the second time that evening.

"An American. Harry Bannon. Do you know him?"

"No. Not under that name anyway."

"You'll soon see. He's running Navachine."

A tiny Zaporozhets 968 came over the Kalinin Bridge in a cloud of exhaust gases. The engine was badly in need of tuning, like every other privately owned car in the Soviet Union. There were no spare parts except on the black market and they cost a fortune. Mechanics were rarer still and cost even more.

"That's them, sir," the driver said.

The Zaporozhets stopped. The exhaust fumes settled like a cloud around it, but Klimenti could see the silhouettes of a man and a woman. They kissed and held the embrace for a long moment.

Lovers, Klimenti thought, wondering at the American's indiscretion. Was she one of Nikishov's honey traps?

The American got out, speaking softly, a lover's reluctant farewell. There was a flare of flame as the woman lit a cigarette. She also had her window wound down and, for a brief second, Klimenti clearly saw her face. His heart missed a beat. Then it pounded so hard it hurt.

Marusya. Marusya. Marusya.

The same face. The same quick toss of head, the impatient flick of hair, the wide, challenging eyes. She was so wonderfully feline, so completely feminine.

In Klimenti's face, Nikishov at first saw the ravage of shock. And then he saw pain.

"Damn you," Klimenti swore. Now he knew why he had been ordered to come along.

"I'm sorry, Klimenti. But you wouldn't have believed it otherwise."

"Damn you!"

The woman was his daughter, Nadya.

6.

Control said, "The Russians might have warned them. But we doubt it. It'd mean they'd have to admit the truth about Lysenko's death, and they're unlikely to do that."

Robert stood at the window. Outside it was dark and the rain was falling. Inside the hotel room it was dry and warm and cozy, quite luxurious really. He was sipping coffee; it tasted good, better than he could remember coffee tasting for a long time. All his senses had been heightened since they had told him his time had come. He saw, heard, tasted, smelled, felt more acutely than he had yesterday, or at any other time in his forty-five years, six months, and twenty-one days.

Knowing it was his time to die, he was experiencing a final feast of life. Was it the same for the unwilling condemned?

He could hear—he could *feel*—the raindrops smashing against the hard, clean glass and atomizing into spray.

Control said, "But even if they did warn them, they'll have no idea who the target is. They'll be more careful, that's all. But not enough to stop you."

Robert believed him. From the day his training began they had told him over and over: Believe, and you will achieve. Believe, and you will obey. Believe, and you are reborn.

Do you still believe in God? they had asked.

No, he'd screamed, aching with the cavity dug by his failed faith.

Good, they'd said. Now we can reduce you to *nothing*. So that we can make you *something*. In your own image.

And they had done it.

He stood there now, watching the rain, rebuilt, reborn, not believing in God but in himself, with the strength to die.

"They won't stop me," he said. "I know what to do."

All day, the media had been carrying the news of the events in Moscow. The so-called Kremlinologists were convinced a power struggle was being fought within the Politburo and they disseminated this propaganda with ill-disguised relish, particularly the conservatives who were afraid of the Soviet leader's popularity among the people. On his last visit, Gorbachev had scored a two-to-one approval rating, making him more popular than a lot of the nation's former leaders had been, and tens of millions of citizens were genuinely concerned about the fate of the man who led the nation that was once perceived to be their greatest enemy.

"What were you?" Control asked, acting out the ritual.

"A priest," Robert said solemnly.

7.

A t No. 2 Dzerzhinsky Square, Nikishov gave Klimenti a file he had prepared on Bannon and busied himself at his desk, turning his back against the light. It was a thoughtful gesture and for a moment Klimenti was caught in a turmoil of anger and gratitude, wondering how such a basically decent and prudish person as Nikishov could have got himself involved in such a filthy business as sexual blackmail.

How had any of them got involved in the whole damn business of deceit and betrayal!

Never before had Klimenti made such moralistic and emotional judgments on what after all were merely the basic practices, crafts, and tools of their profession. It was dangerously irrational and he recognized this, but he could not help it. They had made his daughter a vixen, a honey trap. They were using her as sexual bait and Klimenti was consumed with outrage.

"Does she know?" he asked Nikishov. It was unthinkable that his Nadya, his daughter, was a willing participant in such a sordid business. But Klimenti was afraid of the answer.

"No," Nikishov said, unblinking. "She knows nothing."

With great relief, Klimenti believed him, reviling himself for his doubts. Even so he was unwilling to open the file. He had seen such files often enough to know the possibilities—the infrared photographs showing the ludicrous contortions of limbs and faces in the throes of

44

passion, the tape recordings of animalistic grunts, the demeaning litany of lust. Klimenti had always left such work to his subordinates. But it was he, Klimenti, who had ordered the nests to be baited, believing the ends justified the means. He had done it with distaste—but how pathetic that emotion now seemed against the scald of his own shame.

Pray God they were not using video cameras in his daughter's bedroom. But he knew that if they had the opportunity, then they most certainly would.

There were only five black-and-white photographs. Three showed Nadya and the American at different restaurants. Another showed Nadya and Bannon walking arm in arm into an apartment block. Her head was resting against his shoulder, a posture that told him more clearly than words that they were lovers.

The fifth photograph was a close-up of Bannon, shot with a long lens in daylight. It was enlarged to show every crease and blemish. It was a face of strong features, thin and thin-lipped, more masculine than handsome. But it was the eyes that held Klimenti's attention. The photographer had caught Bannon just as he was about to turn his head and his eyes had already flicked sideways, narrowing with concentration, animating his face with distrust and suspicion. They were the eyes of a man who was full of tension and aware of a threat; they were the eyes of a dangerous man.

Harold Alexander Bannon, thirty-five, single, cultural attaché with the American Embassy, had arrived in Moscow on October 9. He met Nadya Amalrik, twenty, student at the Moscow Institute of International Relations, on December 2 at a cocktail party given by the Deputy Minister for Culture at the Hotel Rossiya to a group of American jazz musicians. Nadya Amalrik was one of a number of young women invited by the Deputy Minister's daughter, Yevgenya Stepanov, commonly known as Zhenya, her flatmate and a translator with the Foreign Department of the Central Committee. On the night of December 11, their fourth meeting, Bannon and Amalrik became lovers. Surveillance had been intensified.

Klimenti flushed. He knew only too well what that meant.

On December 21, Bannon was photographed making a secret rendezvous with Navachine.

It was the barest of summaries and it obviously had been heavily vetted by Nikishov. There would be more, much more.

"Why didn't you tell me earlier?" Klimenti's voice was thick, the words slurred with bitterness. The scar tugged his mouth down and, in startling contrast, his eyes elongated and slanted upward. There was Tartar in his ancestry, and it came through in flashes; he was dark, hungry-faced.

Nikishov said, "You would have warned her. And we couldn't allow that."

It was shocking and simple and quite straightforward.

This was hard for Nikishov, too, but he could not allow himself the indulgence of sentiment. He said, "The possibility that Bannon's involved in Lysenko's assassination made it inevitable you'd eventually find out. Otherwise we wouldn't have told you."

We! Of course. The decision would have had to be taken by the Chairman or the Deputy Chairman at the very least. How beautifully that collective pronoun absorbed responsibility, freeing the individual of guilt, investing it all in the huge, impersonal, and impartial State security apparatus. *We*, the system! The word was a wondrous mouthful, swallowing all blame.

Klimenti knew it well. He had been using it, sheltering behind it, all his career, just as Nikishov was using it now.

"It's got to stop," he said.

Nikishov stared up at him, saying nothing, his face clenched tight against the sympathy he felt. Seeing this face of implacable silence, Klimenti knew what it signified, and he shrank within himself.

"How much longer will it go on?" he asked, a reduced man.

"I don't know," Nikishov said. "But as long as necessary."

The warning was clear. Klimenti was not to tell her; he was not to interfere. Nikishov took the file to the safe and locked it away.

"I'm sorry," he said, "but that's how it is. No one pushed her into bed with him."

"She's only twenty," Klimenti said, knowing it was absolutely meaningless. "She's a student."

Major Kharkov came in and slumped wearily into a chair. "Navachine's a closet Jew. They found out and threatened to expose him. The point is, he insists it was the Israelis, not the Americans. And he refuses to admit he had anything to do with Lysenko's death."

Nikishov said, "Of course. He knows it's a firing squad."

"Give him time," Klimenti said bitterly. "He'll remember."

Kharkov stared at him in amazement. Nikishov went to the window and looked down into the courtyard below.

Klimenti collected his greatcoat and left without saying goodnight. He walked the block that took him around the side of the KGB building and into Dzerzhinsky Square. The statue of Felix Edmundovich Dzerzhinsky, "Iron Felix," the Polish revolutionary who founded the Cheka, the first Soviet secret service, looked down on a deserted square. This was the man who had unleashed the first of the many terrors that had purified first Lenin and then Stalin of those mortals who were against them—or who they imagined were—so that millions had died to make great men feel secure.

The bronze eyes were piercing and stern, the eyes of the State, and standing beneath their gaze, Klimenti no longer felt anger or disgust or even shame. Instead he was numbed by a sense of inevitability. For the first time in his life he began to wonder who he really was.

It was a long way to Shabolovka Street where he lived. Even though it was past two in the morning, he could easily have gotten a KGB chauffeur to drive him there. Instead he walked. The streets were drab, and the buildings were worn and decaying. In the winter Moscow was a besieged city, cowering before the cold. Klimenti walked through the deserted city, full of his own emptiness, full of echoes. He arrived at Shabolovka Street without realizing how he had reached it.

When he got inside his apartment, Klimenti did not switch on the lights but sat in the dark watching out the window. He knew that if he went to bed he would not sleep, and he was afraid of the waking dark hours, a time when the bravest are cowards. He sat for a long time and, without knowing it was happening, he fell asleep.

At 6:47 A.M., Klimenti was awakened by the telephone. As he struggled groggily out of the chair to answer it, he found to his surprise that he held a framed photograph of his wife and daughter clutched to his chest. He could not remember getting it.

"Klimenti, are you awake?"

"What is it?"

Nikishov said, "They've killed an American."

8.

Klimenti pressed the buzzer. The door was painted a soft white, with a thin border of gold elegantly tracing the outlines of its four panels. The corridor was thickly carpeted, there was heavy wallpaper with an old-fashioned flower pattern, and the ceilings were high and decorated with artistic whorls of plaster, the work of a Georgian artisan who had helped build the house more than two hundred years ago. It had formerly been the town house of one of the wealthy merchants who had inhabited the Old Arbat district before the Revolution. It had been converted into a number of large two-bedroom apartments, which were occupied by high-ranking officials of the Communist Party.

The door opened a few centimeters, as far as the safety chain permitted. Klimenti saw a slice of a face, a clear gray eye, smooth skin, and blond hair. He was disappointed. It was not Nadya but her flatmate, Zhenya Stepanov, whose family owned the lease on the apartment. She was one of the many influential friends Nadya had grown up with under the careful guidance of the Morozovs. Klimenti had not met her before, knowing her only through Nadya's conversation.

"Yes!"

It was not a question but a complaint at being disturbed. The KGB tabs on the collar of Klimenti's greatcoat did not daunt Zhenya Stepanov as they did most citizens. She was protected and she knew it.

"Is Nadya in?" Klimenti asked politely.

"No," the young woman said curtly, anxious to get rid of him.

"I'm sorry to disturb you. But I'm her father."

A finely etched eyebrow arched in surprise. She regarded him with bold frankness. But the curiosity was short lived.

"Nadya's gone to the university. I'll tell her you called."

She shut the door. Klimenti felt a sharp pulse of anger at her arrogance. His bad temper lasted all the way to No. 2. The Volga that had collected him from Shabolovka Street passed a convoy of armored personnel carriers and trucks heading back to the barracks of Moscow's two home regiments, the Taman and Kantemir Guards. On the Sadovoye Ring Road, a Militia officer, sitting in a glass cubicle raised on a steel pylon above an intersection, answered his phone and frantically punched the buttons on the control panel in front of him, freezing the traffic lights on green. The timing was perfect. A long black Zil, its interior blocked from view by tinted glass and drawn curtains, sped past with a KGB escort car riding herd on its right flank, siren howling, its red roof beacons flashing. The big limousine and the smaller Volga rode together in perfect unison, like a killer shark and its pilot fish. It took a lot of training to drive that well. The drivers and bodyguards were, of course, Radchenko's men, and Radchenko expected nothing less than perfection.

Major Kharkov was alone in the Operations Room. He had been up all night, working with the interrogators, and was unshaven and rumpled. He reported cryptically, "Major General Nikishov is with the Deputy Chairman. Navachine's finally confessed. It's the CIA. They've identified the missile that killed Comrade Lysenko. It's one of ours, an antitank RPG7."

He was brisk and efficient, despite his tiredness.

"Go home," Klimenti said. "Have a bath, get some sleep, eat. Report back at 2 P.M."

He read the Tass Summary, which was prepared each morning for the Politburo and top officials in the Party, government, and KGB. It was a digest of reports carried in important American, British, French, and German newspapers and by Reuters, AP, UPI, and Agence France Presse, and it contained information that the KGB censors denied ordinary Soviet citizens. The leadership realized that, while it was crucial to restrict information going to the masses, it was important that they themselves be fully informed. It was, perhaps, the ultimate irony that they read the Tass Summary first, before their own newspapers. Gorbachev, who was adept at using the Western media, especially television, had his Summary delivered to his apartment, so he could read it at breakfast or on the way to the Kremlin. In emergencies such as this, special editions were issued with every major development. The one handed Klimenti was timed 0800 hours, barely twenty-five minutes old.

The American was Senator Eugene J. Townley III, an American aristocrat, whose father and grandfather had been power mongers within the Republican Party before him. Townley was a skillful demagogue who knew how to pluck America's heartstrings and did so at every opportunity. He stood steadfastly for the flag, God, and motherhood, damning atheists and Communists with equal ferocity. A hard-line conservative, he had led the radical right in opposing any accommodation of the Soviet Union or its foster children, such as Cuba and Nicaragua. As chairman of the nation's most powerful lobby group, the Committee for Nuclear Preparedness, a troika of defense, industrial, and political interests, Townley had led the fight against disarmament, insisting that nuclear superiority was the United States' only guarantee of survival. In every respect he was almost an exact American counterpart to Lysenko.

Townley was killed at 10:05 P.M. Washington time, while on his way home. The assassin drove a car packed with plastic explosive out of a side street and crashed head-on into the Senator's limousine, exploding on impact. Townley and his two bodyguards were killed instantly. The assassin had been completely obliterated.

Nikishov came in. He, too, had been rudely awakened after only a few hours' sleep and tiredness pulled tightly at his handsome features.

"Comrade Gorbachev's already in his office," he said. "He's called a special Politburo meeting. Poluchkin's frantic. Yesterday he told the Chairman and the Politburo he was sure it was the Americans. And now . . . Townley!"

He sat, nervously drumming his fingers on his desk. He produced a packet of Players and lit a cigarette. He had been too busy to fill his treasured gold cigarette case.

"There's no mention of the Vigilantes for Peace," Nikishov said gloomily.

"There'll be a note," Klimenti said. "The Americans have suppressed it. Just like us."

Nikishov nodded sourly, "For the same reasons." His face was pinched with irritation. He cursed, "Blast Navachine! His confession has confused everything."

Klimenti wondered if the poor wretch down in the basement of the Lubyanka would appreciate the irony of this.

They went to get breakfast. The canteen was crowded and noisy. The food was cheaper and better than you could buy in the supermarkets, and many KGB staff, even married officers, preferred to take their breakfast there. The warm aroma of cooking and coffee made Klimenti feel hungry, and he took the sausage and fried potatoes and black bread and margarine. Nikishov took a hard-boiled egg and white bread.

"Do you have warm fresh milk?" Nikishov asked the manager, a buxom woman in her early forties, as her fingers flick-flicked across her abacus, adding up the bill.

"Warm fresh milk!" she exclaimed, arching her pink penciled eyebrows with fearless disdain. She had been in the job a long time and she knew her place in the scheme of things; the least the Major General could do was know his. After all, *they* were running the country. "General, we don't have *any* milk, fresh or otherwise."

For the vast majority of the people *perestroika* was still just a slogan, promising so much but delivering very little.

"I never eat in the canteens," Nikishov said stiffly. "I always take lunch in my office."

They sat in silence while Klimenti ate and Nikishov fastidiously shelled the egg, slicing it lengthways in halves and then into quarters; he sprinkled on salt and buttered his bread, all of it with surgical precision.

"Does Bannon know that Nadya is my daughter?"

Nikishov said, "That's the big question, isn't it?"

"But you're listening in. Surely."

"We're not sure," Nikishov said, lifting his eyes from his plate. "We think she's using her mother's name."

"Morozov!" Klimenti was shocked. It had never occurred to him that his daughter would not use her own—*his*—family name.

Nikishov ate the slice of egg with pleasureless concentration, as if he feared it would poison him.

"I thought you'd be relieved. After all, the name Amalrik is bad news to the Americans."

Klimenti said sharply, "I'll be relieved when it's ended."

"I'm sorry, it's out of my hands." And, as if to signify his helplessness, Nikishov put down his knife and fork and sighed. "It's cold. Is the coffee hot?"

Klimenti pushed his untouched coffee across. He said quietly, "The Americans have strict rules about fraternization. All contact with Soviet citizens has to be reported. No second contact can be made without permission. All sexual contact is forbidden. A kiss, holding hands, gets you on the next flight out of Moscow. With a Marine escort." He leaned forward over the table, his face tight with an intensity Nikishov had not seen before. "He's a professional," he said. "And he's sleeping with my daughter."

The bitterness made him ugly, stretching the skin over his high cheekbones so that his scar quivered. For the first time, Nikishov saw cruelty in Klimenti and it shook him, as if he had seen something terrible and primitive.

Klimenti opened his hand. It was full of crushed black bread. He dropped the bread on his forgotten food.

Nikishov said, "Don't do anything, Klimenti. If you interfere it'll blow up in her face. And yours."

They had hoped he would get the message. Now they were making sure, telling him straight out.

"Trust us, Klimenti. This is not our doing. But we can't ignore it. Especially not now, after Lysenko. After Navachine. Leave it alone and your daughter will come to no harm."

Klimenti shook his head. He said harshly, "He's a professional."

"He wouldn't be the first to go this way."

"Then he's a fool."

"Or in love."

"No," Klimenti said, rejecting it totally, afraid of what it meant.

"She's a beautiful girl. It happens."

Oh yes, it happened, and if it was true of Bannon, then Nadya was doomed. They would use her ruthlessly to manipulate the American. They would taunt Bannon with threats to harm her and promises to let her go free, until he did their bidding, and in the process they would crucify Nadya. She would never be free of it.

It would be much better if Bannon was using her. Then there would be an end to it.

Klimenti felt the same overwhelming sense of inevitability. He remembered a graffito that had been written in bold, challenging strokes on the tiled walls of a pedestrian underpass on Gorky. It had been quickly scrubbed out, but to all those who caught its brief life, it proclaimed:

OBEY

BE SILENT

DIE

He followed Nikishov out of the canteen, sure now that his colleague was concealing much from him.

When they got back to the Operations Room, Major General Tarabrin, the Director of the KGB's Jewish Department, was waiting, bristling with indignation.

"I understand you've made an arrest in my area of operations."

Nikishov shrugged. "There's been thousands of arrests. Ukrainians. Balts. Mormons. Seventh-Day Adventists. Black-marketeers. Parasites. Refuseniks. Dissidents. Undesirable elements. But I assure you, we've got enough headaches of our own without trying to help you solve the Jewish problem."

Tarabrin flushed. It was a dreadful insult. "I intend to pursue this further," he said and marched out.

Klimenti said, "He's got one of the interrogators on his payroll."

Nikishov nodded grimly. "He wants the credit, that's all. The miserable worm." Nikishov went back to work. The encounter had done him good and lifted his spirits.

Klimenti rang Academician Morozov. "Good morning, Alexander Semionovich. How's everything with you?"

Morozov said frostily, "I really don't have time to exchange pleasantries, Colonel. I have important work to do."

So it was no longer "nephew." The old man was still angry. "My apologies, Academician. But could you tell me who was Comrade Lysenko's personal physician?"

"Who else but that toady Fadeyev from the Kremlin Clinic."

"The Academician?"

"Academician! Hah!" Morozov snorted in disgust.

"Those hairs tell you anything, Academician?"

"Of course!" Morozov shouted and slammed down the phone.

Klimenti rang the Kremlin Clinic. Academician Fadeyev's secretary would not put him through until he told her it was do with Lysenko. Fadeyev came on the phone immediately.

"Is this an official inquiry?" he asked with the smooth displeasure of someone accustomed to authority, and using it.

"Yes, Academician," Klimenti lied.

"Then you may present your credentials and an official letter requesting the information you seek at my office at a quarter past three," Fadeyev said.

Blast him, Klimenti thought. The letter was going to be a problem. Had Fadeyev recognized his name and made the connection?

At 9:45 A.M. Deputy Chairman Poluchkin summoned Nikishov. At 10 A.M. Nikishov returned.

"The Chairman wants a new analysis: what'll be the American position? If it's not the Americans then who else could it be?"

"Is that all?" Klimenti said dryly.

"Immediately. But first you'll need to read this."

Nikishov handed Klimenti a report that bore the letterhead of the Moscow Central Institute of Forensic Science and that was signed by Morozov. There were two summaries. The first said that the Vigilantes for Peace note that claimed credit for Lysenko's killing had been typed on Russian stationery, with a Russian typewriter, using a Russian typewriter ribbon. There were no fingerprints.

The second report said soil analysis had identified the plastic explosive that the assassin used to self-destruct as an American product, HMX. It was the most powerful plastic in the world with a detonation wave of 9,000 meters per second, 1,000 meters per second faster than normal plastic, RDX. The plastic mixture was 91 percent HMX and 9 percent linseed oil. HMX was manufactured exclusively for the United States armed forces although it was also supplied to salvage contactors doing defense work. The Israeli special forces had got hold of some HMX, either by secret agreement with the Pentagon or by buying it clandestinely from the salvage contractors. Or stealing it.

Nikishov said, "The explosive is American, available only to Americans and, we suspect, to the Israelis. We've got Navachine admitting he gave information to the Americans about Lysenko's movements."

"If it was your analysis?"

"The Americans number one, the Israelis number two."

"Except for Senator Townley."

"Yes. Except for the Senator."

Klimenti spent the morning working on the analysis. He knew that Poluchkin would almost certainly have ordered similar assessments from the Institute of the United States and Canada, the top think tank on North America.

The starting point was acceptance that whoever killed Lysenko also killed Senator Townley; that seemed to be beyond dispute, even though the Americans had not yet made any mention of a note. The VFP had promised to kill an American and they had delivered, putting a definite signature on both deaths.

Although the circumstantial evidence so far pointed to the Americans, it was overwhelmed by the killing of Townley, who was anti-Soviet, antidisarmament, and pro-CIA and pro-Pentagon. Moreover, there was also no discernible American motive for killing Lysenko. On the contrary the Americans had a vested interest in keeping Lysenko alive, a Russian hawk who justified their own rhetoric and missile program.

The most obvious suspects for the assassination of Lysenko were the Israelis, the Afghans, Ukrainian or Baltic nationalists, or Polish Catholics, all of whom had good reason to want him dead. Only the Israelis had the expertise, resources, and resolution to strike effectively inside the U.S.S.R. and America. But none of the suspects had any reason to kill Senator Townley, especially the Israelis, to whom he had been a devoted friend.

The most obvious suspects for the assassination of Senator Townley were the Nicaraguans, the Cubans, the Libyans, and the Palestinian Liberation Organization, all of whom hated the Americans, and with justification. All had the ability to strike in Washington. None, however, had the capability to strike in Moscow. Nor did they have any reason to kill Lysenko, who was their ally.

The problem: while it was very easy to conceive of enemies who would want to kill Lysenko and enemies who would want to kill Senator Townley, it was difficult to find a common enemy who would wish to kill both.

Klimenti clearly saw the remaining possibility, but he was loath to put it down on paper. Reports like this had a habit of condemning their authors. He seriously considered clouding the issue. At worst he would be accused of stupidity, which was no longer a fatal disease. But he realized they would see through him. Terrorism was his field of expertise, and they knew the caliber of his work too well to be hoodwinked. In the end Klimenti grew tired of his own duplicity. He finished his report, but with foreboding. For the first time in his career he did not find pleasure in the cool analytical process nor pride in his ability to think with ruthless objectivity.

9.

Later, Klimenti took his greatcoat and went down into Dzerzhinsky Square. He had to make a decision about Nadya, and the Operations Room was not the place to do it. He needed air and space. He needed to be away from the KGB. In the streets, everything was back to normal. Women and children thronged in and out of the Detsky Mir children's store. Although there had been no advertising—not even in the store's bare display windows—word had got out that a shipment of Czechoslovakian wool-lined boots had come in, and a queue stretched around the corner. There was plenty of Russian-made footwear available, but no one wanted it. The shoes fell apart too quickly and leaked.

Klimenti went into the underpass beneath Marx Prospekt. The tiled walls rang sharply with footsteps and voices and he came on a young woman consoling her two-year-old daughter and at the same time trying to search beneath the iron drainage grate that ran across the pavement. It was broken across several sections and the child had lost a shoe, one of the wool-lined Czechoslovakian boots her mother had just bought for her in the Detsky Mir; she kicked her red-stockinged foot and shrieked in terror of punishment.

"Hush, hush," the young mother crooned. "It's only a shoe."

Klimenti knelt beside her. "Let me, little mother," he said, trying to get his hands through the broken grate.

57

A crowd gathered, men and women all doing their best to console the child, the mother blushing with embarrassment at all the fuss. A young conscript with a face full of pimples tore off his army greatcoat, pulled up his sleeves, and ordered: "Stand back." He got a skinny arm beneath the grate and with a cry of triumph, as glad and as loud as if he had scored a winning goal, brought forth the tiny shoe.

The crowd cheered and laughed and the child stopped crying. The mother stood there, saying over and over, "Thank you, thank you," and Klimenti got up and brushed down his trousers; he realized he was laughing with the crowd. His red and green KGB tabs and his colonel's rank—and all the power that went with them—stood for nothing: he was simply a Russian trying to help another Russian. It was absolutely wonderful how distress, small or large, brought out the best in them; it was just as well, for few nations have suffered so much. Standing there in the echoing tiled tunnel, Klimenti was almost pleased with himself.

He walked down Marx Prospekt. The air was stale with exhaust fumes and noisy with the bellow of heavy trucks, which constituted a good part of the traffic. With his mind released from its analytical discipline, he began worrying about his daughter. When his wife Marusya had died, Nadya had anchored his strength; in her little-girl helplessness, she had given him purpose; he had absorbed her pain with his love and in so doing had assuaged his own hurt. Now, when his daughter needed him once again, it was he who was helpless. Worse, he was deceiving her. Every moment of his silence exposed her to manipulation by people who would be ruthless in exploiting her vulnerability.

Silence was his treachery. The *apparat* had informed him of his daughter's situation not only because Lysenko's assassination made it inevitable that he would find out, but also because *they trusted him to remain silent*. It was a trust that shamed him.

Marusya, please forgive me. He was shocked to hear the words. He had spoken them out loud.

Why did the *apparat* trust him? Was it because it had trained and conditioned him and respected his professionalism? Perhaps; it was possible this was part of it. But the real reason they trusted him was that they knew that he could not act without destroying himself and his daughter. The moment he warned Nadya, they would know it; her reactions would betray them both. And with Klimenti removed, there would be no one to protect her. They had sent Nikishov to tell Klimenti that he could not change Nadya's fate. But he could reduce its consequences. By cooperating. This was their offer. How vile it was.

Am I really so helpless, Marusya? Me, Klimenti Amalrik, the man you loved! The father of your daughter?

Klimenti had been walking slowly, head down, hands buried deep in his greatcoat pockets, and now he looked up and found that he was outside the Bolshoi. A bus disgorged West German tourists, most of them women. Years ago their menfolk, their husbands and brothers and fathers and uncles, had come almost this far, right to the outskirts of the city, causing immeasurable suffering; and now they swarmed past him into the theater, trusting the two Russian Intourist guides to give them the right orders.

He had not come far, but in another sense, he had come far enough. He turned up and walked up the hill toward Dzerzhinsky Square. Now Russians bumped him as they passed. They were no longer the warm, friendly people with whom he had shared a brief happiness in the tunnel. The street was full of total indifference. Or was it merely that they were Russian and knew the system and cooperated by keeping their silence? Their other side.

Yes, Klimenti thought. That's it. He was not alone, after all. Just isolated, like everyone else, in this great vacuum of no-speak, afraid of the language.

But what if they didn't really trust him to keep silent? What if they had told him because they expected him—wanted him—to tell Nadya about the American?

What did they want him to start, so that they could finish it?

"We salute you, Comrade Colonel," a harsh voice cried.

He had come back into Dzerzhinsky Square. A group of young men barred his way. They wore fur and woollen caps, old army combat jackets, tight trousers, and boots. They were Afghansty, veterans who had fought in the Hindu Kush, a useless war which everyone wanted to forget. But there were those like these young men who could not forget and who would bear its scars forever.

Five of them snapped to attention, saluting. A sixth stepped forward, dragging an abject young man who was too cowed to protest.

He had already been roughed up. His cap had been torn off to reveal long, straggling hair.

"Forgive us, Comrade Colonel. But doesn't this bit of dogshit make you want to puke?"

Klimenti recognized them as Lyuberites, toughs from the ugly, sprawling working-class suburb in the southwest of the city. In Lyubertsy there was no escaping the draft. It was the blood of Lyubertsy that had flowed in Afghanistan, not the blood of the Lenin Hills or Arbat or Kutuzov Prospekt. There were no privileges in Lyubertsy except that of dying for your country, and they were proud of their sacrifices. They had gone away and fought; and when Gorbachev pulled them out and they came home, they felt betrayed by the decadence that had flourished while they wasted their lives in an unwinnable war. Even now, years after the withdrawal, they felt this alienation as deeply as another generation had felt it in post-Vietnam America, for entirely different reasons. They had gone away as boys and now they were men in their middle twenties; they sought their revenge by patrolling the privileged inner-city precincts, playing the role of vigilantes, beating up those who had capitulated to Western amorality.

Their grievances came forth in snarls.

"Look how he grovels."

"You see the courage of this parasite."

"Oh, he's brave all right. When it comes to baring his arse so the Yanks can shaft it right up him."

"I killed better men in Afghanistan."

But they directed their remarks at Klimenti instead of their victim, who stood downcast and trembling. Klimenti remained silent, wishing neither to provoke nor to appease.

People gathered to watch from a safe distance. It was not just fear that restrained them. Many shared the opinions of these embittered veterans and were grateful that someone had the courage to express them so forcefully. It was also generally believed that these gangs had the unofficial blessing of conservative elements among the leadership. Many others examined their own consciences and clothes and gave them a wide berth.

"With respect, Comrade Colonel, this sniveling object needs a haircut."

A pair of scissors was thrust at Klimenti. The toughs were grinning but their eyes were wary and hostile. One of them was older, quieter. He had a mustache that almost hid a harelip. Klimenti was sure he was their leader.

A woman called, "Good for you, comrades. Clean up all the scum, I say."

Klimenti took the scissors and threw them behind him. The toughs laughed. They had no need of scissors; their hands and boots would do.

"Lost your tongue as well as your guts, Colonel?"

"Chickenshit colonels, safe in the bunkers, buggering the blue-eyed boys."

The tough holding the victim flung him aside and he fled gratefully, without so much as a second look at Klimenti. In that moment, Klimenti understood that he had been the target from the outset.

"Take him, lads," the man with the harelip said.

They moved in slowly, disciplined and quiet; all the more deadly because of it. Klimenti had no avenue of escape, for they would quickly run him down. He wondered how badly they intended to hurt him. The harder he fought, the more damage they would do, and for a moment he thought of submitting passively and taking a beating. But the idea of submission filled him with loathing, at himself for even considering it and at these thugs for making it possible. All morning his helplessness had taunted him, and now he raged at it; driven by instinct rather than intelligence, moving with such explosive ferocity he was hardly aware it was happening, he went into them, feinting a kick left and striking right, chopping his hand into the nose of the nearest tough and double-kicking, getting him in the groin with his boot as he went down. Klimenti spun out, scything his left foot in a vicious arc to catch anyone coming in; he crouched, hands out, looking for another opening.

"Come on, you scum," he snarled. "Come on."

He wanted them to come, really wanted it, to gouge and kick and strike at them, to purge his own shame and pain; he went forward again, right hand jabbing, left cutting, turning, kicking, smashing a face, and spinning out, going forward until he realized he was striking at air, his two victims still down and groaning, full of blood. The speed and ferocity of his attack had taken them by surprise. They had never expected that a man in a heavy greatcoat could move so fast, and for a second the toughs held back, unsure now of the man who crouched in front of them, panting his hate.

"Come on," Klimenti spat. "Come on."

Major Kharkov burst in front of Klimenti, pistol drawn. He looked very dramatic and purposeful as he crouched before the gang, holding the Makarov with both hands and unwaveringly.

"Who wants to be the first to die?" Kharkov asked.

In the crowd, a woman screamed. Citizens who seconds earlier had been prepared to watch Klimenti get beaten up now trampled each other in their haste to get away.

"Pea shooter," a tough sneered.

"There's only one way to find out, shitface," Kharkov said coolly.

The gang leader said, "Let's go, lads."

He turned and walked away. The toughs picked up their fallen and followed, jerking their hands in gestures of contempt.

"Shitsuckers," one shouted.

Kharkov straightened and put the Makarov away. "Reporting for duty, sir," he said with a touch of mockery.

Klimenti was breathing heavily. His heart was pumping and his belly was fluttering from the adrenaline. He had forgotten how fear and anger sucked up all your strength and converted it into madness; that was how men fought, and when it was over, it left you trembling like an old woman. The sweat was squirting out of him.

"Thank you, Major," he panted.

"You gave one of them a broken nose."

So he had been watching all along.

Klimenti said, "If you hadn't arrived, they'd have broken more than my nose."

"Where's the Militia? They make themselves scarce when there's Afghansty around," Kharkov said, echoing a widely held belief that the Militia had been told to leave the toughs alone.

As they walked to No. 2, Klimenti wondered how the Afghansty could have been so sure that a full colonel in the KGB would not be armed.

A message awaited him, canceling the quarter-past-three appointment. Klimenti rang the Kremlin Clinic. Fadeyev's secretary said in her coldest voice, "I have been instructed that under no circumstances will the Academician receive your calls."

Klimenti wondered who had got to Fadeyev and warned him. Or had Fadeyev finally remembered his name and what had happened in East Berlin? He unlocked his desk drawer and took out his Makarov pistol and two clips of ammunition. He loaded one clip into the butt of the pistol and put the other clip and the pistol into his coat pocket.

Marietta Pronin wrote this down, noting the exact time.

Nikishov was at his desk, as still as a cobra, watching with unblinking eyes.

He said sourly, "We've got orders from Radchenko."

10.

Major Kharkov drove them to the small-arms range of the Taman Guards regiment, where a captain of the Military Police gave them a jeep. They were in a two-kilometer-long depression that was bordered on three sides by low, bald hills. It was too small to call a valley but it still gave a feeling of isolation, of being locked away from the rest of the world.

Nikishov grumbled, "I can't understand why Radchenko found it necessary for us to be here."

Kharkov put the jeep into four-wheel drive and followed sets of tire tracks that led through the snow to the target butts. There stood another jeep and an army field ambulance. Morozov was pacing up and down; he seemed physically incapable of being still and he had trodden the snow down into ice.

"Ah, gentlemen," Morozov shouted. "At last. Now we can proceed." The Academician led them behind the butts. "It's important you see for yourselves, so you'll have no doubts about what we're telling you."

A fiberglass store mannequin lay in the snow. It had been dressed in the bulky uniform of an ice hockey player, including helmet and face guard. A number of wires were attached. One led into the mannequin's mouth.

"Look closer," Morozov ordered.

Klimenti and Nikishov did so and stood back in horror. It was not a mannequin but the corpse of a man. Kharkov did not bother to look and Klimenti realized he knew already.

"A bit of a shock, eh?" Morozov grinned sardonically. Their reaction pleased him immensely.

"Who is he?"

Morozov shrugged. "I've no idea. After all the trouble I had getting him, I didn't care to ask."

An assistant reeled out electric wire, running it around the other side of the butts. Another began taking photographs from several angles. The camera flash lit the corpse with a cruel light that hurt their eyes.

Morozov said disgustedly, "You'd be amazed how hard it is to get hold of a corpse these days. Once, this country was filled with them. There were so many they had trouble burying the evidence. But we had to literally beg them to give us this fellow."

He lifted the hockey jersey. Beneath it, instead of the normal hockey player's protective gear, was gray wadding with the consistency of putty. It was plastic explosive, molded around the corpse. Even the feet and hands were wrapped around with explosive, in place of gloves and shin guards and boots.

Morozov said, "They got the idea the same way I did—watching ice hockey. All they did was replace the armor with plastic explosive. They stitched it into the vests, leggings and gloves, and headgear. They molded it around the assassin. Just like a tailor cuts a suit."

He pointed to the wire leading into the corpse's mouth. "We made the plastic into a simple mouth guard to take care of the teeth, jawbone, and skull."

"We're ready, Academician," an assistant called.

Morozov led them back to the jeep. He said, "If we sat that fellow on top of a truckload of explosive, we'd get some of him back. The blast would hurl him into the air and the full force of the explosion would miss him. The trick lies in how you distribute the explosive, to get maximum effect. There's only fifteen kilos there, and it's our stuff—not as good as HMX, but I'm willing to lay a wager that it'll do the job."

An assistant summoned enough courage to shout, "It'll soon be dark, Academician."

"Who cares?" Morozov growled. "There'll be nothing left to collect anyway."

They got into the vehicles. None of them wanted to be out in the open, exposed to the fallout that would rain from the sky.

The explosion was no louder than the sharp crack of a big field gun. Klimenti heard the pitter-patter of earth and snow and God knows what else as it fell onto the hood of the jeep. Goose pimples rose beneath the layers of warm clothing he wore; he felt he was freezing from the inside out, and shuddered. He prayed that nothing gruesomely identifiable as human—a head, a hand, or a foot—would land on the hood, right in front of his eyes.

Morozov was right. The explosion had ripped down through the cover of snow and torn into the frozen earth. The hole was not as big as that dug in the woods at Usovo, but the same dark spray lay over the surrounding snow. The corpse in the hockey gear had completely disappeared.

All of them, even Morozov, who had anticipated the results, stared at the stain in silence. Klimenti had a feeling that any words he could utter would be blasphemous. The assistants began taking photographs. It was almost dark now and the camera flash lit up their faces, giving them living the complexions of corpses. They were all paled by the experience.

Morozov broke the silence. "Mush. Human mush," he said and led them away.

At the Taman Guards barracks Kharkov took Klimenti aside. "Lieutenant General Radchenko presents his respects, Colonel. It would give him great pleasure if you would be his guest for dinner tonight. The Aragvi at eight o'clock."

It was a command, not an invitation. Klimenti said gravely, "I'd be delighted." He was pleased to see that Kharkov had enough humor in him to smile. Perhaps he was not such a robot after all.

As they prepared to leave, Klimenti asked, "Who was he, Major?"

"I don't know, Colonel," Kharkov said. "I didn't ask either."

On the drive back into the city, Klimenti was haunted by the photo flashes of pure white light that had stabbed into the drab, dead flesh. The corpse's left eyelid had somehow lifted, exposing the lifeless eye, and each time the lance thrust of light hit, it shone like black marble.

When they got back to No. 2, Klimenti telephoned the headquarters of the First Chief Directorate and got through to Major General Shalnev, the Director of Special Service 11.

"Your client's not responding," Shalnev said. "Our salesmen have gone through all the normal channels but there's no response."

"It takes time," Klimenti said.

"We know it," Shalnev said. "But time is the one thing we haven't got to spare."

Klimenti went back out into the night. He took a taxi to the Prague Restaurant on the corner of Kalinin Prospekt and Arbat Street and walked from there, turning off into several of the narrow streets that twisted through this attractive old quarter.

Once again he was appraised through the partly opened door by eyes the washed-out gray of a winter sky, and as cold.

"Is Nadya in, please?"

"No," Zhenya Stepanov said. "Are you really her father?"

"Of course!" Her arrogance irritated Klimenti.

"Hmmm," she said, regarding him with interest. Klimenti wondered if she would be so bold and haughty if she knew that the apartment, her bedroom included, was probably bugged. He would have liked to tell her, just to puncture her conceit.

The young woman smiled, becoming a different person. "I was brought up to be very careful. I'll tell Nadya you called."

Klimenti went back to Dzerzhinsky Square. Nikishov butted out a Players and emptied the ashtray. Klimenti had never known him to smoke so heavily.

Nikishov said, "The Americans have informed us there was a note. From the Vigilantes for Peace."

"So now they know about Lysenko."

Nikishov nodded. "They're very angry we didn't warn them."

"I can imagine."

"What was the point? They wouldn't have believed us."

"Have the Americans released the note to their press?"

"No. They want to keep quiet about it, too."

Klimenti said, "It'll give them a chance to blame the Nicaraguans. Or the Cubans."

"Navachine's agreed to cooperate," said Nikishov. "He's been released back into the bosom of his family."

Klimenti nodded. He knew it would only annoy Nikishov if he feigned surprise.

Nikishov said, "It was my recommendation, too."

Klimenti laughed. "In that case, we're both geniuses."

Nikishov's handsome face was soured by his sense of grievance. He said, "Why didn't you discuss it with me first? After all, Navachine's my responsibility."

"I was told not to," Klimenti said.

Nikishov smiled bitterly. "That's what I thought."

"I'd like to see the records of interrogation, if I may, Simis Isayevich?"

"I'm sorry, but I can't give them to you." It gave Nikishov pleasure to see the surprise on Klimenti's face.

"May I ask why not?"

"Because, Klimenti Sergeyevich, they told me not to."

Nikishov was enjoying his revenge.

"Specifically," he said.

At 6 P.M. Klimenti went to a deserted secretaries' pool on the second floor and typed a note on cheap blank paper that was used for carbon copies. He got out just as the security guards came around to lock up.

He got a chauffeur to drive him to Shabolovka Street. Lights were on in all the apartment windows, and the odors of cooking and the sounds of television and family conversations seeped beneath doors and into the corridors. The building had been painted two years ago and was quite clean and bright. Each spring the residents formed working parties and washed and scrubbed the building, argued about the small garden out front, and splashed on paint with more gusto than skill, repairing the ravages of winter. Each spring Klimenti worked with them, taking his instructions from bossy young mothers, sensing a sexual intensity in their brief spasm of authority. They were all glad for what they had and protected it as best they could.

Klimenti opened the drawer on his bedside dresser and sorted among the papers and junk inside until he found a blue consular *kartoshka*, the identity card carried by foreign diplomats. It was in the name of a real American Embassy staff official, but the photograph was of Klimenti. It had been stolen while the official was in a restaurant, and the photograph had been exchanged by the KGB forgers in the 14th

Department. Klimenti had used it as a cover several months ago and should have returned it. He was in breach of KGB regulations and was running the risk of a severe censure, but it took time, a lot of paper work, to get false identification and it was a lot easier and quicker to reach into the bedside drawer.

He showered, shaved, and changed into a blue-and-white striped shirt and a dark gray suit he had bought seven years ago on his last visit to England. He chose a maroon tie. The suit still fitted and this gratified him, because it wasn't easy keeping fit. He put on a pair of dark, highly polished brogues. Over this, he wore a heavy, finely woven overcoat his wife had bought him in New York. The American colony in Moscow was very fashion conscious.

Klimenti took a taxi to No. 7 Kutuzov Prospeckt, an enclave of eight high-rise apartments reserved for foreigners. In the event, it was not necessary for Klimenti to present the *kartoshka* to the guard, a KGB officer disguised as a Militiaman. Russians recognized foreigners by the clothes they wore and by the way they confronted authority, usually by ignoring it. A Russian approaching a door sought out the guard; a Westerner strode straight on past, daring to be challenged, and seldom was.

Klimenti took the elevator to the sixth floor, wondering what would happen if he encountered Bannon. Would the American recognize him?

He went to the door of an apartment occupied by an American journalist who was, in reality, a CIA agent. He slipped a sealed envelope under it. Inside was the note he had typed.

It said in Russian: "Bannon is having a secret affair with a vixen."

11.

Despite the cold, a group of hopefuls clustered outside the doors of the Aragvi Restaurant in a cul-de-sac off Gorky Street. Mostly, they were young couples in their late twenties and early thirties, well-to-do and successful enough to afford the fare but not important enough to book a table, even if they telephoned a week in advance. They waited in the hope that some early diners would leave, making a table available for them.

Klimenti banged on the glass panel. The couples stared at him with resentment. The commissionaire pressed his nose up against the glass, inspecting Klimenti with imperious eyes. He was in his sixties, with gray hair fringing beneath his cap, and was tall and aristocratic. He had a flawless instinct for authority and could size up people with the sureness of a Cossack picking a horse, certain of the pedigree. He stood as stiffly as a drill sergeant as he let Klimenti in. The crowd pressed forward, babbling for attention, but the commissionaire shut the door in their faces without giving them a glance.

Klimenti gave his name and the commissionaire took his coat and, with the smooth flourish of a magician, for they quickly disappeared, five rubles.

"Good evening, sir. Lieutenant General Radchenko is waiting."

He led Klimenti into the restaurant, which occupied a cavernous basement. The marble walls were painted with murals of Georgian tigers and peasants and mountains. Chandeliers hung from the high ceilings. A folk ensemble in Georgian national costume played from a balcony overlooking the main room. The restaurant had been built to please Georgia's most famous son, in 1939; in those days there were dancing girls, and Stalin had made it the fashion to throw rubles at them.

Radchenko had a private room, a measure of his influence and also his intent. He was wearing a civilian suit of distinctive French cut; ever since Napoleon, the French had a flair for dressing men of short stature. Dressing the wolf in lamb's clothing accentuated rather than diminished Radchenko's military bearing. His thick, iron-gray hair bristled in a crew cut which gave clean, powerful lines to his broad-cheeked face. He was hard-bellied beneath his coat, and Klimenti remembered that every day Radchenko swam thirty laps of the indoor pool at the Kremlin spa. Once a year he went through the rigorous fitness tests to which every Guardsman was subjected, including a twenty-kilometer run in full combat gear and battle pack in three hours. There was a rip in his left ear, left by a Mujahedin bullet. It was not something you noticed when he wore his large officer's hat; now it had the same effect as a pirate's earring—it drew your attention, establishing his credentials beyond contradiction.

The lieutenant general proved a gracious host; Radchenko the Terrible had learned much since leaving the officers' academy. A bottle of Kinzmarauli, a Georgian red wine that was difficult to obtain, was already breathing on the table.

"Kinzmarauli was Stalin's favorite, you know," Radchenko said as he poured the wine. Klimenti hadn't known. "They had high times in those days. There were nights when the entire restaurant would be taken over by the Politburo and their hangers-on. The whole gang, Khrushchev, Bulgarin, Molotov, Malenkov, Voroshilov, all of 'em so scared they were getting bilious on the only good food in the whole damn Soviet Union. Even those dancing sluts couldn't cheer them up."

He waved an arm around. "And all because Stalin would be in here, having a good time with Beria, sitting at this very table, eating *shaslik* and getting nice and sozzled on Kinzmarauli. Before he got around to signing the lists. They were scared shitless he'd put their names down. Every one of 'em. Drooling and dribbling shit."

"Those were the days," Klimenti said dryly.

Radchenko laughed. "Tonight we're going to sit here, just like Stalin and Beria, eating *shaslik* and drinking Kinzmarauli, and out there everyone's having a good time. There're no lists to scare them shitless, thanks to Comrade Gorbachev."

"Here's to it, General. Comrade Gorbachev. And no more lists."

They drank some more and began dinner with *chkhirtma*, a spicy Georgian chicken soup. For all the battleground vigor of his language, Radchenko sipped his soup and broke the hot bread with the self-conscious delicacy of someone who has been taught etiquette late in life. True to his word, Radchenko ordered lamb *shaslik* and rice. Klimenti chose chicken *tabaka*.

"We country lads have got to stick together," Radchenko said with a disarming smile. "You know, Colonel, it's my firm conviction that a country boy can learn all the tricks of the city. It takes a bit of time, a few knocks. That's all. But a city slicker can never learn the country, no matter how hard he tries, how long he spends at it. The country's born into you. It can't be taught and it can't be acquired. In the country, city slickers are always foreigners."

Radchenko did not get down to business until they had finished eating and were into the second bottle. He said abruptly, "I'm surprised you didn't realize that all inquiries about the Politburo come directly to me, Colonel. It was on my instructions that Academician Fadeyev canceled your appointment."

"You're quite right, General," Klimenti said. "I'm rather surprised myself."

Radchenko laughed. "However, what I'm here to tell you is that a month ago it was found that Comrade Lysenko had cancer of the bowel. He was given six months to live."

"I see," Klimenti said.

"I hope so, Colonel," Radchenko said. All the good humor had gone from his face. "This week Comrade Lysenko was going to retire from all public duties. The gathering at his dacha was to break the news to his personal staff and old comrades. It's ironic, don't you think, that if the assassins had known that his power was at an end, that his influence was finished, they may have spared his life."

"And chosen another victim?"

Radchenko nodded. "Would you go to all that trouble to kill an old man who was dead in his boots, anyway? Whose power and influence were at an end?"

The excellent wine, the superb food, were forgotten. All joviality had gone from the room; it was as if the clammy spirits of Stalin and Beria had seeped from beneath the chair cushions. Radchenko's face was screwed up hard, the eyes hard, the lips hard, the face of a hunter intent only on finding weakness. He would sense it, the way a dog can smell fear.

Was it Radchenko who had sent the Afghansty? He had the power, and the veterans worshiped him; they would obey him without question. Was it really a coincidence that Kharkov, Radchenko's aide, had arrived in the nick of time?

"Perhaps, Colonel, you might explain your interest in Comrade Lysenko's health."

"It was an afterthought, General. No more. Trying to tidy up all the loose ends."

Radchenko said, "Perhaps."

Klimenti said coldly, "I assure you, General, if my inquiry had any other significance, I would have been far more circumspect than to approach an informer like Fadeyev."

Radchenko stared hard, hunting fear. He said, "It was a brilliant analysis, Colonel. I was both impressed by your courage and the clarity of your thinking and shocked by your frankness. But there are those who would regard it as injudicious."

"It was an intelligence analysis, General, not a political appreciation."

"Quite so. But nonetheless you've trodden on sensitivities that the Politburo would prefer to leave undisturbed. No matter how objective you intended to be, the implications you raised are very troubling."

Klimenti spoke very clearly for the microphones that—he was sure—were recording the entire conversation. "Let's get it straight, General. I did not say that the KGB killed Comrade Lysenko and Senator Townley. I said the CIA will *believe* that we did it. There is quite a difference."

"You argued very persuasively, Colonel."

"I gave the American perceptions, General. No more. The Americans believe that Comrade Lysenko was the leader of an Old Guard faction opposed to Comrade Gorbachev's reforms. They believe that

Comrade Lysenko and the Stalinists were plotting a coup to overthrow Comrade Gorbachev and his supporters. That's why they were so interested in the gathering at Usovo. Given their beliefs, it would convince them a coup was imminent. The fact that Lysenko was killed leaving that weekend meeting will only reinforce their conviction that Comrade Gorbachev reached the same conclusion as they did and ordered a preemptive strike, and the KGB carried it out."

Radchenko stared at him, fascinated. "I accept what you say, Colonel. As an American perception. But I can't accept that the Americans would really believe that we would invent these Vigilantes for Peace and kill Senator Townley just as a cover for exterminating Lysenko."

"General, there are Americans who believe we are capable of *anything*. It's why they are so dangerous. Many Americans, including a lot of intelligence professionals, are still convinced that we had a hand in the assassination of President Kennedy. It would be very easy, and also very satisfying, for them to believe we killed Senator Townley."

Radchenko had not expected Klimenti to be so frank, and for a moment, remembering the microphones, he was not sure how to react. Finally he said, "Perhaps, Colonel, you argued too persuasively. There are those who on reading your analysis could not be blamed for being at least suspicious that you secretly believed the Americans are right."

So this was what it was all about. The room was as cold and as empty as a tomb. The warmth and comfort were gone, mocking memories. There was no need to ask who held the suspicions. The Chairman and the Deputy Chairman. Radchenko had not gone to all this trouble merely to seek assurances in his own behalf.

Klimenti said loudly, his voice ringing against the walls, "I assure you, General, that it is most definitely not my opinion."

Rachenko watched him gravely and it occurred to Klimenti that he genuinely wished to believe him. He said, "I accept what you say, Colonel. However, I feel it is my duty to warn you to be more circumspect in the future."

"Thank you, General. You may rest assured I will take your advice."

Klimenti had been warned off. He was sure now that it all went together: the Afghansty, witnessing Morozov's gruesome experiment, this dinner.

"I'm glad, Colonel."

Radchenko stood up so abruptly his chair scraped loudly across the marble. On the tapes it would sound like a snarl of finality. The dinner was over.

They went out into the restaurant, which was crowded and happy; it was noisy with music, chatter and laughter, the clatter of cutlery and the clink of glasses—all warm, reassuring, harmonic sounds. It was good to be out of that room in which so many death sentences had been carelessly signed, splashed with the red blood of warm Georgian wine. Klimenti swore to himself he would never drink Kinzmarauli again.

Major Kharkov was waiting with a chauffeur-driven Chaika. The streets were quiet as they drove. A drunk staggered and slipped on the icy pavement, performing miraculous gyrations to stay on his feet.

Radchenko laughed heartily. "Sober he'd have fallen and broken a leg. God looks after imbeciles and drunks."

A few minutes later he said, "I take it, Colonel, you are aware that the CIA's so-called Kremlinologists give Comrade Gorbachev only a thirty percent chance of surviving. Kissinger is kinder. He puts it at fifty percent."

"It's not new," Klimenti said. "The Americans live in the hope that their propaganda will become self-fulfilling prophecy."

"Not only the Americans," Radchenko said grimly.

The Chaika stopped outside Klimenti's apartment block. Kharkov leaped out and opened the door for Klimenti. Radchenko reached across and took his arm.

He said quietly, "Colonel, you're a country boy who's learned the tricks of the city. But don't forget: good hunters set snares you never see. Not until you're hanging in them."

12.

"These days it's mostly tourists who come to see him," Klaus said. "Once, not so long ago either, there would have been a huge queue of Russians, stretching right around the Square, shuffling forward, never complaining. They'd wait hours, even in the bitter cold, just to pay their respects, a few seconds, that's all, enough for a quick glance and then the guards would move them on."

He sounded sad, buried deep in his overcoat and fur hat and huddled in on himself against the wind that blew across the great expanse of Red Square and polished the ice that crusted the mausoleum in which the embalmed corpse of Lenin, the man who had begun it all, lay in state.

"How suddenly the mighty fall." Klaus sighed, as if the same fate awaited him.

Control said, "It doesn't matter what they think now. He could do with the rest. But in two, three hundred years, when they look back at the history of the twentieth century, it'll be Lenin they'll remember first. Lenin and Einstein. And Gorbachev, too. Lenin turned the world upside down, Einstein turned it inside out, and now Gorbachev's turning it topsy-turvy once more and setting it back on its feet again. Imagine—a Soviet leader with the Nobel Peace Prize. If he can turn the Soviet economy around, if he can only get it working, they'll make him Man of the Century."

If the great weight of Russia didn't crush Gorbachev first, as it had so many before him.

"What about Churchill? Roosevelt? Stalin? Hitler?" asked Klaus.

"Not in the same league. Mao perhaps. And Truman. After all, he dropped the first atom bombs. That must be worth remembering."

"And the Beatles," Klaus said. "Don't forget the Beatles."

"Yes, the Beatles, too. And Picasso, although I hate to say it."

The ceremonial guards stood erect and immobile, young men carefully chosen for their beauty and stature, qualities enhanced further by the simplicity of their unadorned gray uniforms.

Control said, "It's good to know he's back. The embalming wasn't too good and one of his ears deteriorated. They had to take him away and replace it with a plastic one. It was all very embarrassing for them."

Klaus was plump and soft and suave, a Bavarian; he sold the Russians medical equipment. He smiled. "There's something very Russian about that: their greatest hero having a plastic ear."

But Control was no longer listening. He was caught with a memory, immersing himself back in it, of a woman who had been devout, a believer, too, before she fell into despair; and of Panama City where it had begun for him, for both of them: a warm, humid place, so different from frigid Moscow, and not just in temperature—in temperament and mood, too. Not for the first time, he wondered if he loved her. For a while, they had loved, but in need, not willingly, until they found the strength to part. He wasn't sure what love was, except she was part of him, and he part of her, and always would be.

Her time would come soon. They hadn't told him, but he was sure of it.

Control said, "Tell them we're set to go."

"You've seen him?"

Klaus was not permitted to know the names of those they sent to Moscow or anything else about them, and this only served to deepen his sense of awe at what had been achieved in Moscow and Washington. He envied Control, who could get close to them, who sent them to their death. What an honor, a privilege.

Control nodded. "Briefly. They chose well. Both of them."

"I'll tell them."

In Moscow, Control was the key to it all. There had to be someone else doing the same job in Washington, but that wasn't Klaus's responsibility. Moscow Control was. His life had been placed in Klaus's hands. I'm his lifeline, Klaus thought with satisfaction. He was not afraid, and this made him feel good. One of the few. Yes.

He said, "I've brought instructions."

Control waited, wishing the Square was once again filled with stoic pilgrims shuffling forward, a step at a time, to see Lenin. He missed them. Their patience had always impressed him; it taught you a lot about them. That was their strength—their ability to abide. It's why we fear them, he thought. We know they'll abide and we're not so sure about ourselves.

Klaus said, "The ones we engaged to solve our transportation difficulties. Can you get to them?"

"It takes time but it can be done. But only if it's absolutely necessary."

"It's necessary."

"Why?"

But Control knew. He had been hoping they would send in someone else to do it. He shivered.

Klaus had soft brown eyes. Everything about him was soft. Even his voice. He too shivered. With excitement.

He said, "Kill them."

13.

In the morning, Klimenti threw caution to the winds and telephoned Nadya.

"You've just missed her," Zhenya Stepanov said. "She's working very hard."

"Will you please tell Nadya that her grandfather is coming to Moscow. To ring me. At work is all right. She has the number."

Zhenya Stepanov must have sensed his suspicion, because she said, "I've passed on all your messages. Really, Nadya's working very hard."

When Klimenti got to Dzerzhinsky Street, he rang Shalnev, the head of Special Service 11.

"Anything from our client?"

"Nothing," Shalnev said. "Our salesmen think it's possible he's fallen ill."

He meant arrested. "I doubt it," Klimenti said. "He's very careful about his health."

"Aren't we all," Shalnev said wearily. "We'll keep trying."

Squirrel's unexplained failure to operate the dead-letter drop would make life very difficult, breeding suspicion, the voracious cancer in the bloodstream of every secret service. Even if Squirrel had a perfectly innocent explanation for his behavior, the seed of doubt was already sown. Such was the virulence of the cancer that the more reasonable his

explanation, the more Squirrel would be suspected of having manufactured it. They were afraid that Squirrel had at last been found out and
had become a double agent to save his own skin. Or had he been a
double agent from the very beginning? It was like a maze of mirrors,
each of them reflecting images distorted with paranoia. This was the
incubus of all intelligence agencies, their deepest trauma, that they
were being betrayed from within.

Klimenti deeply felt the burden of concern for Squirrel. They met
once a year in out-of-the-way European villages, to renew the personal
commitment that was so important to Squirrel, who needed to be
reassured that Klimenti was still his control.

Squirrel once told him, "The CIA's the KGB by another name, the
same beast. And I *know* you can't trust them. But you won't let your
beast betray me. Not you, Klimenti."

Klimenti had never understood the basis of this trust, but he did not
question its sincerity. Their meetings lasted only a few hours, usually
over lunch, giving them both a whole morning to reach the rendezvous
and the afternoon to return from it. Yet they were precious hours,
nourishing eleven years of risk. Such trust scalded both of them whom
it embraced, and Klimenti could not accept that Squirrel had betrayed
it.

Stick with me, Squirrel.

Marietta Pronin informed Klimenti that he was to join Nikishov
immediately in the Deputy Chairman's suite of offices. Radchenko was
there too, upright as a cadet officer. He nodded coolly to Klimenti,
putting last night's dinner behind them. Nikishov cast a nervous glance
at Klimenti before snapping his eyes down to stare fixedly at
Poluchkin's desktop. Poluchkin's bad eye was covered with a black
plastic patch to give it some relief from the light, a sure sign of stress.

Poluchkin said, "Colonel, we've offered the Americans an open
and frank exchange of information and resources. We feel that this is
the best way to allay any mutual suspicions that might arise."

Klimenti was careful not to show the relief he felt. The decision
was a vindication of his analysis—and it could only have been taken by
the Politburo.

Poluchkin said, "Both we and the Americans agree that the aim of
these madmen is to destabilize our relationship. *Why* is open to
conjecture. But whatever the reason, it gives us a common enemy, a

shared objective. So we have agreed to cooperate to expedite their elimination."

He paused, to give his words emphasis. "Secretly, of course."

Poluchkin took off his glasses and slid a finger beneath the patch, stroking his sore eye. Considering the time differences between Moscow and Washington, he must have been up most of the night to get the details of the agreement worked out.

Poluchkin said, "You're to be our liaison officer in Moscow."

So, Klimenti thought, they're pushing me out onto the sidelines, and he wondered if it had been Radchenko's recommendation, a decision reached after last night's dinner. They don't trust me, he thought, and was surprised at the weight of disappointment he felt, that his loyalty should be questioned.

Poluchkin turned his awful gaze to Nikishov, who was fastidiously inspecting his fingernails, an obvious sign of embarrassment. "Major General."

Nikishov straightened. His words were clipped and precise. "The Americans have already nominated your opposite number."

Poluchkin and Radchenko were watching intently. There was tension, expectancy among them. Nikishov was pale and he looked up to hold Klimenti's eyes, and Klimenti had the feeling that it was an act of courage and decency.

Nikishov said, "Harry Bannon."

Bannon came to the meeting in a taxi. He came five minutes early. He didn't want to walk in on any unpleasant surprises.

Klimenti waited in the mezzanine floor, which overlooked the lobby of the Rossiya Hotel, giving him a clear view of the entrance. Uniformed hotel guards stood in the well, between the double weather doors, checking everyone. You needed a hotel pass showing room and floor number to get past the guards, who were there to deter ordinary Russians from venturing in for a cup of coffee and a glass of cognac. There were exceptions, however. The guards did not argue with members of the Communist Party or important officials; both categories had sufficient privileges that they could be trusted not to be seduced by contact with foreigners. They also did not bother to check foreigners, and Bannon walked past the guards, ignoring them.

It offended Klimenti that foreigners had more freedom, more

rights, more privileges than Soviet citizens. So much for *glasnost*, when hard currency was worth the humiliation of your own people.

Bannon was taller than Klimenti had imagined. Klimenti saw the same wariness that had been caught so dramatically in the photograph Nikishov had shown him; it wasn't so much nervousness as watchfulness, an expectancy of threat. He would be a difficult man to take by surprise.

So this was the man who was making love to Nadya. The American who had put his daughter in jeopardy. Klimenti prickled with a sensation of coldness. He had come early to give himself an opportunity to size up the American, to prepare himself psychologically.

They met by the elevators, as arranged. "Colonel Raikin," the American said, giving the name Klimenti was working under.

"Mr. Bannon," Klimenti said with equal formality.

Neither offered to shake hands and Klimenti was grateful for it. They exchanged no other greeting. They took the elevator to the tenth floor in a silence made easy by the presence of several Swedish businessmen, both looking straight ahead at the elevator doors. Their frostiness made it easier than Klimenti had expected. Even so he wondered how long it would take the Americans to react to his note. Since the scandal of the Marine guards, they were supersensitive about fraternization with Russians. A week at the most. They would whisk Bannon out of the country, and the threat to Nadya would be ended.

Unless, of course, Bannon was acting on instructions. In which case he undoubtedly knew Klimenti's real identity, that he was Nadya's father. The thought made Klimenti cringe inside and it took all his discipline to conceal his rancor.

In the hotel room Bannon put a tape recorder on the coffee table and pushed the record button. "OK, Colonel, let's get started."

His attitude was businesslike, neither rude nor polite, and showed a contempt for the hypocrisy of diplomatic nicety. They were, after all, enemies in a very real sense. Whatever relations were on the surface between their two countries, even in times of cordiality, the secret war never let up; it went on ceaselessly in the deep and dark recesses, away from the public gaze and conscience. It was not uncommon for CIA agents to display evangelical commitment, deeply and sincerely regarding the KGB as the embodiment of evil. Perhaps Bannon was such a man.

Klimenti was also carrying a tape recorder. Bannon watched with a bemused stare as he set it up. The KGB had recently used the hotel to set a homosexual "raven" trap for a French journalist it wanted expelled, and it had made scandalous reading in the West.

"Why bother?" Bannon indicated the television set. "The room's bugged already, videos and all."

"Better quality," Klimenti said curtly, turning his tape recorder on.

Bannon laughed softly, appreciating the irony, but the humor did not reach his eyes. He had the leanness of a former athlete who has kept fit: moving, he was both physically elegant and arrogant.

They got down to business. The Americans had made the same assessment as the KGB: the assassins were well organized, well equipped and motivated—brainwashed it seemed, to an extraordinary degree. They had self-destructed to remove all traces of identity and to strike psychological terror; they would strike again, and it would be almost impossible to stop them from succeeding. In this, the Americans with their more open society faced a greater problem, but it was only one of degree.

Bannon said, "Colonel, so there will be no misunderstanding, let me give you our perspective. In the States, they gave this problem to a think tank to work over. They put all the possibilities and probabilities through a process of elimination and the conclusion they came to was that it had to be either the KGB or us—and we know it isn't us!"

"That's why we're meeting."

"On the other hand, the assassinations have been considerably to the benefit of President Gorbachev. He has to cut military spending as a matter of economic survival. If he doesn't, the Soviet Union will go bankrupt. Between them, Lysenko and Townley could have fouled him up. And it just so happens that Lysenko was plotting a palace coup. The assassins showed nice timing, wouldn't you say?"

Klimenti hoped he would be there to watch the Deputy Chairman's reaction when the tape was played back to him.

Bannon held up two fingers. "The ball game's just begun and already the score is two nothing for the KGB."

Klimenti said coldly, "We came here to exchange information, not opinions."

He handed over Morozov's analyses, identifying the materials used in the VFP note as Russian and the plastic explosive as American HMX. Bannon did his best to cover his surprise.

"We won't accept this analysis on the plastic unless you give us the original test materials."

Klimenti handed him a plastic evidence bag half filled with soil. "Our experts say this will be enough."

"We have no way of verifying that the samples come from the blast area." The lack of argument made Bannon uneasy.

"You're doing tests on the explosive used by Senator Townley's assassin?"

"Of course."

"I think that'll be all the verification you need."

Klimenti presented Bannon with evidence relating to the RPG7 missiles that had killed Lysenko. Morozov's assistants had found a base plate with a serial number and the computers of the Arab specialists, the Eighth Department of the First Chief Directorate, had traced the antitank missile to a shipment of armaments delivered to the Palestinian Liberation Organization. The cache had been captured by the Israelis when they drove the PLO out of Lebanon in 1982.

Klimenti said, "The Israelis sell captured Soviet weapons to the CIA."

"We won't accept this without independent verification," Bannon snapped. "And that's not possible."

"That's not true," Klimenti said, passing Bannon a photograph of the base plate, clearly showing the serial number. "Your own records can confirm it. You supplied the captured weapons to the Afghans and the Contras in Nicaragua."

Bannon strode to the window, which offered an unrivaled view of the Kremlin and Red Square. But it was of no interest to the American. He drummed his fingers on the windowpane in a slow, methodical tattoo.

"There's more," Klimenti said and gave him Morozov's analysis of the four hairs he had found at the blast site. Examination by a microscope revealed the assassin was a Caucasian male. The hairs were placed in a mass spectrometer, then exposed to positively charged ions and passed through magnetic fields to measure the molecular structure of material that had impregnated the hairs. This was made difficult by the saturation of the hair with plastic explosive. However, the mass spectrometer tests were still able to determine an unusual quantity of bromine, one of the basic elements used in tranquilizers.

The mass spectrometer also revealed the presence of tetraethyl lead, which is absorbed into the hair from automobile exhausts. Tetraethyl lead is added during the refining process to improve the octane rating and is normally composed of four isotopes in fixed percentages—52.4 percent of isotope 208, 24.1 percent of 206, 22.1 percent of 207, and 1.4 percent of 204. But the mass spectrometer showed that the tetraethyl lead absorbed by the four hairs from the assassin's head was different. It had 10 percent less isotope 208 and 10 percent more isotope 207. No refineries in the Soviet Union or anywhere in Eastern Europe produced gasoline with this isotopic balance. In Morozov's opinion it would be unusual even in the West.

Conclusion: the assassin was a white male who had spent the last four to six months outside the Soviet Union, most of it under unusually heavy sedation—possibly in a psychiatric institution—in an area exposed to pollution by a rare composition of lead isotopes. Soviet embassies and trade missions had been instructed to find out which Western refineries produced gasoline with this specific isotopic balance.

"We'll want to do our own tests," Bannon said defiantly. "We'll need some hair samples."

Klimenti handed him a sealed evidence bag. Bannon gingerly held it against the light coming in from the window. The outline of a strand of hair could be clearly seen through the transparent plastic.

"It's enough," Klimenti said. "Our scientists say that if you look carefully enough, you should find some hair in Washington. We're confident they'll verify our evidence. We would also appreciate your help in locating the oil refinery."

"If there's hair to be found, we'll find it." Bannon was defensive now. "The same goes for the refinery."

"We hope so," Klimenti said coolly. "So far, all the hard evidence available shows that the assassin came from outside the Soviet Union, the plastic explosive was American, and the rocket launcher was supplied either by the Americans or by the Israelis. Quite frankly, Mr. Bannon, we'd appreciate your independent confirmation, because it makes nonsense of your so-called perspective."

Klimenti felt good. Thanks to Morozov he had punctured Bannon's arrogance. In comparison, all Bannon had to present was photographs

of the assassination scene in Washington and a summary of eyewitnesses' accounts. Klimenti read the report. It was his turn to be
surprised.

"That's right," Bannon said. "The assassin was a black."

When Klimenti got back to the Operations Room at No. 2, he wrote his
report and made a copy of the tapes. He gave them to Marietta Pronin
to take to Poluchkin.

"I'd like you to put this in the safe," he said, handing her the
original tape.

"Certainly," she said with a smile. She was efficient and pleasant
along with it. Klimenti watched as she went to the safe, twisted the
handle, and swung it open. She secured the combination lock only
when she left the office for lunch and when she went home in the
evening, before the security guards locked every office and tested all
the safes. It saved a lot of fiddling around during working hours. The
secretaries and librarians were constantly warned against such laxness,
but good security bred overconfidence and thus its own destruction. It
was a relief to know that even the otherwise perfect Marietta Pronin
took shortcuts.

When she was gone, Klimenti opened the safe. Quickly he searched
through the folders until he found the summary of Navachine's confession.
He had given Bannon the names of Lysenko's weekend guests. Bannon
had wanted Navachine to plant bugs in the dining room to record the
conversation, but he had refused. He would not have an opportunity
himself and he could not trust anyone else to do it for him. Bannon had not
asked when Lysenko was expected to depart back to Moscow and
Navachine had not included this information in his report, which he had
left in a dead-letter drop on Sunday, the day before the assassination. The
interrogators, at first refusing to believe that this was all the Americans
wanted, had questioned Navachine intensively—the euphemism for rough
stuff—but he had not changed his story. It was the interrogators' opinion
that he was telling the truth.

Navachine had made them a list of the names he gave to Bannon.
There were fifteen guests. Four were Politburo members, including the
Minister for Defense; three were candidate members of the Politburo,
including the junior ministers for Defense and for Internal Security; six
were chairmen of committees on the Central Committee, the real

government of the Soviet Union; the last two were an air force general and the army commander of the Moscow Military District.

These were not the old friends and comrades who peopled Radchenko's version of the dacha weekend, gathered to say farewell to their feeble and dying mentor. These were ambitious men who commanded immense power. Bannon was right. Far from getting ready to retire, Lysenko had been energetically plotting against Gorbachev.

For the first time, Klimenti fully understood how precarious his position had become.

14.

Klimenti went home at seven o'clock. His apartment was on the fourth floor of a six-story building which had been constructed during the NEP, the New Economic Policy, when the Revolution was still trying to impress the world. It had an ancient cage elevator that terrified the residents with its wild rattles and lurches. But the rooms had high ceilings and had tall windows that gave him a glimpse of the Moskva River and Gorky Park. He had two bedrooms, a combined dining-sitting room, a kitchenette, and a bathroom—unheard-of living space for a single man. The second bedroom was Nadya's, but she had not lived there for a year.

The apartment belonged to his wife's family, the Morozovs, who had insisted Klimenti take it up when he returned from America with Nadya. He had accepted it for the sake of his newly dead wife and his living daughter, although it went against the grain to take anything he had neither earned nor paid for. His father had never understood how it came about that the Morozovs could have two apartments and a dacha when whole families, sometimes three generations, were forced to live in a single room, like mice in a hole. His father's difficulty was that he was an honest man who believed in the struggle of the working class, to which he was grateful to belong. Klimenti's grandfather had been a landless and illiterate peasant and his father had known extreme hardship.

Klimenti rang Nadya's number. There was no answer. He opened his mail. There was a letter from his father confirming his travel plans, posted in the village of Vado three days ago. He was taking the overnight train from Arzamas and would be arriving in Moscow at 8:06 A.M. on Friday. Klimenti wished he could telephone, but his father did not have a phone. This convenience, which Khrushchev had given to the masses, had been denied his father because he shared the *izba* Klimenti had grown up in with his old army pal, Sabotka, who had done twenty-five years in the Gulag and who was—as far as the officials were concerned anyway—a thoroughly discreditable person. A telephone, they argued, would only make it easier for Sabotka to do whatever it was they suspected he was doing, although they had never been able to tell Sabotka exactly what this was supposed to be. Besides, telephones were for workers, not social parasites, and Sabotka didn't have a job. No one was brave enough to employ him. Even today they still treated former *zeks* as lepers. Survival in the camps had taught Sabotka many skills and he made a living—and a good one at that—as an odd-job handyman, paid on the sly, sometimes in cash, often in farm produce, which was worth a lot more.

Klimenti's father said, "You can live without a telephone. But you can't live without a friend." Klimenti was proud and loved him.

Klimenti showered and dressed—slacks and a dark turtleneck sweater and a pair of fur-lined Italian boots he had bought on his last trip outside the Soviet Union. He rang Nadya's number twice more. The first time it was busy. When he rang back five minutes later, no one answered. He felt frustrated and rejected.

He put on a jacket of soft, fine Italian leather and a fur hat and took a pair of gloves. Before he went out into the cold, he tucked his Makarov pistol into his waistband and put an extra clip in his jacket pocket. He did not want to be on such unequal terms should he bump into the Afghansty again.

He walked to the river and followed it. The Moskva isn't a great river and in summer it sometimes stinks. But, like all rivers, it soothes the human condition. For Klimenti the Moskva was a confirmation of the continuing thread of existence, outlasting all the cataclysms that had shaken the city. He was not a poetic man but he understood the river in the same way the peasant in him understood the land; it was part of him, and he was part of it. It was very simple.

Dawdling by the river also gave Klimenti a chance to discover that he was being followed by two men in a Volga.

Klimenti took a taxi to the Hotel Belgrade on Smolenskaja Street. There were twin hotels on either side of the street, rectangular stone-and-glass blocks, which had been modern and bold in Khrushchev's era but now showed signs of long neglect. The display windows were empty, except for dust and torn backing paper. One of the outer weather doors had a loose hinge and crashed against its neighbor. There was mud and slush from melted snow in the weather trap.

The guard at the door took him for a foreigner and Klimenti walked through unchallenged. A group of pretty girls wearing expensive Western clothes stood by the cloakroom. They were prostitutes who had bribed the guard to let them in out of the cold, hoping to catch a foreigner. They preyed on them like hungry butterflies and they watched Klimenti with sly and hopeful eyes. One came across and took Klimenti's arm with easy familiarity, as if he were already her lover.

"Please, they won't let us in because we're Russian," she said in good English, looking up at him with dark and appealing eyes. "But if we go in with you, we can get a table. *Pozhaluista.*"

It was a clever ruse, appealing to the gallantry of foreigners to help a Russian damsel in distress, and it worked more often than not, which is how the girls got money to buy their flashy clothes from the hard-currency *beryozka* stores.

"I'm sorry," Klimenti said in English, disengaging her from his arm. "I've come here on business."

"My name is Marina," she called boldly. "My conversation is most interesting." Her friends laughed at her audacity and she laughed with them, quickly shedding her disappointment.

Klimenti took the stairs to the first floor where unmarked doors sealed off the restaurant. Everything worthwhile was behind closed doors. Coveted. If something was on public display, it was only because no one wanted it. The restaurant manager sat guard at the reception desk, ignoring several couples who clustered nearby, waiting for tables. The restaurant was dimly lit, white tablecloths on darkly burnished wood. Waiters floated through the electric twilight. It was a warm, rich place, full of laughter and pleasure and humanness, a contradiction of all that lay without in the wintry barrenness of the city, and it came on you like a gust of balmy wind.

"We're full." The manager indicated the couples. "They've been waiting all night. Try another time."

"I'm with Fedor Yustinovich."

"Who?"

"Tabidze."

"Who's he?"

The manager turned away, surveying his domain with grand hauteur.

"We, you and me, know him as the Ferret."

"You might, but I assure you I don't."

"Oh, you know him all right, comrade," Klimenti said softly. "He comes here every night. He drinks Jim Beam whiskey and smokes Marlboro cigarettes. He wants to be a cowboy. He sells you contraband liquor he smuggles in from West Germany."

The manager made a great show of inspecting his reservations list.

"Oh yes," he said suavely. "Follow me, please."

He led Klimenti to one of the heavily cushioned alcoves that were set against one wall. They were separated by carved wooden lattices, which gave them an air of seductive secrecy.

"You'll be dining, sir?"

"Not before Fedor Yustinovich," Klimenti growled.

"Of course, sir. Perhaps some champagne?"

"Bring me two hundred and fifty grams of vodka."

"Certainly, sir."

He slid off, as smooth as an eel, snapping his fingers for a waiter. The Ferret certainly had a lot of influence. Klimenti was sure he was doing a double deal, bringing in contraband liquor and cigarettes and picking up meat, vegetables, and dairy products, which the manager stole by falsifying his books, and which they sold to the *fartsovshchiki*, the black-marketeers.

The vodka came and Klimenti poured a little. The band began playing popular Western songs with feeling and energy. The small dance floor filled. Marina and one of her friends came in with two foreigners and were soon drinking champagne.

A woman had drunk too much and was slumped over the table, fast asleep. Most of the diners were foreign businessmen or Communist Party and government officials. A number, however, were young men and women, Moscow's yuppies, the sons and daughters of the ruling elite. They were physically attractive, sleek, and self-assured, the first Soviet generation that had known neither war nor want; their powerful parents protected them from both. Like their parents, they clung together, a self-perpetuating ruling class, jealous of their power.

Klimenti watched the door, which was in semidarkness. He was looking for a man by himself. He would leave his companion in the car, to watch the front door.

The singer was even better than the band. Now it was Russian rock, mixing wildness and despair and longing; the singer was so caught up in it that her voice pulsed, heavy with sensuality. She was tiny but she was full of the bigness of the land; her voice was full of black earth. The more Russian the music got, the more excited the dancers became. It was as if a mighty wind from the East had blown across all the Russias and overwhelmed the insinuating zephyrs from the West.

"Hello," Zhenya said.

It was the first time Klimenti had got a good look at her. She was standing by the lattice, holding it. Her arms were slender and bare, something that struck him as intensely feminine.

"Hello," he said coldly, remembering her rudeness.

"Nadya's not here," Zhenya Stepanov said, a challenge.

"I'm not looking for Nadya. Well, not here, at least not right this moment."

Zhenya met his eyes boldly. "A man by himself in this place is usually looking for a woman."

Klimenti shrugged, a gesture of disinterest, an attitude this overconfident young woman was not accustomed to. But she was unperturbed by his disdain. Instead there was a glimmer of amusement in her eyes.

"May I?" she said and sat down before he could reply.

"Zhenya!" A young man had gotten to his feet several tables away. He was good looking, with a proud and autocratic air, and was also a little drunk. Two handsome young couples sat at the same table. Her dinner companions.

Zhenya paid him no heed. She picked up Klimenti's glass and tapped it against the carafe. Her pale eyes were clear and fearless, taunting him.

"If you don't give me a drink, I'll have no excuse for not going back."

"Zhenya." The young man was not used to being ignored.

"It's up to you, Klimenti Sergeyevich," she said, mimicking Nadya, catching exactly the overbearing tone his daughter used when she wanted to bully something out of him. She tapped the glass against the carafe again. Klimenti did not respond, and this time there was a flicker of doubt in her eyes. She was no longer so sure of herself. She was quick-witted and perhaps brazen but rejection was a new enemy. Klimenti wondered if she had come over to amuse herself at his expense.

Zhenya shrugged and put down the glass.

"It's on your head," she said. She slid out of the seat and was on her feet and going away when Klimenti reached up and caught her hand, feeling her tautness. She came back easily, with the fluency of a dancer curling out of a spin, hair tossing. Klimenti was not sure why he had done it. Now that he had recaptured her, he was uncertain what he wanted to do with her.

The young man stared at them in amazement. One of the young women laughed, a scornful tinkle, mocking him cruelly.

"Have some vodka," Klimenti said, pouring.

"Thank you," Zhenya said, and laughed. She was quite sensual and Klimenti understood the young man's hot jealousy. She emptied the glass in one toss, the traditional way, showing her boldness. Klimenti liked the way she did it. She was older than Nadya, perhaps twenty-five, and he had a feeling that tonight she was playing many roles, an actress posing for the mirror. It would be interesting to know why. Perhaps she just liked being reckless.

This time he poured on her command. She gave him a sly look. "Are you afraid?"

"No, but I don't want to get caught in a lovers' quarrel."

"You won't, Klimenti Sergeyevich," Zhenya said, just as Nadya would when she wished to admonish him. "We'll share it," she told him, pressing the glass against his lips, full of complicity. He was sure she was teasing him and it shocked him a little. After all, she was his daughter's friend and flatmate.

"You're very good," he said. "You sound just like Nadya."

She laughed, delighted by his praise. She was quick in her responses.

"Why not? Languages are my business, and I'm good at accents.

And Nadya talks about you all the time. Klimenti Sergeyevich did this or Klimenti Sergeyevich said that. She insists you're too interesting to be a real father."

Klimenti flushed with pleasure. He was paying her so much attention he almost missed the man who slid out of the darkness by the reception desk. Klimenti was sure he had a harelip.

The music stopped and Marina came past, arm-in-arm with her foreigner.

"Hello, Marina," Zhenya said, full of friendliness.

Marina blushed and pulled the foreigner in a little tighter, defiant. She was ashamed at being caught out.

"Hello, Zhenya," she said and hurried off.

"Damn. I embarrassed her."

"You know her?" Klimenti was surprised. Daughters of government ministers did not usually associate with prostitutes.

"She's a translator. I worked with her when I first came out of university. She's got a great talent for languages."

"She's putting them to good use."

Zhenya took the vodka from Klimenti and swallowed it. "What do you know?" she demanded and tapped the glass against the carafe. Klimenti poured.

Her eyes were serious, another surprise. "She's doing it because she wants to meet foreigners," she said. "She wants to get out of the Soviet Union and the only way she'll ever do it is by getting a foreigner to marry her. She's not a Jew. She's not even a dissident or a refusenik. She's got no one in the West yelling on her behalf. She's just a Russian girl trying to beat the system, using the only weapon she's got."

"Not even foreigners marry prostitutes."

"I don't like the word," she flared.

"They ask one hundred dollars but they'll take fifty. Traveler's checks or cash, as long as it's hard currency. Anything but rubles."

"You've been with her?"

"They sweeten the bite by changing hard currency at five times the official rate. In the end, it's dollars well spent."

"So it's true."

"No. Where would I get fifty dollars?"

The girls all reported to Nikishov. Tomorrow morning Marina would be on the telephone, reporting the conversation, supplying evidence of illegal money changing. Nikishov seldom acted immediately on the information. If he did he would have to arrest half the foreigners in Moscow. But it all went into the dossiers, to be resurrected whenever Nikishov wanted to nail someone. If the girls didn't work for Nikishov they ended up doing ten years' hard labor for being social parasites.

"There's a better currency than dollars," Zhenya said darkly. "The only privilege she inherited she's sitting on. You want to deny it to her?"

"I hope she makes it," Klimenti said. "I hope she marries a rich foreigner and goes to live in the West."

Even then Nikishov would not let go. He would use her past to blackmail her into cooperating. Klimenti took the glass from Zhenya and lifted it in a toast. He said sardonically, "To the West. Where money can buy everything. Except happiness."

"Don't mock her. They should let her go. She means no harm. She just wants to be happy."

"You're right. They should let her go." Everyone wanted to be happy. Klimenti asked, "Don't you want to go too?"

Zhenya lifted her eyes to Klimenti. "I've got privileges. I'm Russian."

The way she said it was all the answer that was necessary. It was another quality he found himself admiring. Her honesty. She was not afraid of what people thought.

"Why'd you come over?"

"I don't know. An impulse."

"You always act on your impulses?"

"Only when I'm drinking. Then I'm very Russian. I want to argue." Zhenya laughed, a nice sound. She was right. She was very Russian, full of contradictions.

A huge figure cut across Klimenti's line of vision, walking slowly with the relaxed assurance of someone absolutely secure in his domain. Klimenti focused his attention on the man who preceded the giant. At first it was difficult to make him out, but as he drew closer the light from the table lamps fell onto his face and showed the contempt and cruelty riven there. They were criminals, the shambling Big Dog and the sleek Ferret.

Zhenya said, "I came to tell you Nadya really is working very hard. She's a brilliant student."

Klimenti hardly heard her. He was unable to take his eyes from the beautiful face in the lamplight; he was standing there, his body arched like a matador's, cock-proud, showing them the full measure of his insolence.

Zhenya recognized them and sat with unnatural stiffness.

Klimenti said, "You've got to go. It's their table."

For a moment, Zhenya's eyes were wide with surprise and then they flared with anger. She didn't like being dismissed so peremptorily.

"Business, Colonel?" she asked coldly. "Is that how *you* get the dollars?" She had a hard, proud temper. She slid out of the seat and walked past the Ferret and Big Dog without giving them a glance. She strode with long-legged gracefulness and a lot of men, the two criminals included, watched her go.

"You're wasting your time with her, comrade," the Ferret taunted. "She fucks only the born-to-rule brigade."

"Move," Big Dog ordered, towering over Klimenti. "You're not welcome."

"I hope not," Klimenti said. He did not move.

"Take it easy," the Ferret said, making a great show of placating Big Dog. "This is a tough guy." He sat and pointed at Klimenti's scar. "A guy's got to be real tough to walk around with a face like that." The Ferret pouted and laughed. He had a beautiful, sensual Tartar face, soft skinned and wide mouthed, and dark eyes with long delicate lashes which were much envied by women. However, there was nothing effeminate about the Ferret, who had the explosively muscled physique of a gymnast. He was quick with a knife he carried strapped to his ankle. The underworld had given him his gang name because he was vindictive and murderous. Big Dog, on the other hand, was entirely without malice. Left to himself, he would not hurt anyone. He was, however, also slavishly loyal to the Ferret. They had grown up together in Cheriomuski, the vast complex of flats Khrushchev built in Moscow in the days when he dreamed of giving the workers a little bit of paradise, at least one room to each family. Before Stalin reached from the grave and corrected the error of his ways. It was now a slum in the sky.

Two wraithlike young women slid in next to the Ferret and Big

Dog. They shed expensive fur coats. Beneath, they wore sleeveless cotton tops with their nipples stabbing through like rose thorns. They lit up Kent cigarettes and stared around with vacant-eyed disinterest. Despite their air of worldly weariness, Klimenti was sure they were no older than schoolgirls.

The Ferret waved languidly toward the girls. "You'd fall out of your seat if I told you who their fathers were. Take your pick. They know all the tricks."

"I don't doubt it," Klimenti said. "But it's you I've come to see. Unfortunately."

A waiter arrived with champagne, another with black caviar and thin slices of toast. The girls began eating and drinking immediately, spreading the caviar and nibbling. Like mice, Klimenti thought.

"Fillet steak," the Ferret ordered. "With the blood running."

"The same," Big Dog said. "And a double order of potatoes fried in onions."

"More caviar for the young ladies."

"Vodka. Five hundred grams."

The Ferret put a ten ruble note on the table. The waiter smiled happily. It was almost an entire night's pay.

"Don't let it get cold in the kitchen."

"No, sir."

When the waiter had rushed off, Klimenti said, "Out the back."

"It's warmer here."

"The cold'll help your concentration." He stood up, waiting.

"What about my steak?"

"It'll be cold and overdone anyway."

"You're right," the Ferret sighed.

He slid out of the booth with startling quickness and stepped close to Klimenti, slicing in with his hand, pulling the blow at the last moment so that it brushed Klimenti's stomach before he could block it. It could have been a knife. The Ferret grinned and held up his hand, palm open, to show it was empty.

"Zip," he grinned, slicing his finger across Klimenti's jacket. "Your guts just spilled out."

"Ha, ha, ha," Big Dog howled. "Guts all over the floor."

"How're your balls?" Klimenti said. The Ferret looked down and saw the Makarov pistol Klimenti was holding only an inch from his crotch and swore.

"Shit," Big Dog said in a hushed voice.

"Don't ever try that again," Klimenti said. He was trembling. For a split second he had believed the Ferret had a knife and he had anticipated the awful coldness of steel in his belly, remembering how it cut. He had come close to pulling the trigger. Despite the warmth of the restaurant, Klimenti was bathed in cold sweat. He tucked the pistol back into his waistband.

The Ferret laughed, but it was an uneasy, dangerous sound.

The music began playing as they walked past and went through the door that led to the band's dressing room. The band leader nodded, acknowledging the Ferret's right of entry. Klimenti turned and looked down the restaurant. The two couples at Zhenya's table were on their feet, heading to the dance floor. The young man was drinking grimly, drowning his sorrows.

Zhenya sat by herself, erect, staring at Klimenti. He had a feeling she had been watching him all the time.

Buried among the diners, Harelip, too, was watching.

15.

The Ferret took Klimenti down to a basement that contained the coal-fired furnaces that heated the building. Big Dog stayed outside, guarding the door. The basement was clean and orderly, kept by a workman proud of his labors. Cartons of contraband liquor were stacked against a wall. The Ferret had made a trip recently.

The Ferret sat at a small desk that doubled as the cellarman's morning tea and lunch table. There was only one chair. Suspicion and resentment smoldered in his dark eyes. His dossier said he was twenty-nine but he was aged beyond his years.

"What're you after?"

"A one-out shipment, most likely through West Germany. Something the size of a copying machine. Maybe two of them."

"You guys, you're so afraid of the printed word, how come we waste so much bloody money and effort teaching people how to read!"

"A special shipment, Ferret. A new consignee and a new drop-off, doing it for the first time. But it'd have to be an old hand who brought it across, so it'd come in on a regular run, American software and Japanese computers for us, West German machine tools and American microchips for the Department of Defense and jeans for the *fartsovshchiki*. And a special shipment for someone else."

The Ferret shook his head. "These days, no one's going to risk a stretch for a couple of fucking copying machines."

"It'd be worth a lot of money. Hard currency. Dollars."

"You think it's the Americans?"

Klimenti said softly, "If it was the Americans, they'd have used you, Ferret, wouldn't they? And you would have told us. Wouldn't you?"

The Ferret sneered. "I do my duty. I let you know what's coming across and who's carrying it. I did a lot of business for you when you were in East Berlin, remember. Shit, I ought to get a medal."

His eyes were full of hatred. Playing both sides was a dangerous business. He made a lot of money selling marijuana and hashish to the rich kids. The drugs were supplied through a Turkish tobacco front by the CIA, who hoped to subvert the children of the leadership; the Americans were every bit as adept as the Russians when it came to blackmail. The KGB was willing to turn a blind eye, as long as the Ferret continued to be useful in beating the American embargo on defense technology and as long as he gave the KGB the names of all his customers. If the rich kids didn't buy it from the Ferret, they would buy it from someone else. There was plenty of the stuff coming in through Afghanistan and Georgia. This way they were able to control the situation and use the Ferret's talents for their own profit.

The Ferret's alternative had been a bullet in the back of the head, but he was not psychologically capable of a sense of gratitude. "What's in it for me?"

"Heroin's not part of the deal, Ferret. If the *nachalstvo* ever find out what you're selling their granddaughters, you're a dead man." Klimenti was sure the two young girls in the restaurant were users.

Tabidze's eyelids snapped back. They were indeed the eyes of a ferret, vicious and full of venom. He snarled, "Your mother fucked Germans."

Klimenti said pleasantly, "Ferret, one day I'm going to clean out your mouth. With a 7.62mm slug."

Big Dog came through the door, calling, "Hey, there's a tart up here wants the Colonel." He was cursing as he dragged Zhenya Stepanov after him.

"Get your hands off me," she said, kicking him.

"Let her go," Klimenti ordered.

Big Dog threw up his hands in disgust. "Let her go," he snorted. "Goddamnit, I'm protecting myself."

"Shut up, you oaf," Zhenya snapped.

The Ferret leaned against the wall, grinning maliciously. Klimenti went up the stairs, took Zhenya by the arm, and drew her into the corridor. "What in the hell do you think you're up to?" he demanded.

"You're hurting me." She tried to shake off Klimenti's hand but he gripped her harder and thrust her along the corridor.

Big Dog and the Ferret came out of the cellar door. The Ferret taunted, "Maybe I was wrong about her, eh, comrade!"

The fire door at the end of the corridor swung open. Klimenti saw the glint of blue steel.

"Behind you," he yelled and flung Zhenya to the floor. She screamed, but even so Klimenti heard the distinctive cough-cough of a silenced weapon. Big Dog grunted as the bullets hit him.

Klimenti drew his pistol and fired twice into the dark beyond the gaping fire door. The fall had winded Zhenya and she was curled up, gasping for breath.

"Move," the Ferret screamed.

He kicked Big Dog clear of the cellar door. Two more shots came out of the dark. There was no muzzle flash. The Ferret dived into the cellar as the bullets clipped into the ceiling on an upward trajectory. The gunman was firing from the ground. Klimenti fired four more shots, aiming just above the floor line, methodically spacing the shots to hold the gunman back. He could not move without exposing Zhenya, and firepower was his only protection. But no more shots came out of the dark. Quickly Klimenti loaded in a new clip, putting the used magazine into his pocket. Zhenya's knees were drawn up in a fetal crouch, her head buried in her arms.

Big Dog was down on his knees, his right arm dragging, his left arm clawing at the wall as he tried to get back on his feet. He grunted, a wounded-animal sound, and began shuffling forward on his knees.

"Ferret. Ferret."

Klimenti dragged Zhenya to her feet. She saw Big Dog and screamed, struggling to break free. Big Dog had reached the cellar door but he knew he would not be able to negotiate the stairs. He made no plea for help. He slumped against the wall, waiting his fate, and there was a stoic quality Klimenti could not ignore.

"Help me," Klimenti shouted at Zhenya. He got his hands under Big Dog's left armpit and hauled him to his feet. Big Dog crashed his wounded right side against the corridor wall. He grunted in pain but stayed on his feet. Klimenti swung Big Dog's good arm around his neck. They staggered forward, locked together. It was not until they reached the fire door and fell out into the night that Klimenti realized Zhenya was on the other side, holding Big Dog by the waist, grunting in unison with the wounded man.

They lurched out into an empty alley. Several garbage bins had been placed as a low barricade. Klimenti saw holes where his bullets had penetrated. A black Volga was parked near the door. Klimenti propped Big Dog against the wall.

"Hold him up," he ordered Zhenya and went to the car. It was locked. He swung up his pistol to smash the side window.

"Wait," Big Dog gasped. He reached across his body with his left hand and patted his right jacket pocket. "I've got the keys."

Zhenya dug them out and threw them to Klimenti. She thrust herself under Big Dog's good arm but he held back, doubting her strength.

"I can do it," Zhenya said. She looked ridiculously small against the big man, but she got him to the car and, with Klimenti's help, into the rear seat.

"Oooh, shit," Big Dog groaned as Zhenya slammed the door shut. She scrambled into the front seat as Klimenti skidded the Volga out of the alley. She got onto her knees and leaned over the seat to tend Big Dog, who was quiet now. She was panting. There was blood on her arms and on her dress.

"I think he's passed out."

"No," Big Dog groaned. "But I wish to fucking hell I was."

"We've got to stop the bleeding," Zhenya said, her voice urgent and strained.

She took off her silk blouse. She was wearing nothing beneath and Klimenti saw the dark rosettes of her nipples against the smooth creaminess of skin as she wadded the blouse against the wound, which was high on the shoulder. Her hair fell around her face and she seemed to be totally unconscious of her nakedness, absorbed in what she was doing.

"Here," Big Dog said and reached for a flick knife from a sheath on his leg. She sliced the sleeve out of his coat and cut the cloth into wads, which she pressed on top of the already blood-soaked blouse. She lifted his good hand to hold the wads in place.

"Forget the pain," she ordered. "The tighter you hold them, the better."

Big Dog grunted, "You've got nice tits, lady."

Zhenya hugged herself, not to hide her nakedness but because of the cold. Klimenti stopped the car and put his leather jacket on her. It was warm from his body and she smiled gratefully when he zipped it up.

"Can you put the heaters on, please?" She was trembling, the onset of reaction.

Through his pain Big Dog said, "Lady, you're OK."

"We've got to get him to a hospital."

"No, lady! No hospital."

Big Dog tried to lean forward to grab at Klimenti but the pain forced him back. He gasped, "You know the drill, Colonel."

Klimenti said, "If I was taking you to a hospital, I'd have called an ambulance."

Zhenya stared at him in astonishment. "What are you saying? If we don't get him to a hospital he'll bleed to death."

"If we take him to a hospital, he'll be arrested."

Big Dog croaked, "He's right, lady. The only hospital they'll take me to is in the Big House."

Zhenya was aghast. She was just beginning to realize what was going on. She said angrily, "I don't think I want to get involved in this."

"I'm sorry, lady," Big Dog said, and meant it.

Klimenti asked, "You got a doctor who can handle it?"

"The Ferret has," Big Dog said sourly. "But the way he was moving, it'd take us a week to find him."

Zhenya's anger was short-lived. It surrendered to the cold. She began shivering uncontrollably. "I can't do any more," she said through chattering teeth. She huddled against the door, hugging herself.

Klimenti drove to Shabolovka Street. Big Dog's face was a sickly, pallid hue, drained of blood and strength. His cheeks seemed to have collapsed. His thick lips were white blubber. Despite his great bulk, he was shivering as badly as Zhenya. Klimenti opened the rear door and with a great effort got Big Dog onto his feet. He moaned quietly but he did not once cry out as Klimenti and Zhenya dragged and carried him into the ancient elevator which took them, trembling and lurching fearfully under the strain, to the fourth floor. Klimenti was grateful for Big Dog's courage; one cry would have brought out the other tenants, who were only too anxious to pry into each other's affairs. By the time they had got to Klimenti's apartment, all three of them were exhausted and splattered with Big Dog's blood.

Klimenti took Big Dog into the bathroom. He threw down some towels and laid him on the tiled floor. "I'm sorry," he said, "but I don't want them finding your blood all over my apartment."

Zhenya leaned against the door, on the point of collapse and beyond protest, even though she had difficulty accepting what was happening.

Klimenti got towels and sheets. He draped a blanket over Zhenya and another over Big Dog, who lay with his eyes closed, breathing in shallow gasps. Gently, Klimenti peeled away the blood-soaked wadding and blouse. They had done their job and the blood was congealing. With scissors, he cut away the front of Big Dog's shirt and undershirt. Two bullets had sliced the muscles and plowed up through the shoulder, scalping it, chopping it into raw meat. The bullets had passed through, making a bigger mess on the way out than they did on the way in.

Klimenti went up to Zhenya, who was leaning against the door, shivering, her eyes big with shock. He shook her gently. "I need your help," he said. "I can't do it without you."

For a moment, she stared at him stupidly. He shook her again and, with sudden irritation, she knocked his hands away. "What do you want?" she said, hugging herself beneath the blanket. "Tell me."

"Clean the wound," Klimenti said.

He went to the kitchen and put on a kettle. Zhenya, lost inside Klimenti's jacket, began working on Big Dog. She was covered in blood and still shivering. He went to take over but she knocked his hand away.

"No," she said defiantly. "I can handle it."

Klimenti made some coffee and topped it with brandy; he filled a hot water bottle, which Zhenya tucked beneath Big Dog's good arm, against his chest. She sat back on her heels, sipping the laced coffee.

Propping folded towels beneath Big Dog's head, she gently slapped his face. His eyes opened.

"You're going to live," Zhenya said, smiling tiredly.

Big Dog croaked, "That's a relief."

Zhenya fed him some laced coffee. She helped Klimenti bandage the wound with strips torn from linen sheets. Klimenti got a camping tarpaulin and laid it on the bed in Nadya's room. They got the naked Big Dog to his feet and rubbed him down with dry towels, then put him on the bed and warmed him with the hot water bottle and blankets and an eiderdown.

"Thank you, lady," Big Dog whispered. "You're a real Florence Nightingale."

They left him to sleep. Their clothes were sodden with water and blood, and they were both shivering. Zhenya slumped at the dining room table, exhausted. Klimenti poured a glass of brandy and she sipped it slowly, watching him, her eyes dark-ringed and big, full of a quality Klimenti had not seen in a long time; there was a lostness in them, and there was also trust.

Zhenya said, "I'm cold. So cold."

She was gently pulled to her feet without resisting. Klimenti led her to the bathroom where she stood passively as he took off the leather jacket and then helped her peel off her wet skirt and underclothes. She made no protest when Klimenti stripped and stepped into the shower with her. There was absolutely no question about taking it in turns; they needed equally to be warm and clean and after the events they had been through together it seemed natural that this, too, should be shared.

Klimenti washed the dried blood from her body. She stood upright, eyes closed, the water beating into her face and chest, moving her limbs, turning, obeying the gentle pressure of his hands. Klimenti scrubbed her skin with a washcloth until it was blushing from the friction and when his hands came down to her belly and hips he stopped and she opened her eyes and stared at him, waiting; she was neither submissive nor denying, leaving it to Klimenti to decide, and he recognized in her the calmness of those who are overwhelmed by events, the quiet acceptance of fate. He handed her the soap. She showed no surprise but gave him a quiet, secretive smile that was hardly more than a quiver of her lips, a smile that could have been gratitude or regret, and washed between her thighs, lifting her long legs to the side of the bath to reach her ankles. Klimenti scrubbed himself clean, catching her in glimpses, a taut body, breasts stabbing, tightly cupped buttocks glistening wet, the belly flat and hard, and rising below with a lush swelling of blond pubic hair. She reached up to wash the soap from her hair, arching her body, and with her eyes squeezed shut against the shower jet she looked like an endearing half-drowned pixie.

Klimenti gave her the last two dry towels. "Thank you," she said, the first words that had been spoken since they came into the bathroom. But their silence had said more than words.

"There's a wardrobe full of Nadya's clothes," he said.

"I'll find something," Zhenya said and handed him one of the dry towels. She wrapped the other around her and slipped out. Klimenti stood in the hot steam, treading on cold and bloody towels, and as he dried himself he felt that an opportunity had come and gone; it had been there for his taking and he had chosen not to and was not sure he had done the right thing. He stood there, remembering the touch of her skin and the smoothness of her belly.

He wrapped the towel around his waist and went out. The door to Nadya's room was ajar and he caught the rustle of movement as Zhenya went through his daughter's wardrobe. He went into his bedroom and sat on the bed, empty now and uncertain, trying to put his thoughts together again.

"Klimenti Sergeyevich," she said and Klimenti turned and saw her standing by the door. She looked so tiny and neat in bare feet, with her wet hair plastered against her skull, and it seemed impossible that she had helped him carry Big Dog. Her eyes were solemn and watched him unwaveringly. She had not changed. The towel was still wrapped around her.

Klimenti got to his feet, fearful that words would change the decision she had made for him. Zhenya came across the room and stood before him, looking up with her serious and trusting eyes.

"I'm cold," Zhenya said and dropped the towel and wet her fingers between her legs and rubbed her musk against his lips so that he could taste her readiness.

"Oh, Klimenti," she gasped, taking him, licking the hot, moist words into his mouth. "You're so hard, so hot."

Later they slept deeply, entwined like puppies.

16.

Klimenti got up before dawn to check Big Dog, who slept restlessly, inflamed with a high temperature. He bathed his forehead but there was little else he could do. When he slipped back into bed, Zhenya murmured in her sleep and curled into him, enveloping him with warmth and a pleasant body scent that was a mixture of sweat and perfume and lovemaking; he drifted back into sleep.

In the morning it was different. Zhenya was not beside him. Klimenti went into Nadya's room and found her bathing Big Dog's forehead. She was dressed in Nadya's clothes, a pair of old jeans and a sweater, and she did not see or hear him at the door. She had showered again and her hair was wet. She looked fresh and young, and with a rush of memory, of the feel and smell and taste, remembering the sweet depth of her, Klimenti understood it was not the time to intrude and quietly took his nakedness away.

Zhenya had cleaned the bathroom. She had rinsed out the bloody towels and sheets and wrung them as dry as she could. She had done the same with her own clothes and folded them into a plastic shopping bag, ready to go. Klimenti stood under the hot water, accepting once again the overlordship of inevitability. His skin was smooth with her smoothness, the dried slick of lovemaking, and his pores were tangy with her flavors; he stood under the steaming water and soaped it all away, as she had done to him, preparing himself for what had to be done.

He put on jeans and a woolen shirt and made coffee. It was 6:48 A.M. Zhenya was sitting beside Big Dog, waiting for him, putting the wounded man between them, a bulwark against what they had shared last night; Big Dog was her barricade.

"How's his temperature?" he asked.

"Too high. I've given him the last of the aspirin. But he needs a doctor."

She drank the coffee and turned away from Klimenti to bathe Big Dog's brow. Neither of them had uttered one word, made one gesture— a quiver of a smile, a flicker of an eye—to acknowledge the intimacy they had shared and the knowledge they now had of each other. She was outwardly demure but he sensed she was ready to fight him.

Zhenya said, "It's ridiculous. Aspirin! For a wound like that."

"Don't get upset."

"I'm not upset," she said, facing up to him. "I just don't want to get any further involved."

She meant: in any of it—Big Dog or you.

Klimenti understood. "You've done all you can. More than you had to. It's not your problem anymore."

"I'm not sorry about last night," she said, holding his eyes, defying him.

"It just happened," Klimenti said.

"No," she said, shaking her head. "It didn't just happen."

With every word they became strangers again. How deeply they had known each other, to end with this hollowness.

Zhenya said, "It's too complicated. I don't understand any of it. I don't want to and I'm not going to try."

She shook her head and Klimenti wondered what memories she was denying. The shooting. The bathroom. Or the bed. Perhaps all of them. She lifted her head, wide eyed and direct and challenging, the eyes he had seen on their first meeting.

"All I know is that it's dangerous. All of it."

Zhenya stood up. She looked smaller than she really was, like a young girl. Her wet hair and clear skin made her very appealing, innocent almost, until you sensed the audacity and sensuality coiled within. She came soundlessly across the room and stood in front of him, so that he could smell the freshness of soap and herself and sense her vitality; she reached up and touched his lips with her fingers. This time, however, it was not the beginning of something, it was an ending and she was taking a memory with her.

"Especially you, Klimenti," she said softly and went past him and out of the room. It was some time before he had the will to move, standing there with his own memory, the touch of dry fingers on his lips.

When he went out, Zhenya was pulling on a pair of Nadya's old snow boots. She put on a bright red ski jacket and a woolen cap. He did not offer to get her a taxi. It would be better if no one remembered her leaving.

"Why did you come after me at the hotel?"

Last night was already another lifetime. But he asked, anyway, out of genuine curiosity.

She smiled sadly. "Another impulse."

She picked up the shopping bag with her wet clothes. She paused at the door. "You probably think I'm promiscuous or frivolous," she said, challenging him again.

"Why?" Klimenti said and tried unsuccessfully to hide a smile. Her blush deepened and she glared at him.

"Well, I don't care," she said and slammed the door.

When she was gone, the apartment was once again empty and desolate. He felt her loss and yet he was glad. Zhenya was right. It was too complicated. He was sure she was not as tough or as cynical as she had tried to make out.

Klimenti gently shook Big Dog awake and fed him more coffee and brandy. He was delirious but not beyond the realm of comprehension. He looked around with fevered eyes.

"Where's the little lady?" he asked hoarsely.

"She's gone," Klimenti said, and there must have been a ring of finality in his voice because Big Dog understood what he meant, and his face showed his disappointment.

He whispered, "If it was me, I wouldn't let her go."

He lay back exhausted and Klimenti let him sleep again. He put on boots and an overcoat and his fur hat and took the wheezing elevator out into the cold morning dark. His battered Zhiguli was in a vacant lot across the street. It spluttered and hiccuped but gradually the tough little engine warmed up and began to pull. As he drove, Klimenti tried to remember the last time he had made this journey and found he could not; the neglect was his, all those opportunities surrendered. Now he came as a mendicant. Klimenti did not like it at all but he did not know what else he could do.

A fat, elderly housekeeper answered the door. She eyed Klimenti with animosity, as jealous of her authority as any sergeant major.

"The Academician doesn't receive uninvited visitors," she proclaimed, ready to slam the door.

"I'm a relative," Klimenti said hastily.

She peered at him closely. "I don't remember your face. And I know all the family."

"I'm Nadya's father."

"Nadya!" She stared at him suspiciously. "Is it true?"

"I'm Klimenti Sergeyevich Amalrik."

"You can prove it?" She didn't want to believe him.

Klimenti showed her his KGB pass. Immediately the old witch became contrite and servile. All her life she had served authority in one form or another and she groveled happily and naturally before it.

"Oh, Nadya's such a darling. We all love her so dearly. Please, please, you must come in immediately."

She drew him in through the door and held Klimenti's hand in her spongy, fat fingers. Her face, at first so fierce, was now wreathed in a simpering smile.

"Klimenti Sergeyevich! Who would imagine it? Forgive my impertinence for mentioning it, but I was a maid with this family when your wife was a little girl. A sweet and beautiful angel. How we adored Marusya. She was always the Academician's favorite niece. And now there is Nadya, so like her mother. Oh dear . . ."

The old woman was quite overcome. She shuffled off in her worn carpet slippers with remarkable energy. The apartment was beautifully furnished and spotlessly kept. Morozov was a widower, and Klimenti sensed that everything had been maintained exactly as his wife had wanted it before her death three years ago. The mantel above the fireplace was crowded with family snapshots, and Klimenti immediately recognized one of Nadya, a color portrait taken at the end of the school year when she was about fifteen. The young had so much to live for, and it was all there in her smile and her eyes, the wonderful spirit of boundless hope and unthinking confidence. He had the same photograph at home and it was one of his favorites too. He put it back and was about to turn away when his eye caught an old black-and-white photograph that made his heart hurt.

It was Marusya. It could only be Marusya with that secretive, sidelong glance and teasing smile she had, even as a young girl. She wore a silly white frilly frock, the kind that girls once wore to communion, before they turned the churches into museums and granaries. It was a photograph Klimenti had not seen before and as he examined it, he felt a confusion of pleasure and pain: here he was, eleven years after her death, meeting this young Marusya for the first time—a moment from her past come to him now—long after her life had ended.

"She will always be a little girl to me," Morozov said. "My little Marusya." The Academician came across and took the photograph from Klimenti and read the inscription on the back.

"Ah, yes," he sighed. "Her tenth birthday. We had no children of our own, as you know, and it was our pleasure, my wife and I, to give birthday parties for all our nieces and nephews."

He put the two photographs side by side. It was unnerving. Frozen in different moments of time, the mother was forever younger than her daughter. The likeness was so strong they could have been the same person at different ages.

"I'll get a photographer to make a negative and give you a copy."

"Thank you."

"Is it Nadya you've come about?"

"No."

"It's just that, well, in all the time I've known you, you've never approached us unless it was something to do with Nadya. You've come only on her behalf, never for yourself."

"It's the truth, Alexander Semionovich, and I'm sorry for it. I wish it could have been different, but it's the way I am."

"Proud and stubborn," Morozov grunted. "Admirable qualities. But your trouble, nephew, is that you're too independent, too much of a lone wolf."

It was an old grievance against which there was no argument.

Morozov smiled kindly. "What is it, nephew, that's so important that you have honored me with a visit so early in the morning?"

"I need your help," Klimenti said, relieved at how simple it was.

"Good," Morozov exclaimed. "It's about time."

Morozov inspected Big Dog's wound and said, "In Stalingrad we sent them back into the front line with wounds worse than this. And they went willingly."

"And look what happened to them," Big Dog growled. "If the Germans didn't kill them, the commissars did."

"Do you know who I am?" Morozov barked.

"No," Big Dog growled back, resenting all authority. "And I don't fucking well care either."

"That's good, because if you did, I'd leave you to look after yourself."

Morozov opened his medicine bag and took out bandages, syringes, and a set of scalpels. Big Dog cringed.

"Oh no," he protested.

"Oh yes. If you want to keep the arm."

"Shut up, Big Dog," Klimenti said. "He's taking a big risk fixing you up."

Morozov worked deftly and with pleasure. It had been more than forty-five years since he had last treated gunshot wounds but he had not forgotten, and as he cut away the makeshift dressing he was once again a young man in the stinking and dark cellars, with the dust falling into open wounds and dead eyes, as the battle raged above. After a while he began to whistle tunelessly as he worked, a hiss of a song Klimenti did not recognize.

"It's a clean wound, nice entrance, clear exit. The deltoid muscle's been torn and the humerus is almost certain to be chipped. There's no way to be sure without an X ray, and that's out of the question."

He prepared a syringe. Big Dog eyed it fearfully. "What's that?" he demanded suspiciously.

"Pethidine. One hundred milligrams."

He rolled Big Dog over on his good side and injected it into his buttock.

"You're lucky," Morozov said. "In Stalingrad, we had to do worse jobs than this with no anesthetic at all." He slapped Big Dog's buttock, taunting his fear. "Soon you'll be feeling no pain."

True enough, within a few minutes Big Dog was smiling lopsidedly. He became talkative, paying Morozov no attention as the doctor prepared another syringe and injected five milliliters of lignocaine into the wound and went to work with the scalpel.

Big Dog babbled, "My grandfather was killed at Stalingrad. Defending the tractor works."

"Oh?"

"It's the truth. His name's up there in granite, on the memorial."

"You've seen it?"

"Oh yes. We've all been to see it."

"They were all heroes," Morozov said and meant it.

"She had nice tits," Big Dog murmured. "Real nice tits."

"That pethidine's great stuff," Morozov chuckled. "I only wish we'd had it in Stalingrad."

Big Dog shut his eyes and lay back, a ridiculously contented expression on his face. It didn't take a lot of imagining to work out what he was thinking about. He had an erection.

"It's one of the more beneficial side effects," Morozov said.

When he was finished, he gave Klimenti twelve capsules. "Ampicillin, an antibiotic. He's to take one three times a day. The bandages should be changed once a day. He can have liquids, but don't let him eat anything solid until tomorrow."

"When can I move him?"

"When he wakes up. If you have to."

Klimenti drove the Academician back to his apartment. The gray, glum light of day had fallen into the city, bringing no warmth. Street and building lights burned, and traffic pressed through roads with headlights peering through the fumes. Everywhere, people were scurrying or queueing for buses, heads down, shoulders hunched against the dismal prospects of the day.

Klimenti wanted to apologize. "Alexander Semionovich, I know you don't like this one bit, and neither do I."

Morozov waved a huge, bony hand dismissively. "You're wrong, nephew. Oh, I admit I came only because I couldn't refuse without making a hypocrite of myself. But it's been good for me. It's reminded me of a lot of fine young men and how lucky I've been to live so long, when so many didn't."

He smiled self-consciously and got out, then leaned in through the window. "It's good, after all this time, to be able to do something for his grandfather."

When Klimenti got back to the apartment, Big Dog was awake again. Klimenti asked him, "Who's trying to kill the Ferret?"

"Who isn't!"

"What's it about, Big Dog?"

"Maybe it was you they were after."

"No. He shot for the Ferret. And you."

Big Dog thought about it. "Yeah, you're right."

"Who?"

"I don't know."

"I don't believe you."

Big Dog sighed. "Listen, Colonel, if I did know I wouldn't tell you. I'm no *stukach*, that's for sure. But I'm telling you the truth. I don't know. Who or why."

Klimenti believed him. He said, "What's he been up to, Big Dog? What's new?"

"I just told you, I'm no informer. So drop it." Big Dog's face was set in grim, sulking defiance, the face he presented to police interrogators and outsiders generally.

"The Ferret ran out on you, Big Dog. Your *paichan*"—he invested the slang term for gang leader with withering contempt—"your boss left you to die like a rat."

Big Dog looked away, scowling.

Klimenti sneered, "He used you as a shield. And then he scuttled off and left you to take it."

Big Dog lay back against the pillows, brooding.

"Some *paichan*! Some mate!" Klimenti's scorn was real and Big Dog felt it deeply.

"Shut up," he said but it was more a plea than a curse.

"Go back to sleep," Klimenti said and went to the door.

"Colonel." Big Dog's face was screwed up and Klimenti was surprised to see it was with anguish, not anger or pain. "Why didn't you scuttle too?"

Klimenti was not sure he knew the answer.

"Why'd you scrape me up, you and the lady with the nice tits?"

Big Dog was genuinely disturbed; in his entire background, there was nothing to give him an inkling of why Klimenti would have done what he did.

"I wanted information," Klimenti said and Big Dog nodded, accepting it. This he could understand. It confirmed his prejudices and dismissed the unsettling uncertainties. Klimenti thought he saw a flicker of disappointment in his eyes.

"Yeah," Big Dog growled, stronger already.

Klimenti said, "Don't use the phone. It's sure to be tapped."

As he dressed for work, Klimenti turned his radio into the BBC's shortwave foreign service broadcast. The Vigilantes for Peace had claimed responsibility for both assassinations. They had sent the BBC copies of the Russian and American notes and accused the two superpowers of complicity in concealing the truth from the citizens of the world.

The VFP had finally spoken to the world. It could only mean they were ready to strike again.

17.

Control heard the news on the Voice of America shortwave broadcast. He felt a surge of exultation. At last the spark was struck; it would ignite the world. He listened to the broadcast, trembling with emotion and aware that he could not betray himself to the microphones buried in the walls of his apartment.

Now, with the world alerted to their cause, their work began in earnest. And so did the danger.

The VFP statement said in part:

The fact that both the Soviet Union and the United States lied about the reasons for the assassinations is indisputable proof of their hypocrisy. It shows they are afraid of the truth and alarmed by the desire of all mankind to live without the threat of nuclear extinction. They conspired to deceive the peoples of the world because they felt their own selfish interests were imperiled. They cannot be trusted.

It is better that the guilty few die, so all may live.

It was their litany. Hearing these fateful few words addressed to the world, Control felt sure they would succeed. He had never doubted it. But now he was absolutely sure.

In this moment of triumph, Control felt his loneliness acutely: he was overcome by a surge of compassion for Gerald, who had gone to his death alone; and for whoever it was who had done it in Washington; and for Leonardo, who at this moment was in his hotel room, making his final preparations. Alone. They were all of them alone and yet together, sharing conviction and commitment and sacrifice. No one could compare with them on this matter of brotherhood; it was their deepest faith.

His telephone rang twice and then fell silent. Exactly a minute later, it rang twice again. The Russian wanted a meeting.

Control got dressed and went out into the morning cold. He took an underpass across Kutuzov and went into the main lobby of the Ukraine Hotel. A billboard flashed a poster of some beautiful and leggy dancers in daringly cut Western costumes, naked buttocks cupped, pelvises thrusting, nipples peeking—the hotel's ballet corps who performed each night in its crowded nightclub. Control had caught their act a month ago and, by Western standards, it was pretty restrained. Even so, it took away the breath of its Russian audiences, who went crazy over anything remotely erotic.

He went to the washroom and into a cubicle and waited until the two Russians using the urinal had departed. He left the cubicle and used a key to open the door to the toilets' storeroom. Thanks to bad draftsmanship, the storeroom was much larger than intended. The Russian had given him the key and they had used it once before. Even so, Control carefully went over the place, looking for electronic bugs. He trusted no one. The Russian came in.

"What's the problem?" Control said severely. "I told you, no contact unless it's absolutely necessary."

"You didn't tell me who it was," the Russian whispered frantically.

Control said, "It makes no difference."

"It makes no difference! Are you insane? A member of the . . ."

Control crushed his throat, choking off his words.

"No names," Control hissed.

The Russian nodded, his eyes bulging with fright. Control slowly released the pressure. The Russian rubbed his throat.

"I can't do it anymore," he gasped.

"You've got no choice."

"Please. I've done all I can. All you've asked."

In his terror he had forgotten himself and begun to lisp. His breath was rancid. Spittle had dried in the corners of his mouth. His lips trembled. Control had never seen a man so afraid.

"They're questioning everyone who's been out of the Soviet Union in the last twelve months."

"It's routine. They'll never suspect you. That's why we picked you."

"Please. I can't go on. My nerves will betray me."

He was on the verge of tears, a cringing, abject figure, beyond shame. Control put his arm around his thin shoulders and felt his trembling frailty.

"Calm down," he said soothingly. "I didn't understand it was so bad."

"Please," the Russian sobbed. "I'm not up to this."

"It's OK, it's OK," Control said softly, as if he were hushing a child. He took out his handkerchief and gave it to the Russian to cry into, holding the sparrow-body and feeling the pathetic heartbeat and pitiful little shudders.

"We'll do what you want," Control said. "There's no more reason to be afraid."

18.

Klimenti and Bannon met in the same room on the tenth floor of the Rossiya Hotel. They both produced tape recorders.

Bannon said, "The VFP statement hurts our credibility."

"It's very effective propaganda," Klimenti said, knowing the American preoccupation with credibility.

Bannon said sourly, "Only in the West."

He had a point. The Politburo had imposed a total media ban on the VFP statement. The only Soviet citizens who knew about the Vigilantes for Peace were those who, like Klimenti, listened to foreign broadcasts. In the West, however, the assassinations and the Vigilantes for Peace were leading the news, and their statement revealing Soviet and American complicity in suppressing the true intent of the assassinations had caused outrage. Already the American media and Congress— including some members of the President's own party—were demanding an explanation. It had dismayed other Western leaders, particularly the British, French, and West Germans, who had also been deliberately misled.

They watched each other with cold, appraising eyes. Klimenti said, "Eventually it'll seep through. It just takes more time."

Bannon held up three fingers. "Maybe. But it's only the second inning, and from where I sit, the score is KGB three, us nothing."

Klimenti asked wearily, "You brought me here just to tell me this?"

"Just as long as we understand each other." Bannon sat back and pushed a file across to Klimenti. "We found some hairs. Our tests show the similar lead and high bromine content. And they confirm exactly the same isotopic composition of the lead."

Klimenti felt a rush of excitement. Morozov's hairs, which they had all scoffed at, had produced a definite connection between the two assassins. It was incredible that scientists could learn so much from so little.

"So we have two assassins with two factors in common," said Klimenti. "They received the same medical treatment. And the likelihood is they underwent it at the same place."

"We've got the location," Bannon said. "Well, the general area anyway." He passed Klimenti a Michelin city guide.

"Rome!"

"That's right. The Eternal City. The ruins are being eaten away by lead fumes from automobiles. The Italians wanted a case to make unleaded gasoline compulsory, so they got the oil refineries that supply Rome to change to a distinctive isotopic composition that could be easily monitored."

"When?"

"It was a six-month program. It ended last month."

"There's nowhere else they could have absorbed it?"

"Nowhere. Rome's the only place in the world where they've sold gasoline with that isotopic balance."

"So there's no doubt. They were trained in Rome."

Bannon nodded. "Playground of the Red Brigade."

The implication was plain. The Italian terrorists were fanatical, ferocious, and courageous, and it was commonly believed by Western antiterrorist experts that they had received training, equipment, and financial support from the KGB. Klimenti was in a position to know it was true.

Klimenti said, "The Red Brigade are finished. They were betrayed. Their leaders are in jail or dead."

Bannon said, "They've regrouped before. With help they could have done it again."

"It's possible. But do you really believe that a group of fanatical world revolutionaries and anarchists like the Red Brigade would involve themselves in a disarmament campaign?"

Bannon did not answer immediately. With elaborate care, he put the map and the reports back into the file and handed it to Klimenti. "We've got a basic problem here, Colonel. Our analysts don't accept that any rational person could seriously believe they can force the superpowers to disarm through a campaign of terror and assassination. We've been negotiating about nuclear weapons for more than thirty-five years and have hardly got anywhere. It took years of continuous, exhausting negotiations to get the Strategic Arms Reduction Treaty. And do you know how many missiles that got rid of, Colonel?"

"A lot more of ours than of yours," Klimenti said dryly.

"A lot less than the fifty-percent cuts they were talking about." Bannon was unmoved by Klimenti's sarcasm. "A hell of a lot less. There's still more than sixteen thousand strategic warheads in the silos and submarines, armed, ready to go. Do you think that any rational human being could really believe that we could get rid of them overnight? Sixteen thousand! With another thirty thousand tactical warheads to back them up. Even if we wanted to, even if we started now, it'd take years. Decades maybe."

Bannon's eyes challenged him, hard, distrustful.

"Do *you* believe it, Colonel?"

Klimenti had to answer. He said, "I don't know."

Bannon switched off his tape recorder and stood up, a tall and dangerous man, moving with brutal smoothness. He was satisfied. He had just hit his first home run for the Americans.

On his way back to Dzerzhinsky Square, Klimenti came to a decision. He would give the Americans five more days to react to his message alerting them to Bannon's affair with Nadya. If they did not remove Bannon from Moscow, if he was still in the Soviet Union when the sixth day dawned, Klimenti would kill him.

The decision calmed him. He knew he could carry it through, and this put an end to a lot of the doubts that had been troubling him. Most important of all, he no longer felt helpless.

Klimenti rang Special Service 11 about Squirrel. Shalnev reported, "Nothing from Washington. We're sure they've got him."

Klimenti said, "If they'd taken him, they'd keep him in the game. They'd force him to maintain contact, so they could play us along."

"Well, what is it then? You tell me. You know him better than anyone else."

Once again, Klimenti had only one answer: "Wait."

At lunchtime, Klimenti walked one block downhill to Neglinnaya Street to a government food and department store. He joined the women who were queueing at the men's winter wear department and waited twenty-five minutes before it was his turn. There was a limited choice of extra-large clothes, and he bought a track suit and a woolen jacket and queued again to pay for them.

"*Perestroika!* Bah!" a matron scoffed. "It's all hot air, as usual."

Klimenti caught a taxi to the Kalinin Metro station and took the Blue Line one stop to Smolenskaya station. He went up into the street and across to a vacant lot where a family of farmers, taking advantage of Gorbachev's relaxation of the laws on private enterprise, had set up a *shaslik* stall. The sons barbecued meat on coals glowing in a metal drum cut in half, while their mother, wearing a white apron and chef's cap, sold it from a tent at premium prices—two rubles fifty kopecks for one hundred grams. But none of Moscow's meat-starved citizens argued and the *shaslik* stands did a brisk trade. The State took 90 percent of their profits; even so, the peasants would soon be rich.

Klimenti stood at a chest-high table and ate the charred meat on a paper plate with raw onions and barbecue sauce and two slices of black bread. It was hot and delicious despite the cold wind. A young woman wearing her most elegant clothes stood next to Klimenti, gnawing at thick chunks of meat with the gusto of a savage, concentrating on enjoying this simple luxury. When she finished, she licked her manicured hands, gave a burp of satisfaction, and went away.

By the time he finished eating, Klimenti was sure he was not being followed. He took a taxi to Shabolovka Street. The elevator clanked and hissed like a living creature.

His apartment was empty. Big Dog was gone.

Quietly, careful not to move anything, Klimenti began a systematic inspection of the apartment. Nadya's bed was unmade. Big Dog's clothes were gone and so were the antibiotic capsules. The electric heater was switched off. Nothing was missing from Klimenti's wardrobe; even his biggest coat would have been too small. There were no signs of a struggle or of a forced entry.

Big Dog could not have left without getting a new set of clothes and he was too weak to have gone by himself. The problem was, had he gone willingly or under duress? Had Big Dog ignored his warning and telephoned some cronies to fetch him and then let them in? Or had the KGB intercepted the call—and arrived first?

If the KGB had gotten to Big Dog, Klimenti would know soon enough. It was a matter of waiting and staying calm. He had a lot of experience at both.

But this time everything was different.

19.

Academician Fadeyev, Chairman of the All-Union Congress of Neuropathologists and Psychiatrists, addressed them in Deputy Chairman Poluchkin's office. Also present were Klimenti, Radchenko, Nikishov, and Major Kharkov. Fadeyev was a small man in his late sixties, perfectly bald, his scalp slicked with oil and shining. He had a thin face and bright, quick dark eyes. He wore beautifully tailored clothes but made no attempt to compensate for his lack of physical stature. He was sure of himself but did not bristle with it, the way many small men did.

He was the most authoritative expert in the Soviet Union, and thus the world, on the use of punitive psychiatry. He had been in charge of the twelve Special Psychiatric Hospitals for "especially dangerous mental patients"—dissidents—that had been run by the MVD, the Ministry of Internal Affairs, under Brezhnev and Andropov. When Gorbachev came to power he had closed the SPHs and released their patients.

Fadeyev's work in the SPHs had been required reading in East Berlin during Klimenti's term there. "Mental illness," Fadeyev had written, "is the absence of social adaptation." Dissidents were "antisocial misfits," usually schizophrenics, who needed "corrective treatment." Fadeyev regarded psychoanalysis as an "essentially reactionary tendency in psychiatry." Instead he advocated "scientific resolutions

124

on the basis of Marxist-Leninist philosophy." Fadeyev wrote: "The purpose of corrective treatment is to inflict suffering, thus forcing the patient's complete subjugation and the ultimate recanting of his former antisocial beliefs."

Fadeyev treated dissidents with overdoses of neuroleptic drugs normally reserved for schizophrenics and violent maniacs. His favored treatment was with the drug haloperidol, which caused muscular rigidity, sensitization of the skin, chronic convulsions, dryness of tongue, neck, and mouth, sensitization of the mastication muscles, an irritating physical restlessness that made it impossible for the patient to find any comfortable position. Overdoses of haloperidol, Fadeyev wrote, made it difficult for the patient to sit, to walk, to think, to talk, and impossible for the patient to lie down. "It induces unimaginable anxiety, groundless fears, sleeplessness." It was, Fadeyev concluded, very effective.

The scar on Klimenti's chin throbbed at the memory.

Fadeyev remained seated. He spoke without reference to notes and softly, the voice of a sympathetic man. "There is no such person as a typical terrorist. There is no common terrorist personality, even among terrorists who belong to tightly knit, well-disciplined groups sharing narrow but highly defined goals. They're all individuals, all different, even though they might share a number of common factors. Usually they are young and impressionable with poorly developed values systems in which violence has frequently been seen as a solution to problems. Usually they share common backgrounds such as nationality, religious or political beliefs, common social factors such as poverty, deprivation, suppression, or a common, detested enemy who is seen as the cause of all their problems.

"It is commonly believed that these factors in various combinations are sufficient to produce an endless supply of terrorists. It is an erroneous belief. These factors are sufficient to indicate the target, but they are not in themselves strong enough to produce a terrorist. For instance, millions of Palestinians have suffered deprivation, humiliation, outrage, poverty, occupation, brutality, the death of a family member, at the hands of the Israelis; yet only a minuscule percentage of them are prepared to become terrorists. On the other hand, the Baader-Meinhof and Red Brigade terrorists were comprised of people from different nationalities, social and political backgrounds whose only common factor was their belief in their mission. So it's obvious that all terrorists have different personality patterns before they go to their group, and this remains the case even after they have been subjected to the same group conditioning process—what is commonly known as 'brainwashing.' "

Fadeyev paused to let them absorb his words. His style was clinical and impersonal, like his experiments. Yet he had caught their interest and knew it. "The first lesson about terrorists is that they are very human creatures, sensitive and full of frailty, even the worst—or best—of them."

Klimenti remembered them, all different, all of them seekers. He had sensed it in them. But what had they sought after? It haunted him to this day. What? Why?

Fadeyev said, "We have to go deeper, much deeper to find the secret motivational forces, the personal values systems, that produce human beings prepared to commit the most horrendous crimes in the name of their 'cause.' And this, of course, is very difficult. It takes a large amount of time, money, and expertise. The simple truth is that terrorist groups don't bother. Why should they? They've got someone prepared to kill. Why waste time trying to find out the deep-seated motivations behind their behavior? Instead, they expend their energy on control, on enforcing a group behavior that is self-sustaining. They force the individual to bend to the group will, and the most common way of achieving this is to make the individual dependent on the group.

"This is done by isolating the group, removing it from anything that could challenge or contradict the group's exclusive social reference, its code of behavior and morality. Their training excludes all other reference points that would enable them to make comparative judgments and it exploits the group frustrations. The aim is compliance, a submissive mental condition—which, in fact, is what 'brainwashing' is all about.

"To make killing easy, it is necessary to dehumanize the victims. They're not killing people but 'pigs.' The Nazis did it very successfully and on a massive scale by describing their victims as 'subhuman vermin.' If innocents are to die, it is necessary to believe that they are being *sacrificed* for the global good.

"Each group also needs a system of incentives and rewards. They need 'hero' models to inspire them, the promise of fame, and rich rewards. Most terrorists don't expect to die. Their training is carefully channeled to emphasize the *task* rather than the *risk*. Once, it was believed that it was possible to produce human automatons who could be conditioned to act on command by activating a subliminal psychological 'trigger' implanted during the conditioning process. All these programs were disasters."

Once again Fadeyev paused to make his point. Not once had anyone thought to interrupt or question him.

"The second lesson about terrorists—and one of the most significant—is that the durability of their conditioning is limited. It needs to be constantly reinforced by group behavior. Terrorists are vulnerable when they leave the nest, when they go beyond the group, outside their own exclusive social reference. Immediately, they are challenged by different values systems and codes of behavior and the group begins to lose control. The time factor varies, of course. It might take months, weeks, days. There are cases where it has taken only a few hours away from the group for a terrorist to change his mind. So the group can't be sure about any of its members once they've left the hive. For this reason, most terrorist acts are carried out by teams of self-inciting terrorists; quite often drugs are used either to excite or to calm them, as the occasion requires. The terrorist who is permitted to operate alone, at long distance, over considerable time frames is very rare indeed. Usually they are professionals, on hire to terrorist groups whose members they use as their cannon fodder."

Fadeyev fixed his bright eyes on Klimenti. There was no sign of recognition. Yet Klimenti was sure he remembered him and the scar. Or was it possible that he had conducted so many experiments it was just another incident, quickly overtaken by others?

"Professional terrorists don't commit suicide. They get others to do it for them. The lesson here is that we are confronted by assassins who, on the little evidence we have so far, contradict much of what I've told you, who break all the rules and yet are successful, with a degree of commitment and self-sacrifice that is rare indeed. Whoever they are, wherever they come from, they are remarkable individuals. And, needless to say, so are those who are responsible for their conditioning."

Fadeyev stood up and his audience immediately realized why he had remained seated: standing, he was dwarfed by the conference room table, which reached to his waist. It gave Klimenti satisfaction to realize that Fadeyev was more sensitive about his lack of size than he pretended to be.

"There's no more I can tell you," Fadeyev said. "But bring me one of these remarkable people—alive!—and I will tell you all there is to know about them."

Fadeyev was smiling, and it shocked them all.

At 4 P.M., staring out the window into the brightly lit courtyard that led to the doors of the Lubyanka, Klimenti came to the decision that it was time to grasp the nettles. Perhaps it was the onset of the winter night, guillotining the day so early and completely. Part of it lay in the uneasiness he felt about Big Dog's fate, whatever it was. He had a feeling that he was so far out on a limb now it mattered for nought whether he was bold or timid; the tree would shake and he would either fall or survive. It was better that he did the shaking.

"I'm going to see my daughter," he told Nikishov and walked out.

The afternoon felt good. The streetlights looked cheery and friendly. Now that he was going to see Nadya he no longer felt alone. The people rushing to catch the underground were no longer voiceless or indifferent: they communicated urgency and desire; they had direction and purpose and their greatest anxiety was missing the next train; they had forgotten about Stalin's lists and they dared to dream dreams. Every day, life was getting better, freer. Knowing at last what he was going to do, Klimenti felt sure of this.

He got a taxi and ten minutes later was standing in the warmly carpeted and wallpapered corridor, pressing the doorbell. If Zhenya was home, he would simply act as if nothing had happened between them. But the eyes that stared out through the chain gap were dark, not sandy gray; her hair was dark, too, her skin creamy olive, and she was as wide mouthed and fine nosed as a Gypsy.

"Papa!" Nadya opened the door and threw her arms around him, a storm of wild impulses, hugging him tightly and kissing him, saying, "Oh, Papa, it's so good to see you," as if she were a girl again and not a young woman; and Klimenti felt wonderful and stood there grinning like an idiot.

"Hello, daughter," he said with mock formality, part of the ritual that had developed between them long ago when he had realized with a shock that his young daughter ruled the roost, manipulating him with a cleverness beyond her years, with a cunning that could only have come to her naturally, through her genes, from her mother.

"Come in, come in, take off your coat."

Nadya coiled around his arm, unwilling to let go, and drew him into the apartment, claiming him with the same enveloping possessiveness of her mother; it was remarkable, this fusion of mature woman and reckless child, and it was one of her most attractive qualities. She was indeed her mother's daughter, headstrong and spoiled.

"I got your messages. Oh, Papa, I'm so sorry I haven't rung you but I've really been busy."

She took his coat and threw it aside, uncaring, concerned only with Klimenti. The apartment was all that he had expected, richly appointed and modern. The decorations included several icons and paintings that would fetch a fortune in the West.

"Is Papasha really coming?" She loved his father dearly and was genuinely excited.

"Tomorrow morning."

She clapped her hands with pleasure, a little-girl gesture. It was difficult to believe that she was sleeping with a CIA agent.

"And Sabotka. Is Grandpapa bringing that old reprobate, too?"

"He won't come without him. He's afraid of what he'll get up to if he leaves him by himself."

Klimenti realized he had been unconsciously watching the corridor that led to the bedrooms, looking for Zhenya.

"I'll be there to meet them," Nadya promised. "I'll come around first thing tomorrow and make sure everything's just right." Now she was playing the Little Mother, so full of good intentions and womanly bossiness, and he adored her for it.

"I'm so glad they're coming," she said and he knew she meant it.

"Yes," he said, smiling, feeling wonderful. "It's good."

"Oh, Papa!" Impulsively, she kissed him and swirled away into the kitchen, calling, "I'll make coffee, *real* coffee. Zhenya's family's got the most marvelous housekeeper and she gets it for us."

Yes, he could see that. This luxurious apartment was a showcase for the failure of socialism; almost everything in it, except the icons, had been imported from the capitalist West. Like so many other indulgences, it was carefully hidden from public scrutiny. Envy, after all, had been one of the many motivating forces for the original Revolution, and the *vlasti* weren't taking any chances.

Seeing his inspection, Nadya said, "It's your first visit."

"It's very nice."

"Oh, Papa, I'm such a selfish, thoughtless beast."

The coffee smelled wonderful and tasted as good. While he drank it, she watched him lovingly, fondling him with her eyes, seeing the things only a woman can see; her eyes went over his face with the same attention a cat gives to licking itself, missing nothing. At times like this Klimenti was overwhelmed by her womanliness, her secret strength, so unexpected in someone still so young. Sometimes she made him feel like a juvenile; she was aware of it and knew how to use it.

"You look tired, Klimenti Sergeyevich," she said, admonishing him gently, and for a moment Klimenti had the strange feeling that Nadya was mimicking Zhenya mimicking her; the way they both said his name was almost identical. "You're not taking proper care of yourself."

"We're storming." Storming was frantic overtime work to make up monthly quotas.

"No one storms at the beginning of the month."

"In the KGB we storm all the time."

"Oh, Papa!"

The apartment contained so much electrical equipment—stereo, video, television, spotlights, even a sun lamp—it would be a pushover for a professional bugging squad. Did Nadya bring Bannon to this apartment? If she did, then the chances were Nikishov was listening in on them at that very moment.

"I'm working very hard, Papa. So you'll be proud of me." Nadya looked very determined and serious, her convent face gleaming, so endearing.

There was the sound of the latch turning and Zhenya walked in, wearing a fur coat and tossing her hair, which she had just freed from a fur cap. She looked very sophisticated and self-possessed, quite different from the young woman who had fled his apartment that morning.

"Oh!" she said, stopping abruptly. She was carrying a box wrapped in expensive paper emblazoned with the trademark and name of a famous Paris couturier.

Nadya pounced on her, grasping the box and holding it up for inspection.

"So, Zhenya! He's reduced to bribes."

She shook the box, which was as light as a feather. "It'll be exotic French underwear. It always is."

Zhenya's face was flushed from the cold but she blushed a deeper shade. Klimenti stood up, setting his face in what he hoped was a polite, impersonal smile. He remembered her standing quietly before him, eyes big and full of trust and her fine body trembling with the cold and exhaustion as he removed her wet underclothes. Yes, they had been French, too.

"Good evening," he said with faultless formality.

"Hello," she said and rescued the box from Nadya. "Not now," she pleaded.

"Don't be embarrassed because of Klimenti Sergeyevich." Nadya laughed good-naturedly. "He understands such things."

"I'm not embarrassed. Excuse me, I'm going to take off my coat."

She fled out of the room. Nadya called after her. "Suit yourself, but it's not everyone who has a fiancé in the Foreign Service."

There was a knock on the door.

"Damn," Nadya said. "Who can it be?"

It was Major Kharkov, so handsome and upright in his uniform, his officer's hat in his hands and his eyes full of admiration for Nadya.

"Excuse me, Colonel. But it's urgent."

"Damn," Nadya said. "I haven't properly introduced you to Zhenya."

Klimenti was glad Kharkov had come.

20.

Kharkov did not drive to Dzerzhinsky Square. Instead he turned off at the Valdai Café into Malaya Molchandovka Street, which runs behind the high-rise buildings facing onto Kalinin. After the noise and traffic of the main thoroughfare, it was quieter here—mostly women on foot, going to Kalinin to catch their trolley cars or rushing to get to the New Arbat supermarket before it closed. They all carried shopping bags stuffed with even more shopping bags, even the men; you never knew when you might chance on something you wanted and they were always ready to buy up in bulk, their purses and pockets full of wads of rubles hoarded for such rare opportunities.

They're Russian, the Militia officer had said at the roadblock. *Always full of hope.*

The street was narrow and turned sharply. The apartment buildings were three- and four-storied and older. They were, however, in reasonable repair and several had been torn down to make small playgrounds for children, deserted now and somehow barren in their emptiness. The naked oaks stood like mourners at a graveside. A toddler's broken plastic car lay half buried in the snow. It had a touch of pathos, as if it were a broken child and not merely an inanimate toy. Lights glowed from windows, promises of warmth and coziness, accentuating the dark cold outside.

The building at which Kharkov drew up, however, was derelict, an old warehouse that was being converted into apartments. It was directly behind the October Cinema. Several Militiamen stared sullenly at the Volga, recognizing its KGB plates, and opened their road barrier so it could pass through.

There were a number of Volgas parked behind the barricade. And one Chaika. They all had KGB registration. The Militia had been ordered to keep their distance, the reason for their resentment.

Radchenko and Nikishov stood by the Chaika. Another barrier had been erected a few meters past it, at the entrance to a driveway that led into the deserted warehouse. The gatepost was broken, the gate gone, and a car was parked in the shadow of the building. It was a dun-colored Volga M-124, a five-seater modeled on the American Plymouth, and it was in beautiful condition, reflecting back the bright, harsh glare from the portable lights that had been run out from the KGB cars. Whoever owned the M-124 could not only afford to pay five years' salary for it but obviously also had the privilege of a garage in which to keep it out of the harsh weather and away from the envy of vandals. Klimenti thought of his own key-scratched and scarred Zhiguli and how he had to remove the windshield wipers to prevent their being stolen.

The lights illuminated Academician Morozov as he stooped and inspected the dead man in the car.

"Who is it?" Klimenti asked.

"Take a look," Radchenko said, an order.

Klimenti went and stood beside Morozov. The dead man was Major General Tarabrin, the commander of the Yevsekzia. The Jew hunter. The Academician pushed the corpse back in the seat, so he could better inspect the neck. He had to use considerable strength because Tarabrin was already stiff and cold. The dead man's face was remarkably composed. His eyes were shut and there was no disfigurement of strain, shock, or even pain on his features. At first glance, it appeared he had died peacefully. In repose Tarabrin's features had the fineness of female beauty. He was wearing a heavy civilian overcoat and a fur hat.

"Hello, nephew," Morozov said. His dark eyes were hooded and brooding and, Klimenti thought, full of warning. Morozov stamped across to deliver his report.

"He was murdered," Morozov said bluntly, knowing it was what they least wanted to hear.

"Murdered!" Nikishov exclaimed. "A KGB Major General! A few meters from Moscow's busiest cinema!"

"You're certain?" Radchenko asked.

"Of course," Morozov said brittlely.

"He looked so peaceful," Nikishov said, not daring to challenge Morozov directly. "The Militiaman who found him reported it was a heart attack."

"Perhaps you should get this policeman to do the autopsy," Morozov said sarcastically. Nikishov wished he had held his tongue.

"Poison?" Radchenko asked, expressing Klimenti's immediate suspicion. It was obvious that Tarabrin had died without a struggle. Poison also raised the possibility of suicide, which was preferable to murder.

"No," Morozov said. He took off his gloves and held up his two huge, bony hands, spreading the fingers like talons.

"Hands!" Nikishov exclaimed.

"Like this," Morozov said and reached forward and grasped the lapels of Nikishov's greatcoat. With a brutal twist, he turned his knuckles inward, so that they lay against Nikishov's throat. Nikishov was helpless in that powerful grip.

"My knuckles are right against your carotid arteries," Morozov growled into Nikishov's face, extracting his revenge. "One thrust—and you're dead."

He released his grip and stood back. Nikishov's gloved right hand went involuntarily to his throat. Morozov gave him one last sour look of satisfaction and turned to Radchenko.

"He was a trained killer. He used Tarabrin's lapels to anchor his grip, to maximize the thrust. He knew what he was doing."

"The Afghans used knotted silk cords," Radchenko said.

"Hands are faster," Morozov said. "Just as long as you know how to use your knuckles. Or your thumbs. A second's pressure and they're out."

He spoke with all the detachment of a scientist. The carotid arteries were situated on both sides of the larynx and carried blood to the brain. Blocking them, cutting off the blood supply, caused the victim to faint almost instantly. It was the simplest, quickest, and most effective way of disabling someone.

"But it didn't kill him," Morozov said. "To do that, the killer would have had to maintain the pressure for at least four minutes, causing him to die of cerebral anoxia. In that case, there'd be outward signs of distress. Discoloration. A protruding tongue perhaps. Facial distortion."

He stared around at them with his cold, analytical eyes. At Usovo he had been excited, as wild as a bear. But today he was as frigid and emotionless as a mortuary attendant.

"But he's as pretty as a virgin. I can't be sure, but it's my guess he died of vaso-vagal shock. The vagus nerve is one of the most important leading from the brain to the heart. It regulates the heartbeat, the rate at which the engine pumps the blood. If you're in danger, the brain flashes the signal down the vagus nerve, the heart pumps fuel faster. You're asleep, the vagus nerve tells it to slow down. It's like a spark plug, firing the heart. Shut the brain down and it is possible for the vagus nerve to be completely traumatized. The heart stops beating. It'd take only a few seconds."

"Could the killer have anticipated it?"

"Perhaps. If he knew a lot about the human body."

"Or killing?"

"Yes. Or killing. But it's more likely Tarabrin had a weak heart and the murderer found the job was over quicker than he expected."

Nikishov said, "If the killer used his knuckles, he attacked from in front. That means he was sitting in the car with Tarabrin. So Tarabrin knew him. It's possible he even trusted him."

"You don't have to be strong," Morozov said. "Just quick. As long as you know where to apply the pressure."

"I'll remember it, Academician," Radchenko said laconically.

Radchenko walked over for a second inspection of Tarabrin's corpse, his interest rekindled. After a moment's hesitation, in which the dictates of good taste fought and lost out to curiosity, Nikishov followed.

Klimenti told Morozov about Big Dog's disappearance. He said, "If it was the KGB, they'll want to know who patched him up."

"He doesn't know who I am. He can't tell them anything."

"How many doctors are there in Moscow who I know, who're aged seventy, with a headful of white hair and built like a lumberjack? And experienced in gunshot wounds."

"I should have worn a turban."

Klimenti chuckled. The old man's sardonic humor was unquenchable.

"They might want to question you. If they do, tell them the truth. How I came to you."

Morozov said somberly, "I talk bravely, Klimenti. But the truth is I don't want to go through it again. I'll do my best but I tell you, I've seen it before, when I was younger and stronger. It frightened me then and it frightens me now."

"I'm sorry I got you involved."

"Don't be. I owed it to his grandfather. Remember." The Academician sighed. "It's just that for a few years, we were all able to forget what it was like to be afraid."

Before he left, Morozov asked, "Klimenti, if it was the KGB, why wouldn't they interrogate you? After all, it was your apartment. You took him there."

"They might not want me to know they've got Big Dog."

"Why?"

"I don't know. But it's a possibility."

"In that case, I'm safe too."

"Perhaps. But don't count on it."

"I'm an old man, Klimenti. I'll put my trust in you." Morozov reached up and placed a great paw on Klimenti's shoulder, then shook him gently, as if to reassure him.

"In Stalin's time you could trust no one. Not even your closest friends. Sometimes not even your wife or your children. Your own brother. You had their hearts, but Stalin and Beria took their courage and their souls, and love was not enough." He shook Klimenti again, imparting his strength, and said gravely, a command, "Don't let them do it to us again, nephew."

He walked away with unaccustomed slowness, his head hung in thought. Or was it sorrow?

Major Kharkov went up to Radchenko and saluted smartly. "I've commandeered the cinema manager's office, sir."

"Right," Radchenko said curtly and strode off. If he was impressed by Kharkov's initiative and efficiency he did not show it, and Klimenti realized it was no less than he expected of his handpicked men.

Tarabrin's body was taken away by an ambulance from the Serbsky Institute. Nikishov and Klimenti sat in the Chaika, waiting for Radchenko to return. They were both self-consciously aware that they had no real purpose here, but neither of them expressed it.

"Where's the *Sluzhba*?" Klimenti asked. Tracking down Tarabrin's killer was the responsibility of the Political Security Service, which ran the KGB's criminal investigation bureaus.

"Radchenko sent them packing," Nikishov said.

"He gave them a reason?"

"He told them to telephone the Chairman."

"Oh!"

"Oh, indeed," Nikishov said dryly.

"It could be the Israelis," Klimenti said. "Or it could be a Jew out for revenge. Tarabrin had a lot of enemies."

"It's possible." But neither of them believed it.

Radchenko came back with Kharkov. They got into the Chaika. Radchenko turned to Nikishov.

"I want you and Major Kharkov to find out if Tarabrin had a file on Navachine. If there is a file, I want to know who sold him to Tarabrin, even if you have to haul in every informer who worked for him. I want it done tonight, before the word gets out."

"We're on the way," Nikishov said and slid out of the car, followed by Kharkov.

"I underestimated him," Radchenko said, staring after them. "I thought he had no heart for the hunt."

He sat in the car, once again using silence as a weapon.

Finally, Klimenti said, "Did Navachine name Tarabrin?" He remembered how upset—and anxious—Tarabrin had been when he burst into the Operations Room to demand they turn Navachine over to him. He had wanted to control the interrogation.

Radchenko gave him a sly look. He said, "No. Navachine believes he was recruited by the Israelis. He thinks they passed him on to the Americans."

"But you think Tarabrin was behind it?"

"Tarabrin was a Jew hunter. Navachine's a Jew. Someone had to dig him out of his closet. Who better than one of Tarabrin's *stukachi*?

It's possible Tarabrin then sold him to the Americans. They sent in one of the Israelis they keep on their payroll to set him up."

"Why would Tarabrin work for the Americans?"

"Why do Americans work for us?"

"Money usually. Sometimes revenge. Because we're blackmailing them. Never commitment."

Except Squirrel.

"You've got your answer. Tarabrin was a nasty little shit. I'd say greed. If he was working for them. We'll probably never know for sure now."

"Did Tarabrin know we'd turned Navachine around?"

"No."

"So he wasn't trying to warn them."

"No."

The job had all the elements of make-believe, even when it was played in deadly earnest. It was difficult to know what was real and what was shadow. Deception, the necessity for it and the fear of it, was so deeply embedded in everything they did it was sometimes impossible to know where it began and ended, who was deceiving whom.

Radchenko said harshly, "Say it, Colonel!"

Klimenti said, "If Tarabrin was working for the Americans, then it's unlikely they killed him."

"That's right. If he was working for the Americans."

If! If! That was the second time Radchenko had questioned his own suspicions. Radchenko, the man of tough words and even harder opinions, was making considerable play of his uncertainty in a most uncharacteristic way.

Unless he was doing it deliberately. Teasing the truth.

Klimenti stared out the window, not wanting to face Radchenko, sensing it would be a test. In the glare of the lights, the snow looked more surrealist than real; then the lights went out and Klimenti blinked against the sudden dark that fell over the street and saw it all very clearly, for in the shadow world only shadows are real.

Radchenko had got rid of the Sluzhba before they started asking awkward questions. Radchenko was going to control the investigation, from start to finish. Why? He had enough on his hands. His job was protecting the Politburo, not chasing a murderer.

Klimenti believed he knew why. Tarabrin had been killed by a professional. In the Soviet Union, it was the KGB who trained professional killers. Tarabrin had known his killer and trusted him. And who would Tarabrin trust more than a fellow KGB officer?

Tarabrin's name had not been on Navachine's list of those who went to Lysenko's dacha. But that meant nothing. The conspirators' very existence signaled they had support—and where would they seek it first? In the KGB, where Tarabrin, a toady, a conservative, the Jew hater, a man who sought patronage, would be a natural ally. Klimenti was surprised only that Tarabrin had the nerve. Perhaps he had hoped to ride the tiger and dismount if it got caught in a trap; that was more like Tarabrin.

"We'll go on," Radchenko said to the driver, who pumped his brake pedal and flashed the rear lights as a signal to Radchenko's bodyguard in the Volga behind. The man who guarded the Politburo went in fear of his own life. Both cars slid backward out of the lane with the smooth precision of long practice, like ice skaters dancing.

It was dark in the rear of the Chaika. They rode without speaking. Radchenko was buried in the seat, staring out the darkened window, deep in thought, his eyes hooded and heavy. Klimenti was astonished by the measure of the man who was becoming increasingly revealed. His uncouth exterior concealed subtleties that were all the more dangerous because they were unsuspected. Gorbachev must have seen this long ago, when he picked Radchenko out from the herd and made him his protector.

Radchenko was playing a double game. Klimenti considered this possibility. Radchenko wanted everyone in the KGB to be asking questions, in whispers, so that they would spread like a contagion. They had killed Tarabrin *with their own hands*, literally, so that everyone would know who had done the killing, and whisper it. Radchenko had got rid of the Sluzhba so that everyone would know it, and whisper it. Radchenko had called in Klimenti, who ran American agents, and Nikishov, who hunted Americans, so that everyone would suspect he was trying to frame the Americans, and whisper it. Radchenko had sent Nikishov and Kharkov after Tarabrin's informers, so that everyone would feel vulnerable, and whisper it.

Radchenko was using Tarabrin to carry a message on his corpse. He was issuing a warning to them all that Gorbachev and his supporters were prepared to kill to protect themselves. He was warning them to stay away from conspiracies. Beware!

First Lysenko. Now Tarabrin.

But the President needed a smokescreen. It was a measure of Gorbachev's insecurity that the KGB no longer dared be brutally obvious. There were so many powerful men involved in the plot against Gorbachev that Radchenko was not confident he could move against them without mobilizing the forces he sought to dispel. So Radchenko fought in the shadows, with whispers.

But would Gorbachev—for none of the killings could have been done without his approval—really let Radchenko kill a United States Senator as part of their smokescreen? Klimenti, for all his experience, was shocked by the thought. *Gorbachev!* For the first time, Klimenti gave serious consideration to the possibility that the Americans—and Bannon—were right.

The Chaika and its escort Volga did not use the customary sirens and flashing rooftop beacons. Instead the two cars slid swiftly through the city, and the silence of their passing struck Klimenti as ominous.

Klimenti knew how to fight in the shadows. You stood still, not even a muscle quivering, so still it became a torture—and you waited, with all the patience of a statue; in the shadows, you had to be inhuman because it was human to move, and movement was the betrayer. The first man to move revealed himself, and then you killed him.

That's how you fought in the shadows.

They were all waiting, listening to whispers.

21.

M arietta Pronin was still on duty in the Operations Room. She was thirty-five and married to a civil engineer. They had two children and were prosperous, even though the housing shortage condemned them to live in a one-bedroom flat. They had their own refrigerator, washing machine, clothes dryer, and color television set and a wardrobe full of clothes. They had paid ten thousand rubles to buy a Zhiguli—and two years later were still waiting for delivery. Last year they had been given a KGB-subsidized holiday to the Black Sea. In several years, if they both maintained their so far exemplary records, they would get a two-bedroom apartment with a subsidized rent and probably would be allowed to join a group tour outside the Soviet Union. It was prospects such as these that kept Marietta Pronin working late, without complaint.

"There was a telephone call for you," she told Klimenti. "Twenty minutes ago. A young lady. She didn't leave her name or a message."

She watched him carefully, wondering at the private life of this colonel in whom she sensed an aloofness that had nothing to do with arrogance but instead, she had decided, had everything to do with his own apartness. He was a different man, and it made him quite attractive, even with the scar.

"Thank you. It was probably my daughter."

If it was his daughter, Marietta Pronin thought, why wouldn't she leave her name or a message? It would go into her report.

Zhenya, Klimenti thought. It had been Zhenya who phoned, and there came a rush of memories, the taste of her and how she had stood before him, anointing him with her musk, and the hot wetness of her loving, and her clean-scrubbed, little-girl morning face. An impulse, she had said, and he smiled again at her brazenness.

Klimenti went home and changed into a work shirt, jeans, boots, and a heavy woodsman's jacket. He dug a cardboard shoe box out of the bottom of his wardrobe, removed a metal security box and unlocked it. Inside was twelve hundred American dollars in hundred-dollar bills. He removed three and unwrapped a Walther PPK 9mm pistol from its protective chamois cloth, along with three magazines and a box of ammunition. It was a beautiful weapon, made by the Germans for the Luftwaffe and Gestapo, and Klimenti had got it from the Hungarians. He inserted a seven-round magazine and took two extras. If guns were to be used tonight, he did not want the bullets being traced back to his service-issue Makarov.

His battered Zhiguli had taken on a list; the right front wheel was gone. Klimenti swore and kicked the axle.. The job probably had been done by an amateur, most likely another Zhiguli owner who had had one of his wheels stolen by another unfortunate Zhiguli owner who had had one of his wheels stolen by . . . a chain reaction of theft. The shortage of spare parts made scavengers and thieves of them all. The professionals who stole for the black market would have driven the car away and stripped it bare. When his anger died down, Klimenti was grateful the thief had been considerate enough not to rip open the rear trunk and steal the spare wheel and his tools. It took him fifteen minutes to put the wheel on.

He drove to Cheriomuski, Khrushchev's egalitarian dream, which was now revealed as high-rise poverty. It was a vast complex, a mistake. Even now, after several generations, the people who lived there had feelings of disassociation and isolation. The civic authorities were constantly running programs trying to instill some sense of civic pride. The people's response lay in front and behind the buildings in broken furniture and junk they had hurled out into the sky. "Killer litter" they called it.

Klimenti found the block he was seeking and parked the car,

hoping the wheels would still be on when he returned. The walls were disfigured with graffiti. Here, in the womb of the State's meager generosity, lives were consumed with personal hatreds and vendettas against those who shared their misery; the sour odors of overcrowding and the shrieks of family arguments and lovemaking all seeped through the thin walls into the adjoining apartments and corridors; they intruded on each other and offended each other. So they hated and fought and wrote filthy messages on the walls: *Vladimir sucks cocks. Masha fucks. Screw perestroika. Don't send my son home in a coffin. Welcome to the Workers' Democratic Paradise.* Sometimes they got drunk enough to kill each other.

Klimenti caught a whiff of cabbage before he reached the first floor. After that he was never free of it. On the third floor a gang of kids stood in the corridor, smoking cigarettes and talking. There were eight of them, boys and girls, aged between ten and fourteen, escaping the tyranny of their parents and the confinement of one-room apartments. They had punk haircuts, tight jeans, heavy boots, and an air of defiance and menace. They stared wordlessly at Klimenti as he paused to catch his breath; he was sure that had he ventured along the corridor, into their territory, they would have attacked. He continued up the stairs and heard behind him the shrill contempt of their laughter.

By the time he reached the sixth floor, Klimenti was sure Big Dog could not have made it, even with help. He found the door he wanted and knocked, listening to the sounds of other people's lives. Mostly he heard the muted voice of many television sets.

She was old and wrinkled and tiny and she looked up at him through the partly opened door with suspicious eyes.

"Good evening, Little Mother. I'm a friend of Anton Anisimovich."

Big Dog's real name sounded strange on his lips. He'd got it and this address from the files the Industrial Security Directorate kept on its smugglers. The old woman was his grandmother and she had lived too long in this lousy place to trust strangers. She looked at his face and then at his hands and Klimenti saw she did not believe him.

"He doesn't live here," she shrilled. "He hasn't lived here in years, the layabout." She went to shut the door but Klimenti held up a wad of rubles.

"I know he lives here," he said. "Otherwise he would not have told me to come here. To give him this."

The gesture checked her. But it was not the money that interested her. Her eyes went from it back to Klimenti's face and he saw her true anxiety.

"You've seen him?"

"This morning at breakfast. Before I went to get the money."

She was unsure. She was worried about Big Dog but she had long ago learned to distrust hands that were not callused by hard work and faces not worn with suffering.

"He said I could trust you, Little Mother. He said you were the only person in the world he could trust."

A flare of pleasure lit her eyes, and for a brief moment Klimenti saw them as they had been when she was young, dark and full of fire.

"You speak too well," she said, still undecided. "Your accent. Your words. The look of you. You're not one of us."

"Anton helped me. Now I've come to help him."

"He's in trouble?"

"Yes."

"Come in," she said, stepping back, her hesitation gone.

The one-room apartment shone with cleanliness and order. It was partitioned at the end, where the window would be, to make a small sleeping quarters, barely big enough for Big Dog to lie down in. A sink with a single tap was set against one corner, where the walls carried a small square of glazed tiles. Next to it was a gas stove and a bench underneath a small set of wall cupboards. There was a compact Swedish refrigerator on which sat, of all things, a German microwave oven. There was a divan, which probably doubled as a bed, and a comfortable armchair with a pretty primrose pattern cover, obviously imported. A carved footstool with an embroidered cushion sat in front of the chair, near an electric heater, also imported. The walls were freshly painted, and there were two Georgian rugs on the floor and one on the wall. There was a small table with a lamp on it and one of those paintings of the Virgin Mary, Mother of Christ, set in a cheap plaster frame, which are sold by the hundreds of thousands in Catholic countries. And a telephone.

"He brings me something each trip," the old woman said. "He's a good boy."

It didn't concern her that the appliances were stolen from consignments ordered by the State-owned special stores. What counted was the way in which they were given, and that obviously was with love. It was a side of Big Dog that Klimenti had not suspected.

"His grandfather, my husband, was killed in Stalingrad. In the tractor factory. His mother died in childbirth and his father drank himself to death in sorrow. I sewed overcoats to keep us alive."

She said it calmly, a litany of disaster that had become her living strength. The burden had bowed and almost broken her body, but not her spirit. She had square, strong hands with spatulate fingers, work thick and swollen now with arthritis. He remembered how she had looked at his hands, recognizing him for what he was. And at his face. It wasn't the scar that made her suspicious. It was his intelligence.

"What has he done?" she asked with infinite forgiveness.

"A bit of smuggling," Klimenti lied. "Nothing serious at the moment. But it could be."

Relief flooded into her eyes and she turned away to hide the tears that came quickly. Klimenti gave her his handkerchief and for a moment she held his hand; he was surprised at how soft her fingers were, despite their tough, horny appearance.

"When did you last see him?" Klimenti asked.

"Two days ago. In the morning. I wasn't worried when he didn't come home last night because I know he sometimes has a girl. He tells me it isn't true but I can smell them on him." She smiled at her grandson's well-intended deception, finding love in this also. "But he usually telephones me the next day. To make sure everything's all right, to see if I want anything."

"Has anyone rung? Any of his friends?"

"Do you mean Tabidze? The Ferret?" She spat out the name, her face full of venom, revealing the dark side of her strength.

"Him too. But anyone."

"No. No one has rung. Especially not the Ferret. He's afraid of me, and with good reason."

She would kill him, Klimenti thought. If she had a gun or a knife or a club, she would use it on the Ferret. If the strength was still in her fingers, she'd strangle him.

"No one has come here?"

"Only you."

Klimenti believed her. He took out the three one-hundred-dollar bills. Her eyes spread wide in amazement.

"What is it?" She held back, as if it was from the Devil.

"American money, Little Mother. It's for Anton Anisimovich."

"American money!" She was horrified. It was indeed from the Devil.

"Don't worry, Little Mother, it's good money, better than rubles. If Anton's in trouble, it can save him."

Klimenti pressed the money into her hand. Big Dog could get a safe passage into the West with American dollars. The old woman's curiosity took over and she examined the notes, turning them over and fingering their texture.

"They're not at all like rubles." She pointed to the picture. "Who is it?"

"Benjamin Franklin, a great man."

"I've not heard of him."

Klimenti laughed out loud. "That's all right, Little Mother. He means nothing to you."

She laughed too.

"You must tell no one about the money. Only Anton Anisimovich." He had trouble remembering not to say Big Dog. "If his friends learn about the money they'll steal it. And if the authorities hear of it they'll arrest you."

She nodded, watching him with bright, intelligent eyes, excited now that she believed she was doing something to help her grandson. "What will I tell him?"

"Tell him there's more. Enough to solve his problems."

"How much?"

"Enough."

"Who are you?"

"Excuse the language, Little Mother, but tell him it's from the friend of the lady with the nice tits."

She giggled, a little girl conspirator now, surprising Klimenti once again.

"You're a good man, whoever you are. Your hands are a disappointment but your face is good." She reached over and touched the scar with her work-worn soft fingers and Klimenti had the sudden feeling that he had been blessed.

"Do you pray, Little Mother?"

"I never stopped," she said with pride. "Not even for Stalin."

Klimenti wrote down his telephone numbers at the KGB and at home. He put them down backward, explaining it to the Little Mother, knowing that this simple device would not be detected by anyone who was not trained in similar deceptions.

"Tell Anton to ring me, seeking a job as a house cleaner for his mother. If anyone comes here asking for him or telephones for him, you telephone me, asking for the job for yourself."

On his way out of the building Klimenti remembered the touch of the old woman's hands on the ugly welt below his mouth and he felt the pain of a memory; it was of his mother, but it was not of a face or even a person, really. She had died when he was five, worn out by the war and privation. All her energy had been consumed in holding on while her husband fought the Germans back to Berlin in a Guards' tank regiment, and when he had returned to their village in November of 1945, she had blossomed briefly, full of happiness and laughter and liveliness. Two years later, Klimenti was born. But his mother was a flower consuming the last of her sap, and perhaps she knew it. She wilted and died with a suddenness that his father still did not understand, even all these years later.

There was no surviving photograph so Klimenti remembered his mother as a series of sensations, of warmth in the night when they slept on top of the iron stove together, and the clean soap smell of her washing in the morning. Sometimes she came to him as the sizzle of fritters frying, and other times he heard her voice singing softly while she sat in the sunshine and repaired their meager clothes. But he could never identify the song nor see the face; and in these moments Klimenti felt a sense of hurt that wounded him sharply; the callusing of life, the birth of his own child, even the loss of his own wife—none of this had diminished his boy-wound, which would never heal, no matter how long he lived. Klimenti was troubled by a suspicion that his lack of conscious memory was a repudiation of his mother, punishment for the pain she had inflicted by leaving him. Of course, he had not done it deliberately, but such things happen, even to adults, and children did not have the strength to bear scars.

"Klimenti Sergeyevich." A voice called his name softly across the night and Klimenti realized that he had left the building and crossed to his car, blinded by his memories. He turned quickly and saw the Ferret standing close by, with his beautiful Tartar face and the dark almond eyes that women so envied. They were feral.

Once again he had let the Ferret in too close; now he came in to finish it, his right arm swinging low and upward so that the knife would disembowel Klimenti, as he had promised in the restaurant. It was impossible to step away from the knife, so Klimenti jackknifed over it, going forward to intercept the blow, scooping for the blade with both hands, catching the Ferret by the wrist and falling onto it so that the momentum of the blow had to fight against his entire weight. He felt the knife punch against his belly and wondered at the lack of pain.

The Ferret cursed and tried to wrench his knife arm free, but Klimenti kept driving forward, pushing him off balance; and when he felt the Ferret swinging sideward, Klimenti turned against the arm and smashed it across his knee and heard the Ferret scream. The Ferret pulled back, trying to free his arm to stab again, and Klimenti went with him, driving the Ferret's arm upward with all his strength until it was shoulder high, and then he pivoted and wrenched against it, reversing the arc and catapulting the Ferret through the air. Klimenti tried to hold on, knowing his only chance was in staying in close, where he could use his strength against the Ferret's superior speed; standing off, the Ferret would stab and slice, chopping him down. But he was wearing gloves and the momentum of the Ferret's somersault broke his grip. Klimenti moved to close in and kick the Ferret before he regained his feet, but he slipped on the snow and fell. He rolled frantically, kicking at the air where he expected the Ferret to be, rolled again, and came up onto his feet in a sprawling charge that bounced him against the Zhiguli.

The Ferret was standing three meters away, hunched over, holding his sore wrist. He straightened and snarled and transferred the knife to his left hand. His body arched backward, his hand curling high over his head, and Klimenti thought it was the most beautiful and deadly human movement he had ever seen, and then it slashed down, releasing the knife. But the upswing had warned Klimenti and he dived sideward into the snow and heard the knife smashing against the car door, where his belly would have been.

When Klimenti regained his feet, the Ferret was already thirty meters away and running with a swiftness Klimenti could never match. Even so he gave chase, tugging out the Walther. He fired, but it was a hopeless shot—on the run at that distance—and then the Ferret cut around the corner of an apartment block and disappeared from sight. Klimenti ran to the corner and rounded it carefully, keeping a meter between himself and the wall, just in case the Ferret was waiting in ambush. But there was nothing, only the shadow of the building. Klimenti listened for footfalls but heard nothing. A spear of yellow light flared out from the darkness and Klimenti saw the muzzle flame of the second shot before he heard the blast of the first and he jumped for the corner, firing before he rounded it. He heard the cough of a car motor starting and he ran around the corner, crouching low, pistol aimed. Again it was too far for a shot, and then the car was onto the road and gone.

Klimenti ran back to his Zhiguli. The knife lay on the snow. Klimenti picked it up with his left gloved hand and saw that it had blood on the handle and, panicking, he remembered the blow against his belly. He tore open his jacket and shirt and saw he had no wound; his thrust against the Ferret's arm had stopped the knife's momentum sufficiently for the thick woolen jacket to absorb the blow. The blood was not his.

Klimenti found the body lying in snow dark with blood. There was a gaping puncture wound behind the right ear, where the Ferret had struck with the knife, twisting and jagging it to sever the larynx. Klimenti turned the head so that he could see the face. The lips were stretched back in a death snarl hideous to see. There was a mustache that almost, but not quite, hid the bitter slash of a harelip.

Klimenti shuddered, feeling again the coldness of steel, so cold it burned. He put the knife beside the dead man and opened his jacket. A Makarov pistol nestled in a shoulder holster. He had obviously been taken by complete surprise. Klimenti found a pass embossed with the Sword and Shield emblem of the KGB. He was Captain Karl Pavlovich Shileiko, aged twenty-seven. Klimenti was certain he was one of Radchenko's men. He put the documents back. He did not open Shileiko's wallet. There was no time, and he did not want the burden of even a brief glimpse into the dead man's personal life.

Shileiko had got in the way and the Ferret, who had a gun, had used his knife because he needed to kill him with stealth. But with Klimenti, there was no reason for not using the gun. Had the Ferret used it at such point-blank range he would undoubtedly have succeeded in killing Klimenti.

The Ferret had chosen to use the knife because killing Klimenti was personal, something he would do with pleasure, and killing an enemy with a knife was a very intimate thing to do.

22.

Zhenya saw him through the small patch of clear glass she had wiped out of the condensation on the windshield. The rest of the car had been frosted in for more than an hour and the Zaporozhets' thirteen-horsepower engine trembled with the effort of keeping running. It was worn out and needed badly to have its pistons rebored and an oil change and a lot more; it was making a nasty sound just keeping the heaters going. The warmth and the tinny panting of the engine had begun to get claustrophobic as her anxiety grew that he would not come, or that she would miss him, and she made sure the small patch of glass in front of her was kept clear.

Klimenti stopped, recognizing Nadya's car through the cloud of exhaust fumes. Now that he had come, Zhenya was more nervous than she had been waiting and she was determined not to show it. She huddled down inside her fur coat, her fur cap pulled deep over her ears. She looked older, more composed in the fur-embrace, and she knew it.

Klimenti walked over and got in.

"Hello," he said, as if they had met like this every night of their lives. His voice was strangely flat.

"You're not surprised?" she said, off balance immediately.

"Nadya has a key. She'd wait inside." He was calm and still, sitting in the darkness, his shoulder touching hers.

Sometimes he's like a cat, Nadya had said. *You get this unearthly feeling that he sees everything without looking.*

"I went up and knocked. But, of course, you were out."

He did not reply and, remembering how she had abandoned him that morning, Zhenya thought he was angry. His face in the faint luminescence that came from the dashboard instruments was pale and drawn, his eyes pulled tightly back into his skull. She sensed again the remoteness that had drawn her to him, but this time it was so strong it was almost threatening.

"You telephoned my office?" His voice was toneless, and it was impossible to tell if he was exhausted or just uninterested.

"How did you know it was me?"

"Nadya would have left her name."

The fuel gauge was hovering around empty. Klimenti switched off the engine. "You can't come up," he said. "Big Dog's gone. Someone came and got him and they might not have been his friends. The place might be wired."

"Wired?"

"Listening devices, so they can hear everything that's said. And happening."

Zhenya stared at him, remembering the gasp of their loving, so beautiful in the throat of passion but shameful in any other context.

"Oh!" She felt violated. She looked quickly across at Klimenti but he was inspecting his hands, holding them out in front of him, fingers splayed, and she realized he was looking to see if they were trembling.

Holy Mother of God, she prayed, what is it this time? She felt overwhelmed by panic.

Klimenti put his hands away. They had not been shaking.

"It's all right," he said. "If there are bugs, they'd have put them in today when they took Big Dog."

He was glad she did not know that the KGB most probably already had her on tape in her own apartment. Wealthy young bachelors in Foreign Affairs didn't bring young women sexy lingerie from Paris unless they expected to see them in it, and then help them take it off; and she was young and greedy for life and full of need.

Now that she believed she had escaped the microphones, Zhenya was outraged. She also wanted to shake his calm. "It's filthy. Disgusting," she flared. "I don't understand how you can be part of it."

"Don't try. It's a fog. Keep out of it."

He spoke quietly, almost with detachment, and she shivered even though it was still warm in the car. In the morning, when she had fled, she had been glad to get away, and yet all day she had been troubled by his uncomplaining acceptance. She had respected him because he seemed to understand and she thought that showed real character, real maturity. But now Zhenya believed it was merely indifference on his part and that she had done only what he wanted her to do, and it diminished and hurt her.

"Why'd you come?" he asked.

Zhenya wound down her window. She took off her fur cap and shook loose her hair. She held her face into the cold night air to take the heat from her cheeks. She was beautiful with her face set against emotion.

"You wouldn't have come unless it was important," Klimenti pressed.

Zhenya said to the open window, "When I got home this morning, two Militia officers were waiting. They had my fur coat and hat and snow boots. I'd left them behind in the cloakroom at the Belgrade." She laughed, hard now. "There wasn't time to collect them."

"You were very brave," Klimenti said.

Involuntarily, Zhenya put her hand to her breast, remembering the cold and her nakedness in the car. Later, when they made love, she had felt scalded, and the heat that had been in her belly now seemed to be burning her nipples.

"They're very expensive, a gift from my father. They have my name and address on the labels."

"They were investigating the shooting?"

"They didn't say so directly, but they wanted to know why I'd left such beautiful clothes behind on such a freezing night. I told them I met an interesting man and went home with him. I couldn't get my coat and hat without my boyfriend knowing what I was doing."

She pulled a wry face. "In a way, it was the truth."

"They wanted a name?"

Zhenya nodded. "I told them it was none of their business who I slept with. They didn't like that. Then the telephone rang. It was for them. You should have seen their faces. When they hung up, they were

very angry, the way people are when they feel they've been humiliated."

The way the Militia felt every time the KGB pulled rank on one of
their investigations.

"I thought I should warn you."

He said nothing. She shrugged. "It might have been the KGB.
Who else would dare interfere with the Militia?"

Klimenti wondered how much he should tell her. He asked, "Was
Nadya there?"

"She has an early lecture every Thursday. She had already left."

Zhenya saw his relief and smiled sourly. She had been unnerved by
the Militia but she had kept her courage and not given them his name,
and she felt cheated that he had not recognized this.

He said, "You were right in coming. Thank you."

Zhenya shook her head, repudiating his timid gratitude. Somehow
it shamed her. She started the car engine. It wheezed and spluttered and
she gave it full choke and pumped the accelerator, knowing what she
was doing.

"I want to go now. I'm very tired."

Klimenti said, "You're not to telephone me under any circumstances."

She laughed at his bluntness, mocking it, to show she didn't care.
"You needn't worry on that score. I won't make the same mistake
twice."

"If they come again, they'll be KGB. They might be wearing
Militia uniforms but they'll be from the KGB."

"It's illegal," she said, but it was not a protest. She had learned a
lot in the last twenty-four hours. Her perspectives had been changed,
forever. No longer did she feel protected by privilege and inviolate. She
was learning what 99 percent of her fellow citizens already knew. In
that sense it was the beginning of her real education.

"If they question you, tell them the truth. They'll know most of it,
anyway, and it'll be to your credit."

"Even about the apartment? Big Dog?"

"Everything."

"About us?"

"Yes."

Zhenya turned away from him then, staring out the window into the gray night. The engine was misfiring and she had to keep revving it to stop it expiring altogether.

"If anything happens, if anyone comes to see you, you're to let me know."

Zhenya laughed at that, too, this time with a touch of scorn.

"Certainly! I'll shout it across Dzerzhinsky Square. That way, they'll never know."

"You're to come here and wait. As you did tonight."

"No. To hell with waiting on you," she said vehemently.

"I understand your anger. But this is something different."

"To hell with your understanding too."

He said harshly, "Listen, this isn't a game of musical beds for the amusement of rich kids. This isn't about impulses. This is about staying alive. Tell me, Zhenya, what's the price for your wounded ego? A life?"

Klimenti could see her eyes in the glow of the instrument panel and in them there was a hurt her words and her courage would not admit to.

"Whose life?" she asked softly.

Klimenti did not answer. He got out of the car. Zhenya leaned across and wound down the window.

"I'm neither promiscuous nor frivolous," she said defiantly. "And I didn't come on an impulse."

The tiny Zaporozhets spluttered into action, hiccuping on the misfiring cylinder, throwing out its tail plume of exhaust as she drove off. He watched the car all the way down Shabolovka Street.

In his apartment, Klimenti drank two glasses of Scotch while he cleaned the Walther and returned it to its chamois in the metal security box, along with the diplomatic *kartoshka*. He put the security box into a plain shopping bag and went down to the basement, where each tenant had a small wire-mesh cubicle in which to store their belongings. He chose one that was crammed with household odds and ends and suitcases, picked the lock, and buried the shopping bag beneath a carton of books.

Klimenti checked his clothes for blood and found none. He had a shower and climbed into bed naked. After a while he got up and dug out a pair of pajamas that he had not worn for years. He was uncomfortable wearing them but he did not want to be naked when they came for him.

He lay awake, thinking about the dead man with the harelip. Shileiko had led the Afghansty. He had followed Klimenti to the Hotel Belgrade. It was almost certainly Shileiko who had taken the shots at the Ferret and Big Dog when he saw that Klimenti was onto them. Shileiko had gone to Cheriomuski to finish the job, and had got his throat cut. Shileiko worked for Radchenko. Why would Radchenko want the Ferret dead?

There could be only one reason. Radchenko had used the Ferret to bring in the American plastic and the RPG7. Radchenko was behind the assassinations and Tarabrin's death. It was almost certainly Radchenko's men who had taken Big Dog from Klimenti's apartment, to shut his mouth, too.

Radchenko was Gorbachev's man. *Gorbachev!* Was it possible? Why not? To survive, he had to be as ruthless as his enemies.

For the second time in less than twelve hours, Klimenti was appalled by his suspicions. The fears that had first assailed him at the scene of Tarabrin's murder now seemed corroborated by Shileiko's death. He waited, unable to sleep. How long would it be before they found Shileiko's body? Then they'd come. To find out how much he knew.

It was a long, sleepless wait. Major Anatoli Stepanovich Kharkov banged on his door at 5:15 A.M. He was tired and angry.

"Lieutenant General Radchenko's orders," he snapped, paying no deference to rank. He would take Klimenti at gunpoint, if necessary. "You're to come immediately."

It was a relief, a release from the terrible night.

Klimenti shaved and showered again, taking his time over his toilet, refusing to be flustered. Kharkov chafed at the delay. "The general's waiting," he said but Klimenti ignored him, putting on a fresh uniform. When they went out into the cold dark, Klimenti saw another Volga parked behind Kharkov's car. The search party.

"What's it about?" Klimenti asked, but Kharkov's only reply was a curt: "General's orders."

"Sir!" Klimenti snapped. He'd had enough of the major's surliness.

"Sir." Kharkov bit out the word through clenched teeth. Perhaps Shileiko had been his friend. They rode the rest of the journey in silence.

Radchenko was waiting in the Operations Room. He had not slept. Klimenti smelled the sour odor of sweat and stale cigarette smoke. Radchenko noted how fresh and smart Klimenti looked and scowled at Kharkov as he left.

"Reporting for duty, General—as ordered," Klimenti said blandly. "Ready and willing."

Radchenko's scowl deepened. Klimenti did not look or sound like a man who was cowered by the threat of interrogation. "That's good, Colonel," he growled, "because I want you to tell me what you were doing at the Hotel Belgrade two nights ago." He slapped down a file and took out a photograph of the Ferret. "With this scum." Radchenko's eyes were bleary and dangerous. And vengeful. With Radchenko hunting him, the Ferret was as good as dead already.

Even though Klimenti was prepared, it was still a jolt. The only way Radchenko could be so sure that the Ferret had killed Shileiko was because he had sent Shileiko to kill the Ferret. It confirmed all Klimenti's suspicions, and it shook him.

"Who was under observation, General?" Klimenti asked sourly, sure now that he had to fight back. "Tabidze? Or was it me?"

"I'm asking the questions, Colonel. And I want an answer."

"Is this a formal interrogation, General?"

"Do you have a problem with the question, Colonel?"

There was a deadly formality in their words. Two hard, cold-eyed men. Unblinking.

"It's my right to know."

Radchenko glared, realizing that Klimenti was not going to be intimidated. He said, "We've interviewed Zhenya Stepanov."

They knew it all.

Klimenti said quietly, "Tabidze's a professional smuggler. He's also an informer. I thought he might be able to give us a line on who brought in the plastic and RPG7 used by Lysenko's assassin."

He wondered where she was now. In this building somewhere? Or had they taken her across the courtyard, into the Lubyanka, to really scare her? She would come to no harm. She was the daughter of a deputy minister, and these days that stood for something.

"You think Tabidze was involved?"

There it was, out in the open. Radchenko was anxious to find out how much Klimenti had learned from the Ferret. How much he knew,

and how much he suspected. Klimenti realized his own life was
balanced on his answer. If Radchenko grasped that he suspected the
Ferret's involvement, then Klimenti too was dead mutton.

"Tabidze?" Klimenti hoped he sounded surprised. "No, not
Tabidze. His hide depends on us. Even a ferret doesn't chew off the
hand that feeds it. But he's got a keen nose, a regular *stukach*. And he'd
sell anyone out, even his own mother."

"Did he have any information?"

"We were interrupted."

Was that a flicker of relief in Radchenko's eyes?

"Why did you go alone, out of uniform, without a witness, without
a warrant? Without telling anyone?"

"Tabidze would have cleared out the moment he saw a uniform. Or
anyone else."

"You know him well then?"

"I recruited him."

"He trusts you?"

"He trusts no one. He's afraid of me."

"Why?"

"One day I'll walk him to a firing squad, and he knows it."

Radchenko nodded. That he believed. "Why did you help his pal,
Big Dog?" His tone was flat, relentless.

"Tabidze took off. I had Big Dog, so I hung onto him."

"Why did you take him to your apartment? Why didn't you bring
him here for a proper interrogation?"

"It was the fastest way of getting his cooperation. Convincing him
he had nothing to fear. Winning his gratitude."

How feeble it sounded. Radchenko didn't believe it.

Klimenti said, "I felt it was worth trying. If it didn't work, I was
going to bring him in."

"Did it work, Colonel? Did he tell you about Tabidze?"

In Radchenko's small eyes, Klimenti could see neither malevolence nor mercy. But he was sure he was on trial. For his life.

"No. He was unconscious most of the time."

"You didn't bring him in, did you, Colonel?"

"No, sir. He got away from my apartment."

"Got away?" For the first time, Klimenti sensed a tone of mockery.
"Why didn't you report it?"

"It was a bloody mess. As far as I knew, no one was aware I was involved, so I thought it best to keep quiet. I didn't want it on my record." It was a humiliating lie but Klimenti felt no hesitation in telling it. He withdrew into his armor of professionalism.

For a long moment, Radchenko sat in silence, watching Klimenti with his gimlet eyes, probing, sensing. Suddenly Radchenko blinked and there was tiredness in his face, and Klimenti realized it was all right. This was not Radchenko's killing face.

"You were stupid, Colonel. Worse, unprofessional. If you weren't needed to liaise with the Americans, I would recommend immediate and severe disciplinary action. I'm afraid that will have to wait. But rest assured, Colonel, that your future conduct—the proper execution of your duties—will help determine the extent of the charges against you. Do I make myself clear?"

"Yes, General." Klimenti could hardly believe he had got off with a reprimand.

"After all," Radchenko said dryly as he left, "we are on the same side. Aren't we?"

For the first time since he had trodden the snow in the silent forest at Usovo, Klimenti thought that it could be the truth. He had been confronted with his own fate and, in consequence, the realities that governed his continued existence. Yes, if Radchenko was acting to protect Gorbachev, then he was on Radchenko's side. He was against the Stalinists. If it came to a showdown—*it had come to a showdown*—then he was prepared to condone killing. The difficulty was, Radchenko had not invited him into his bunker and he was still out in no man's land, caught in the crossfire, among the mine fields. One wrong step and . . .

For the second time, Radchenko had warned him to keep out of it. There would be no third warning. Nor would Klimenti require one. Henceforth, Radchenko could kill whom he wished. Klimenti would keep out of it. Klimenti remembered the graffito in the underpass. Never before had he so clearly understood its bitter message:

OBEY
BE SILENT
DIE

He would do his duty. He would obey. He would be silent. So that he would *not* die.

It wasn't cowardice: it was common sense. Survival. And in the final count, he agreed with Radchenko. He was on his side. All he had to do was look the other way. Nadya was his only concern, not Kremlin plots and counterplots. *Nadya*, his daughter.

Klimenti picked up a telephone and dialed.

"Hello," Zhenya said.

She was back in her apartment. She had been sitting by the telephone, waiting for the call.

"Who is it?"

Klimenti sensed a quaver of anxiety beneath the calm she was trying to impose on her voice. He put down the telephone without speaking. He didn't want his voice on the tape.

23.

Leonardo rode the *elektrichka* to Studencheskaya station. He had used the system every day to acquaint himself with it and had several five-kopeck tokens in his pocket. It was the fastest way to get around Moscow: the metro trains ran quietly and on schedule and were clean and modern. Leonardo had never seen any graffiti; the people were polite and orderly; it was very civilized.

So Leonardo was surprised when he got out at Studencheskaya and saw the word SUK written large in crayon on the freshly painted station bricks. It stood alone, declaring itself to every alighting passenger, a statement of defiance. It was quite thrilling to see the language of revolt in the West being used in Moscow. The Soviet young were hungry. For new ideas, for innovation. For everything, perhaps even freedom. They were even using a new language.

Leonardo walked one block down Kievskaya Ulitsa alongside the deep cut that carried the railway tracks. The footpath was raw, frozen earth covered with packed snow, and twice he slipped and almost fell. This was a poor, semi-industrial area and the drabness was depressing. Everything was scoured by the weather, so that even relatively new buildings seemed worn out and exhausted. Passersby paid him no attention. They walked with their heads down, watching their footing, chins tucked into collars against the cruel fingers of winter.

He came to a fenced-off area that was used by the municipal

authorities as a parking lot for street-working equipment and snow-plows. Next to it, outside the fence, was a sagging brick structure, which had once been used as a garage until it had become too dangerous. It was shuttered and locked. Opposite it was an electrical substation with its own parking lot. No houses full of prying eyes looked out onto the derelict garage. Control had chosen well.

Leonardo walked on past. He knew the area thoroughly already; Control had coached him from a map and Leonardo's confidence grew as he mentally ticked off the names of the streets as he went past them. He had learned his lessons well. By the time he came out to the Kiev railway terminal he was feeling quite proud of himself.

It was good. It was positive. He was being definite, doing things, working to get it right.

He walked onto the Borodino Bridge and stood for a while staring at the frozen river. He would have liked to see it moving. He would like to see a living river before he died. Leonardo became aware of an intense longing for the warmth and sweetness of spring, for green foliage and the tiny creatures that lived among it. But he would be two months dead when trees bloomed again in Moscow.

He turned and retraced his steps past the Kiev terminal square and walked down Bolshaya Dorogomilovskaya Street to its junction with Kutuzov Prospekt with its massive granite sculpture of a soldier, a worker, and a woman fused together in sacrifice, the heroes of the Battle for Moscow; it was dramatic and powerful, yet—for all their resolution and courage—the sculptor had managed to give the figures a sense of tragedy.

Life was different along Kutuzov. You could see it immediately. The apartment buildings were painted in pale yellows and ochre, with occasional flashes of blue; they were substantial and impressive, giving a sense of security and well-being. Most of them had small playgrounds and areas for parking cars. Young nannies pushed high-wheeled prams containing their heavily swaddled charges.

In two blocks he passed two food stores, a supermarket selling general goods, a number of smaller shops selling clothes, and at least three coffee shops, a concentration of services unheard of elsewhere in the Soviet Union. At the doors of a *beryozka* shop, a small group of working-class women were pleading with a gray-headed doorman, who was refusing them entry. They had no hard currency to buy with and merely wanted to look at the wonders within. The old man's medals announced he was a veteran of the Great Patriotic War, and Leonardo thought it was sad that he should be so resolute in turning away the generation whose future he had fought to secure. It made a mockery of the monument he had just passed.

It was not difficult to find the apartment building he sought. It was huge, eight stories of granite blocks stretching three hundred meters along Kutuzov. It was, Leonardo noted, the same color as No. 2 Dzerzhinsky Square. In front was an elevated glassed-in traffic controller's post, which gave the Militia operator a clear view of the broad avenue. There was no intersection and pedestrians crossed in an underpass. The sole purpose of the post was to stop the traffic whenever a curtained-off Zil limousine called to pick up or drop off one of the occupants of the apartment block. The profiles of two of the building's most famous former tenants were embossed on big bronze commemorative plaques at each end of the block. One was of Leonid Brezhnev, the other of Yuri Andropov, both former rulers of the Soviet Union. Plastic flowers lay in cages at the bottom of each plaque. Their surviving families still lived here.

This was No. 26 Kutuzov Prospekt. Leonardo did not cross the street for a closer examination. He had already noted the two young KGB men lounging out front, stamping their feet and beating their hands, doing their best to pretend they weren't there. They could be a problem.

One of the second-floor apartments had a window box, empty except for a glass jar which contained two naked birch twigs. It was a simple and soulful offering that caught the anguish of a Russian winter. Leonardo was not the only one who longed for the coming of spring, and this knowledge comforted him.

24.

"So!" Sabotka declared for the umpteenth time. "This is Moscow." He stood at the window of Klimenti's apartment, staring out on the street below, his seared face completely devoid of expression, as frozen as the permafrost. It was what Klimenti's father called "Sabotka's Siberian look," the face of bitter survival. There were times, Sabotka had told them in one of his rare moods of retrospection, when you only had to smile, to blink, let a muscle quiver, and some mongrel killed you, so you became a mask, mute through all suffering. But both Klimenti and his father understood it was more than that. Sabotka had endured so much, the cost of staying alive had been so high, he was careful not to let any of it show, fearing it would tear him and his face to pieces, such was his hunger for revenge.

"So," he said, "this is the center of the universe."

Sabotka's words, unlike his face, were allowed their freedom and they were full of contempt, a judgment delivered. This was where they had written down Sabotka's name, long ago. This was where they had settled the fate of millions of people, "Stalin's chips," flying from the ax of the Great Woodsman as he felled forests of humanity.

"It's full of rotting buildings," Sabotka said derisively.

Klimenti's father sighed. Sometimes Sabotka tested even the almost measureless patience of his oldest friend, Sergei Ivanovich

Amalrik, who was also his only friend, because Sabotka would admit no other. "I don't know why you bothered to come," he grumbled.

"It's falling to pieces," Sabotka said with immense satisfaction.

"So what'd you expect?"

"What they promised us. Paradise!" Sabotka's eyes were aglow with hate.

Even now, after more than two decades of freedom, Sabotka's body was still withered with the hunger of the Kolyma and it showed particularly in his face, which was rat-thin, beyond feeding, beyond filling. He had been twenty-two when they took him east and forty-six when he came back over the Urals: he had been an old man all the years in between, snap-frozen into old age by a process that was instant, premature, and permanent. But it had also invested Sabotka with a quality of agelessness, taking him to the limit where further weathering was impossible. His iron-gray hair was thick, and he still wore it in a stubby bristle. He walked with the broken-kneed gait of a man who for too long had borne an unbearable burden. His voice was strong and harsh and often forbidding. His eyes had the power to reach out and bite you, as quick and as deadly as a scorpion, full of poisonous claws. They had lost none of their strength and were as clear and as pure as venom.

In contrast, Klimenti's father had a kindly face. He, too, had a headful of thick hair and his body, thinner now, was still strong from his work as a mechanic who kept the tractors and trucks running for the municipal authorities. He had the slow, watchful eyes of a country man, not suspicious but careful. He was both proud and grateful that socialism had sent him to school and made him the first of countless generations of his family to learn to read and write. It had taught him a trade. It had trained him to fight and given him the weapons to defeat his enemies. It had taken his only son from an obscure background and sent him to the most important university in the land, an honor his own father would not have believed possible. It had made his son an important man and he was thankful.

"My apologies, Klimenti Sergeyevich," Sabotka said. "I'll shut up now. In fact, if you don't mind, I would like to use your bathroom, which, seeing you've got running water and a seat you can sit down on, could be regarded in some quarters as part of the paradise they've so selflessly provided for us on earth."

He was totally incorrigible and didn't give a damn for anything except his past, or anyone except Sergei Ivanovich, whom he loved. He was completely without respect for any laws other than those necessary for survival. Yet, for all his faults, there was one that Sabotka did not possess. He was not capable of betrayal. He would die before he forsook a comrade. In the gulag it had not been possible to survive alone; it needed collective strength to haul each man through, so you were careful who you shared your courage with, asking what you gave, and there was no room for shirking or holding back or theft; a man who stole your strength stole your life, the last betrayal, so you chose with great care. If you knew this, it was possible to understand Sabotka's devotion to Sergei Ivanovich, who had unhesitatingly opened his door to the scarecrow who had identified himself as his old comrade, Sergeant Nikolay Andreyevich Sabotka of the 176th Tank Regiment of General V. I. Chuikov's Third Shock Army, returned from the grave, and worse.

Klimenti's father and Sabotka had served in the same tank platoon, which had been overrun in the initial German assault on Stalingrad in September 1942. Sergei Ivanovich's T34 extricated itself but Sabotka's tank was knocked out and he and his other three crew members were taken prisoner. After two months in a prisoner-of-war compound Sabotka escaped and made his way back through the German lines to the Russian defenses. It was a remarkable feat of endurance, determination, and skill, for the Germans were everywhere. Sabotka, however, was immediately arrested and charged under Section 1, Article 58 of the Soviet Criminal Code with "treason to the Motherland." He was accused of winning his freedom by agreeing to spy for the fascists. At the time Sabotka had been considered lucky to escape the death sentence. Many others, also falsely accused, were shot on the spot. It depended entirely on the commissars; the more terrified they were, the faster they shot, hoping to build a bulwark of corpses between themselves and their own impending doom.

Sergei Ivanovich sighed, as he had on many other occasions, full of forgiveness. "He's an old reprobate. But he's had a hard life."

Klimenti said, "I have to go out again. Work, I'm afraid."

His father said, "You're not to worry about us. If it's your duty that calls, then it has to be done. We can wait."

But he was disappointed and Nadya saw it.

"For you, Papasha," she said and with a flourish produced her surprise—a walnut cake, Sergei Ivanovich's favorite. He lived simply, cooking the plainest of foods for himself and Sabotka, and a walnut cake—any cake—was a rare luxury. When Sabotka returned from the bathroom, his eyes lit up, as greedy as a child's.

"Thank you, *dochka*." Sergei Ivanovich's face was composed and grave, a certain indication that he was moved. He was a man of great privacy and in moments of intense emotion became shy and withdrawn.

"Oh, Papasha!" Nadya exclaimed and threw her arms around his neck, ready to die for him, and Klimenti thought, my God, *little daughter*! She's more like a little mother! And once again he was astounded by the fullness of her womanhood, the depth of her female mystery and strength, marveling that she was indeed his daughter.

Despite his shyness, his father was not a recluse and there had been several other women with whom he had maintained discreet relationships, an achievement in the intrusive scrutiny of village life. He treated his partners with respect and honesty, making it clear he was not interested in marriage. Klimenti wondered if he, too, shared this same obstinacy of love. Both of them had been widowed at relatively early ages and both had kept faith with their dead wives. He felt an affinity of the soul with his father, as strong as the bond of blood, stronger, perhaps, because it was a recognition that they both shared the same pain.

"She's like her mother," Sergei Ivanovich said, stroking her hair. "Impulsive and domineering. A dear little commissar."

"Commissar, indeed!" Nadya exclaimed. But she was nonetheless delighted. "If that's what you think, then you're to obey instructions and get some rest."

"Yes, I'm a little tired."

"He didn't sleep," Sabotka said. "The carriage was full of prattling women and he's forgotten how to sleep sitting up, like a soldier."

"The reason I didn't sleep isn't because I couldn't. It's because you wouldn't let me, with all your incessant yap about Moscow. You kept the whole carriage awake."

"I don't know what you're talking about," Sabotka growled, doing his threatening best.

"Don't let him fool you," Sergei Ivanovich said. "His suitcase is full of pamphlets on Moscow. Where to go. What to see. I tell you, for all his scorn, he's as excited as a child."

"Nonsense!" But Sabotka's eyes belied his denial and they saw it and laughed, and Sabotka gave up all pretense and laughed with them. It was a good moment.

Nadya took his hands, which were huge and broken and awkward. "Come with me, *Siberyaki*. We've got hard labor to do."

"Yes, Commissar," Sabotka said, as tame as a pet lamb, and went with her into the second bedroom.

"I've never seen him so meek," Klimenti's father said with satisfaction.

Once a year, Sergei Ivanovich came to Moscow and spent a fortnight with Klimenti, two weeks out of fifty-two, no more than a morsel of anyone's lifetime, that's all, a small bite, and for the rest of the year, for most of his life, he was left alone, this man who was his father, his own flesh, who had given him his blood and his features. Sabotka was more family to his father than his own son.

It was an old guilt and it was not assuaged by the fact that his father had refused all Klimenti's attempts to get him to share the empty apartment in Moscow. "They wouldn't let Sabotka live in Moscow," Sergei Ivanovich had said. "And I couldn't leave him by himself."

Sabotka, who had survived everything, would not survive loneliness. Sabotka had sealed his father's fate.

Klimenti had seldom been back to his home village, Vado. His marriage, America, the death of his wife, his career, had created a gulf not so much between Klimenti and his father as between the urbane KGB officer and the community he had grown up in. His former friends eyed Klimenti with suspicion or jealousy, and often the latter inflamed the former, for Klimenti had escaped. Others treated him with disgusting servility, angering him, and some regarded him with loathing or fear, forgetting that he had once been a young boy who ran barefoot with them.

"It's good to see you, Father," Klimenti said, kissing him on the cheeks, and Sergei Ivanovich smiled and nodded and patted him on the back, comforting his son, knowing Klimenti's pain and wanting to spare him that, too.

He went into the bedroom where Sabotka had already claimed

the mattress Nadya had got him to put on the floor. "No, no," Sergei
Ivanovich protested. "You take the bed, a guest in my son's
house."

"I like to sleep hard," Sabotka growled. "This is mine and you're
not getting it, you old buzzard."

25.

Klimenti rang Major General Shalnev at Special Service 11. Squirrel still had not cleared any of his dead-letter drops.

Shalnev said, "It's the fifth day. I'm going to ask the Chairman for permission to abandon all attempts to contact. We can't take any more chances."

"He hasn't turned," Klimenti said. "We can trust him."

"How can you be so certain?" Shalnev demanded angrily. "If it was you out in the field, would you want us to take the risk? On the intuition of a colonel who is safely back in Moscow?"

It was a scathing insult but Klimenti made no retort. Instead, he said quietly, "General, I don't think the Chairman will appreciate you being so reckless with Squirrel's safety."

He heard the sharp intake of Shalnev's breath. His barely veiled threat troubled the major general. He was aware of the extraordinary precautions surrounding Squirrel's identity and resented them. They had been so bloody careful to hide Squirrel from sight he had disappeared completely and was beyond their reach—and that was breaking one of the basic rules of his craft. Never lose control. But Shalnev was also aware that Squirrel was permitted to operate on his own terms because he was one of the most important agents the KGB had ever recruited.

"You'll go to the Chairman?" Shalnev demanded.

"Only if you force me to."

There was a long silence. Then Shalnev said, the words heavy with rancor, "One more day. I'll give him another twenty-four hours."

He put down the telephone before Klimenti could reply. Shalnev was a small, pugnacious man who swam in ice pools in winter to defy nature and contradict God, and he would not forgive Klimenti this humiliation. Klimenti had made a powerful enemy in his immediate superior officer but this did not concern him as much as Shalnev's attitude to Squirrel. Henceforth Shalnev would take a personal interest in undermining Squirrel as a way of attacking Klimenti.

Moscow Center never abandoned their men in the field. They always got them back. It was part of the contract, the compact of trust. But Squirrel was not really Moscow Center's man. He was Klimenti's, and Moscow Center had never really trusted him, despite his great value and service.

Klimenti wished Squirrel would make contact, for both their sakes.

Nikishov came in. His handsome features were haggard. He was wearing his heavy greatcoat and did not bother to shed it as he sank wearily into his chair. He took out a packet of English Players. He had long ago emptied his treasured gold cigarette case and he was too tired to be bothered refilling it.

"He's good," Nikishov sighed. "A real professional."

Nikishov had been up all night with Kharkov going through Tarabrin's files. He had spent the last two hours in a surveillance van, watching a rendezvous between Bannon and Navachine, the first contact with the American since Navachine's treachery had been uncovered. It had taken place at 8:30 A.M. in Gorky Park.

"Bannon's instructions haven't changed," Nikishov said. "He wants Navachine to report on the Politburo's movements. He particularly wants guest lists."

So Bannon was still seeking evidence of the conspiracy against Gorbachev.

"We'll make sure he gets all the lists he wants," Nikishov said.

"You need some sleep."

"You're right."

But Nikishov made no effort to leave. He sat there, hunched in his greatcoat, staring moodily at his cigarette. Finally he said, "We instructed Navachine to tell Bannon he had heard rumors that Tarabrin was dead. Nothing confirmed, of course. Just office guff that he'd died of a heart attack. Or something."

"What was Bannon's reaction?"

" '*Who* is Tarabrin?' "

"He's a professional. You saw it yourself. If Tarabrin was one of his agents, Bannon wouldn't give himself away."

"It was worth a try."

"You got your man?"

"Eh?" Nikishov shot him a startled glance.

"The *stukach* who informed on Navachine. You and Kharkov went through Tarabrin's files."

"It was his wife's cousin," Nikishov said with acerbity. "He's also her lover." Nikishov's distaste surprised Klimenti. They all detested informers but they used them frequently and ruthlessly. He felt there was another emotion involved in Nikishov's reaction.

"Does Navachine know?"

"Of course not," Nikishov said bitterly. "They're always the last to know."

"What's the going rate for a Jew?"

"A cabin for two on the *Shota Rustavelli.*" Nikishov's mouth curled with contempt. He was taking it personally and Klimenti wondered why.

A Pacific cruise. Of course. What else? Rubles were worthless. For an important Jew, you got the Pacific. For a clerk, it was the Baltic. Why not? The country was a gigantic bureaucracy and there had to be forms and requisitions, even for Jew-sellers.

"They gave him up to Tarabrin?"

"Not directly. The cousin reports to a major. Naturally the major took such an important catch directly to his director, wanting the credit."

"Tarabrin took over?"

"No. But he gave instructions that Navachine wasn't to be pulled in. The major was to use him as bait, to see if he could catch even bigger herrings. Nothing was to be done against Navachine except on Tarabrin's direct orders."

"Normal."

"Perfectly, and good trade craft. Tarabrin was careful not to put a foot wrong. He had Navachine on a leash and he could play him at arm's length. And if the major got suspicious about the Americans, Tarabrin would be the first to know."

"Is there any evidence of a direct connection between Tarabrin and the Americans?"

Nikishov frowned. He had already reached his own conclusions and didn't like them being questioned.

"Nothing. But the circumstantial evidence against Tarabrin is so strong it can't be denied."

Klimenti did not argue.

At 11 A.M., Deputy Chairman Poluchkin summoned Klimenti to his office, where he handed over a Tass special bulletin. It was the latest statement of the Vigilantes for Peace and had been carried verbatim by the BBC on its 7 A.M. London-time radio news exactly one hour ago. The statement had been monitored by Tass. It read:

The CIA and the KGB, the bitterest of enemies, are secretly working in close cooperation to destroy the Vigilantes for Peace. It is the first time they have cooperated in a covert operation. The immense resources of the world's two most powerful and repressive intelligence agencies are being coordinated in an effort to destroy those who are fighting to prevent a nuclear holocaust. The joint CIA-KGB offensive proves that both superpowers believe it is in their mutual interest to destroy those who seek to force them to disarm.

Despite expressions of good will and peaceful intentions by the presidents of the United States and the Soviet Union, the entrenched ruling cadres are interested only in world domination through the ruthless exploitation of nuclear terror. They are equally the enemy of all mankind. Their oppression must be ended.

It is the sacred duty of all human beings to assist the Vigilantes for Peace in this struggle.

It is better that the guilty few die, so that all the innocents may live.

Poluchkin was still wearing a patch over his wounded eye. His good eye was red and sore from strain. They were all starting to show signs of stress.

Poluchkin said grimly, "They've got someone on the inside. How else could they know? But why tell us? Why reveal they've got an agent in the enemy camp?"

"They've discredited the Soviet Union and the United States," said Klimenti. "It puts us and the CIA at each other's throats. They're sowing discord, suspicion, creating public distrust. All in all, General, it's very effective."

Poluchkin nodded. "Everything you say is true. But it's not enough. Think of the effort they must have expended to recruit the man in the first place. The risks they took doing it. And then to throw it away in a public announcement over the BBC. I tell you, Colonel, it goes against every instinct I know. All my training. Unless . . ." Poluchkin let the word hang dramatically on the air, a verbal left jab. "Unless they've got nothing to lose and everything to gain. If their agent has been exposed. If he's dead!"

"Tarabrin!"

"Who else?"

But there was no evidence that Tarabrin was working for the Americans. For a moment Klimenti was going to make the point. And then he remembered his interrogation by Radchenko and all that it foreshadowed. He was through asking awkward questions. If they wanted him to believe that Tarabrin worked for the Americans, he was not going to argue—even though he didn't believe it. But Klimenti's respect for Radchenko grew. Tarabrin's corpse was humming with messages, with Radchenko's hand on the key.

Poluchkin said, "We must convince the Americans the leak isn't our doing. We want you to stress that it's possible the agent is a German or a Briton, or whoever else the Americans have briefed. It can't hurt to cast some doubt into their own camp."

"The liaison will continue?"

"In secret, of course." Poluchkin smiled grotesquely. "How else can we convince the Americans it isn't a KGB plot?"

26.

A cademician Morozov rang. "I've got family affairs to discuss. I'll see you in the Slaviansky Bazaar in ten minutes." He put down the telephone before Klimenti could argue.

Nadya! Or had they come to see the Academician about Big Dog?

Klimenti checked that the Makarov pistol was in his greatcoat pocket. The last time he had gone for a lunchtime walk he had been caught unprepared. It would not happen again.

"I'm going to get some fresh air," he told Marietta Pronin, who noted down his departure.

Klimenti took the pedestrian underpass beneath Dzerzhinsky Square. It was crowded, making it difficult to see if he was being followed. A road gang was at work on Marx Prospekt, clearing away the snow heaped against the curb by the snowplows. All of the workers wore secondhand quilted army jackets and trousers and peaked caps with the ear flaps tied under their chins; it was difficult to recognize them as women. They used their snow shovels with slow and easy grace, letting the long hafts do the work for them, the sure sign of veterans. The only man in the team sat in the truck with the heaters running, cap off, smoking a cigarette and reading a newspaper.

Klimenti walked along to the huge gate tower, which had been one of the main entrances to the sixteen-century city walls, part of which had survived the ravages of 1812, when Muscovites burned their city to deny it to Napoleon, a sacrifice beyond imagining outside Russia. He waited for several minutes before he was sure he was not being followed and then hurried into 25th October Street.

The wind had turned and was coming now from the east, a dry wind that pinched icy fingers into nostrils and eyes. Even so, the street was crowded. Pedestrians overflowed the footpaths. Government cars taking important officials to lunch drove slowly among them. The street cut diagonally for several long blocks across to the GUM department store and Red Square and was popular with city workers for lunchtime diversions and shopping. A noisy group crowded around a street hawker who was selling transfers of Mickey Mouse and Goofy as fast as his hands could take the money and hand over the change.

The Slaviansky Bazaar once had been Moscow's greatest literary restaurant. Chekhov and Tolstoy had dined there often. So had the composers Tchaikovsky and Rimsky-Korsakov. But the Revolution was no great respecter of tradition or fame and it had withered, enduring the final humiliation of becoming a cafeteria. In the Sixties, during the Khrushchev Spring, it was restored into a huge room with soaring rafters and a domed ceiling, three stories high and decorated in traditional Slavonic style with beautifully carved and brightly painted woodwork. A fountain played in the center.

Morozov already had a table. Klimenti could see his mane of white hair across the room, shining in the wan sunlight that came in through the lace curtains. As soon as he was seated, a waiter in a high-collared white smock, loosely belted at the waist, produced a menu with a flourish. Normally you waited a good half hour before a waiter deigned to give you his attention. Here they ruled; this was their dictatorship.

"The manager believes he has a weak heart," Morozov confided. "He's convinced he can survive only if he gets a pacemaker. But, of course, Soviet medicine is not yet ready to give pacemakers to restaurant managers."

"Unless he knows someone who can get him on the list."

Morozov shrugged. "Perceptions are everything. He believed he was about to die. Now his name's on the list, he believes he has a chance to live—and he's looking a lot better already."

The waiter waited patiently, ignoring the pleas from other tables. Even the foreign businessmen could not entice him away with hard-currency bribes, placed beguilingly alongside their Intourist coupons. He had been told it was worth his job to displease Morozov.

"The fish soup is excellent," Morozov said and Klimenti let him order for both of them. As soon as the waiter was gone, Morozov leaned forward and whispered, "Could they record our conversation?"

"Only if the table itself is bugged. Or one of us. There's too much background noise."

Morozov was relieved. He said, "I took my report on Tarabrin's autopsy to the Deputy Chairman's office."

Tarabrin! Here he was again, more active as a corpse than he was alive.

"The Deputy Chairman read it with great interest. He instructed me to tell no one of my findings. He was very emphatic. Almost threatening, in fact."

"Poluchkin smiles, it's a threat."

"I know the difference. And he wasn't smiling, I assure you."

"In that case you're taking a great risk if you talk about it."

"So are you if you stay to listen."

"I'm staying to eat fish soup."

Whatever Morozov intended obviously did not rest easily with him. The waiter delivered a tureen of steaming soup with chunks of fish and potatoes and leeks. Despite his curiosity, Klimenti was unwilling to press Morozov. It had to be his decision.

After several mouthfuls, the Academician said, "There were no surprises about the cause of death. I was right the first time. It was vaso-vagal shock. What was interesting, however, was that, apart from the damage I expected to find to the carotid arteries, I found some swelling in Tarabrin's lymph nodes."

"The result of strangulation?"

"No. It wasn't caused by bruising. He had adenopathy of the lymph nodes, a condition which could suggest that there was something wrong with Tarabrin's immune responses. It's not very definite, just a possibility, and I was almost tempted not to bother."

"But you did?"

"I took ten milliliters of blood from the femoral vein in his crotch. I gave it to the immunologists at the Serbsky and got them to run an ELISA test. They haven't done a lot of them. There's not a big demand for ELISA tests in the Soviet Union. In the West, yes. But not here. Not yet."

Morozov peered at Klimenti. "Do you know what an ELISA test is for?"

"No."

"Hmmm. That's interesting. They tell me that in the West even the schoolchildren know what it's all about. There's been a huge education campaign, you see. But here there's hardly been a whisper."

Morozov went back to eating his soup, tearing at the bread, ladling the fish and potatoes into his mouth with gusto. He seemed to have forgotten Klimenti altogether.

"All right, Alexander Semionovich," Klimenti sighed. "What's it all about?"

"Acquired Immunodeficiency Syndrome," Morozov said, his face alight with triumph. "Commonly known the world over as AIDS."

Klimenti forgot about his soup. He stared intently at Morozov.

"Oh yes," Morozov chuckled. "I thought it'd interest you."

"Tarabrin had AIDS?"

"The first test showed up yellow. Tarabrin was antibody positive, which means he'd had contact with someone who had AIDS. He had the first stage of the infection in his blood. Still dormant but there, waiting to consume him one day. His killer did him a favor. Tarabrin was going to die a humiliating and terrible death. Very slowly."

"You're absolutely sure?"

"An ELISA test isn't foolproof. I got the immunologists to do supplementary testing, what's known as a Western blot, an analysis in greater detail. Much more specific. It takes eighteen hours and it *is* certain. It showed up black. Tarabrin was definitely infected."

"Am I right in saying that most people who have AIDS are either homosexuals or drug addicts?"

"Most of them. Or bisexual. And Tarabrin most definitely was not an addict. Not an intravenous user, anyway, and that's the risk factor. There wasn't a puncture mark on him."

"You believe he was a homosexual?"

"I'm sure of it."

No wonder Poluchkin had ordered Morozov to keep quiet. The Soviet Union had laws against homosexuality. The severe penalties made any Russian homosexual, particularly a major general in the KGB, vulnerable to blackmail.

Klimenti asked, "What were Tarabrin's chances of contacting AIDS inside the Soviet Union?"

"It's a possibility, of course. But the restrictions on overseas travel have largely quarantined us against the disease."

"You're saying Tarabrin contracted the disease outside the Soviet Union?"

"Most probably. Either that or he had a homosexual contact with someone who has been outside the Soviet Union recently."

"It shouldn't be hard to find out."

"I already have," Morozov said, looking rather pleased with himself.

"You! How?" Surely Morozov didn't have access to Tarabrin's file.

"I telephoned his wife. If you want to know about someone, ask his wife. Especially if you're a doctor. They trust us too much. We're their surrogate priests."

He finished his soup and burped loudly to show his satisfaction. He tore the napkin from his neck and wiped his mouth vigorously, like a man drying himself with a towel. He was not a man to dib and dab with a napkin just as he was not a man to sip his soup.

"I want you to understand it wasn't just curiosity. I had very strong medical imperatives for talking to Tarabrin's wife. You see, there's a chance she could also be antibody positive. If she'd been having sexual relations with her husband."

"Had she?"

"No, thank God. Not for quite some time. She's a lucky woman."

"Did she know Tarabrin was a homosexual?"

"He never admitted it. He was probably afraid she would use it against him. But she knew. I think she felt sorry for him. I think he missed out on something there."

"Had Tarabrin been outside the Soviet Union recently?"

"Six months ago. Which is just about right."

"She told you where?"

"Of course."

Morozov was enjoying himself, making Klimenti drag every fact out of him. It was his revenge.

"Where?"

"Rome."

Rome! Where the assassins had been brainwashed. The headquarters of the VFP. And now Tarabrin! It was a shock.

"Ah-hah!" Morozov snorted in triumph. "So it does mean something!"

Oh yes, it meant something all right! Had it been a casual homosexual contact, two men seeking each other out, desire their only motivation? Or had Tarabrin been caught in a honey trap baited with a raven, a beautiful young Italian boy he would not be able to refuse?

"It means something?" Morozov repeated, frowning now, worried for his triumph.

"The Eternal City," Klimenti said, trying to recover.

"Of course it's the Eternal City. Everyone knows that. But does Tarabrin being in Rome mean anything?"

"Should it?"

"Nephew, don't fool with me."

Klimenti smiled. Obviously what was good for the goose was not, in Morozov's case, good for the gander.

"Not particularly, except that it would be a good place for Tarabrin to have a homosexual relationship."

"He did, nephew. Believe me."

"If it was Rome, then you have no cause for further worry."

Morozov scowled. He did not like this evasion at all. He said sternly, "My interests in informing you were never medical."

"What were they then, Alexander Semionovich?"

"I felt it was important that you know, considering the conversation we had yesterday."

"It is, and I thank you."

"Don't thank me," Morozov said irritably. "I thought we were in this together."

"We are. But I assure you that apart from the fact that it's possible Tarabrin caught AIDS there, Rome has no significance in relation to his murder."

"You're sure?" Morozov was clearly disappointed and doubtful.

"Absolutely," Klimenti said, holding the Academician's stern eyes with an expression of frankness. He hated lying to Morozov but it was in the old man's best interests. He was too deeply involved already and the less he knew, the better.

"Thank you for the soup," he said. "It was excellent."

"I detest eating alone," Morozov growled. "Old men spend too much time with just themselves for company."

"You've met my father?" Klimenti was glad to change the subject.

"Once, a long time ago. A fine man."

"He's in Moscow. Nadya and I would like you to join us tomorrow night. At my apartment."

For a moment, the Academician's long face was alight with pleasure. Then he frowned and shook his head. "Thank you, but I'd be interfering."

"How?"

"Well, he's your father, Nadya's grandfather, your closest family."

"You're invited, Alexander Semionovich. Nadya and I will be offended if you don't turn up. And so will my father, when I tell him you refused."

"Well . . ." Morozov wanted to accept but was strangely shy.

"You're family, too," Klimenti said. "You're very important to Nadya."

"I'll come," Morozov said, beaming. "With pleasure."

Before they parted, Klimenti asked, "Did you tell Tarabrin's wife he had AIDS?"

"No. The poor woman has enough distress for the moment."

"And she told you all that? On the telephone?"

Morozov grinned. "It's remarkable, isn't it?"

"It's absolutely astonishing."

"Mind you, I'm very persuasive," Morozov called, happy now.

After the warmth of the café, the cold air was refreshing. Klimenti walked slowly, deep in thought. Tarabrin! Rome! Homosexuality! A deadly troika.

Whoever killed Tarabrin had believed that the secret of his homosexuality would die with him. In all likelihood they had never even considered the possibility of AIDS. But now, thanks once again to Morozov's brilliance, Tarabrin's corpse accused his murderers, threatening them from a refrigerator box in the Serbsky morgue.

Klimenti doubted that the VFP—not even the Americans—could

have known about Tarabrin's homosexuality. KGB officers traveled abroad under false identities. They did not announce themselves. The odds on Tarabrin being picked up at random by agents of the VFP—even the Americans—were beyond calculation.

Yet whoever it was in Rome had been waiting, the trap baited. They had known Tarabrin was coming. They had known who he was and what he would be seeking.

The statue of Felix Dzerzhinsky came into view, dominating the square in front of the KGB, and as Klimenti lifted his head to confront the stern visage, the bronze eyes seemed to pierce him, stabbing for the truth he had been unwilling to consider until the long-dead commissar confronted him, scorning his fear.

The only agency that could have known about Tarabrin, his movements, his weaknesses, was the KGB. Had it sent Tarabrin into a trap of its own baiting and made him the tool of its own sinister foster child, the VFP?

Perhaps Tarabrin had realized who his blackmailers were and had sought to escape to the Americans. His revelations would have been devastating confirmation of the suspicions the Americans had about the KGB and the VFP. But it wasn't easy to change sides. Tarabrin would have had to move slowly and the Americans would be even more cautious, suspecting a trap. Tarabrin would need to excite their interest, to increase his value. At the same time, he would be careful not to show his hand until he was safely on the other side.

How much had he told the Americans before Nikishov got onto what he was up to and told Radchenko?

How much did Bannon really know?

In this world of shadows and whispers, in this mirror maze of distortions, it was not possible to know what was true, what was real, what to believe, or to see the way ahead. Klimenti felt he was walking blindly, and at each step the path became more treacherous.

Klimenti became aware of the weight of the pistol in his greatcoat pocket. How long would it be before he could stop carrying the Makarov around? Weapons did not bother him particularly. He had carried them in a number of countries and had always been glad to have them. But it troubled him that it was necessary to go armed in Moscow, the city he had always regarded as a sanctuary, where he was safe from his enemies. Now he was no longer certain who his enemies were. He was sure of only one thing: he had to be careful that Radchenko did not see *him* as an enemy. There were no guarantees, no sanctuaries, not anymore.

Klimenti walked with his hand deep in his right coat pocket, the Makarov clenched tightly in his fist.

27.

Poluchkin and Radchenko told Klimenti and Nikishov about Tara-brin later that afternoon. No doubt they had conferred with the Chairman first. And no doubt the Chairman had conferred with Comrade Gorbachev. Increasingly, Klimenti began to realize that if he was correct in his suspicions, then Gorbachev was deeply involved.

Nikishov was staggered by the information. It was one of the few occasions in which Klimenti had seen him completely surrender his mask of urbanity. Nikishov frequently used ravens for entrapment and probably realized more completely than any of them the full ramifica-tions of Tarabrin's homosexuality. Yet there was no doubting his repugnance.

Klimenti, who had to feign amazement to protect Morozov, was glad of his reaction.

"Rome!" Nikishov exclaimed. "The home of the VFP. It can't be a coincidence. It's our first real evidence the Americans are behind the VFP."

No, Klimenti thought, it's not a coincidence. But he didn't believe it was the Americans.

"And they're trying to make out it's us," Radchenko said. Klimenti, believing he was acting, was impressed.

Nikishov recovered some of his composure. He sat stiffly, his mouth and eyes slitted with anger. "Last night was nothing. I'll tear Tarabrin's department to shreds."

"No," Poluchkin ordered. "We want you to proceed quietly. Tarabrin may have recruited a network. There may be other American agents in his department."

Nikishov flushed. The fact that Tarabrin, a KGB major general, had been working for the Americans right under his nose was disaster and humiliation enough. But an *entire network*!

"We don't want the Americans to get any idea we know about Tarabrin," Poluchkin said, softening the blow.

"Use Major Kharkov," Radchenko said. "He's already got some familiarity with Tarabrin's operation. And we want to restrict the information as far as possible."

Once again, Klimenti was filled with admiration at the manner in which Poluchkin and Radchenko were twisting and turning, manipulating the evidence to their own advantage, controlling it, two master puppeteers. The only problem was that he, too, was attached to one of their strings, jerking and dancing on command.

With Nikishov and Kharkov gone, it fell to Klimenti to remain behind as duty officer. When he telephoned his apartment, Nadya said gaily, "We're already into the vodka and pickled cucumbers."

"Papa too?" His father seldom drank.

"Well, not a lot. But Sabotka and I are making up for him. Listen, Papa, we're all missing you. We want you here."

"I'm sorry, darling. I'm going to be late."

"Oh no, Papa. Not tonight."

"We're storming. You go ahead and enjoy yourselves."

"Damn. We were all looking forward to it. It's been a long time since we sat down and had a *dusha-dusha*." A heart-to-heart talk.

"Too long," he said, putting down the telephone and wishing he could be with them. How long was it since he had gone home to an apartment that wasn't empty? How long since he had had his family around him? Too long. Much, much too long. He had come to a resentful acceptance that Nadya's nights belonged to Bannon and he felt a fierce pleasure that tonight his daughter would be with him and not the American. He felt a sense of triumph, an emotion more befitting a jealous lover.

The thought shocked him. Yes, he had been jealous of Bannon.

Finally he admitted it. It wasn't just the jeopardy Bannon had placed Nadya in, although that had fired his anxiety to a dangerous degree. She was so like Marusya; mother and child shared the same secrets, the same beguiling mannerisms of body language and expression that pierced his heart cruelly. But it was a cruelty he loved for it gave him back his wife, and in these moments, woman and child, lover and loved, became one, fused with longing and—now he saw it for the first time—fear. Possessing his daughter, he still embraced his wife; Maursya lived again, before his eyes as well as in his heart. There was no carnality in it, there was only his needing and his terror.

Whoever stole Nadya from him also stole Marusya; whoever took Nadya was putting Marusya back in her cold grave, beyond his reach, emptying his life.

This was why he was going to kill Bannon, and once it was in his head, he could not stop the thought. It was thunder inside his skull, piercing his self-deceit. It shook him to realize that he could be so primitive, such a wild animal. Now he understood why each time he contemplated killing Bannon it gave him satisfaction.

Not knowing where his thoughts had stolen from, Klimenti remembered Zhenya and her voice on the telephone. "Hello"—just one word, a farewell. The interrogation had released Zhenya, expunging the secret that had bound them. There was no longer any need for her to wait on him in a parking lot, uncertain, afraid, overcome by events that had come onto her so unexpectedly. No doubt, she had been impulsive in her relationships before, and why not? Who was he to judge such matters? She was young, beautiful, and privileged, and therefore careless. This time, however, she had paid for her willfulness and she had learned that she was not inviolable. It had given her a bad fright, but that was all. She was lucky and she was intelligent enough to know it.

You're free, Zhenya, Klimenti thought, wanting to believe it. Instead he found his fingers on his lips, once again seeking the taste of her musk and finding only the sourness of the dead day.

Nikishov returned at midnight. He opened his desk drawer and took out a bottle of vodka. He arched his eyebrows, a sardonic question mark. Don't be so surprised, his expression said—but Klimenti was, nonetheless. He could not have been more surprised had Nikishov pulled a cobra out of his drawer.

"It's Wyborowa, real Polish vodka," Nikishov said. "None of that Russian piss."

Klimenti laughed softly, once again observing that everything about Nikishov, even his vodka, was foreign. Only his flesh was Russian. And his soul. Nikishov poured vodka into two of Marietta Pronin's gleaming coffee cups.

"Anything?" Klimenti asked.

Nikishov shook his head. "Tarabrin's files are perfect. He was a real clerk, a pen pusher."

Nikishov swallowed the vodka without flinching, pouring a second cup before Klimenti was halfway through his first, and Klimenti learned something he had not even suspected. Nikishov was a heavy drinker; the bottle in his drawer was no oversight. Klimenti wondered how long it had been going on, and why. All the years he had known Nikishov he had been an abstemious man, as careful in his habits as he was in his manners and dress, shunning overindulgence. The unusually heavy-smoking Klimenti put down to the unrelenting pressure of the last few days. But it did not explain the drinking.

Nikishov stared into his vodka, brooding. He sighed, a decision made. "Earlier today I received a report from inside the walls of Chaykovskogo Ulitsa." Chaykovskogo Ulitsa was the address of the American Embassy. It was studded with Nikishov's listening devices. "There's been a flap. An American and a Russian girl, so we presume it's Bannon and your daughter. If there's another couple, then we don't know about them."

All Klimenti's tiredness, the burden of the day, was forgotten. At last the Americans had reacted to his note. "It had to happen," he said. "Ever since you seduced their Marines, they've watched their own people like hawks."

Nikishov smiled faintly, accepting the compliment. "We're not sure exactly what the situation is. Whether they've just learned of the relationship or whether they've just learned that *we know* and have got them under surveillance. There's a significant difference."

Klimenti said too sharply, displaying his hopes, "Either way, if they're playing it straight, they'll put him on the next plane out of Moscow."

"Normally, yes." Nikishov sighed, letting the doubt hang between them, knowing that Klimenti would be unwilling to take it further.

Then he said somberly, "There's something else you should know. Bannon and Nadya were using an apartment off Sverdlova Square. It belongs to a young man in the Foreign Department, Leonid Lyubimov, who's fortunate enough to spend most of his time in Paris. The point is, Lyubimov returned to Moscow over the weekend to do an internal course to qualify as a Second Secretary. So Bannon and Nadya have had to find a new place, and that's not easy."

French lingerie, Nadya had teased, shaking the gift from Paris. And Zhenya had blushed. So his name was Leonid Lyubimov.

"Since Saturday, they've been using the apartment Nadya shares with Zhenya Stepanov. The daughter of the Deputy Minister for Culture."

"Does Zhenya Stepanov know about Nadya's relationship with Bannon?" Klimenti used her full name, as if she were a stranger. He knew almost nothing about her except how she tasted and how she made love and the tautly muscled silkiness of her body, and how totally she responded, quick to excite, an easing of tightness. And something of her impudence and her fear.

"No," Nikishov said. "They've managed to get away with it because Zhenya Stepanov sleeps *most* nights at Lyubimov's apartment." The emphasis was delicate but unmistakable. Nikishov knew about his relationship with Zhenya and was warning him to be careful.

What a mess! An American spy using the apartment of a daughter of the Deputy Minister for Culture as a love nest! Screwing the daughter of a KGB colonel, while the colonel screwed the Deputy Minister's daughter, while she screwed a foreign affairs diplomat. How sordid! And dangerous. They wouldn't dare keep it from the Chairman.

Klimenti wanted to tell Nikishov it was finished, a one-night stand, but he could not bring himself to say the words. They could only cheapen matters further.

Nikoshov put the vodka bottle away in his drawer and locked it. When they went out into the corridor, Klimenti saw Nikishov had forgotten his greatcoat and told him.

"I'm not going anywhere," Nikishov said and walked to the door of one of the small cubicles in which officers slept overnight during emergencies. He looked vulnerable and quite miserable. "I've got no home to go to," he said. "Well, not what you'd call a home anyway. My wife and I have separated."

"Oh!"

Klimenti could not remember how long Nikishov had been married. They had two adult sons. Klimenti recalled Nikishov's wife at a KGB dinner last year, a quick-witted and intelligent woman, young for her age, attractive and secure in her sophistication and social standing.

"Well, that's one way of putting it. The truth is, she's gone to live with someone else. An admiral." His mouth curled with bitterness. The word was a poison. So this was the pain behind the shadow in his eyes. This was the reason he had been so bitter about Navachine's betrayal by his wife and cousin.

"I'm sorry," Klimenti said, feeling inadequate. But there was nothing else he could say. Despite their long association and mutual respect, they had never been really close, each of them a man apart, their emotions shackled by a long-ingrained habit of covertness and self-control. With dismay Klimenti thought, there's part of my brain that should be able to dictate an acceptable human response to Nikishov's dilemma, something beyond mute sympathy. But the brain cells have been crippled by disuse; I've let them die. Part of my humanness has withered.

Klimenti would have liked to put an arm around Nikishov and say, "I'm with you, old friend. You're not alone." But he did not know how to do it and was afraid it would embarrass them both.

"It's been a difficult day," Nikishov said and stepped inside.

28.

The Zaporozhets was in the parking lot, dull with frost. Despite his conviction that Zhenya would not come, Klimenti found himself looking for exhaust fumes. It would be impossible in this cold to wait without the heater on. There were none. Klimenti was disappointed and the emotion annoyed him intensely. She was in bed with Lyubimov, making love. This thought annoyed him even more.

Nadya had gone to bed but his father and Sabotka had waited up, a nearly empty bottle of vodka before them. As usual Sabotka had been doing most of the drinking.

"So the Tartar returns," Sabotka declared. Klimenti bore signs of his heritage in his cheekbones and eyes and Sabotka had not missed it. He had eyes as sharp as a bird's, pecking away at you all the time.

"Nadya tried to keep awake," his father said, "but I'm afraid Sabotka wore her out."

"You're damn right," Sabotka said proudly. "It's obvious she's not used to wild country boys."

Nadya was in his bed, curled into the pillow the way she would sleep with a man, and Klimenti heard a soft murmur of breathless words, indistinguishable but nonetheless recognizable in tone, a lover's caress; he felt like an intruder and made to leave. Nadya tossed and flung out an arm and cried out and Klimenti heard the word this time, as clear as a pistol shot, "Harry!" He paused in shock, afraid she would awaken and find him there. But she curled back into the pillow, sighing, and Klimenti stepped out of the room, feeling a sense of shame, a thief who had stolen something very private and very important from the person he most loved.

He had not won. Bannon was with her tonight, even here, in his own bed.

Sabotka had retired to the kitchen and was cooking an omelet. His father gave him a glass of vodka. "Believe me, it's easier to eat whatever he cooks," Sergei Ivanovich counseled. "Otherwise you'll be arguing all night."

"I know best," Sabotka called out. "The vodka will put fire in your belly and the food will put it out."

That was the sum of life, getting food into your belly. Everything else was pure luxury.

Klimenti drank the vodka while his father told him about their day with Nadya. Sabotka, working in the kitchen, drinking vodka in quick gulps, was content mostly to listen.

"She's a good girl," his father said.

"Tough, too," Sabotka added appreciatively, an expert.

Sabotka had insisted they visit Lenin in his mausoleum. This surprised Klimenti, and he said so.

"Lenin was OK," Sabotka said gruffly. "If he'd stayed around, everything would have been all right. It wasn't Lenin who betrayed the people. It was that Georgian fox, our Little Father."

The omelet was excellent and Klimenti ate it with relish, surprised at his hunger.

"He's a good cook," Sergei Ivanovich said, proud of his friend.

Sabotka sighed. "Paradise, real paradise, the only one I know of for sure, the only one that counts, is a full belly and warm, sticky balls."

He grinned, and seeing the cunning sneak into his face, sly and cruel, Klimenti once again understood something of what had kept the old *zek* alive all those terrible years.

"Warm, wet balls, fresh from the cunt," Sabotka said, leering disgustingly, remembering.

"You've got a filthy mouth," Sergei Ivanovich sighed.

"I know," Sabotka admitted, beaming around. It was an old argument, worn smooth with habit and affection. The truth was,

Sabotka was proud of his filthy mouth and used it shamelessly to shock people. It was, he said, one of his few pleasures, setting him above those whom he despised.

"Fresh from the female oven," Sabotka said defiantly, declaring war, knowing his friend was appalled by his attitude toward women. Sabotka's regard for them was confined to his loins. Stalin's purges and the war against fascism had produced a rich crop of widows and lonely women and Sabotka harvested them ruthlessly. He had an uncanny ability to touch the depths of their sympathy and he exploited it shamelessly. He was a wounded creature who had limped in from the forests, and they sought to hold him in their cages with soothing love and soft flesh, only to discover that he was wild and devouring and beyond capture. As soon as his belly was full and his loins emptied, Sabotka moved on. At first Klimenti's father had believed it was the natural reaction of a man too long denied. As the years passed, however, Sergei Ivanovich saw that his repudiation of feminine love was seated in fear, not of women themselves but of all that came with them—the goods and chattels of love, responsibility and children—all of it weighing you down, heavier than ankle chains.

"He's an animal," Sergei Ivanovich said and then, as always, immediately excused his friend. "But it's not his fault."

"That's right," Sabotka said and the two old friends chuckled together.

Klimenti made up the divan that opened into a bed, and his father helped him, pointedly ignoring Sabotka, who was sending him impatient messages, nodding, winking, shaking his head in exasperation and, finally, in disgust.

"Listen, Klimenti Sergeyevich," Sabotka said in a fast burst, "today there was talk. Some people were saying they'd heard that Lysenko was assassinated—by a mad bomber who blew himself to smithereens." He paused, the first time Klimenti had seen Sabotka short of breath.

"Heard?"

"The BBC," Sabotka said with the hush of someone revealing a great secret.

"I told him not to ask," Klimenti's father said. But in his eyes, too, Klimenti saw a hunger. He wanted to know almost as badly as Sabotka.

"You know these things," Sabotka said, his eyes hooked into Klimenti, refusing to let go.

"The BBC, you say?"

His father and Sabotka nodded.

"Have you ever listened to the BBC?"

"How could we listen to the BBC?" Sabotka asked, almost contrite now, behaving himself, his eyes desperate with hope.

Klimenti went to his bedroom and returned with a radio, a Taiwan-made Sony WA-8000 he had bought in France. The KGB men who searched his apartment could hardly have missed it. No doubt they reported it. So what? Klimenti didn't know a KGB man who didn't have his own shortwave radio. He handed it to Sabotka.

"This is a Sony," he said. "It's got seven shortwave bands. Right now it's tuned for the BBC. But you can get them all: Radio Free Europe. The Voice of America. Peking, Frankfurt, Radio Moscow even."

Klimenti flicked a switch. The lively sounds of jazz filled the room, bright and zestful.

Sabotka was overwhelmed. "It's beautiful," he said and indeed it was, black and smooth and compact with bright red and silver markings, a digital clock, a tape recorder and a dial showing its ranges and the seven shortwave bands. On the back, it even had a map of the world showing all the different time zones. Never had he held a radio of such excellence and versatility and power. The music was coming all the way from London. It excited him tremendously.

"I don't waste the batteries listening to the music," Klimenti said dryly.

"Of course," Sabotka said and hastily switched it off. After the jazz, the room seemed dull and empty, but he knew how hard batteries were to come by.

"Tomorrow, I'll give you the schedules and the frequencies and you can listen all you want."

Sabotka nodded, fondling the radio, his fingers itching to make it work again, to hear sounds and voices from outside the Soviet Union. This radio was his ticket to freedom. At last he could reach past the bosses and hear a different tune.

"Son-nee." He said the name. It didn't sound heroic but it was, an enemy of repression.

"There's several conditions, Sabotka."

There were always conditions. With great but deliberate delicacy, as if he had been offered an unacceptable bribe, as if a camp commandant was once more trying to turn him into a stoolie, Sabotka laid the radio on the table. More than words, his gesture rejected everything.

He sat waiting, calmed now and dignified, wearing his camp face, watching them with *zek* eyes.

"You're to keep your mouth shut about it."

"Simple. That's the one thing I know how to do."

"And no more questions. You listen all you like but you figure it out for yourself. I don't want to—I won't—discuss it with you."

"All right." Sabotka sat stiffly, waiting.

"Well?" Klimenti asked after a minute.

Sabotka's eyes lit up. His whole body was infused with a new hope. "That's all?"

"That's all."

Sabotka's hands darted out and seized the radio. "You have my word, Klimenti Sergeyevich. I won't waste the batteries. I'll be as mute as a lamppost. I won't ask anything. I won't argue."

"Does the arguing cover me, too?" Klimenti's father said, proud of the way his son had mastered the situation. "Does it cover all subjects?"

"I'll shut up," Sabotka promised. "You won't even know I'm here."

In the morning Sabotka announced excitedly, "They call themselves the Vigilantes for Peace."

Sergei Ivanovich had listened in, too, and Klimenti could see his father was troubled to discover how much information was still being withheld from Soviet citizens. Sabotka's defiance was that of an animal, instinctive, baring its teeth, snarling its rage or fear. Sergei Ivanovich's defiance was quieter, calmer, and all the deeper for it.

Sergei Ivanovich said, "I don't support their methods but it's hard to argue with what they say they want. Total nuclear disarmament."

"Their methods are fine by me," Sabotka snorted. "They're doing us all a big service. They should kill *all* the bastards, the whole damn gang."

What power, to execute the executioners! Stalin had left the dirty work to someone else. But not Sabotka. He'd not only write down their names, he'd stand staring into their pallid faces, letting them know who was doing it, *Sabotka the* zek, *you turds*, and he'd pull the trigger as well, looking right into their eyes, not flinching. Oh yes, he could do that.

"They should have kept you in the Kolyma," Sergei Ivanovich said. "You're not fit for civilization."

"They did their best, the stoolies. And, my friend, if this is civilization, then I sometimes wonder why I bothered to come back."

"To disturb my peace. That's why."

"Damn right," Sabotka cried out. "That's the reason!"

They glared at each other—and burst into grins, good friends, real comrades, the fiery and embittered Sabotka, thirsting for revenge, and his quiet and hopeful mate, wishing for justice.

Nadya, who had gone shopping, telephoned. "Papa, the Zapo's finally packed up."

"What's the problem?"

"How would I know? The Zapo's a mystery to me. I'm surprised it's lasted this long."

Klimenti told his father about Nadya's car. He was eager to start work immediately.

"If it's fixable, he'll fix it," Sabotka said proudly. "And even if it isn't. Sergei Ivanovich isn't just a mere mechanic. He's a physician, a healer of wounded metal, a mender of broken parts, a doctor to faulty hydraulics, a surgeon on fuel injection systems."

"Enough!" Sergei Ivanovich growled.

"You should be made an Academician of the Internal Combustion Engine, my friend. It's no less than your due."

The Zaporozhets was half a block from Nadya's apartment. The engine had cut out as she was parking. Klimenti's father spat on his hands and buried himself in the engine, humming happily. Klimenti lingered, caught by this familiar memory, remembering the rich smell of dirt and engine oil and human sweat and, sometimes, when his father hurt himself, blood, and always the coarse voice humming, a sound that he had come to love.

"It's as I thought," his father said, coming up with a handful of spark plugs. "This car isn't going anywhere until it gets four new spark plugs."

"Not on a Sunday," Klimenti said.

"No problem," Sabotka grinned. He took a plug and strolled off, whistling.

Sergei Ivanovich sighed. "If I thought it'd do any good, I'd try to stop him." He broke into a grin. "I'd better get to work. When Sabotka comes back with his spark plugs, he'll want instant results."

29.

The weather turned worse than usual, and after fixing the Zapo they all returned to the apartment, where Klimenti and his father spent the afternoon helping Nadya prepare *zakuski*, platters of gray Beluga caviar, with chopped egg and onion; smoked red salmon, white sturgeon, and pickled herring in mustard sauce; Hungarian pepper salami; mushrooms in sour cream and dilled cucumbers; rye bread and butter and several cheeses. Sabotka took the Sony radio into the bedroom and twiddled the dials, listening to any foreign broadcast he could pick up.

Klimenti and his father loved watching Nadya at work. She had her mother's gracefulness, long limbed and easy moving, sometimes deft, sometimes sensual, always confident. Everything she did seemed natural, as if she was born to it. She could perform the most delicate and complicated tasks seemingly without concentration, as if she were guided by instinct and not her eyes, and with flair, not satisfied merely to get the job done but needing to do it with a flourish, a physical pronouncement of success. She had her mother's style, the part of her that was aristocrat, and her father's stubbornness, the part of her that was peasant. The fusion was at times enthralling.

As they worked, Klimenti's father recounted to Nadya all he had heard on the BBC that morning.

"Disarmament! Pssh! They must be crazy," Nadya said. "They're never going to get rid of nuclear weapons."

Sergei Ivanovich thought she was probably right.

Sabotka emerged and announced angrily, "It's amazing! The Americans are saying they're anarchists. I tell you, for a while I thought I was listening to Radio Moscow. *Anarchists!* But it was Radio Free Europe. That's the Americans, isn't it?"

"The CIA," Klimenti said.

"They're no bloody different," Sabotka exclaimed in disgust. "They even sound the same."

"They might be right," Klimenti said and wished he hadn't because Sabotka turned on him.

"It's always been the anarchists. Anyone who challenges those bastards is an anarchist, and all anarchists are KRs, *kontr-revolyutsioni*, and all KRs are 58s." He was referring to Article 58 of the old Soviet Criminal Code. "Shit on them all!" he shouted. "Don't you see it? They're all the same."

"Maybe that was true before Gorbachev," Klimenti's father argued. "But things are changing."

"Screw Gorbachev," Sabotka raged. "Screw *glasnost*. Screw *perestroika*. In Stalin's day it was *perekovka*, a reforging, and millions perished, sent to their deaths by the fat cats in the Kremlin."

"Calm down," Nadya coaxed. But even her power over him was diminished and he stood there, fretful and glaring around.

"It's changing," Sergei Ivanovich insisted stubbornly. "Tell him, Klimenti."

"It's changing," Klimenti said.

"It'll be changed," Sabotka said, "when we no longer have to listen to the BBC to find out what's going on."

None of them, not even Sergei Ivanovich, had an answer.

Sabotka sank back into his chair, dispirited. All his life, what had passed for truth had come to him from thousands of miles away, from Moscow to the frozen Kolyma, a multitude of channels, from the Ministry down through the flunkies to the Department and its flunkies to the camp commandant and his flunkies and then down through the trusties until, finally, coming from the Moon or Mars maybe, it got to the *zeks*. Each processor distorted it, so the *zeks* disbelieved everything they heard and believed only what they themselves experienced at that very moment, for the next minute might bring something even worse. A prisoner transport, for instance, to some even greater hell.

Now Sabotka was in the same room as the truth, only a meter from it, and they were still saying it was the anarchists. The liars!

"The truth is that, even today, Klimenti Sergeyevich is afraid to tell us the truth."

"Shut up," Nadya shouted, surprising them all. She stood over Sabotka. "Don't you talk like that, not in this house."

Sabotka was shrunken and quite miserable, unable to look up into Nadya's angry face.

"You've got a foul and cruel mouth," Nadya stormed.

"I apologize," Sabotka said miserably. "I'm ashamed of myself."

It shocked them. Never had anyone heard Sabotka admit to shame. He continued in a laggardly voice, "The truth is, I can't restrain myself. The truth is, people have already forgotten, and I find that hard to stomach."

He was wretched, and it stirred their pity.

"It's the vodka," Sergei Ivanovich said.

"No," Sabotka said sadly, "it's not the vodka. It's Russia, the *Rodina*." The Motherland! The mother of all their sufferings. They could not argue.

"I'm sorry I shouted," Nadya said and took Sabotka's huge, broken hands and caressed them. "Lie down," she soothed. "Take a nap."

Sabotka obeyed her meekly and slept until shortly before Morozov arrived with a bottle of French cognac, "For later, when we have coffee to sober up."

The exchange of greetings by Morozov and Klimenti's father was performed with a formality that was almost old-fashioned in its grammar and gravity. They had met only once before, many years ago, but they knew of each other through Nadya, who often told Morozov about Papasha, and vice versa, and the two objects of her admiration were aware of what they shared and treasured it. Such was their greatness of spirit that they saw themselves not as challengers in competition for her love, but as allies in a common cause.

Sabotka was full of gaiety now. His powers of recovery, his resilience, were remarkable.

"I'm hungry," he said, rubbing his flat, hollow belly. "Let's eat up before the sight of all this food drives us crazy."

"That's Sabotka!" Sergei Ivanovich said, relieved.

They devoured the *zakuski* and then *kotlety*, spicy ground meat patties, and *oladi*, thick fritters stuffed with mushrooms. The vodka whetted their emotions and when Klimenti put on records and Nadya sang for them, tears trickled down the cheeks of Klimenti's father and Sabotka and, surprising them all, Morozov too. It was a sad country love song, right from Russia's womb. Nadya was sloe-eyed and brooding as she sang, and this affected them too, to see such sorrowing beauty.

"So big shots bawl, too," Sabotka said approvingly to Morozov, who grinned a bit self-consciously and dried his eyes.

"No tears, Klimenti?" the Academician said, feeling much better, a big relief. "You're not Russian unless you can weep a little and cleanse your soul with tears."

Klimenti smiled wanly and offered no answer. He had felt that Nadya was singing for love, a love she didn't yet know was lost, and he felt guilty that he was responsible for her pending heartaches. Oh, daughter, he thought, it's a lousy deal you're getting, but it has to be.

"He's Russian all right," Nadya said proudly, making him feel even worse. "He's just a little different, that's all."

Klimenti's father sighed. "We weep not just for sadness, although there's been too much of that. We weep for happiness, too. But what's really remarkable is how little it takes to make us happy."

It was a wonderful evening, in the bosom of his family. Klimenti wanted to embrace them all.

At one o'clock in the morning Nadya announced she was going home to sleep at her apartment and insisted on driving Morozov. Klimenti was caught by surprise. He had expected that he would once again sleep on the divan, while she took over his bedroom.

"No, Papa," Nadya said firmly. "We've all got beds to got to. Besides, I'll be back first thing in the morning to make breakfast."

"It's got nothing to do with getting our breakfast," Klimenti retorted a little sharply.

"Then what is it to do with, Papa?"

How could he say it without making an absolute fool of himself?

And shaming Nadya! Klimenti shrugged, tongue-tied. Nadya's eyes were filled with curiosity. Was she beginning to suspect?

"Do you think I can fit into your Zapo?" Morozov asked, settling the argument. He was quite drunk.

Klimenti put on his coat and accompanied Nadya and Morozov down to the car. "Goodnight, Papa," Nadya said brightly and kissed his cold cheeks, ignoring his mood. She smelled good, a perfume he recognized. *Zhenya!* So they shared the same perfume, just as they cooperated in conspiracies of love. And why not? Weren't they young and beautiful? It was natural, their right. But not with an American.

Morozov got his bony frame into the tiny car. It rocked and sank alarmingly on its puny springs.

"Goodnight, nephew. It's good to be a family."

The Zapo lurched forward in a cloud of exhaust fumes. Klimenti walked across to his Zhiguli. He drove to Sverdlova Square and turned off and parked where he could observe Lyubimov's apartment building, a solid, three-story pre-Revolution structure. Most of the lights were out. Klimenti estimated there were four apartments on each floor, two facing the street, two facing the rear courtyard. A single man who had an apartment in such a building had a lot of *blat*. Zhenya had chosen well. The inbreeding of the privileged, the new nobility, would progress uninterrupted. Like the old aristocracy, they had already succeeded in insulating themselves from the common herd. When it came to grabbing and holding on, there was nothing the old dogs could teach the new.

A car came into the street and Klimenti ducked as it drove slowly past. At the bottom of the street it turned around and parked. Klimenti saw a silhouette. A man alone. Normally they worked in pairs. He did not like it.

Klimenti waited. The man did not get out of the car. Like Klimenti, he was waiting and watching.

They did not have to wait long. The Zaporozhets steamed into the street and parked outside the building. Nadya got out, walked straight to the door, and, using a key, disappeared inside. Not once did she look around.

After five minutes, the man got out of the car and walked across the street. Klimenti's heart sank. Despite the heavy overcoat the man was wearing, Klimenti recognized his walk—easy, yet somehow tense, coiled, ready to spring. It was as he feared. The man was not a KGB agent detailed to keep watch on Nadya.

The man pushed open the door, which had been left unlocked for him, and went in.

It was Bannon.

30.

L eonardo rose early. He had taken half a sleeping tablet and had slept for six hours without dreaming and without waking. It was a blessing. He was not without fear and dreaded the loneliness of the early morning hours. He switched on the radio. The program was in Russian, but Leonardo was glad of the broadcast. Silence stretched time, making it last, and time was his enemy now. Each hour was a burden and every moment of idleness or introspection only made it harder.

It was important to keep his energy flowing, and he went briskly about his tasks, shaving and showering and dressing and packing his few clothes. In the lobby, he paid his hotel bill with his American Express card. They also took Diners, Eurocard, Visa, J.C.B., and Kultakortii. The cashier was a buxom woman in her middle forties and her fingers flicked deftly across an abacus. As always Leonardo watched with pleasure. In his time in Moscow, this simple and ancient apparatus, the first of all computers, had been the only instrument of the state that had worked swiftly and efficiently and in whose adjudication he had any confidence.

Leonardo ordered two cups of black coffee at the buffet but declined the breakfast, which was much the same fare that was on offer for lunch and dinner: black and white bread, margarine and jam; cheese, boiled eggs, and salami; smoked red salmon, smoked halibut or sturgeon, and caviar; a horrible sausage, so pale it looked bilious, and made Leonardo so; and a small selection of stale cakes.

At 7:30 A.M., Leonardo donned his camel-hair overcoat and took his suitcase to a waiting Intourist car, which took him to Sheremstyevo Airport. On the way the driver pointed out a ten-meter-high X-shaped concrete structure. "Tank trap. *Kaput*," he said in a mixture of accented English and German. It commemorated the defense line where the Russians had stopped the Germans. It was the people's strongest unifying force, this pride they felt in their victory over the Nazis, won at such great sacrifice.

Leonardo wondered if this pride was felt by the man who was waiting for him at Sheremstyevo Airport. It was possible, even though he was seeking to flee the Soviet Union.

The flight indicators confirmed Aeroflot flight SU241 was due to depart to London on schedule at 9:50 A.M. The customs officers were taking their time going through the departing passengers' luggage. They were polite but thorough. Beyond, Leonardo could see the partitions that hid the passport checkpoints from view. Coming in, Leonardo had been confronted by a thin-faced, handsome young man in a glassed-in cubicle. He was blond with clear blue eyes and he regarded Leonardo with a glacial stare that had shocked him with its total lack of humanity. He had stared at Leonardo, his whole body as frigid as his eyes, for more than a minute, much longer than was necessary for recognition, before stamping his passport.

Travelers leaving the Soviet Union were subjected to the same intimidating scrutiny, and this worried Leonardo.

At 8:10 A.M. he went to the men's washroom and into a cubicle. He set the suitcase on the toilet seat and changed into the Russian clothes and shoes Control had given him. He put his clothes into the suitcase and sat down, waiting, trying not to hear the sounds of people defecating in the cubicles on either side. The sounds, never pleasant, annoyed him intensely. It was a warning that his emotions were sensitizing him despite his outward calm. He had to be on guard against himself.

At exactly 8:21 A.M., Leonardo left the cubicle and went to the washbasins. He put the suitcase down by his left leg and draped the overcoat over it. He ran some water. A minute later, the man he was waiting for walked into the washroom. He was dressed as Control had said he would be, in an Italian jacket of light tan leather with dark trousers and Italian shoes. He was slightly bigger than Leonardo and thicker, but the English overcoat was two sizes too big and would fit him comfortably.

The Russian went to the basin on Leonardo's left and ran the water; when he lifted his eyes to the mirror, Leonardo was shocked at how pale and nervous he was. He had big dark eyes that seemed to have shrunk deep into his skull, as if they were trying to retreat from reality. If he reached out and touched the man's face, it would be greasy with the slick of terror.

My God, Leonardo thought, he's going to his freedom and yet he's more frightened than I am.

Leonardo walked away, knowing he would carry with him, right to the end, the memory of the fear he had seen in those dark, burning eyes. Could they survive the unwavering, inhuman blue eyes of the striking young man who protected the frontier? At the door, he looked back and saw the Russian pick up the suitcase and the overcoat.

Leonardo went out of the airport. He was glad to get outside where it was snowing. He began walking, welcoming the cold.

31.

Klimenti had not slept well and he sat at the window, looking out on the dismal street below, irritable. The morning was well advanced and, despite her promise, Nadya had not yet arrived. The thought of her still with Bannon in Lyubimov's apartment gnawed at him. Was Bannon crazy? Nikishov had said the Americans were aware of what he was doing. And he had walked in, as bold as brass, right through the front door. Was he so besotted he was prepared to risk his career, perhaps even his freedom?

Or was it something else?

Nadya was in a trap and unaware of it, and the knowledge that he had not warned her preyed on Klimenti's conscience.

It was a relief when she telephoned. "I'm sorry, Papa. I'm not feeling well." Her voice was sore and husky. Had it been a lovers' farewell? Hope surged, and Klimenti felt even more of a hypocrite.

"It's a woman's thing, that's all. I'll take something and stay in bed for a while. Tell Papasha and Sabotka I'll make it up to them this afternoon. I'll be their devoted slave."

"She's all right," Klimenti told his father. "Just exhausted by all the excitement."

Later, Sabotka emerged from the bedroom in a state of tremendous excitement, brandishing the Sony, his passport beyond the Soviet Union. "It's begun," he shouted. "It's started."

Klimenti and his father stared in amazement as Sabotka jumped around, his face alight with a fervor that tore away the cruelty and the hardness, making him young again, a man full of hope.

"What are you raving about? What's begun?" Sergei Ivanovich demanded.

"What's begun?" Sabotka shouted. "I'll tell you what's begun. The people are marching. They're in the streets, shouting, 'Down with the Soviet Union. Down with the United States. Down with the imperialists.' "

"Imperialists! They're calling us imperialists?" Sergei Ivanovich was shocked. "*Us!* The Soviet Union!" The revolts in the republics worried him.

"That's right, comrade. *Us. Them.* Down with the superpower imperialists!" Sabotka hopped around the room.

"All my life I've waited," he shouted. "All my life I've wanted to march. I've wanted to shout it out. Down with the Fucking Shitheads! Down with the Fucking Hypocrites! Now they're marching, and I'm with 'em."

He leapt around. "Down with the Fucking Fuckers!"

"You've gone mad."

"Who's marching?" Klimenti asked when Sabotka paused for breath. "Where are they marching?"

Sabotka stood there, panting, his eyes alight with an unholy fire. "Everywhere," he said. "The whole world's marching."

He was, of course, exaggerating. The BBC Russian Service had carried the World Roundup program, which reported that an estimated one and a half million people had marched in fifty-two cities in thirty-eight countries, including the United States and all the NATO countries, in demonstrations against nuclear weapons and the superpowers. In twenty-five countries, including the United Kingdom, France, Japan, Canada, India, Australia, and New Zealand, the demonstrators had carried placards supporting the VFP. In several cases they paraphrased the VFP credo.

"If you don't believe me, come in and listen," Sabotka said, and Sergei Ivanovich accepted the invitation.

Klimenti was glad to be left alone. He had some hard thinking to do. Although no one had followed Bannon or Nadya, he was certain that Nikishov had Lyubimov's apartment under observation. It wasn't necessary to post men to do it. All Nikishov had to do was to remind the *upravdom*, the apartment block "warder," of her duties in regard to reporting on all visitors and then point her in the direction of Lyubimov's apartment. A gentle threat to sharpen her wits and a little salacious gossip to whet her curiosity, and she'd be all eyes and ears—a lynx, missing nothing, mad for the scent. Nikishov had probably also planted a bug in the bedroom.

What then? Wait. It was all he could do.

Once again Klimenti was pinioned by his powerlessness; it was an iron stake driven through his belly, nailing him into immobility. There was nothing he could do except sit it out. But it was getting harder to do it. He was tense and frustrated, dangerous signs, and something else, something more insidious, more poisonous, a growing feeling of bitter resentment toward the men who were so callously using Nadya. To Nikishov, who was perhaps a friend, who had his own problems. And to the mother service, the KGB, which he had served faithfully all his adult life, which had nurtured him and rewarded his loyalty and ability with promotion, travel, interesting work, and privileges, which valued and protected him. The KGB had been his life and he had been proud to serve. But now there was a canker in his gut, vile and rancorous. He had to tear it out, quickly; he had to resolve the threat to Nadya before resentment festered into malice—and malice into hatred.

Klimenti closed his eyes to cool his brain. But the eye-dark brought no relief; it was shot through with stabs of hot light. It was no good letting his emotions control his mind. He had to be calm, analytical, professional. He could do it—and every time he was calm, analytical, and professional, all those things, he came to the same conclusion. It wasn't hysteria. It was the cold, hard truth.

The KGB was a threat to his daughter, and anyone who threatened Nadya was his enemy.

Not just Bannon. But the KGB, the *apparat*, the whole damn system. Bannon he could kill. But what could he do about the KGB? About Nikishov? All of them!

He had reached an emotional point of no return. How quickly he had journeyed there. In less than a week. But what a week, the worst in his life since Marusya died. A week of shame and humiliation, sitting by like a lamb while Bannon screwed his daughter and everyone watched the video tapes and listened to the sound tapes—*filthy*—and schemed and *used* her, like a slut. Oh, they gave them fancy names—vixens, swallows, honey traps, *situations*—but it was all to dress up their own guilt, so they could pretend they hadn't stooped as low as you could go, so they wouldn't be too embarrassed about the hard-ons they got when they watched and listened. And how they watched and listened! Oh yes.

It was dark and cool now against his eyes. The shrapnel bursts of light had stopped. He would have liked to spend the rest of the day like that, hiding behind his eyelids. He would have liked to sleep.

He opened his eyes and blinked against the light. It was time to confront himself. His fear. His shame. It was time to commit himself to Nadya. He was through with waiting. He was through with being helpless.

The moment he made the decision, he felt better, a whole man again.

Klimenti parked the Zhiguli down the street from Nadya's apartment and walked several blocks to the offices of the Ministry of Foreign Affairs. It was bitterly cold, a wind blowing from the east. Even so the park ponds and the river were crowded with skaters. Skiers were heading to the Metro, brightly colored back packs stuffed with bread, thermos flasks of hot soup, and bottles of cheap brandy. Cars passed with skis strapped on roof racks. Some were heading for the Moscow hills, which would be hopelessly overcrowded. Others were going to the city's outskirts where they would cross-country ski through the whitened forests, stopping to pile dead wood into huge fires to sit by while they ate their lunch. That was a cheering moment, even on a dismal day: the leaping flames; the bright, wind-burned faces; the wonderful warmth of the soup; and the hot bite of alcohol. Klimenti had done it many times with Nadya and it had always made him feel good, before she came to an age where he felt an intruder and began to lose her to her friends.

He went into the streets behind the Ministry. Here the courtyards of the old merchant buildings were packed with Ministry Volgas, idle during the weekend. There were no guards; chained gates were considered security enough. Klimenti chose a building that needed repairs where the unfired clay bricks on the shoulder of a corner had crumbled, sagging the tiled roof. Obviously no one of any importance worked here, for the condition was not recent. It took Klimenti no more than five minutes to pick the padlock on the gates, open the door of the dispatching office, take a set of keys, and steal a Volga.

He drove to Kutuzov Prospekt and parked opposite the Ukraine Hotel, outside the huge complex of apartments that housed foreigners. Bannon's apartment faced onto the Taras Shevchenko Embankment and the Moskva River, around the corner from Kutuzov. Klimenti removed his gloves, took the Walther from his pocket, and cocked it. Before leaving his apartment, he had used a small file to cut diagonal grooves across the nose of each bullet. The dumdums hugely increased the hitting power and at the same time warped the ballistic markings, making it impossible to match the bullet to a particular gun.

It would take him no more than four seconds to fire all seven rounds into Bannon, and that would be controlled fire. When he opened the door, at point-blank range. First the chest to punch him backward and then, when he was down, the head, a deliberate, aimed shot, the *coup de grâce*.

He wanted to be absolutely sure.

So what was the problem? Why, then, was he delaying, sitting there, holding the gun? He had never had to fire the killing shot before, but that wasn't it. It was because this killing was personal, and Klimenti knew it. No matter how detached, how dispassionate Klimenti was, no matter how professionally he carried it out, he could not escape the truth that he was going to kill Bannon for purely personal reasons. No so long ago, even as late as last night, he would not have believed he was capable of it.

He had, in fact, believed it to be wrong. Now it was different. He could do it.

At the last moment Klimenti remembered the rubber glove. He had almost gone ahead without it, the first indication that he wasn't as calm as he believed. He dug the glove out of his pocket and pulled it on. It was an ordinary household waterproof cleaning glove and it was a tight fit. The glove would absorb the blowback that would normally impregnate his gun hand with tiny specks of gunpowder from the cartridge, and barium and antimony from the percussion cap. Scrubbing his hand after the shooting wouldn't remove the evidence, which was invisible to the eye but could be revealed by swabbing the hand with a solution of hydrochloric acid, demineralized water, and acetone.

It was time to go.

A figure loomed up beside his car. The passenger door opened. Klimenti aimed the pistol.

"Hello, Klimenti," Nikishov said, a calm Sunday greeting. He was not surprised to see the pistol. "It's cold out here," he said and slid into the Volga, shutting the door. He tugged off his fur hat and stared straight ahead, saying nothing. His film-star features were pale and composed.

Klimenti lowered the pistol and took off the rubber glove, which seemed to condemn him more than the gun. He slipped the clip out of the Walther and put it into his pocket. He did not want them to see what he had done to the bullets. He put the pistol on the seat between them. Nikishov made no move to pick it up.

He's too embarrassed to look at me, Klimenti thought. He's embarrassed *for me*.

"You worked it out from the phone call?" Klimenti asked. Before he left his apartment, he had dialed Bannon's apartment number and hung up the moment he answered. The call had lasted only a few seconds. They could have known he was making it only if they were tapping his phone as well as Bannon's.

"You were making sure he was in." Nikishov smiled apologetically and shrugged. He had eloquent body language, even in a heavy greatcoat. "You were also observed in Sverdlova Square early this morning. It was obvious it had become a crisis for you. The call to Bannon was the trigger. My first thought was that you were going to confront Bannon, hoping to scare him off. You might even have threatened him. But the more I thought about it, the more I became convinced it wasn't your plan."

"Why?"

"Too theatrical. Threats aren't your style. It left the matter undecided, the resolution beyond your control, in Bannon's hands. You'd expose yourself with no guarantee of success. It's not like you at all."

Klimenti nodded. It was all those things. And distasteful.

"It was simpler to kill him. A better result," Nikishov said. "That's more like you."

"Why didn't you pick me up? Why wait till the last second?"

"I wanted to be sure."

Nikishov picked up the Walther and ejected the bullet already in the breach. He ran his fingers over the cross-cuts and nodded, a professional who understood the significance of the grooves and perhaps even admired the handiwork.

"I'm sure," he said and held out his hand. "The clip."

Klimenti gave it to him. Nikishov extracted the six remaining bullets and put them into his pocket. He slammed the magazine into the butt, pulled the trigger to fire down the hammer, and handed the pistol back to Klimenti.

"You're going to report it?"

Nikishov shook his head. "This is between you and me. No one else."

I should be grateful, Klimenti thought. But he wasn't. Relieved, but not grateful. He didn't want to be under an obligation to Nikishov. Any of them. He was not through yet, not while the threat to Nadya still existed, not while Bannon was still fucking her. For the video cameras.

An old woman stopped to stare, regarding them with unabashed curiosity. Nikishov brutally jabbed a gloved finger, a command to move on. But the old auntie refused to budge, staring at him brazenly. Nikishov sighed and wound up the window. The old auntie lost interest. She spat onto the footpath, to show her contempt for bully boys, and hobbled painfully away on swollen feet.

Klimenti said, "Why, Simis?"

Nikishov stared after the old woman until she turned off into one of the apartment blocks for foreigners. The KGB agent disguised as a Militiaman gave her a friendly nod. She was a domestic servant, each day struggling painfully from her hovel of a room to clean what must have seemed to her the marvelous palaces of those who, so she had been told all her life, were the enemies of the Soviet Union. Sometime, in a moment of fatigue, she must surely have paused to wonder why the Soviet State rewarded its enemies so richly and its loyal citizens so poorly. Of course, she augmented her earnings by reporting to the KGB, but that was also her duty, and the amount she received for spying was only a pittance.

Old auntie, poor soul, doing her patriotic best. For kopecks! Nikishov wondered what her reaction would be if she realized the man she had spat at so contemptuously was her paymaster.

"It's a matter of conscience," he said. "I feel responsible. You shouldn't have been told. It's too much to expect of a father."

Conscience! Responsibility! These words from the man who was despicably using his daughter in a honey trap. What made it worse was that Nikishov meant them. Klimenti felt bitter, angry, but he kept quiet.

Nikishov asked, "Why didn't you warn Nadya? It might have worked."

"I was too ashamed of my silence to break it."

The wind was stronger now, whipping up loose snow and hurling it in little flurries. It plucked at the clothing of people on the street, working into their body warmth, so that they shrank into themselves and tried to walk faster. It was a bitter day.

"She wouldn't forgive me. I'd lose her."

For the first time, he was seeing it clearly. Now he understood the power of the confessional. Emptying the heart, shedding its secrets, exposing its hopes and fears, was an essential process in clearing the brain. You had to get rid of all that heart muck that clogged the brain, miring its beautiful clarity, before you could begin to understand anything. The heart was hot and steamy, condensation on the cold purity of the brain, fogging it. He had thought—he had been convinced—that his brain had been in charge, when in reality Nikishov was right—it had been his heart all along, clouding his perceptions, refracting his vision.

Now he saw it. The reason he had to kill Bannon was not just to save Nadya, but to save himself. From banishment from her heart. He was as afraid for himself as he was for his daughter. Perhaps even more afraid. He had been too craven to face the alternative. He had never thought of himself in these terms before. He wasn't at all surprised, nor shocked. He didn't care. Against the reality of his fear, it was meaningless.

"You really thought you could get away with it?"

"No," Klimenti said. "Not really."

Nikishov believed him. It wasn't a factor, he thought. Klimenti simply didn't care. Killing Bannon, that was it, that was everything. He stared at Klimenti, seeing a different man, a man he didn't know. What torment he must have endured, be enduring, that he was prepared to sacrifice himself for his daughter. *Him too!* Somewhere deep inside, an old wound hurt. Nikishov thought of his wife and her lover, the admiral, and his own empty apartment, entombed in its echoing loneliness. They hadn't made love in a long time and all night, well into the dawn, he had lain awake, remembering how it had been when she was eager, knowing that was how the admiral was getting it, now, right now. His distress had been so acute he had involuntarily cried out, "No!"

How the word mocked him.

Klimenti wound down the window and turned his face into the cold wind. He had the blood of Tartars in his veins, the wildness of the steppes in his soul. Yes, he was perfectly capable of killing to protect his own, and Nikishov felt a pang of envy and sorrow that he did not share this savagery; he was sure it had the power to cleanse, a blood release. He was sure it would free him if only he too had it.

Klimenti said, "Bannon went to Lyubimov's apartment alone, unaccompanied, no tail. None of ours. None of theirs."

Nikishov took out his Italian gold cigarette case and lit a Players with his gold Dunhill lighter. They were beautifully burnished, a soft, rich color, gold, the color of civilization. It reassured him to hold them. They were the symbols of success.

"The *kartoshka*," he demanded, hand out.

Obediently Klimenti passed over the blue diplomatic pass. Nikishov ignited it with the lighter and held it gingerly while the flames chewed through Klimenti's photograph. He dropped the remains into the snow.

"Simis, they warned him off. You said so. Keep away from that little bit of Russian cunt, they said. Your cock's in charge of your brain. Grow up."

Who was he punishing with these cruel and arcane words? Himself?

"He came alone, no one tagging along to make sure he was a good boy, just out for the fresh air. Can you believe that, Simis? Not one watchdog."

Surely Nikishov saw what it meant?

"They sent him, Simis."

Nikishov threw the cigarette into the street where it continued to burn, his contribution to the Greenhouse Effect. Russia could do with a little more of it. "He's going. Tomorrow. The next day. We don't know yet. But he's going." He glared at Klimenti. "We'll make sure of it."

Klimenti snarled, "And they're giving him a last fling. Is that it?

A farewell romp in the spirit of *glasnost* because, suddenly, over there at Chaykovskogo Ulitsa they've all got hearts like Walt Disney and, real suddenly, they're full of shit. You too, Simis."

The words were foul and scathing. Accusing. This time they worked. Nikishov's mouth crimped with distaste.

"Nadya's in no danger. I assure you."

"You assure me," Klimenti sneered.

Nikishov paled. This was too much. "Listen, you've been fool enough. Don't make it worse. Don't interfere. In another day or two it's going to be over. Bannon's going. I'm not *assuring* you. I'm *telling* you. So listen! Shut up! Keep out of it!"

They could hear each other breathing. For a long moment, that was all they heard, angry breathing. Hostility became a physical force between them, so strong it was palpable.

"It's you they're after," Nikishov said at last. "Not Nadya. They're using her to get at you."

Finally, the truth. Why had Nikishov lied for so long?

"And they almost did it, Klimenti. They almost succeeded."

Nikishov was right. Klimenti had come close to self-destructing. If they neutralized Klimenti they would also neutralize Squirrel. He would trust no one else. Klimenti wondered how long the Americans had known this. And how?

Nikishov said, "Sending Bannon last night was a last toss, a final provocation."

"They know *that I know*?"

"Yes."

"Bannon knows?" Klimenti shivered.

"We're not sure about Bannon. They might not have told him. It'd be less pressure on him."

Yes, it was possible. Even so, Klimenti wished he had killed Bannon. Not with a bullet, but with his hands!

"Who told them she was my daughter, Simis? Who told them I knew?"

His eyes were cold and accusing. You, Simis? Was it you? Playing your clever little games of double-deception?

Nikishov did not flinch or avert his eyes. "They've been after you a long time, Klimenti. Since Washington. They've had a lot of time to learn everything about you. They're patient. Painstaking. Thorough. They know how to wait."

It was possible.

Nikishov said, "But why now? That's what we need to know. Why they've decided to act now."

Klimenti wanted to be free of it, to get away. He wanted to escape from himself. "Are we going anywhere?"

"Go where you like. It's Sunday."

"I've got to return the car." How ridiculous it sounded.

"Don't get caught," Nikishov said. On any other day, it would have been worth a laugh. "Will you drop me at Dzerzhinsky Street first?"

Klimenti nodded. In gritty silence he started the engine and drove onto the Kalinin Bridge. When they were halfway across, Nikishov ordered him to stop. He got out and went to the rampart and threw the bullets into the icy river below.

32.

A woman came out of Nadya's apartment building. She wore boots, an ankle-length woolen coat, and a fur hat and she had wound a scarf across her face to protect it from the wind. She went along the street, going away from Klimenti. Even in the heavy boots and clothes, he recognized the walk, and could imagine the body beneath, taut, silken against his mouth.

The last time he had seen her was in the parking lot at Shabolovka Street. In the trembling Zapo, her eyes huge and hurting. He could have had her and he hadn't. It was less than an hour after the Ferret had tried to kill him with a knife. But that wasn't the reason. She had come to him, a beautiful young woman, and he had sent her away. To an interrogation! But why?

The interrogation had released her. They were free of each other.

Even as he thought this, Klimenti got out of the Zhiguli and followed Zhenya. He quickened his step to shorten the distance between them but made no attempt to overtake her. He didn't know what he wanted, or why he was doing it. His feet took him after her, drawn along behind. She wasn't going far because these were the narrow back streets and there was no public transport.

Zhenya turned right. Half a block down there was a small church, a low building of deep burnt ochre and blue, a graceful spire no more than three stories high and a beautiful cupola, vivid against the drabness of the street, the awnings and window shutters and doors painted white, giving the building a sense of drama and character. No sound came from within and the windows and doors were closed. It gave every indication of being deserted, shut down under lock and key.

Zhenya opened the door and entered, shutting it behind her. Klimenti hesitated. The only churches he had been in had been converted to museums or public libraries. He was not sure of what awaited him behind the closed door. But he had come this far, driven by instinct. He opened the door.

What confronted him inside the church overwhelmed him the moment he crossed the threshold. The effect was immediate; he was not prepared for it, there was nothing in his whole experience to forewarn him. In the flickering light of many candles flashing on gold and silver, Klimenti stood holding his fur hat, enthralled, his senses alive and pregnant. The beautiful, unbelievably sweet and gentle voices in song gave him instantly an understanding of worship as if he had known it all along, latent inside him. There was no music except that in the voices themselves and Klimenti tingled at this human beauty; he felt it alive in him, like electricity. The voices and the smell of human warmth, of sweat and cheap soap, and the steam of damp clothes and the smoke of the candles gave him back his mother, sleeping curled inside her embrace on an iron stove. The odor he identified instantly with love and protection; and the soft light, moving and swaying, dancing, full of shadows, full of living texture, was the light she read to him by, swaddling him in her sonorous voice.

What overwhelmed him most of all was the sense of intimacy. There were perhaps fifty worshipers, no more, but the church was small so they stood against each other, swaying and bowing, not in unison, but each in their own time, heads bobbing and hands fluting. He watched the black-clad women singing and praying and *sensed* them, was not shy, and was among them, and did not feel a stranger. Their coarse faces, wrapped in head scarfs, for a moment did not remember hardship and were at peace, and their thick, work-worn hands fluttered with gracefulness in obedience to their ceremonies. This was their moment of beauty and they treasured it beyond accounting.

An old man, stooped and stinking, in rags almost, stood by the door, bowing and scraping, his cap in one hand, the other out, begging; he sang with the women in a deep, strong voice kept low, almost a whisper, as if he knew that this was a woman's place and he did not wish to intrude. Klimenti gave him a handful of kopecks and the old man mumbled his thanks, picking up the hymn in the next breath; he worshiped as naturally as he breathed.

The priest was old and gaunt and wore the unmistakable brand of the camps. He had suffered for his beliefs.

Klimenti could not see Zhenya.

And then, without any sense of climax, it was over and the women immediately broke into gay chatter, gossiping. Some knelt before the statues of saints and told them their personal prayers and fears and wishes, asking for their protection, their reverence genuine and deep. Then, with the quick and meddlesome care of a *babushka* cleaning an infant, they took out handkerchiefs and wiped away a speck of dust or a smudge of candle smoke, cleaning the noses of saints, totally familiar and unafraid, unawed. They broke out bread and cake and some women put up a samovar and they ate and drank hot tea out of chipped cups, calling shrilly, laughing as they worked, arranging things their way. This was their church, these were their saints, this was their God.

Their self-assurance, their secureness, was astounding.

Some women bossily shoved their way through the hubbub, using as a battering ram a trolley on wheels, the kind used in hospitals to carry stretchers, and on it lay the waxenlike figure of an old woman, child-sized and clothed in her best, a starched white headcloth across her forehead and under her chin. At first Klimenti thought she was a plaster saint about to be propped into place, and then he realized she was real, a corpse, a grandmama. Her grandsons and sons came and stood by the coffin, uneasy and a little afraid, awkward in their coats and ties, unsure where to put their hands and their feet, or their eyes. The women ignored them, bread clutched in one hand, fingers of the other touching the dead woman's forehead in blessing, chewing and talking and straightening the burial clothes, so that she was perfect. This was how they would be one day, and not too far away either, and they fussily arranged the corpse exactly in the way they themselves would like to be laid out. They set up candles all around the coffin and pushed the ungainly and ignorant men around and the men shuffled without argument, dark eyes downcast.

It was all very natural, without fear. These people did not grovel before their God, fearful and despicable, but stood up and talked to Him, face to face, full of confidence even in the presence of death.

Their audacity stunned Klimenti. It was not what he had been taught to believe.

Two fingers touched the old woman's forehead and flew upward in the sign of a cross, touching another forehead, this one living, strands of blond hair escaping from a headcloth and tumbling across her eyes. It was Zhenya, her face imprisoned in black lace. In the soft golden light her eyes seemed even bigger than he remembered them and they regarded him solemnly. Klimenti sensed a tranquillity that was totally foreign to all else he had seen in her. She was drawing strength from the women around her; she felt their sureness and their familiarity and drew it into herself. She looked away and spoke to an old woman, kissed her cheeks, and walked to the door, passing Klimenti without another glance. She gave the old man some rubles and he bent almost to the floor in his gratitude, slobbering praise and blessings.

Klimenti watched her go out into the daylight, into a different world. When he followed, the old man opened the door and enveloped Klimenti with his overpowering stench. His eyes, Klimenti saw in a sudden lance of daylight, were not at all obsequious, but full of rage.

Zhenya walked to Arbat Street. When Klimenti came out onto the wide paved concourse, she was waiting. "You're following me," she said straight out.

"Yes."

"Why?" Her eyes had not lost their solemnity. She was still in the sway of the church.

He shrugged. "I don't know." It sounded pathetic and he was aware of it. But it was the truth, and he owed her that.

In her eyes there was now a flicker of anger. "You're a hypocrite," she said and walked on, fast now.

Klimenti did not follow. He stood, staring after her. Thirty meters on she stopped and turned and stared back at him. Then she walked into a café. Klimenti went after her.

Zhenya stood with her back to the door, waiting while her coffee was prepared. She took her coffee to a table and sat with her back turned to Klimenti, who ordered black coffee and two cognacs. He sat opposite Zhenya, who continued to act as if he wasn't there. The only other people in the café were two middle-aged matrons who were talking softly and exchanging photographs of their children.

Klimenti pushed a brandy in front of Zhenya, who ignored it. He sipped his own cognac, watching her averted face. It was warm, and Zhenya took off her scarf and hat and shook loose her blond hair.

"Does your father know about the church?" Klimenti asked. Even though the Soviet Union now guaranteed religious freedom and people were openly going to churches, there were still many in power who did not approve of what they saw as "primitive Christian superstitions."

Zhenya did not respond.

"They'll go to him," Klimenti said. "A deputy minister. They'll expect him to influence you."

"It's none of your business," she said.

"No. You're right."

He drank some more brandy and then some coffee and wondered why he didn't feel foolish, sitting there, forcing his unwanted company on a cold and hostile young woman.

"I'm waiting for someone," Zhenya said. "He'll be here soon."

Lyubimov. Klimenti wondered if he knew about the church. He said nothing, sipping his coffee and brandy, watching her, waiting.

"Why?" Her eyes were still angry.

"I was coming for Nadya. I saw you leave and I followed. I don't know why. An impulse." Or was it compulsion?

"An impulse. *You!*"

She smiled at that, scornfully. She simply didn't believe it. He wasn't surprised. He, Colonel Klimenti Amalrik, the cool, aloof agent from the KGB with a heart full of ice and a head full of analysis. Impulse! The word was hot; it throbbed with life and recklessness and didn't belong with him, not in his dead-fish heart, not in his silicon-chip brain.

He said, "It's different now."

Since that night in the Zapo. Her cheeks burned with the memory. She had gone to him, wanting his strength, and he had been indifferent.

"Different! Oh, it's different all right. They've interrogated me." She picked up the brandy and drank half of it in one swallow.

"You know," she said, wondering at his lack of reaction.

"They told me."

Zhenya stared into the brandy, holding the glass in both hands.

"Why not?" She lifted her eyes to accuse him. "After all, you're one of them."

She wasn't wearing any makeup. Her lips were soft and clean and the color of the brandy with light striking into it; he wanted to touch them.

"I tried to warn you," she said. "I knew Nadya was at your apartment so I went to the parking lot. The Zapo was there but it was locked."

"You came!" Klimenti didn't—couldn't—believe it.

"I tried to wait but it was too cold."

"How long?" he asked quietly.

"An hour. Until midnight. My feet began to freeze. I had to go."

An hour, exposed to the wind and with the temperature at least minus thirty degrees celsius, conditions to break the hardiest of men, while he'd been drinking vodka with Nikishov. He felt ashamed that he had misjudged her so poorly.

"Zhenya," he said softly.

She shook her head.

"Look at me, Zhenya."

"No," she said.

"I didn't know."

She looked up now, accusing him. "But you told me to come."

"I thought you were too frightened."

"You *thought* . . . !" She spat the word.

He had thought she was free of him, released by the interrogation. But she wasn't. Not then. How wrong he had been.

Zhenya said, "I thought you'd be expecting me. When I went there, I thought you might actually be waiting. Even then, I still believed you'd come. That's why I waited. As long as I could. I believed you'd come." Her eyes were full of bitterness too, slitting them. "But you already knew. You didn't need me to warn you. So you didn't even bother."

Not for one minute had he believed she would do it. Not for a second had he considered that she might go to the parking lot to warn him. He had underestimated her courage and her character. He flushed with shame.

Zhenya said, "He'll be here any minute. Please don't make it difficult."

She was free of him. Not that night. But now.

Her lips were darker now, full of blood and youngness. Her eyes were steady and unforgiving. She pushed away the half-drunk glass of brandy, a gesture that dismissed him from her life.

"Life's for living," she said. "It won't wait on yesterday."

As he went out, Klimenti believed he knew what she meant.

A note awaited him in his empty apartment. "Zapo lives! Gone for a grand tour. Love, Nadya."

The telephone rang. Nikishov said, "Radchenko wants us."

"Where?"

"The Lubyanka."

33.

It was the first time Klimenti had crossed the courtyard. He had looked down on it a number of times and he knew its bloody history. But he had never had to venture into it or to cross to the blank steel door that awaited up a short flight of steps. The Lubyanka was not part of his working realm. It belonged to those whose enemies were perceived to be within the Soviet Union, to those charged with protecting the Soviet State from its own citizens. The people who were brought here were not foreigners. Nor were they criminals. They were people whom the protectors of the State had adjudged to be subversives. There were times when all it required to become a saboteur was an innocent question, a doubt expressed, the mildest criticism. Klimenti had no doubt that of the hundreds of thousands of men and women, and sometimes children, who had been destroyed within the Lubyanka, most were innocent. The only justice within the Lubyanka was that some of the judges and executioners had eventually followed their victims.

There was no mercy within the Lubyanka. There never had been. Klimenti did not expect to find it now.

The cobblestones had been freshly swept of snow and his footsteps rang, echoing back from the cold stone walls that rose over him on all sides. After the Revolution, when the purges began in earnest, they had built a sandbag wall against the bricks and mortar to protect them from the executioners' bullets. They used Maxim machine guns, very messy, very indiscriminate, and the heavy-caliber bullets did a lot of damage to the stonework. Even so, those who were killed in the courtyard were lucky. It was a quick death compared with the inhumanities that awaited within the Lubyanka. If you leaned back and stretched your neck, you could see the sky, a better sight to take to the grave than the concrete ceilings and walls of the cells within the prison, and the cold, bored faces of the executioners. Here you could at least escape your torturers; the air was fresh; you didn't have to breathe the same foul vapors that had been the last breaths of countless dead, and that were the living breath of the jailers.

Was he crossing the courtyard to face a new set of interrogators? Klimenti was once again acutely aware of how inconclusive Radchenko's interrogation had been. It was too gentle, he had been let off too easily. Now they were mocking him by inviting him to his own interrogation. It was brutal and clever in the one stroke, making him a willing victim. They knew he would come because there was nowhere he could run to. But by *asking* him, rather than coming for him, they were making him the principal in his own humiliation.

They knew what they were about. In matters such as these, they were the experts, the best in the world, not by any innate ability or particular proficiency for the job but simply because they had had a lot more practice than anyone else.

With foreboding, Klimenti pressed the buzzer on the steel door that led out of the courtyard and into the Soviet Union's most dreaded prison. The sliding hatch in the door opened and a fresh-faced young man peered out. He was whistling but broke off when he saw Klimenti's rank.

"Good afternoon, Colonel. *Spravka,* please."

Klimenti handed him his KGB pass and the young man squinted at it and then at Klimenti. Satisfied, he disappeared from view to check his list. After a few minutes the door opened and the young man stood aside, saluting as Klimenti walked in. He wore the uniform of a prison guard. There was a desk and chair at the head of the corridor. The guard indicated a ledger.

"Please sign, Colonel," he said pleasantly, and when Klimenti had done so, the guard wrote down the time and countersigned it. He took a pass and wrote Klimenti's name and rank on it.

"Please don't misplace it, Colonel. There are heavy penalties. The only people in here without a *spravka* are the prisoners."

"I'll remember it," Klimenti said. "Where am I to go?"

"I'll get someone to escort you. This is not a place to get lost," the guard said cheerily, without a hint of irony.

The escort was older, grown plump in the job. He wore rubber-soled shoes and moved soundlessly. All the cell doors had peepholes and, seeing them, Klimenti remembered the stories Sabotka had told him about his time in the Lubyanka, before they shipped him east and north and into the Kolyma in the Arctic Circle. The prisoners were instructed to sit perfectly still and silently on their cell bunks, staring at the peepholes. The guards came intermittently to look through the peepholes and if they caught a prisoner whose attention had drifted, he was taken away and beaten. That was why they wore rubber soles, so that the prisoners could not hear their approach and be warned.

The worst thing, Sabotka said, was that the guards sometimes did not come to check for days on end. But the prisoners sat there anyway, staring at the peepholes, waiting, listening for footfalls they would never hear.

Remembering, Klimenti walked through the torturous silence. It lay in the corridors like a terrible weight, crushing the spirit. Klimenti had never known that silence could be so intimidating and oppressive.

They went down two floors. The only other guards Klimenti saw were posted at desks on each floor. They checked his pass, even though he was escorted. They looked more like clerks than guards.

It got colder. They were deep under the prison, locked in the frozen earth. Each floor was an exact copy of the others, spotlessly clean and bright with electricity.

The escort stopped at a cell door. The sound of his knuckles on metal was soft and hollow, like a distant drum. An eye peered through the peephole.

"Colonel Amalrik," the escort announced.

The cell door opened. The escort departed, quickly and sound-lessly. A young man in a white hospital jacket said, "Come in please, Colonel."

Klimenti stepped in. The cell door closed behind him. He heard the bolts shooting into place. Involuntarily he shivered.

A single strong light bulb burned in the ceiling. Unlike the gleaming corridors, the walls were scarred concrete, dark with slime and age and God knows what else. The ceiling was low, the same filthy concrete. The floor was wet. If it had been a few degrees colder, it would be slicked with ice. The air was foul with the stench of rot and dampness. And something else. It was no exaggeration: you could actually smell it, the stink of fear, of death, of pain.

It was an evil, malevolent, and disgusting place.

Klimenti stood stiff with shock, seeing all this and the poor wretch standing naked beneath the light bulb. He was shivering uncontrollably. His head was bowed, so Klimenti could not see his face. He was overweight and soft, and his private parts had shriveled with the cold and fear. He moved his trembling hands to cover himself and the man in the white jacket, who was standing next to Klimenti, said gently, as if he was correcting a loved child, "Don't."

The hands jerked back, as if the man had been stung by electricity, and, seeing this, Klimenti knew they had already begun to work on him. Only intense pain and the terror of it could incite such a spasm. The man looked up and Klimenti saw his eyes were black and liquid with fear. His ankles were chained to the floor. Chains with wrist shackles hung from the ceiling. They were swaying. They had already been used.

Radchenko and Nikishov stood to one side, their faces set against mercy. There were three men in white coats. Two of them wore surgical gloves that reached to their elbows. These days, the torturers were physicians and psychiatrists and dentists and other specialists with degrees from Moscow University.

It wasn't Klimenti who was to be interrogated. It was this poor wretch. He felt a surge of relief.

"Stand over here," Radchenko said in a voice Klimenti had not heard before; it was full of death. He went across, surprised at how stiff his limbs had suddenly become.

Nikishov did not acknowledge his presence. He was staring past the prisoner, as if he were trying to see right through the thick stones saturated with centuries of suffering. There were no windows. The place was sealed tight, like a coffin.

"Who recruited you?" one of the white-jacketed interrogators asked in a quiet, bored voice. He was a specialist interrogator, probably a psychologist, and knew that sympathy got you more than pain. If you had the time.

The prisoner whimpered, "I've told you. I don't know who it was."

"That's right. You've told us that many times now. And I'm afraid we just don't believe you."

It was the gentlest of reprimands and it gave the prisoner false hope.

"Please. I don't know."

"Would you like us to put you in the chains again?"

The prisoner sobbed in despair. He tried to speak but his fear was too great and the words slobbered around in his throat and mouth. It was not a human sound.

He was not marked. It was more disturbing than finding him bloodied and mangled. Then you could understand such fear.

The interrogator said, "We'll have no choice. Unless you tell us who it was."

The prisoner shook his head. Spittle drooled from his mouth. Steam rose from beneath his legs. He had defecated. He stood there, in the hot stink of his own shit, slobbering and dribbling, and the full measure of his fear was that he did not once move his hands from his sides.

"Show him the photograph again," Radchenko said.

"Was it this man?" the interrogator asked.

Klimenti leaned forward but he could not see the photograph.

"No," the prisoner gasped. "I've told you. I've never seen him before."

"You're afraid he will harm your family?"

The prisoner shook his head, his eyes downcast. Radchenko took the photograph from the interrogator.

"He can't. Not anymore."

The prisoner shook his head again. He was breathing in great gulps, like an animal.

Without a word, Radchenko handed the photograph to Klimenti.

It was Tarabrin.

"You see, he's dead," the interrogator said.

The prisoner was one of Tarabrin's Jews. His head jerked up and this time it was not fear that glistened in his wet eyes. It was hope, and they all saw it. With his eyes, the Jew betrayed the dead Tarabrin.

"Ah yes," the interrogator said. He was a handsome young man with intelligent eyes and a sympathetic face.

"No," the Jew screamed. "No."

"Show him these," Radchenko said, passing across two more photographs. One showed Tarabrin dead in his car. The other showed him stretched out on a slab in the morgue.

"Look at them," the interrogator said.

The Jew shook his head, moaning.

"You're a courageous man, trying to protect your family. Believe me, he can't hurt them. Not now."

The interrogator stepped across until he was only inches from the Jew. He said softly, "But we can."

He reached out and with the gentleness of a man stroking a butterfly he put his finger on the Jew's chest.

The Jew shrieked. His hands jerked up across his chest. He stood there, hugging himself, his eyes popping, biting his mouth until the blood flowed.

"The chains," the interrogator said and the other two men in white coats took the Jew's arms and unlocked them from his chest. He made no move to resist as they lifted his arms and fastened them in the dangling wrist shackles. The Jew slumped against the chains, as if he were glad to have their support, and hung there, his chest heaving, his jaw clenched. But his respite was only momentary. The men in white jackets went to the wall where there was a drum with two handles. They began winding, tightening the chains until the Jew was stretched as taut as a bow string, his feet raised several centimeters off the floor.

In the old days, they had done this so they could beat a man from any direction, in all parts of his body, or use other instruments of torture without hindrance.

The Jew shut his eyes and waited, panting with fear. He was going to make an effort not to scream again. But they all knew he would.

One of the white-jacketed men, the one without surgical gloves, took out of his coat pocket a smooth ebony box the size of a cigar case. It was lined with bright red velvet and contained a variety of long, shiny needles.

Acupuncture. That's how they did it without leaving marks,

stabbing needles into nerves that shot unbearable pain straight to the brain. It was devastatingly simple and effective. Apart from the excrement and the urine and the slobber, it was also neat and clean. They probably thought they were being humane.

The acupuncturist had thick gray hair. He was an elderly man, a grandfather. He had a kind face and his fingers, as they carefully selected a needle, were beautifully manicured.

The Jew opened his eyes, unable to resist his fate; he saw the needle and shuddered, biting harder so that the blood ran again.

"Wait," Radchenko said and led the way to the door. Nikishov shot the bolt and dragged it open with all the strength of a man escaping. As they went into the corridor, Klimenti turned and, before the door shut off his vision, he saw the Jew stretched taut in the chains, his eyes fixed hypnotically on the long, exquisitely tooled needle held in hands a noblewoman would treasure.

"No," the Jew pleaded. "Please. No more."

The door shut. They began walking. They had not gone ten meters before they heard the scream, muffled by steel and concrete.

34.

Radchenko didn't beat about the bush when they were admitted to the Deputy Chairman's office. As soon as they sat down, he reported to Poluchkin, "We've caught a Jew who's working for the VFP. He's identified Tarabrin."

The Jew worked for the VFP!

Klimenti saw again the Jew's unmistakable recognition when they showed him the photograph of Tarabrin. He had no doubt that Tarabrin had recruited the Jew. And now Radchenko was saying the Jew worked for the VFP!

"It's proof that Tarabrin was working for the Vigilantes for Peace as well as the Americans," Radchenko said. "Tarabrin's the common denominator." He stared at Klimenti, stabbing the words at him. "The Americans are running the VFP!"

Klimenti was astonished. He had come to the conclusion that the VFP was the creation of the KGB—and here was Radchenko, the man to whom he gave all the credit, saying he had proof it was the Americans.

Nikishov displayed no reaction. He obviously was in the picture and agreed with Radchenko.

"The Americans! I knew it all along," Poluchkin said.

"Who's the Jew?" Klimenti asked. Radchenko's eyes glimmered

with dislike; he was losing patience with Klimenti. He turned to Nikishov, who was waiting, notebook on his lap, and nodded.

Nikishov said, "The Jew was picked up at Sheremstyevo this morning, trying to board a plane to London. He was using a passport and visa papers, claiming to be an Italian." He checked the notebook. "Leonardo Ruffini, aged forty-five. A tourist. What interests us is that there really is a Leonardo Ruffini. He came in from Rome five days ago, on Monday, the day Lysenko was killed. He arrived at 6:05 A.M., was checked through customs at approximately 7 A.M. and was in his hotel room before the roadblocks went up. They anticipated our reaction. Their timing was perfect."

There was a note of reluctant admiration in Nikishov's voice.

Radchenko said, "We're sure the Italian's still here."

"Why?" Poluchkin demanded.

"Because Leonardo Ruffini is the next assassin. That's why he came to Moscow."

"Explain it," Poluchkin ordered harshly.

Radchenko said, "Like all good plans, it's basically very simple. Instead of running the considerable risks of smuggling assassins into the Soviet Union, the VFP bring them in the way the Italian came in, as a tourist. One man among thousands, using the most legitimate, commonplace cover of all. It means Ruffini can move openly while he is in Moscow, obviating the difficulty of keeping him in hiding. Everything is simple. A tourist is a person least likely to stir suspicion. We watch them, but not very closely. Certainly not close enough to stop Ruffini making a contact in Moscow."

Yes, Klimenti thought, it's a good plan.

Radchenko went on, "But there's also a drawback. Since the assassin has come to kill and then self-destruct, he won't depart the Soviet Union when his visa expires. So someone has to leave in his place—or we start looking for him. That was Tarabrin's job. Providing the stand-ins. He had an endless supply—Jews who've been refused permission to leave the Soviet Union because they've held jobs in top security areas."

Yes, Klimenti thought, a brilliant plan, admiring its simplicity. *But it could still be the KGB*. Radchenko was still the person best placed to set it up. He could have used Tarabrin, just as he was describing it, and then killed him, realizing he was more use to them dead than alive.

Poluchkin frowned. "What's the point, especially since the assassin is going to blow himself to oblivion?"

"Because if we've got an assassin on one hand and a missing tourist on the other, we've got an obvious suspect and a visa photograph to work with. And that's the last thing they want us to have."

"The assassin's visa papers," Poluchkin exclaimed, seeing it. "Of course, that's it."

"That's right. To get his tourist visa, the Italian had to supply two photographs of himself. One for the visa. One for our files."

"We've got his photograph." Poluchkin was so excited he was shouting. He leaped to his feet, forgetting his war wounds. "My God! They can get forged documents. But the visa photographs have got to be genuine."

Radchenko said, "We'll have the Italian's photograph within the hour. And then we'll know who we're hunting."

A third assassin? That didn't fit. If there was a third, there would have to be a fourth. There'd have to be two more killings, an American as well as a Russian, to keep the balance, to maintain the myth of the VFP. Klimenti was sure the facts didn't support their theory. Two more assassinations were an unnecessary complication. Radchenko had already got away with it. Why more killings, when so much could go wrong?

The Italian didn't fit.

In that moment, Klimenti understood it and wondered at its perfect symmetry and deadly deceit, this creation of Radchenko's. The Italian fitted all right—perfectly! There wouldn't be any more assassinations. Radchenko would capture the Italian before he could strike—and the Italian would confess that he was working for the Americans. Radchenko probably had him safely tucked away somewhere, waiting for the right moment to produce him. The Italian would expose another assassin in America and Radchenko would give the Americans the information that would lead to his capture. And the second assassin would also confess that the VFP was the creation of the Americans.

In fact, both would believe it utterly. Fadeyev would have seen to that. At last Fadeyev had triumphed, recovering from his failures in East Berlin. This time they had sent him to Rome.

The great beauty of the plan, however, was that the real villain,

Radchenko, the man who had conceived this brutal mischief, would emerge as the hero. Gorbachev would be saved, the Americans condemned.

But even as he saw it, Klimenti sensed there was something imperfect about it. If he was right, Poluchkin would have to be part of it—and yet there was no doubting the Deputy Chairman was genuinely amazed by Radchenko's revelations; and the old Commissar, whatever his other qualities, certainly was not an actor.

Nor was Radchenko. Klimenti sensed in him a ravening anger that didn't fit the picture either. Smugness, perhaps—but not this smoldering rage that had the Guards' Commander up on his feet, a wild animal stalking a cage, smelling the blood spoor, frantic to be let loose. Klimenti could feel his strength; it came off him like a wave of heat, carrying the smell of sweat. Poluchkin and Nikishov sensed it too and all of them watched in fascination as Radchenko stumped up and down, his head down, shoulders bunched, a squat and dangerous man. At that moment, Radchenko held them all in his thrall.

"To summarize the evidence against the Americans," Radchenko said, punching forward a clenched fist, thumb raised. "One: Navachine, a closet Jew, is blackmailed into working for them."

A stubby finger speared the air. "Two: Tarabrin, the head of the Jewish department, is murdered. We take his department to pieces and find Navachine's name in his files. It's not proof, but at the same time it's enough to raise a strong suspicion that Tarabrin is working for the Americans and passed Navachine onto them."

Radchenko raised another finger. "Three: Tarabrin was a homosexual who was caught in a raven trap in Rome. We already know the VFP have been operating from Rome. We suspect the VFP were blackmailing him."

The fist broke open, splaying four thick fingers, the thumb now tucked against the palm. "Four: This morning, we capture a Jew trying to sneak out of the Soviet Union as a stand-in for a VFP assassin—and the Jew identifies Tarabrin."

Radchenko stared around in triumph. "We've come the full circle, everything's clear at last. Tarabrin's the common denominator." He splayed his hand. Klimenti was surprised how small it was, like a fat pig's trotter. "Five: We capture this Italian assassin and we can prove *beyond doubt* who's behind the VFP."

He spun on his heels to face Nikishov, commanding him.

"The Americans," Nikishov declared.

"Damn right!" Radchenko exploded.

He really believed it!

Watching him, feeling his heat, smelling it—believing his anger—Klimenti felt his theories about Radchenko falling to pieces. And then he realized something else. The plot he had conceived and attributed to Radchenko was an echo: *It was exactly what he, Klimenti Sergeyevich Amalrik, would have planned.* That's why he saw it so clearly, felt it so sharply. It was how he would have run it!

Klimenti was sweating, body-steaming again. He no longer was sure of anything, not even his fears. He was in the shadows, fighting, and he was losing his way. No, he was already lost.

"You're right," Poluchkin said, coming to his feet in his excitement. "I'm convinced."

Radchenko turned to Klimenti, a challenge.

"Colonel?"

"The evidence points to the Americans," Klimenti said carefully, inwardly cursing his stubbornness. Why, why couldn't he just come out and say Radchenko was right, even if he wasn't sure? It was the only sensible, the only sane, attitude to take. What could he hope to gain by dissembling? Didn't he want to live? He had seen the putrid silence of the Lubyanka and he did not want to become part of it. So what was wrong with him?

Radchenko's eyes flashed. Klimenti was sure he saw contempt. Radchenko had smelled his fear. Soon, unless Klimenti was more careful, he would come for his throat; the scent of fear drove animals insane.

"Tell us, Colonel. Why would the Americans sacrifice one of their most powerful politicians? Why would they murder a man who is a friend of the Pentagon, the CIA, the NSC, the entire military-intelligence-industrial troika, a superpatriot?"

For a moment, Klimenti felt suspended in a vacuum, aware only of a feeling of deep respect for the man who stood before him, the man with a peasant's body, a peasant's face, a peasant's cunning, a man whose parents had been illiterate. How many times had he warned himself not to underestimate Radchenko, and each time the Lieutenant General of the Kremlin Guards had leaped ahead and taken him, all of them, by surprise. He had a quality that overwhelmed minds better trained intellectually. It was audacity.

Klimenti said, "They would sacrifice Senator Townley only if they had more to gain by his death. A lot more. If the prize was right."

Poluchkin sat immobile in his chair, holding his breath. A Players burned forgotten in Nikishov's fingers. Only Radchenko seemed to have the power of movement. He leaned forward, his heavy brow only inches from Klimenti's face. His small eyes had the hypnotic quality of a snake's. In that moment, it was easy to believe that Radchenko mesmerized his victims before swallowing them.

"In your opinion, Colonel, what prize would be right? What prize is worth the sacrifice of Senator Townley?"

"There's only one, General."

"Who, Colonel? Who?" The voice was commanding, insistent.

"The President of the Soviet Union," Klimenti said calmly, completely unafraid, in the eye of the storm.

"Yes," Radchenko said.

"Gorbachev!" Poluchkin came to his feet, shouting it.

"Gorbachev?" Nikishov sat bolt upright.

"Mikhail Sergeyevich Gorbachev," Klimenti intoned, a litany of respect.

It was possible, after all, that Radchenko was right.

"It's inconceivable," gasped Nikishov, ever cautious.

"They wouldn't dare," Poluchkin shouted, smashing his mighty fist onto the desk. "They wouldn't dare."

He stood, glaring at them with his fire-streaked eyes, demanding to be right.

"They dare," Radchenko growled. "The Americans sent the Italian to Moscow to kill Comrade Gorbachev!"

35.

A t 4:30 P.M., Leonardo was in the Metelitsa Café on Kalinin. He had come in to escape the cold and himself. The Metelitsa was huge, more than a hundred tables, and most of them were already occupied, predominantly by young people who rushed to get in early before the hot food, mostly sausage, ran out. Black bread, salami, cheese, and cold smoked sturgeon made bleak fare on a midwinter's eve, even if there was plentiful and cheap brandy to wash it down.

A television positioned so that it could be watched by those in the queue was showing a Russian historical epic. Leonardo bought himself a brandy and two coffees and he was starting on the second coffee when he heard two words that froze his hand in midair.

The television said Leonardo Ruffini.

The cup fell from his nerveless hand, splashing coffee on the table. The young couple he shared it with gave him a sharp glance and turned away, wanting nothing to do with him. Leonardo's face filled the television screen, many times larger than life. Then, thankfully, the cameras picked up the news reader who repeated his name, "Leonardo Ruffini, a psychiatric patient," and Leonardo realized they were hunting for him.

His first impulse was to get as far away as possible from the condemning screen. His photograph flashed on again, his visa photo, and he wanted to throw up. Leonardo began walking, his head ringing,

237

Leonardo Ruffini, psychiatric patient, weaving among the people in the queue, going faster and faster until he was almost running. He was panicking, losing control, a sure way to draw attention to himself, and he willed himself to slow down. He wiped his face. It was damp with sweat, the way the Jew's face had been slicked in the washroom at the airport, and it was remembering this that restored his control, seeing once again the dark eyes swollen and wet with fear, eyes that were so eloquent, eyes that had betrayed them both.

He saw again the young KGB passport officer with the face of an angel and the eyes of Satan.

Leonardo walked to Kalinin Station and caught the Arbatsko–Filyovskaya line to Studencheskaya. Caught among the crush of people, he felt part of humanity again and was grateful that he was no longer cut off. The shock of seeing his own face on Moscow television had ejected him out of himself and he knew he would not return.

At last Leonardo had found his living river, a river of people, and he stood in its mist of stale breath and sweat, absorbing their stubborn, enduring strength, and for the duration of his journey beneath the streets of Moscow he was happy.

At Studencheskaya the graffito "SUK," the password of rebellion, was no more. The station staff had scrubbed it away. No matter, he thought. A word cannot be destroyed. Their fear made "SUK" immortal.

Leonardo walked alongside the railway embankment as the trains rushed along below, bright worms in the dark. The garage looked totally derelict. No one would hunt for him here. He unlocked the padlock with the key Control had given him. Inside, it was bleak and forbidding. He sensed a dull gleam and reached out and found the freezing smooth metal of a car. He edged around the car, got in, and found the flashlight Control had told him would be there.

The car was a Zil, one of the luxury limousines reserved for cabinet ministers and top Party officials. The upholstery was smooth and pliable, real leather. An eiderdown and a small traveling pillow were on the rear seat, which was big enough for him to lie down with his knees curled up. Leonardo covered himself, glad of the security of the car, burying himself in the eiderdown. He was very tired. He wanted to sleep. For a while, he thought of the train and how good it had been to be among people again, one of them. It made him a little lonely.

36.

It was Radchenko's theory that a cadre of hardliners within the American intelligence establishment was mortally afraid of Gorbachev's popularity and influence in the West, especially since he had won the Nobel Peace Prize. In many countries, citizens had a higher regard for the Soviet President than they had for their own national leaders. In most countries, Gorbachev rated higher than Bush—dangerous stuff if you sincerely believed that the Soviet Union was still the enemy.

Radchenko did not believe the American President was involved; Bush was too proud to admit Gorbachev had created an influence gap. What the hardliners feared most of all, Radchenko argued, was the approval Gorbachev had won with his initiatives on disarmament. There were Americans who believed disarmament was the biggest threat to the United States' security and its superpower status. They were afraid Gorbachev was going to retain dominance on disarmament issues and push America into a corner, where it would have to either go along with his initiatives or become pariahs in world opinion. They saw the United States isolated, disrespected, disliked.

In Radchenko's scenario, getting rid of Gorbachev would solve the problem and at the same time it would be a devastating blow to the Soviet Union. It would throw it into destructive turmoil, especially at a time of ethnic unrest and nationalist fervor for independence among its constituent republics. The world would plunge back to confrontation, a new arms race that would bankrupt the Soviet Union and reduce it to Third World economic status. It would be forced to abandon Gorbachev's economic and social reforms. The Old Guard Stalinists would take up the reins again; repression would return. Americans, feeling threatened, would rally behind their President. The West, feeling equally threatened, would flee back into the American embrace. So would Japan, perhaps even India. China would move closer to the West.

Instead of the United States, it would be the Soviet Union that would be isolated.

That's why they had sent the Italian to Moscow.

Klimenti was convinced Radchenko really believed it. In that case, Radchenko could not possibly be behind the VFP, or be responsible for the deaths of Lysenko, Senator Townley, and Tarabrin. But Klimenti could not let go of his doubts. Their roots went too deep, right into his psyche.

There were six telephones on Poluchkin's desk, all of them secure lines buried more than a meter beneath the pavements and streets of Moscow so that they could not be monitored by American spy satellites. An olive-green telephone was the *vertushka*, his direct link with the Chairman of the KGB. A red telephone was the *kremlevka*, which connected directly to the Kremlin.

As Klimenti and Nikishov went to leave, the red phone rang. They all stared at it. Poluchkin's eyes swung slowly to Radchenko, who sat upright, perceptibly stiffer. They had been expecting the call, with some trepidation. It rang again. Poluchkin nodded to Klimenti and Nikishov, an order to leave, and waited until they exited before he picked it up.

In the corridor Klimenti said, "The *kremlevka* doesn't ring every day."

"No," Nikishov said and walked on.

Klimenti shrugged. Something was on, but neither he nor Nikishov wanted to discuss it further. The silent corridor, the watchful guards, discouraged conversation.

"I'll have to meet with Bannon," Klimenti said, and Nikishov nodded and walked on in silence. He was worried that Klimenti would complete the mission he had interrupted only a few hours earlier. But

Klimenti was right. The Americans had seen the Italian's photograph on television and they would require an explanation. Klimenti's absence, a new man in his place, would only make them suspicious that the Soviets were onto them.

It was perhaps perverse, but Klimenti found himself actually looking forward to coming face to face once again with his quarry. He was certain within himself that Nikishov had only interrupted the inevitable. Unless the threat to Nadya was quickly resolved, he would go after Bannon again and this time Nikishov wouldn't be able to stop him.

"I'll go unarmed," Klimenti said, sensing Nikishov's fears. "You can search me if you wish."

"That won't be necessary," Nikishov said stiffly. But he was obviously relieved.

Klimenti and Bannon met in their usual room on the tenth floor of the Hotel Rossiya. The American examined Ruffini's photograph for a long time. "He's got the face of a man who's suffered," he said finally, a strange thing to say.

Bannon was right. The Italian had a sad, introspective look about him. Klimenti had a feeling he knew Ruffini—not *who* he was, but *what* he was. Bannon was more perceptive than Klimenti had imagined and it irritated him.

There was something hungry in Bannon's look, a gauntness in him. He had the face of a hunted man, Klimenti thought with a vindictiveness he found satisfying. He hoped the Americans had been interrogating Bannon about his relationship with Nadya. The thought that Bannon might know he was Nadya's father—that Bannon had been laughing at him all the time—was never far from Klimenti's mind, even though Nikishov had reassured him they had got more information from Chaykovskogo Ulitsa and were now sure it wasn't so.

"The Italian's the catalyst," Bannon said, flat-voiced and nasal, almost a snarl. "Unless you fabricated the whole damn story. The Jew. The exchange of identities at the airport. Unless you're running the whole damn show. The Italian included."

Klimenti said coldly, "You'll be able to see the Jew. As for the Italian, he'll present his own proof. Either we get him or he kills. One way or another, you'll know."

Bannon nodded. Klimenti's refusal to argue impressed him.

"How'd they recruit the Jew?" Bannon asked.

"We're waiting for him to tell us," Klimenti lied. He had not told Bannon about Tarabrin. Nor would he. But if Radchenko was right, then Bannon already knew about Tarabrin and was probing to see how much the KGB knew.

"He will," Bannon said, more tired than aggressive. The American, too, was under a lot of strain and it was beginning to show. He looked older, thinner, more worn. Perhaps, like Klimenti, he suspected his own people weren't giving him all the information they had. An agent was trained to expect and accept this, but it didn't make it any less stressful.

Klimenti said, "The Italians have agreed to cooperate. They'll put Ruffini's photograph on television and in the newspapers in the hope someone will recognize him and come forward with his real identity. Then we can start backtracking."

The KGB believed that the same exchange system had operated for Lysenko's assassin. They had formally asked national police forces and intelligence agencies in the West to track down every male Caucasian foreigner who had departed the Soviet Union in the three days before Lysenko's death. The KGB was supplying the names, addresses, and photographs from the visa applications. Eventually the Western agencies would come across an identity that no longer existed, either dead or disappeared, and they would have a visa photograph of Lysenko's assassin and his country of origin. They would show it on television and start hunting down his real identity, just as they were doing with Ruffini.

Bannon said, "Thank God it's not the tourist season."

The telephone rang. It was Nikishov. He gave his message cryptically, with instructions from Poluchkin to pass it on to Bannon.

Bannon was watching Klimenti with a strange intentness.

The pain in the Lubyanka was ended. "He's confessed," Klimenti said. "He's identified Ruffini as the man he exchanged identities with."

"The Jew in the Lubyanka?"

"Yes."

The Jew in the Lubyanka. Klimenti had not been able to say it.

"The poor bastard," Bannon said softly. He went to the window and stared out on the city below. "What will happen to him?"

"He'll be sent to the Kolyma."

"The Kolyma used to be a death sentence."

"Not anymore. It's hard work but these days they look after them."

"Why'd he hold out for so long?"

"He thought he was protecting his family."

"He thought?"

"It doesn't happen that way anymore."

In the end, it had not mattered. In the end, all the Jew had believed in was the needles. And those beautiful hands.

Bannon turned from the window. He put away his tape recorder and regarded Klimenti with cold, appraising eyes. "I'm sure you're aware, Colonel, that every Thursday the Politburo convenes for its weekly meeting. At 9 A.M. sharp. Once a week they get together and take a vote on all the big decisions. A collective leadership, with Comrade Gorbachev the first among equals. But only as long as he commands a majority in the Politburo." Bannon was being deliberately provocative. This was planned. "If he loses out? Well, who knows until it happens." Bannon shrugged, as if it was a matter of complete indifference to him. "They let Khrushchev live."

Klimenti said nothing, waiting.

Bannon continued. "But yesterday the Politburo didn't turn up. Yesterday, for the first time since 'Comrade' "—he said it mockingly— "Gorbachev became President, the Politburo failed to meet. As far as we know, Comrade Gorbachev hasn't been sighted or heard of since Tuesday."

The day after Lysenko was assassinated.

"I wonder why?" Bannon said and turned and walked out of the room, not needing an answer.

The *kremlevka*!

37.

Klimenti took a taxi from Razina Ulitsa to Dzerzhinsky Square, paid off the driver, and walked past the front of No. 2. It occupied an entire block, an island surrounded by a moat of three streets and the square in front. Along its one-hundred-meter frontage there were only two doors. One was the Chairman's entrance, a massive granite portal in the center of the building topped with a balcony overlooking the square. The balcony connected to the Chairman's third-floor suite. The portal enclosed double doors of polished oak that were used only by the Chairman and his deputies. Their personal staff used the second door. All other KGB personnel used the side and rear doors.

Two bronze profiles were set in wall plaques, one of Karl Marx and the other of Andropov, the former KGB Chairman who had become leader of the Soviet Union, the secret policeman who had paved the way for Gorbachev. Of all the men who had used the third-floor suite, only Andropov and Dzerzhinsky, its first occupant, who still dominated the square in bronze, had received any public tribute.

In between, there was only silence and darkness. Would it return?

If Gorbachev was in danger, if the Politburo had gone to ground, the tanks and the Guards would be in the streets.

But people walked past, as they did every day, on their way home, heads down against the cold. There were no Guards in sight. Lights glimmered. The KGB never slept. Klimenti turned the corner and looked across to the office block that housed the Secretariat of the Central Committee of the Communist Party, the real government of the Soviet Union. This was where the Politburo met every Thursday, inside the anonymous slate-gray building. Here, too, they worked late into the night and lights shone. Everything was normal.

Klimenti walked around the KGB building until he came to the Lubyanka side. People were leaving the government food store across the street, their carrier bags and arms full of cans of tomatoes. A shipment had come in from Georgia and they were buying up all they could carry before the supply ran out.

Nothing's changed, Klimenti thought. And nothing's ever going to change. Not even Gorbachev was strong enough to overcome the dead weight of Russia, anchored in the cement of centuries of inertia; not even Gorbachev could get it rolling. At that moment, Klimenti found this reassuring.

He was glad to get inside, escaping the strangling night and its smothering dark.

In the Operations Room, Nikishov was dictating a summary of the Jew's confession to Marietta Pronin, who took it down in shorthand. There was nothing in Nikishov's report to shock her; it was, after all, only a digest of what the Jew had said. It made no mention of how he had come to say it.

I don't even know his name, Klimenti thought. He's just "the Jew in the Lubyanka."

Major Kharkov rushed in, flushed with excitement. "Rome's come through with the Italian's real identity."

He passed the message to Nikishov, who read aloud, "Antonio Augustus Donatello, aged forty-five. A writer."

"How'd they get onto him so quickly?"

"He's got a police record."

"A criminal!" Criminals usually had only one cause—their own welfare. They were not the types to make self-destructing assassins.

"No," Nikishov said, reading on. "He's not a criminal. He killed his family."

"He killed his family and he's not a criminal!"

"In a car accident. He was drunk. His wife, a daughter aged twelve, a son aged ten. He was sentenced to eight years in jail for manslaughter. He served three."

Kharkov was furious. "He killed his wife and two children and they let him out after only three years."

"In the West they're soft on crimes against people," Nikishov said.

"Three years! It's criminal."

"Crimes against property are a different matter. Rob a bank and you get life."

"It's corrupt. Christ, and they criticize *our* human rights record."

Kharkov was full of righteous anger. His training had armored him but beneath it he was still a young man with much to learn and full of hope, the fuel of life.

Nikishov said, "He tried to hang himself in his cell."

"It's a pity he failed."

"Now he's trying again," said Klimenti. "This time with a suit made of plastic explosive. A human bomb."

Nikishov said, "Is that it, do you think? Is that what they went looking for, people wanting to die? Tell me, Klimenti, from your experience in Berlin, would you trust such a difficult mission to someone who is so obviously unstable?"

"Suicide's an act of cowardice," Kharkov declared, full of young courage and hatred for the drunk who had killed his family and contempt for the system that had let him off so lightly.

Klimenti said, "These assassins aren't cowards."

Kharkov glared. He didn't like it at all.

"Millions of people have done it," said Nikishov. "Died for what they believed in."

"Dying for what you believe in is not the same thing as *sacrificing* yourself," said Klimenti. "Most ordinary people are prepared to die for someone or something they love—but only when there is no other alternative. As rational human beings, they will have first satisfied themselves that there is indeed no other way. Fate overtakes them. It's a decision forced on them. Or it happens on the moment, in the heat of action, without thought. Usually we call them heroes."

"What's the difference?"

"With assassins who are prepared to sacrifice themselves it goes much deeper. No one is forcing death on them. They're volunteers. They choose to die. Death is not a desperate, unavoidable resort. For them, death is their fulfillment, a goal. They choose how and where and the circumstances of their death. And why. They are not overtaken by fate. Instead, they make death their destiny, and there is a huge difference. They train to die. The energy of their life is devoted to perfecting the manner of their death. Preparing for it. Then performing it."

I speak for the living dead and the soon-to-die, Klimenti thought. They require respect.

"You trained psychotics?" Nikishov demanded.

"Rational people don't train to die. They train to kill and stay alive."

"So I'm right. They were psychotics."

"The best of them were."

Nikishov was appalled. "Where'd the VFP get their psychotics?"

"The same place we get ours."

"The loony bin," Kharkov said sarcastically. He didn't like what he was hearing.

"Where else?" Klimenti said wearily, aware of their shock. "In Iran, they recruit them in religious institutions. They call them zealots. Young men with an obsessional love of God. The PLO recruit them in refugee camps. Young men with an obsessional hatred of the Israelis. They exalt them to martyrdom. They promise them paradise. Unfortunately, we can't offer Soviet citizens paradise after death. We don't believe in God and we've already given it to them in life."

Kharkov's eyes flashed with anger. He did not like to hear the Soviet Union mocked.

"With foreigners, there's a huge pool of hate to recruit from. Palestinians. Libyans. Cubans. South Americans. Armenians. Turks. Black Africans. Black Americans. Even in a real paradise, the South Pacific. We use them all. With Russians, it's more difficult. These days, we can't even offer them a cause to love, an enemy to hate. All the Bolsheviks are dead. The Americans are human after all. It's all too gray, too murky. We're all bureaucrats. There's nothing to inspire a Russian to sacrifice. So we have to take them where we can."

"Sick, pathetic people. Failed suicides!" Nikishov really was disgusted.

Klimenti knew it was pointless trying to explain. Who could understand who had not known them? Standing in the snow with Radchenko at Usovo on that first day, he had remembered their faces. Now he heard their voices, speaking to him across that great barrier of time. He was shocked; amid the chorus he heard laughter, *real laughter*.

Yes, he remembered now. There were moments when they had actually been happy.

Klimenti could never tell anyone about their laughter and their gratitude. They would think it indecent. He could not blame them. When he was recalled to Moscow, he was glad to get away. Yet he had never been able to completely rid himself of a sense of guilt. He felt as if he had abandoned orphans.

He looked again at the photograph of the Italian with his sad and wise face, full of wistfulness. He too was an orphan.

"We do this? We use these people?" Kharkov was horrified.

"While they're in control."

Kharkov swore softly. "What happens if they lose control?"

"We take them back to where we found them."

"It'd be kinder to kill them. And good sense." Kharkov meant it. Now he believed what he had heard.

"You're right," Klimenti said and walked away, not wanting to tell them more.

Kharkov sat at his desk, studying the photograph of the Italian. After a while he came across to Klimenti.

"What sort of writer do you think he was?"

"Does it matter?"

Kharkov was a little embarrassed. A few minutes ago, he had thought only of the Italian as someone, *something*, who needed to be killed. Now he was wondering who he was. He had remembered his own training and had begun to understand part of what had happened to the Italian during his reconstruction into an assassin. They had made it clear to Kharkov that he could be called on to kill, without question, without compunction.

"No," he said and turned away. He went back to his desk and sat down. Kharkov was sure he could kill this writer. He was sure it had to be done. But he was no longer sure he wanted to do it.

Radchenko strode in, filling the Operations Room with his presence. Kharkov snapped to attention, so keyed up he forgot he was indoors, without a cap, and saluted.

"Sir!"

"It's on," Radchenko barked, surprising Klimenti with his sense of drama.

"Yes, sir," Kharkov shouted back, overjoyed as any Young Pioneer.

"Colonel, you're to report immediately to Deputy Chairman Poluchkin."

"Yes, General."

"Major, come with me."

"Yes, sir!"

Radchenko strode out, followed by Kharkov. Klimenti went across to Nikishov.

"What's on?"

Nikishov cast a warning glance at Marietta Pronin. "General Poluchkin'll tell you." He began clearing his desk.

In the corridor, Klimenti passed Guards' technicians carrying in extra telephones and collapsible map tables.

The eye patch was gone. Behind the thick lens, Poluchkin's terrible eye was red and swollen and uglier than normal. But the Deputy Chairman was not feeling the pain; he was too excited. Adrenaline had washed away the irritability and tiredness of the past few days. Poluchkin had removed his uniform jacket, his tie was pulled down and his shirt sleeves rolled up, and there was on his scarred, suffering face a look of immense satisfaction. He was a happy man.

"We're going into action and, my God, it's about time," Poluchkin said. "It's been so long, I'd almost forgotten what it's like, commanding troops instead of clerks. I tell you, Colonel, those were the days. With death and destruction all around, you knew you were alive and you were grateful for it."

He was alive again, Poluchkin the fighting Commissar, the legend, the man who had lain down in the freezing mud with his troops so that they could see he led by example, the man who had bared his body to Nazi steel and had survived to tear their throats out. The years fell away and he was full of energy and strength and certainty; Klimenti saw in him the qualities that had inspired his men.

That's what the call on the *kremlevka* was about. Orders.

Poluchkin picked up his packet of Gauloises. It was empty. He crushed it and threw it against the wall. This was no longer an office; this was his command bunker. He took a fresh packet from his desk drawer and ripped it open. He sucked the strong smoke deep into his lungs.

"You're not surprised, Colonel?"

"No, sir."

"Of course not. I've read all your reports. Brilliant stuff. You grasped it from the beginning. You understood what Lysenko was up to. Perhaps you understood too quickly."

He gave Klimenti a hard look. "That's why you thought we'd killed him."

At last the accusation, the confrontation. At last they were saying it straight to his face. Klimenti's throat was very dry. What did it matter, anyway? His name was either down or it wasn't. He was ashamed of his fear and duplicity.

"The truth is I wasn't sure of anything, General."

It was a relief to get it out. To hell with them.

Poluchkin nodded in satisfaction. He, too, was glad to have it out in the open.

"It's a list, isn't it, General? Of people to be arrested."

No more lists, Radchenko had said, toasting it in Stalin's wine, blood-red Kinzmarauli. And he had known all along it was a lie; they had been writing down the names even as they ate and drank.

"You think your name's on it?"

Klimenti felt the sweat run out of his armpits and trickle down his ribs. But he was no longer afraid.

"What's another colonel on a list like that?" Among the millions of voices already silenced.

Poluchkin nodded somberly. "That's right. What's another colonel? Among four members of the Politburo and three Candidate Members. Sixty-three members of the Central Committee, eleven generals and forty-two colonels. Two of the generals and nine of the colonels are KGB officers. Our own men."

Poluchkin smashed the list onto his desk, a paper truncheon. He had no need to read it. He had composed it and the numbers tripped off his tongue with savage fluency. Betrayal was a grim and dirty business and he had been through it before. He took off his glasses and rubbed his swollen eye. It was itching; there was never a minute when it did not remind him of his affliction. Sometimes he wished he had the courage to pluck it out.

"One hundred and twenty-three traitors. And there's more to come. You can be sure of it."

Poluchkin brought the list across. When Klimenti had come into the office, he had been striding around with the energy of an angry buffalo. Now he limped.

"Read it, Colonel. Your name's not there. In fact, it's on another list. The conspirators' list." He smiled sourly. "You're in good company. I'm included. So is the Chairman, Radchenko, Nikishov. And Comrade Gorbachev."

Klimenti took the list. But he did not attempt to read it. It was too long.

Poluchkin said, "President Gorbachev was due to fly to Jerevan tomorrow for talks on the Armenian situation. He was to be accompanied by several of his most loyal supporters in the Politburo. And, of course, the Chairman and Lieutenant General Radchenko." He paused, his scarred cheeks quivering with anger. His voice grated. "They were going to put a bomb on board and blame it on the Armenians."

A bomb! So, at last, it was revealed. The *Russian* plot to kill Gorbachev. From the beginning, it had been the first thought on their minds, their uppermost but unvoiced fear on the Chaika ride to Usovo that first morning.

"The arrests were going to start immediately after the bomb went off. *Their* list included all senior officers who were considered likely to oppose the coup."

"What were they going to do?"

"What else! Those bastards are Stalinists. They were going to shoot us."

Poluchkin laughed, a hard, unhappy sound. "Don't be shocked, Colonel. Now that you're going to live, you should be proud your name's on their list. I congratulate you."

"What's going to happen to them?"

"Not a lot. After all, they're important people. They'll be allowed to retire and be isolated."

But Poluchkin wasn't happy about it. He preferred more permanent solutions.

"The President's a lawyer, a stickler for legality. He wants it clean and above board," Poluchkin growled. "Things have changed."

Behind its fortress-thick lens, the maimed eye blinked, a living creature. Klimenti had not seen it do that before.

38.

L eonardo came back to consciousness quietly, without panic, remembering immediately where he was. He lay curled up on the back seat beneath the quilt. His body had warmed the seat and he snuggled into it, his eyes closed. His overcoat had become twisted around him while he slept and it constrained him like a . . .

Straitjacket . . . !

He wrenched his body around, tearing at the coat, full of fright, remembering the bright lights that never went out and the observation windows that never ceased their scrutiny, and his helplessness. His legs were caught up in the quilt, but he did not mind; they had never imprisoned his legs. He got his arms free and lay back panting, surprised at how quickly the panic had come and how strong it had been. He also became aware of something else.

There was a light in the car, reflecting down from the roof lining. Someone was in the car with him.

Leonardo jerked upright, kicking to free the quilt.

"Hello," Control said. "Did I startle you? I'm sorry."

Leonardo was so relieved he laughed softly, mocking his fear. "No. You didn't startle me. I startled myself."

Control smiled, full of compassion and understanding. The smile of his brother. He had been reading by the light of a pencil flashlight.

Now he reached up and switched on the interior light. It cast a soft yellow glow.

"What about the batteries?" Leonardo said. "We must be careful not to drain them."

"A few minutes won't hurt."

Leonardo was glad of the light. He was glad of the company. Control's hair was rumpled from his cap, which lay on the seat next to him and it made him look surprisingly boyish. He held up two thermos flasks.

"I've brought you some soup. Some borscht and black bread. And a thermos of coffee."

Leonardo laughed and Control stared at him in concern, misunderstanding the cause of his gaiety, suspecting it was panic.

"No, no, no," Leonardo hastened to reassure him. "Borscht is fine. Wonderful, in fact. You see, every night I've been in Moscow I've asked for borscht soup. You come to Moscow, you see the Kremlin, you ride the underground, you drink vodka, you eat borscht soup. What could be more Russian?"

He smiled, feeling good. "Particularly the answer I got every time I asked for it."

"Nyet soupa!"

"That's right. *Nyet soupa, nichts soupen,* no soup."

"It's winter."

"It's Russia! I'm not complaining. But how did you manage it?"

"A can."

"Of course. How simple!"

"Not so simple. First of all, the can had to get here from Hungary."

They sat in the car, their faces softened by the weak light, laughing together, keeping it quiet but laughing nonetheless. They were both aware of how strange it was, full of the unreality of their circumstances. Leonardo had come all the way to Moscow to die and to eat borscht soup made in Budapest.

"I'm hungry," Leonardo said, grateful and surprised that this was so. "Do you mind if I eat now?"

"Of course not."

Control passed across the thermos of soup and an air-sealed plastic container that held some heavily buttered black bread, a few slices of cheese, and a small can of black caviar. The soup was hot and the rich, tempting odor filled the car. The outer and inner lids of the thermos made two cups; Leonardo filled them both and passed one to Control, who demurred.

"Please," Leonardo said. "There's more than enough, and it must be cold outside."

He did not want to eat alone. This would be his last supper and he wanted to share it so that it would live in one man's memory. How he conducted himself now would be his epitaph, inscribed not in stone but in the heart of a man.

"It's delicious," Leonardo said. The soup was thick and tasty. He dunked the bitter bread.

"I put in a lot of cream and some butter."

Leonardo wondered how he had come by the cream. In a Moscow winter. But he did not ask. He was hungry enough to want a second cup. This time he put some cheese on the bread. Control sipped his borscht, watching Leonardo with thoughtful eyes. He had come to a decision.

"Something's gone wrong. The Russians know who you are. They're hunting for you."

"I know."

Control gaped. His reaction pleased Leonardo immensely. It was human to be taken by surprise and he wanted desperately to be sure that he was sharing his last moments with someone who had warm blood in his veins. He was also proud of his calmness. Every minute, he was finding new strength. It was a positive way to end your life, going out stronger than you came in. Few people had such a privilege.

"I was in a café when they showed my photograph on television."

Control exhaled, a whistle of breath. He was impressed by Leonardo's lack of reaction.

"You're amazingly calm about it."

"I assure you, I wasn't then," Leonardo said. But he was pleased by the compliment.

Control scrutinized him intently, making no attempt to conceal his examination. He had another decision to make.

"I can do it," Leonardo said. It was not a plea. It was a declaration. He met Control's eyes with a steady, unflinching gaze and it was Control who turned away. He sat, head down in silent contemplation. He was surprisingly young. Leonardo wondered who he was and where he came from. But they were fleeting thoughts, quickly overridden by his serenity.

"I'm sure they got him at the airport," Leonardo said. "He was terrified. His eyes betrayed him. You couldn't miss it. You could smell the stink of fear on him. The poor fellow."

His sympathy was genuine. He understood the terror the Jew had experienced and he loved him for it.

"I didn't choose him," Control said. "He wasn't in my control."

"It wasn't an accusation."

No, Control thought, it wasn't an accusation. Yet he was aware that, for the moment at least, the initiative had passed to Leonardo. It was subtle and there was nothing changed in their attitudes. Yet Control knew Leonardo sensed it, too; he could feel the power in the Italian.

Tarabrin had picked the Jew. Tarabrin, who had come to him whimpering with fear, pleading for mercy. How long ago was it? Only yesterday, thirty-six hours ago. Even then the Jew's fate was already sealed. And so was Tarabrin's. It had been a mistake killing Tarabrin. But it would have been an even bigger mistake to let him live.

"I was wondering if you were going to tell me," Leonardo said. "You took your time."

"I had to be sure you wouldn't panic."

"And if you weren't sure?"

"I wouldn't have told you."

"You would have let me go on, not knowing the Russians were hunting for me?" It was important that Control should tell him the truth. It was part of the pact, part of their blood-trust.

"No. That would have been foolish."

"What then?"

Control shook his head, not wanting to answer. He could not meet Leonardo's eyes.

"Tell me," Leonardo said harshly now, surprising Control. "You had the courage to do it, then have the courage to tell me."

"You're right," Control said. "I could have done it because it would have had to be done. But, somehow, telling you is a lot more difficult. Somehow, it makes me feel indecent."

"You have to tell me."

"Yes," Control said and took his right hand out of his coat pocket. He was holding a shining black pistol.

"I would have killed you."

"Thank you," Leonardo said and sank back against the seat, suddenly exhausted. They had promised him they would never lie, and they had told the truth.

"If you panicked, if you botched the job and were taken alive, it would do a lot of damage. We can't take that risk. You know that."

Yes, Leonardo knew it. They told you everything, trusting in you. Leonardo did not know it, but another man who shared his destiny, one of his brothers, had exactly the same thought on the eve of his death.

"They won't take me alive."

"I believe you." Control put away the pistol. "They're looking for an Italian disguised as a Russian. They know we're going to try an assassination but they don't know who or where or when. They don't know how we're going to do it, so they won't be looking for a chauffeur driving a Zil. That's why we chose it. A Zil's the badge of power. No Russian would dare stop a Zil."

He smiled, relieved that it was over, wanting now to show his acceptance of Leonardo. "You'd better see if it starts."

Leonardo got into the front seat next to Control. The engine kicked over immediately and purred softly. It was beautifully maintained.

"Is it stolen?"

"Several times. This Zil never officially existed. The factory manager forgot to count as it came off the production line. He probably had a dozen millionaires lined up to buy it. Men who made their money the same way he was making his, by stealing from the State."

"Millionaires! In the Soviet Union?"

"Oh yes. Lots of them."

"I thought they shot economic criminals."

"Not Brezhnev. Under him the *tolkachi* prospered. Everyone was up to their armpits in it, even his own family."

"Brezhnev's own family!" Leonardo was genuinely shocked.

"His daughter, Galina. Her lover was a jewel thief; she manipulated the black market for diamonds. Her husband, too. He was a Militia general and he took a million rubles in bribes. I got someone who knows the black market to find a nonexistent Zil. Then I paid him to steal it. You see, the owner can't go to the Militia. They'll want all sorts of information he can't give them without revealing the car was stolen from the State in the first place."

Leonardo laughed. "I like it."

"In a corrupt system, anything's possible."

"What about the car thief? Won't he put two and two together? Isn't it dangerous for you?"

"He's been taken care of," Control lied. It was another loose end that remained to be tidied up and this time he had only himself to blame. He had tried once and failed.

"Oh," Leonardo said. It was something he had to face: people other than his target would die. The first victim was a car thief. How many would it be tomorrow? He didn't want to think about it.

"He wasn't just a car thief," Control said. "He deserved to die."

"It's all right."

"Tomorrow, on the street, there'll be people. Innocent people."

"I told you, it's all right. I'd rather not think about it. Not now. Not later either, for that matter."

"So far, we've been able to avoid it. But it's inevitable. Each time we strike, it will be harder. Particularly in Moscow."

Leonardo said, "I would have liked to meet some of the others. I'm very curious about them. What they're like. Who they are. Who they were. How many of us there are."

"Yes, I understand. But it's not possible, of course. We have to keep each of you isolated, to minimize the damage if something goes wrong."

"I'm not complaining. Just curious. Somehow, don't tell me why, I get the feeling it'd be, well, good to meet them." Leonardo smiled, feeling a little self-conscious. "It's just an idle thought."

"We have to get you dressed before I go."

Leonardo's body prickled with a cold shiver. He hated the suits.

Control got out of the Zil and went to the rear of the garage. He shone his pocket flashlight on a green Russian army duffel bag, which had the name and number of its former owner stenciled on it. He opened the bag and took out a large battery light, which cast a pale glow. Then he unpacked a one-piece silk overall. Leonardo had worn one many times before, to accustom himself to the discomfort and weight. Even so he shivered a second time, remembering the clammy feeling of the plastic explosive beneath its thin covering of parachute silk. It had the consistency of putty and you could squeeze it, like soft, misshapen flesh.

"You want to go to the toilet, you'd better do it now," Control said. "There's a bucket in the corner."

"I'll try," Leonardo said. He was wearing women's panty hose to protect his legs from the cold and it made it difficult. He had to lower his trousers and pull down the panty hose and he was so embarrassed he was surprised he was able to urinate. He held the bucket up against himself so that the jetting liquid wouldn't make a lot of noise and make matters even worse.

Control put a blanket on the cold floor and Leonardo stood on it and undressed. He was aware the panty hose made him look rather ridiculous, perhaps even pathetic. The overall zipped from the crotch to the neck and it was close hugging, like a wet suit. From his ankles to his neck and wrists, every part of his body was encircled by plastic explosive.

Control unpacked a chauffeur's uniform, which was several sizes too big, and helped Leonardo pull it on. Leonardo found it difficult to get the necktie right and Control helped him with the knot. Then he knelt and fastened on boots, which looked very much like ski boots and weighed about the same because they were lined with plastic explosive.

The three final items, which Leonardo would not don until the last minute, were a set of heavy mittens and a motorcyclist's helmet, both with plastic explosive molded inside, and a mouth guard made of plastic explosive with a thin layer of plastic. Altogether, Leonardo would carry fourteen kilograms of plastic explosive. He clumped around, hating it. It wasn't the weight; it was the feeling that he was wearing someone else's flesh.

"I feel like a deep-sea diver," he said, trying to smile through chattering teeth.

"Get in the Zil. We'll run the heaters to warm you up," Control said. He helped Leonardo into the front seat, wrapped the quilt around him, and poured some more soup.

"This'll help."

Leonardo drank gratefully.

Control gave him his last piece of equipment, a matchbox-sized UHF radio transmitter. It emitted a signal at a frequency of 304 megahertz. The signal had two refinements to block interference by other transmitters that might be in the area. It went out on a band width of 0.1, and it contained a binary pattern generated by a Motorola

MC145026 trinary encoder silicone chip inside the transmitter. The signal was received by tiny receivers buried in the plastic explosive in each item of Leonardo's clothing. In each receiver, an aerial of fine gold wire one centimeter long passed the signal to a silicone chip paired with the chip in the transmitter. The chip, only two millimeters square and 0.1 millimeter thick, was a trinary decoder preset to recognize the unique binary pattern. In a split second, it identified and verified the pattern and completed an electrical circuit powered by a three-volt Lithium watch battery. The battery was connected to a detonator.

A similar device would explode a hundred kilos of plastic explosive in the Zil.

Leonardo put the transmitter into his coat pocket. He did not want it where he could see it. Not yet. Tomorrow, yes. But not tonight. He turned to Control, his eyes bright. Tell me, they pleaded. Tell me.

Control thought about it and shrugged. "His name was Gerald."

"Gerald. He was American?"

"English."

"What was he? May I ask? Surely, it can do no harm." Leonardo leaned forward, as anxious as a schoolboy.

Control remembered Gerald's pale face. He had been afraid but he had the courage to admit it and he had overcome it. Gerald had not displayed such curiosity. But then Gerald was English, and the first.

"A nuclear physicist."

"A nuclear physicist. That's something." Leonardo was genuinely impressed. He asked, "The tanks in the streets the morning I arrived. That was Gerald's doing?"

"Yes."

"And later, the obituary on television. Lysenko. That was Gerald too?"

"Yes."

It's a good sign, Control thought. Leonardo had used his eyes and ears well. A frightened man saw nothing except his fear.

Leonardo hugged himself, pressing the cold plastic explosive hard against his flesh. But this time he did not shiver. "I won't fail you," he said.

"I know you won't." It would have been interesting to see them together, the tortured, curious Italian and the fearful, reserved Englishman. Leonardo and Gerald. "You would have liked him. And he you."

"Thank you," Leonardo said proudly.

"What were you?" Control said, obeying the ritual. It was important that they should not forget how it had been, before their rebirth.

Leonardo sat quietly, his face solemn. He didn't want to say it.

"You have to tell me," Control said, putting his hand on Leonardo's arm, to tell him he was not alone.

"A poet. A failed poet."

Leonardo's words were heavy with sadness and so was his face. To have sacrificed so much and to have been a failure! It was unforgivable. Tomorrow he would make a sacrifice of himself, and it would be his greatest success.

"You won't be a failure now," Control said in his caressing voice, deep and almost a whisper. "Now that they know who you are, after tomorrow you'll be immortal."

Tears glistened in Leonardo's eyes. He took Control's hand and held it, and Control was surprised by the strength he felt trembling there.

"Remember me," Leonardo said and smiled and wiped away his tears. "That's all the immortality I want. One person who remembers me."

"I'll never forget," Control said. "Any of you."

"I'm all right now. I'd like to be alone." Leonardo smiled wanly. "To think on my immortality."

When he went out into the night, Control took with him an image of a frail man with chicken-thin legs shivering in women's brown panty hose. He could not escape the feeling that he had already left Leonardo in his coffin.

39.

Nikishov was at his desk in the Operations Room, watching Radchenko's men at work on the telephones, coordinating the arrests. He had nothing to do, and the inactivity allowed his tiredness to overwhelm him. He had not been home in two days and nights, and his handsome face was grouted with exhaustion. He observed sourly to Klimenti, "It's been a long time since we did mass arrests."

Half a dozen desks had been moved in. About fifteen officers manned telephones. But it was surprisingly calm and quiet. They spoke in subdued tones. Even the signal bells on the telephones had been muted. Marietta Pronin went around, handing out cups of tea from a samovar that had been brought in and emptying ashtrays, as quiet on her feet as a nurse.

"Any reports?" Klimenti asked.

"The arrests are going smoothly."

"The Italian?"

"Nothing yet." Nikishov shrugged. "But it shouldn't be long. Where can he hide?"

Indeed, where could any foreigner hide in the Soviet Union, a nation full of informers? Where could he run to in a nation that had 350,000 specially trained Border Guards to seal its frontiers?

But the Italian wouldn't run. Whoever he was working for—Radchenko or the Americans—he believed he had come to Moscow to fulfill a mission, and he would do it. Klimenti was sure of it. The Italian would do his best to finish what he had come to do. To kill and then self-destruct. To give his death, perhaps his whole life, significance.

If it was Radchenko who was running him, the Italian would be captured at some opportune moment. If it was the Americans, he would meet a different fate. Now that the hunt was on, they would not take the risk of his being captured alive. They would kill him.

The poor, miserable, motherless bastard!

They sat in silence and Klimenti became aware of a mutuality of feeling, a shared understanding. Nikishov felt it too, one of those rare moments of sympathy, when people recognize themselves in others. They were both feeling the weight of the day, the enormity of all they had seen and learned, remembering the Jew in the Lubyanka, and acknowledging the necessity, and knowing the full measure of treachery, and accepting it, and the immeasurable venality and vanity of power, and understanding it.

Nikishov opened his drawer and took out a bottle of vodka, the same one he had opened the other night. Several of Radchenko's men glanced sharply across but Nikishov paid them no attention. He glanced at Klimenti and smiled. To hell with them, he was saying, I need a drink—and so, I'm sure, do you.

He was right. Klimenti did need a drink. Nikishov passed him the bottle without comment.

Sitting there, drinking vodka in comradely quiet, Klimenti and Nikishov wanted time to pass quickly, to steal away from them. They were waiting for the morning so that they could shed the contaminated skin of today and start again. They were exhausted beyond the need for sleep; they needed not rest but comfort, a reassurance of their worthiness, for both felt themselves to be decent men and the Lubyanka had left its wounds.

Nikishov said, "Did you know that during the *Yezhovshchina,* the interrogators used to sleep on the desks in this room? The floor even. They were working around the clock, twenty-four hours a day, dragging them in and giving them confessions to sign and taking them straight out into the courtyard. Bam! A bullet in the back of the head, back in again. Next, please."

Nikishov drank deeply, and it seemed to Klimenti that he was hardly aware of the alcohol. What they had witnessed in the Lubyanka had upset Nikishov more than he had realized and, with this thought, Klimenti became aware that his own distress was more acute than he had been willing to admit. Both he and Nikishov had been holding it down, afraid of the emotion. The sour stench of the cell was still in their nostrils—in the very pores of their skin—and Nikishov had recognized it as the foul breath of Nikolai Ivanovich Yezhov, the "bloody dwarf," not quite five feet tall, one-time secretary of the Central Committee, whom Stalin made chairman of the NKVD in 1936. Stalin's terror reached its height under Yezhov, whose exterminations were so ferocious that the period bore his name, the *Yezhovshchina*. Yezhov trusted no one, including his own killers. In 1937 he executed 3,000 NKVD men. Finally, even Stalin came to fear him, and in December 1938, Yezhov was taken down into the Lubyanka and shot—perhaps in the same cell the Jew had been taken to.

Klimenti was glad of the vodka.

Nikishov said, "Yezhov worked them to exhaustion. But that wasn't the reason they stayed here and slept on the desks and the floor. You see, they were afraid to go home."

He lifted his eyes to Klimenti. They were pale and empty, like an exhausted summer sky. *Like us*, they said. Nikishov gestured. "Here, in this very room. Too terrified to go home because that's where they came for you, in your lousy little unheated room with its blanket partitions and your wife and children imprisoning you, because with a wife and children you can't run, you can't hide, you can only lie awake and sweat it out, knowing they'll come for you, the way you came for others. So they fell down and slept where they could, right here on this floor, as cowed as the men they tortured. Condemned men. It was a terrible time. Some of them couldn't stand the waiting so they walked outside into the courtyard and shot themselves."

Nikishov emptied his cup a second time. "It happened," he said simply, beyond contradiction, and filled his cup again and passed the bottle to Klimenti. "All revolutions devour their children."

"This isn't another *Yezhovshchina*," Klimenti said. "It can't happen again."

Nikishov's thin lips twisted into an acrid smile. "You're forgetting, *it almost did*! Poluchkin told you. I know he showed you their death list, otherwise you wouldn't be here. Your name was on it. So was mine. Don't you realize how close it was?"

Klimenti had never seen Nikishov in such a state. He wasn't excited. On the contrary, what was noticeable was an almost deathlike languor, as if life had already drained out and he was merely waiting for the husk of his body to follow.

"Tomorrow," Klimenti said gravely. "They were coming for us tomorrow night."

"And where are you most Monday nights?"

Klimenti did not answer. He did not have to.

"At home, Klimenti Sergeyevich. At home." Nikishov laughed softly, a bitter sound. "They say an Englishman's home is his castle. For a Russian, it's a prison. The most dangerous place a Russian can be. And if you've got any doubts, why not take a walk across the courtyard and ask the newest inmates of the Lubyanka. That's where we got them tonight, at home, in bed with their wives."

"It has to be done."

"That's what Yezhov said."

"It's only temporary."

"Yezhov said that, too." Nikishov emptied his glass again. "We're just hired gangsters, ready to break the law whenever our bosses give us the orders."

Across the room Marietta Pronin was standing by her safe, staring at them. Several of Radchenko's officers were watching them, too.

"They'll say we got drunk on duty," Nikishov said, smiling sourly once again and pouring more vodka. "I'm working on it."

Three men strode into sight in the courtyard below, two of them in full uniform and caps and the third in bare feet, manacled hands clutching to hold up his trousers. They had removed his belt and jacket and he shivered in his thin shirt, his feet already frozen and hurting.

Klimenti was terrified he would lift his eyes and catch him watching at the window and recognize him.

The steel door opened and the Lubyanka swallowed them.

Zalozny. His name was Zalozny, a colonel in the Armed Service Directorate, which spied on the military. Zalozny and Klimenti had shared a room during a course that gave them their colonelcies, and he had been a bright and cheerful fellow, fond of telling jokes and singing country songs.

Klimenti turned away from the window and its accusing view. Who else did he know among the conspirators? The cold reached across from the Lubyanka and seeped through the double-glazed windows and into his body, making him shiver.

Nikishov's telephone rang. He answered it, sipping his vodka thoughtfully as he listened. He turned his back and spoke quietly, so that Klimenti could not hear what was being said. When the conversation was terminated, Nikishov topped up his cup with vodka and lit a Players, sucking deeply, watching the smoke spiral. Klimenti, who knew only too well how acutely personal distress warped long-held perspectives, wondered if the loss of his wife was responsible for Nikishov's strange behavior.

Nikishov emptied his cup. He offered the bottle to Klimenti, who shook his head. There was only a trickle left anyway and Nikishov grimaced. "Ah, well," he sighed, and straightened himself, a soldier once again.

"There's more news from the Americans," he said. "Bannon's finished. They're flying him out tomorrow."

Klimenti sat upright. At last!

I did it, Marusya. I wasn't so helpless, after all.

"It's a relief." Nikishov smiled ruefully. "I'm sure you would have killed him eventually."

"Where to?" Klimenti was surprised at how hoarse his voice was.

"Rome," Nikishov said, arching an eyebrow. "Interesting, isn't it?"

Nikishov dropped the vodka bottle into a wastebasket. "The forensic evidence," he said and looked sourly across at Marietta Pronin and Radchenko's watchful men. "Although there's more than enough eyewitnesses."

40.

Shortly after midnight, Squirrel broke his silence.

A lieutenant colonel of the Thirteenth Department, the duty officer in the Communications Center at Dzerzhinsky Square, received a Most Urgent, Most Secret signal from the Soviet Embassy in Washington. The message was received by a cryptographic machine which spoke via a satellite link in continuous code, twenty-four hours a day, to a twin machine in the embassy in Washington. It was sent in a code reserved for Special Service 11, whose principal officer in Washington ran Soviet agents within the United States. The signal was delivered in the raw to the Special Service 11 duty officer, who decoded it. The duty officer telephoned to warn the Deputy Chairman and ran to catch the elevator.

Both the Chairman and Poluchkin had made arrangements to spend the night at No. 2 and Poluchkin was preparing to retire when he was handed the signal. Halfway through reading it, he began to sweat and grabbed the green-colored *vertushka* to warn the Chairman.

The signal read:

> Squirrel reports National Security Council convinced Gor-
> bachev is to be removed by armed coup. NSC urged President
> to order DEFCON 2. President 3:30 P.M. Washington time
> postponed DEFCON 2 decision for 12 hours pending devel-

opments in Moscow. President ordered an immediate review of
SIOP 6.

"There's no mistake?" The Chairman was clearly shocked.

"No, sir. The American nuclear forces are about to go onto a
war-fighting alert."

DEFCON was an acronym for Defense Condition, the alert status
of the American nuclear forces. There were five grades. DEFCON 5
was peace. DEFCON 1 was nuclear war. The normal status of
American nuclear forces was DEFCON 3.

DEFCON 2 was a state of full, around-the-clock nuclear war
readiness, fingers on the buttons. It also went by the code name of
"Cocked Pistol" and was exactly that—a nuclear arsenal at hair-trigger
alert. Crews went on war standby in Minuteman ICBM bases between
Missouri and Montana and on mobile MX missile launchers in nuclear
submarines at sea and at Strategic Air Command bomber bases. All that
was required for the crews to arm more than 9,000 strategic nuclear
warheads was a telephone call from the President to the North
American Aerospace Defense Command (NORAD) headquarters buried beneath Cheyenne Mountain, in Colorado.

In less than twelve hours, the world could be on the brink of
thermonuclear destruction.

The Chairman was almost two decades younger than Poluchkin but
he was both shrewd and tough. Now he showed himself to be cool
headed, as well. He picked up the *kremlevka* and relayed the signal
to President Gorbachev in crisp, precise language. Then he informed
the headquarters of PVO Strany, the Soviet Defense Command,
forty-five kilometers from Moscow, which controlled the satellite
and early-warning radar units, the Moscow Defense System of thirty-
two antiballistic missile launchers in eight sites around the city,
the nationwide air-defense system of 9,600 surface-to-air missiles
in 1,200 sites, and 1,200 interceptor aircraft. Nuclear shelters in
Moscow were to be brought to full readiness without alarming the
public.

"We're going to full alert?" Poluchkin asked. He was sweating.

"Only our defensive units," the Chairman said. "The President has
ordered that our Strategic Rocket Forces be brought to fifty percent
readiness."

"Fifty percent! But the Americans are going to DEFCON 2."

"Not yet," the Chairman said. "We've still got twelve hours, more than enough warning. We're not under the same pressure as the Americans are to 'use them or lose them.' If they go to DEFCON 2, we'll be ready."

The Chairman was right. The Strategic Rocket Forces were the main Soviet offensive arm with a throw-weight of more than five thousand strategic warheads on ICBMs in twenty-six launching bases stretching across the Central and Eastern Soviet Union. Unlike the Americans, the Russians did not consider their missile silos to be first-strike targets—the American weapons were not yet accurate enough to guarantee destroying hardened targets—and thus considered they had more time in which to use them. The American ICBM silos, however, were vulnerable to the more accurate and bigger Soviet warheads, putting intense pressure on them to fire their arsenal before it was destroyed.

The Chairman said, "Our nuclear submarines are to prepare to put to sea but there's to be no surging unless Comrade Gorbachev specifically gives the order."

Poluchkin caught his breath. The nuclear submarines carried 2,100 strategic warheads and Gorbachev was risking losing a vital component of his nuclear forces. Because of deficiencies in their nuclear reactors, two-thirds of the nuclear submarines were kept in their home ports, and the Americans regarded "surging"—rushing out to sea—as a first step to putting the Soviet nuclear forces on a war-fighting alert.

"A nuclear submarine can go a long way in twelve hours," Poluchkin said. "We're throwing away their only chance to disperse."

"The President's aware of it," the Chairman said. "But he wants to signal the Americans that he has no intention of launching a preemptive first strike. He's worried the situation could get out of control, that war dynamics could take over."

War dynamics! Each side escalating in turn, moving in fear, trying to head off its opponent, the process gathering momentum until it became unstoppable. Until someone fired the first missile and un-leashed a barrage and counterbarrage of more than 16,000 strategic nuclear warheads, with another 30,000 smaller warheads in reserve. Then it was all over. Everything. Hundreds of millions dead. Hundreds of millions sickened and hurt. The landscape devastated, cities destroyed. Nuclear winter. Civilization perished.

SIOP 6. What a ridiculous acronym for the end of mankind. It's not possible, Poluchkin thought. It was inconceivable.

But it was about to happen.

The Chairman said, "We're to go no further than the Americans, one step back from a total alert."

"Comrade Gorbachev's still in the Kremlin?"

"He's remaining at home."

"But . . ."

"There's to be no panic. We've got twelve hours before Bush makes his decision. And when he does, we'll know."

"But it's SIOP 6, sir. A decapitating attack on our leadership. To take out our entire civilian and military command structure. The target is Moscow, damnit."

"Comrade Gorbachev knows the implications of SIOP 6," the Chairman said.

Poluchkin persisted, "All it'll take is just one of the Trident submarines they've got on station in the Barents Sea. Just one, that's all, and we'll have 288 one-hundred-megaton warheads right on top of us. In less than five minutes from launch. That's not enough time to evacuate the President and the Politburo."

"They have to go to DEFCON 2 first, General. And even if they do, it's no certainty of an attack. They've gone to DEFCON 2 four times before—and pulled back each time because we held off."

"No, they've never fired, thank God," Poluchkin said hoarsely. "But it's almost twenty years, the Yom Kippur War, since they last went that far."

The Chairman said, "Nor did the Americans go to full alert when we did in 1982 over Poland. They are as conscious as we are, General, that simultaneous full alerts for our strategic nuclear forces are tantamount to a mutual declaration of war."

"But it's different this time," Poluchkin said. "This time they've sent an assassin to kill Comrade Gorbachev. That's why they're priming the President to order SIOP 6."

One of Squirrel's greatest coups had been in sending over the American nuclear-war fighting plans, the Single Integrated Operational

Plan. SIOP 6, one of the options, was designed to react to an emergency in the Kremlin, a limited nuclear attack to destroy a chaotic, unstable, and thus—from the American viewpoint—dangerous Soviet leadership. The SIOP 6 aim was to take out the Soviet High Command before the Marshals, fearing the Americans would take advantage of the vacuum in the Kremlin, could launch a preemptive strike on the United States to forestall an American preemptive strike on the Soviet Union. It was so grotesque as to be almost beyond belief. But it was true.

"It's obvious President Bush is being advised by the cadre that sent the Italian to kill Comrade Gorbachev," Poluchkin insisted. "That's their plan—to kill him and make it look like a Kremlin coup. To create the conditions for SIOP 6."

"You believe Bush is involved?"

"Not Bush," Poluchkin said. "If he was involved he would have gone to DEFCON 2 when they wanted it." He saw it clearly. "The assassin's going to strike within the next twelve hours. That's the time frame they've given the President for a Kremlin coup."

"Twelve hours," the Chairman exclaimed. "But where? When?"

"I can tell you exactly," Poluchkin said, absolutely sure now. "At 8:35, when Comrade Gorbachev leaves No. 26 Kutuzov as he does every morning, six days a week. It's the only time in the next twelve hours when he'll be exposed."

Poluchkin felt a surge of relief. This was a problem he could grapple with. The Italian was someone he could combat. This was on a human scale. It gave his brain an escape from the fear of the mad inhumanity, the inhuman madness, of nuclear war, which was something beyond conception, beyond reckoning.

"We should move him now," he said, barking it, an order. The Chairman blinked in surprise and, then, in admiration. Poluchkin was an old man, but still a warrior. Ready to fight, to shove his weight around, for what he thought was right.

"You're right, General." The Chairman reached for the *kremlevka*. While he spoke to the President, Poluchkin remembered with a jolt that the Minister for Defense, Marshal I. T. Batrakov, was one of the anti-Gorbachev plotters who had been arrested that night. The Soviet forces were without their leader.

The Chairman was pale when he put down the red telephone. He said grimly, "Comrade Gorbachev's staying put. He says these are dangerous times. For all of us."

For all mankind, Poluchkin thought. It was what the VFP manifestos said.

For all the innocents!

41.

The telephone woke Klimenti at 6:47 A.M. He sat up, feeling wretched, his mouth sour from the vodka.

"Yes," he croaked.

"Colonel! That you, Colonel?"

He did not recognize the voice. "Who's calling?"

"It's you all right, Colonel. You guys, you're so used to pushing people around, you've got your own way of talking. How's the lady with the nice tits?"

Big Dog! He was alive. Radchenko's men hadn't taken him. He had made his run and got through.

"How's the weather in West Germany?"

Big Dog laughed. "Not as hot as it was in Moscow, I tell you, Colonel. I got your message. Thanks. You're full of surprises."

He had taken the money and told his grandmother to forget about phoning Klimenti. Well, who could blame him under the circumstances? It was exactly what Klimenti would have done.

"How'd you leave the apartment?"

"No deal, Colonel."

"You owe me."

"Yeah, that's true. You and the lady with the nice tits. That's why I'm making this call. One day I'll do something for her too. I pay off. I don't owe."

"Where's the Ferret?"

"Watch it. No names. They listen in."

"I want him. He killed one of our men."

He heard the hiss of Big Dog's breath. He hadn't known.

"You stick with him, he'll kill you too."

"I told you before, Colonel. I'm no *stukach*. No deals on old mates."

"He's no mate. Listen, no one's after you. It's the Ferret we want and we'll get him, no matter where he goes. You do the right thing and we'll forget all about you. But if you don't help us, we'll have to come for you, too."

There was silence.

"How's the shoulder?" Klimenti asked, reminding him of his debt.

Big Dog said, "Colonel, it's not going to work with me. I've got something to tell you, and then we're square."

"We'll come after you, Big Dog."

"Shut up or I'll hang up."

He was indeed no *stukach*. Here was one Russian, a petty criminal, who was not an informer.

"I mean it."

"I believe you."

"OK, listen. A couple of weeks ago we brought in a shipment. From Stuttgart. It's the same old racket. Voentorg buys the stuff brand new in the West, writes it off as damaged stock, and sells it at cut prices to their buddies in the General Staff. This was a truckload of furniture listed as Defense Department office material. No customs checks. That's how we brought in the other stuff. It's a breeze." He laughed derisively. "Shit, and they call *us* crooks. I tell you, it's a fucking insult."

"Stick to the point."

"Yeah. Listen. There were two crates that weren't for the generals. Heavy stuff too. It was the first drop, at a disused garage in Moscow. I knew the address. You see, a week earlier, I'd stolen a Zil and stashed it there for safekeeping."

"A Zil!"

"That's right! A beautiful piece of work. The motor's so quiet you could hardly hear it—and it had enough power to drive a tank. It was only two years old, a 'phantom' that fell off a factory production line."

"Who'd you steal it for?"

"Who else do I work for?"

"What'd the Ferret want with a Zil? They'd throw him into Lefortovo."

"It wasn't for the Ferret, was it? He was paid to get it."

"Who?"

"Shit, Colonel, what do you expect? He didn't say. I didn't ask. He told me where it was kept and I went along with a jimmy one night and opened it up and drove it out and took it to this garage. It was as easy as that. A week later, when we dropped off the crates, it was still there."

"Where?"

"Studencheskaya. In Kievskaya Ulitsa, not far from the Metro. Right opposite the electricity substation. You can't miss it."

Klimenti wrote it down.

"There's more. I got the Zil's registration. MOA 715."

Klimenti repeated it and wrote it down.

"We're square, Colonel. I've paid off."

"Big Dog, wait."

"Give my regards to the lady with the nice tits."

"Big Dog, listen!"

"I've said all I'm going to say."

"We're coming for the Ferret and that means we'll be coming for you, too. Unless you cooperate."

"This is the West, Colonel. This is freedom. You can't operate here like you do back home. Here, it's different."

"Don't you believe it."

"Shit. It'd better be different."

There was a click as he put down the phone.

By the time Klimenti arrived at Studencheskaya, Major Kharkov had already taken a team into the garage and found it empty. With this, Klimenti's suspicion that Radchenko was running the VFP finally collapsed. This was the perfect time for Radchenko to pull the Italian out of his hat. But he was gone, and there was no mistaking the grim disappointment on Radchenko's face as he stood by a Chaika with Nikishov.

"He was here all right and not so long ago," Radchenko said. "There are Zil tire marks in the snow."

Nikishov said, "The Zil's a high-profile trap, easy to identify."

Radchenko said, "He thinks he's safe. He's going to go ahead as planned. He's going to drive that Zil right into our hands."

"If anyone approaches him, he'll self-destruct," said Klimenti.

"That's the difficulty. Taking him alive."

Nikishov said, "We need the Italian, General. So we can shove him down the Americans' neck."

"Our first consideration is the safety of Comrade Gorbachev." Radchenko was the only person among them who knew about the crisis with the Americans. If the Italian was successful and killed Gorbachev, the missiles would start flying.

Radchenko instructed Major Kharkov to drive them to Kutuzov. He had been warned by Poluchkin of the likely time and place and already had two squads of his toughest Guards disguised in street clothes and in place, one at KGB Headquarters and the other at the Kutuzov Militia station, which was closer to the President's apartment. On the radio he went over his instructions one more time. No one was to directly approach the Zil containing the Italian. The nearest squad was to proceed immediately to the location of the Zil and was to take up positions where they could keep it under close observation. No attempt was to be made to arrest the Italian until General Radchenko had taken direct command.

"We believe the Zil is packed with explosives. We know the driver is wired to self-destruct and will do so to prevent capture. So surprise must be total. There must be no attempt to clear civilians from the vicinity," Radchenko ordered. "This will only arouse the Italian's suspicions. Everything must be done to convince him he is in the clear, that everything around him is normal."

Klimenti sucked in his breath. A nervous tic quivered across Nikishov's face. Radchenko's expression was stern and forbidding, a face set for terrible orders. "I repeat, no attempt is to be made to warn civilians or to remove them from the vicinity."

Kharkov drove with skill and speed, inspired by his general's calmness.

Klimenti could sense the Italian out there, waiting, all alone, a very special man. He wanted very much to take the Italian alive, and it wasn't only because he would prove the case against the Americans. Klimenti wanted to talk with him, to know him better.

It was 7:50 A.M. when the Chaika drove into the garage beneath No. 26 Kutuzov Prospekt. Radchenko voiced everyone's thoughts. "I didn't see any Zil," he said, frowning. "Damn. Where is he?"

It was the first and only sign of nervousness.

Another Chaika sped into the garage and braked to a halt by the elevator doors. A bodyguard leaped out and opened the rear door for Deputy Chairman Poluchkin, who limped hurriedly across, dragging his war leg. "Tass just came through with a special bulletin from Washington," Poluchkin gasped. His face was flushed, his afflicted eye bulged hideously behind its lens. He had not had time to don his eye patch. The veins in his face pulsed.

"They killed the Secretary of Defense. An hour ago."

Radchenko could not believe it. The breath hissed through Nikishov's teeth. Klimenti felt his heart had stopped beating.

"Who? How?" Radchenko barked, urgent, angry, and afraid.

"The assassin self-destructed." Poluchkin's voice was as ravaged as his face. He was convinced that a nuclear war was only minutes away and he felt in the grip of a paralyzing terror that comes not from personal fear, but from a sense of horror. Perhaps the missiles were already in the air.

"The Vigilantes for Peace," Klimenti said. His heart was thumping now. He wanted to shout it. "It's the VFP."

"It has to be," Nikishov shouted.

"The Defense Secretary," Radchenko echoed, still unable to believe it.

"It's not the Americans," Klimenti said, and his companions knew he spoke the truth.

42.

O n his last morning in Moscow, Leonardo began to understand his hostility to the light. In Rome he had become accustomed to a light so clear and sharp it leaped into dark spaces with intrusive force. The contrast of light and darkness was strong and dramatic, a clash of wills that gave clear definitions unmistakable in their character, the hot sun to walk and laugh in, the cool shade to sit and reflect, the secret dark for loving.

But here, in Moscow, it was different. This light cast no shadows; it was full of shadow itself. It did not declare itself honestly but was full of murky deceit, a light sly with distrust. It had no definition, it penetrated nowhere. Instead, it seeped and oozed, a slime of light.

With such a light weighing down the people, Leonardo thought, repression was easy. He was parked in a courtyard that gave him a clear view across the twelve-lane highway to No. 26. He had to fill up half an hour. There was nothing he could do to escape idleness, no way he could squander time so that it would pass quickly. He had to sit it out, his senses alive as they had never been before. It was to this test that all his training had been directed. Time, and all that it could wreak in him, was the enemy, filling him with such an intensity of awareness that he felt his whole being prickling with it, electricity in his fingertips.

He was sweating profusely. He could actually feel his pores

opening and letting out the sweat. He had never felt that before. The suit of plastic explosive had begun to weigh on him, pressing into his flesh, like a scab on a wound. He lowered the side window and felt the cold on his eyes, surprised at how hot they were.

A man walked out of No. 26. Leonardo tensed. The man turned right and began walking. He was alone. There would be two bodyguards. It wasn't the target. It was too early.

The glass jar with the two bare twigs was still on its balcony but this morning they seemed more forlorn than hopeful. Thinking about this, Leonardo felt the beginnings of an almost forgotten need.

Three couples left No. 26, all of them elderly. Two young nannies emerged, pushing prams, the servants of the rich.

Leonardo began counting the electric trolley buses but found he couldn't remember the count, his mind afire with an old impatience.

Two girls skipped across his line of vision, holding hands, eyes flashing, talking all the time, their young spirits so animated he could feel it, and he felt like shouting out his thankfulness at this rebirth.

It had been so long, a dead time so deep he thought he had lost it forever. But now it was coming back, a beloved hunger, a peculiar and urgent flow of consciousness, which had always been part of him, the best part, seeing things not just as they were but as he absorbed them: the people in the train last night, his living river; and the little girls dancing, as bright and as fresh as rain droplets in the sun; and the sly and murky light, so full of deceit and decay. All of it was within him and building up pressure, needing its release.

A Chaika went past on the other side of Kutuzov, going quickly. Leonardo almost missed it.

Sometimes the process took only minutes, quick molten lava, but more often it took time and pain, wandering restlessly and without sight, looking only inward. More often than he wished to remember, he failed, and the truth shriveled and howled within, a piteous and bitter dying.

It was then that he drank and, in the end, there had been a lot of drinking.

Now, with his time going fast, he was sure he had the strength to take it all the way. *He knew it.*

Leonardo patted and pressed at his clothing. But he had no paper, no pen; he who had always carried them. He leaned across and opened the glove compartment, searching within, his fingers growing desperate in the emptiness. There was nothing. Control had stripped the Zil.

No! After all the dead years, he could not be cheated now. No!

His hands beat at the steering wheel in frustration.

Across Kutuzov, a couple with a young child came out of No. 26, a family venturing out together. The child was a boy about seven, and he gathered snow into his mittens and hurled it at his father, who grabbed him and swung him in the air. The woman laughed and hugged her husband's arm—an act of possession, content with her men—and they walked arm in arm until they went out of Leonardo's line of sight.

Leonardo rested his arms and head on the steering wheel, his eyes shut, full of despair. He had found himself again; all that had withered within was germinating again; he could feel it growing inside. He was sure he had the strength this time to survive.

He did not have to die!

It was a physical shock, jolting him upright.

He could live!

Oh God! Oh God!

Across Kutuzov, a man stepped out of No. 26 and stood surveying the broad avenue in both directions. Satisfied, he tapped the double oak doors, a signal. Two more men exited. They turned left and began walking. They were a minute early.

Get the transmitter.

But Leonardo's hands were locked onto the steering wheel. He could not break them free. His hands wanted to live, to write again. And he could do it. He did not have to die.

The three men were walking slowly, stamping down on the snow to make sure of their grip on the pavement. The man in the middle was heavier than his bodyguards, and even though he was engulfed in an overcoat and fur hat, there was no mistaking the aura of authority he carried, a man sure of himself.

Move!

If he lived, he could write it all, about his wife and his son and his daughter. He could give them life again, the lives he had taken away. There was so much to put down, of love and grief and redemption; it was all in him, as much of him as his heart beat, thumping inside, and he knew he could get it out.

Start the engine. Go!

His hands would not let go. Were they defying him? Or was he willing them to hold on, to give him back his poetry?

Across Kutuzov, the three men walked out of his view.

They were gone. He would live!

In that moment, Leonardo became calm. He had been seduced by the same selfish conceit that had destroyed him once before. The sting of your grief is guilt, they had told him. You must first empty yourself of guilt, so you can come to terms with your grief, and then you can direct yourself usefully; and they had helped him do this. But they had not warned him against his conceit, which, unburdened of guilt, had resurrected itself.

His hands released from the steering wheel, letting him go.

Leonardo placed the mouthguard in his mouth. He pulled on the heavy mittens. He put on his helmet. He drove out from under the archway and into Kutuzov, turning right with the traffic flow.

At first, he could not see them and he swore foully, cursing himself and his cowardice. He swerved the Zil over to the center lane, heedless of the traffic rushing down on him, anxiously searching the footpath opposite so intently that he did not see the yellow trolley bus until the Zil was directly in front of it, cutting across its path. The bus driver swerved violently and stamped on his brakes, slewing the bus broadside across the avenue as the wheels locked on the slippery surface.

In his elevated command post across Kutuzov, a Militia sergeant heard the screech of skidding tires and turned in time to see the Zil dart in front of the swerving bus, a miraculous escape. He swore. Those arrogant bastards thought they owned the roads. And then he remembered the orders to check the registrations of all Zils.

The big car was opposite him now, back under control. As the Zil passed he read the rear plate, MOA 715, the number he was watching for. In that instant of recognition, he also saw what was wrong about the chauffeur.

He was wearing a motorcyclist's helmet.

The sergeant grabbed the telephone.

Leonardo saw the family of three first, the boy in between the parents now, swinging on their hands like a little monkey, and then he saw the men he was searching for. They had passed the family and were walking quickly ahead.

Leonardo wished they would walk a little faster, to put more distance between them and the family. He slowed the Zil, to give them more time. I don't want to hurt them, he thought. Not a family. Not a child.

One of the bodyguards stopped and turned, staring at the Zil. He had a transceiver held to his ear and he went into a crouch, like a fighter, and there was no mistaking the alarm in his posture. He was only fifty meters away. He shouted something and his companions turned and stared at the Zil, too.

They knew!

The bodyguards grabbed the short man and began running, their feet slipping as they dragged him along.

Leonardo pumped hard on the accelerator and the heavy car slewed sideways as its wheels spun. But the tires got enough grip to surge the Zil forward and Leonardo swung it across the oncoming traffic, missing a Volga by inches. The bodyguards must have heard the noise of the onrushing car because one of them turned, holding a pistol two-handedly, his legs apart, bracing himself, firing while his companion dragged the short man along the footpath, searching for a doorway.

The family turned, gaping in astonishment, the child terrified by the shriek of the Zil's tires, which were spewing out black smoke from the scalded rubber. They were close, too close, but Leonardo was committed now and the bullets were striking into the bulletproof window, plop, plop, plop, opening little star-edged holes in the outer layer, plop, plop, plop, and falling harmlessly onto the hood, and then Leonardo was past the bodyguard with the gun and the Zil jolted as he took it up onto the footpath, getting inside the oaks that lined the curb, and the two men running knew they had lost the race and turned and saw him coming onto them and screamed.

Leonardo ran them down when they were only three meters from the doorway. He didn't see them go under the Zil because the moment before he struck, he took his hands from the steering wheel and reached for the transmitter and felt the impact as they hit and heard them cry out and he threw the switch, thinking, God, I'm sorry about the family, and the Zil hit the building wall and scraped along it and into the doorway.

Leonardo was hurled against the seat-belt straps.

He was still alive.

The Zil, his suit of plastic, had not exploded. The transmitter hadn't worked.

Frantically, Leonardo flicked the switch. Then again. Nothing. He could feel the Zil shuddering from the impact.

"No," he screamed. "No."

The bodyguard who had fired at him was beating at the window with his pistol, trying to break through the bulletproof glass. His face was contorted with the effort. And fear. And rage.

Desperately, Leonardo flicked the switch again. It didn't work.

The bodyguard banged a clip into his pistol and began firing into the metal of the door lock.

Leonardo stared at him helplessly.

The pistol shots were deafening. The bodyguard wrenched the door open and hurled himself into the Zil. Leonardo struck for his face but he was held back by the seat belt and landed only a glancing blow. The bodyguard punched him brutally, snarling, a beast of fear.

"No," Leonardo screamed. "No."

A block away, standing at the base of the massive Hero City of Moscow obelisk, Control took a UHF radio transmitter from his pocket and switched it on.

The Zil exploded.

PART II

—

ROME

PART II

ROME

1.

Two young women spurted across the square on a Vespa motor-scooter, their dark eyes flashing audaciously at Kharkov, who smiled wistfully and sighed, touchingly woebegone. After a week in the Roman winter sun, his skin was already darkening; this heightened his blond Slavic handsomeness and pale eyes and drew beckoning glances from the women. Alas, Kharkov was forbidden to respond and the men, seeing this and wrongly suspecting his motive, pursued him with unblushing ardor, accustomed to rich pickings among the Germans and Scandinavians who migrated south every spring and summer. Klimenti laughed to himself and Kharkov, sensing mockery, cast him an angry look. Klimenti, however, shrugged—too bad!—and Kharkov saw he meant it in sympathy.

Levitin from the embassy said, "He's late."

He had been saying it for the last half hour and was now becoming anxious that he would be taken for a fool or, worse, a fraud, by the colonel from Moscow with the ugly scar slashing into his face. Levitin was young. Rome was his first foreign posting and he dreaded the thought of a transfer back to Moscow in disgrace.

Although it was still winter, the temperature had hovered around eighteen degrees celsius and, even though the day was cooling, the skies were a clear and friendly blue. It was very pleasant sitting outside the *ristorante* in the waning sun, sipping strong Italian coffee, black *espresso* in tiny cups, and watching at arm's length the boisterous bustle of the Piazza Campo dei Fiori market as it closed down for the day.

The air was heavy with the smell of fresh fish and cheeses and salamis and smoked hams; the stalls had been heaped with blood oranges, mushrooms, zucchini, eggplant, asparagus, and lush green and red peppers; they were green with salad vegetables and crimson with tomatoes; herbs hung in tangy bunches. On one side of the square was a baker, from whose shop wafted the seductive smell of hot bread. The variety, the richness and careless abundance, the sheer weight of it, was more than enough to drive a Moscow housewife crazy with excitement.

And the noise! After the frozen muteness of Moscow, Klimenti welcomed the cacophony. If Moscow was like a tomb, then Rome was like a shrill brass band: drums beating, cymbals clashing; the traffic noise coming at you like the throb of a tuba shredded by wild trumpet bursts of sirens and the shrill clarinet screeches of braking tires; none of it in control, the conductor blind and deaf and demented and the orchestra and the audience beyond restraint, overflowing and invading each other, full of argument and pique and sudden flashes of laughter— teeth flashing, eyes flashing, hands flashing, their bodies alive to the music and soul of their city.

Contradicting all this liveliness, the fifteenth-century *palazzi* surrounding the square were surprisingly drab, age- and sun-worn brick— shit brown, Klimenti thought. There was something secretive in the way they hung over the square and the narrow cobbled lanes that twisted among them, shaded arteries echoing with the city's lifeblood of humanity. The ground floors had been turned over to merchants and butchers and bakers and restaurants and *hosterias* and the upper floors had been converted into apartments. What went on behind the heavy shutters was no doubt very ordinary indeed, but the wooden slats brought a sense of concealment and mystery that, since it was difficult to imagine anything sinister or threatening in such friendly sunlight, was delicious to consider. Sometimes, however, the shutters reminded Klimenti of Poluchkin's eye patch, hiding wounds perhaps.

"He comes every day for coffee," Levitin said, repeating himself.

In the center of the piazza, the somber and cowled statue of the Copernican philosopher Giordano Bruno gazed solemnly down from the very place where he had been burned at the stake in 1600 for advocating that the sun, not the earth, was the center of the universe. Here, in the Field of Flowers, many freethinkers had perished in flames that consumed their mortal flesh but not their heresies, which had survived to win recognition in a more enlightened age of science. It was here, on the immortal Bruno's granite plinth, that the first posters had been pasted that very morning, proclaiming two new martyrs.

In huge print, the posters were headed:

I MARTIRI DI MOSCA

The Moscow Martyrs! Directly beneath were the faces of Leonardo and of Gerald. Lysenko's assassin had been identified by the British as an English nuclear physicist, Warwick Edward Montgomery. The likenesses had been reproduced from the Soviet visa photographs, which had been released in the media around the world in an effort to track down their movements in the last six months of their lives. Below the photographs was the proclamation:

Condannate i Colpevoli!
Salvate gli Innocenti!
Disarmate!

Levitin translated. Condemn the Guilty! Save the Innocents! Disarm! It was signed "Rome Action Committee," one of many similar groups formed in cities around the world, usually—as was the case in Rome—as offshoots of already established disarmament organizations. It was still considered too dangerous to support the VFP directly but it said a lot for the effectiveness of the VFP campaign that no other message was necessary. In the streets today there was hardly anyone who was not aware of the Vigilantes for Peace, what they had done and why they were doing it.

In the three weeks since the killing of the American Secretary of Defense and his Soviet counterpart, Marshal Illarion Trivonovich Batrakov, the VFP had scored their greatest propaganda triumph by releasing information to the world media on the DEFCON crisis, which for fifteen hours had brought the Soviet Union and the United States to the brink of nuclear war.

The VFP manifesto had been particularly damning:

The crisis once again establishes beyond doubt that the leaders of the United States and the Soviet Union are surrounded by advisers who are warped by outdated and crippling attitudes of mutual belligerence and distrust, men whose irrational hatreds and insane jealousies have propagated criminal philosophies such as Mutually Assured Destruction, the deathly shadow of Nuclear Winter. Once again, these criminal hypocrites have shown that in the pursuit of their own short-term self-interests they are prepared to ruthlessly risk the destruction of all living kind. The full measure of their cowardly deceit is that they constitute the privileged few who are guaranteed to survive the nuclear devastation they will release *without warning*. They will not pay the price of their betrayal. You will. It is essential for the survival of the Planet Earth that these criminals be replaced by men and women of goodwill who are armed with moral courage to negotiate real disarmanent.

It is just that the guilty few die so that all the innocents may live.

The manifesto had been repeated in newspapers, on radio, and on television in almost every language in every country in the world, reaching an audience of billions.

"He's here," Levitin said, sweating his relief. "At the flower stall."

He did not indicate his quarry. It was not necessary, for the young man's beauty made him conspicuous among the rough, weathered faces of the market crowd. Already two Swedish girls shopping indolently at the adjacent olive seller were eyeing him greedily. He ignored them with such a grand arrogance that it only served to fire their interest, as he knew it would.

"A lousy gigolo," Levitin hissed. He was jealous. The Swedish girls were shapely and promised much.

He was dark even for a Roman and, in a country of small people, was strongly built, well muscled without the unsightly exaggeration of iron-pumping body builders. He dressed simply: well-washed jeans, leather casual shoes, a soft leather jacket over a white shirt, open to expose his chest. He wore lots of gold. His hair was thick and long and combed back like an ancient heathen warrior's, falling around his ears and still damp from the shower. The morning, Levitin had reported, was for sleeping. He ate breakfast when others went to lunch; the afternoons were for leisure and the nights for working. Gigolo was the wrong word. He was a male homosexual prostitute. The Swedish girls were wasting their time, as they soon realized. They shrugged and moved on; it was a small defeat, for Rome was full of young men ready to answer their call. The fair Northerners came seeking dark princes and settled for pallid waiters.

Tarabrin, puny and pale, starved, a sparrow beating against its cage, must have been a pushover for this young sex hawk. Klimenti wondered if the Roman was aware he carried the deadly AIDS virus and was doomed.

The Roman's dark eyes lingered on Kharkov, caressing, questing, promising, and Kharkov turned to stone, his cheeks reddening, and the Roman saw his anger and laughed; but there was also regret in it for Kharkov was beautiful, too, and the Roman had his weaknesses. He sat at a nearby table and ordered *espresso* and pretended to ignore Kharkov, whose pale eyes blazed. For all his toughness and confidence, Kharkov had little experience with blatant male coquetry and it savaged his young manly pride.

"Shit shover," he muttered in Russian, and Klimenti realized he would have to be careful not to let Kharkov take the Roman by himself. They wanted him in good health.

"Thank you, *signore*," Klimenti said to the waiter in his best American. "Your coffee is great. Just great."

"*Certo*," the waiter replied with disdain. *Cretino!* Of course his coffee was excellent.

They walked out of the square, going away from the side the Roman had come from. They came into the Piazza Farnese and the huge *palazzo* from which it took its name. Here they parted, Levitin going to get the Lancia they had parked a block away while Klimenti and Kharkov walked quickly to the via Monserato and stopped at an alley which cut across it. It was only four meters wide and the houses rose steeply on both sides, giving the impression of a small cobbled canyon.

"He lives in No. 27, third house on the left, a room on the top floor," Levitin had reported. He had been following the Roman for three days.

Klimenti and Kharkov went into a small delicatessen and stood at the counter, drinking yet another coffee. They remained there until the Roman walked past and turned into the alley. He was home. Already night was encroaching, the temperature was dropping quickly, and the street was emptying. Levitin drove up in the Lancia and parked it so that they could see into the alley.

Kharkov was a little keyed up. He had no doubt he could do what was expected of him—cosh the Roman unconscious when he came out again. Even so, this was his first go at the real thing. Deep breathing would ease the tension but he couldn't do it without the others noticing and knowing the reason. Levitin was clasping the steering wheel so hard the blood was squeezed out of his fingers, using the wheel as a counterpoise, straining his arm, shoulder, chest, and gut muscles to rip out the tension. Levitin was better trained than he had suspected.

Klimenti was also experiencing some anxiety, although for entirely different reasons. It was fast approaching seven o'clock, when he should be in his hotel room, waiting for the telephone to ring. Once he had initiated the contact, it was essential he maintain the watches. It would be harsh fate indeed if tonight of all nights Squirrel rang. But he had no choice. He had to see this operation through.

The turd stirrer won't know what hit him, Kharkov thought with satisfaction.

A pale blue Alfa 90 Super pulled across the mouth of the alley, blocking it. The headlights went out. They could see the silhouettes of four men seated inside.

"*Carabinieri*." Levitin cursed.

"Quickly," Klimenti ordered, his hand out to Kharkov. "Your pistol."

Three men got out of the sleek Alfa. None of them wore a uniform. They were not *carabinieri*, the paramilitary police. Nor were they from the Polizia di Stato, the national police.

Klimenti took Kharkov's weapon and dropped it into a camera bag, along with his own pistol. Kharkov also passed across a heavy rubber sap. Klimenti locked the bag and passed it over to Levitin.

"It's yours," he said and told Kharkov, "Stay put."

He got out of the car as the three men walked up.

"*Buona sera, Commissario Capo*," he greeted the leader, a round-shaped man of about forty. He was Alberto Spina and officially he held the equivalent rank of colonel in the Italian antiterrorist police, DIGOS, the Direttorato per le Investigazioni Generali e per le Operazioni Speciali, which was leading the hunt for the VFP in Italy. The ranking KGB officer in the Soviet Embassy had assured Klimenti, however, that Spina was in reality an agent for Italian counterintelligence, SISDE, the Servizio per le Informazioni e la Sicurezza Democratica. Spina had been seconded to liaise with the KGB and the CIA and he and Klimenti had already met twice.

"Might I inquire what you and your men are doing here, Colonel?" Spina asked in English. He spoke with exaggerated politeness. His fat-cheeked, good-natured face concealed a quick and dangerous brain.

"Sightseeing," Klimenti said.

"No doubt," Spina said blandly. "It's an interesting quarter."

One of his men went to the door of No. 27 and pressed the buzzer for the top-floor apartment. The name listed against the buzzer was G. Salvatore.

They had been exposed. Spina knew about the Roman, too. But how? The Lancia rocked as Levitin and Kharkov moved inside. They too had realized what was happening and were getting ready for trouble. It occurred to Klimenti that it was a setup, that Spina—an Italian version of Nikishov—had sent the Roman to embarrass them.

"There's no answer," the Italian at the door said.

That surprised Klimenti. The Roman definitely hadn't left the building. Perhaps there was a rear exit Levitin had missed. In that case, they were off the hook.

"Try them all," Spina ordered and the Italian began pressing all the buzzers.

"Please ask your men to step out of the car," Spina ordered.

"For what purpose?" Klimenti asked politely.

"Sightseeing," Spina said testily.

The playacting was over. Klimenti beckoned to Kharkov to get out.

"The driver, too, please."

"He's an embassy chauffeur," Klimenti said, his tone implying, *that's all*.

"I'd still like him to get out of the car."

"Will you please step out, driver," Klimenti ordered.

Levitin slid across the seat and stepped out, holding the camera bag.

"Any objections if I look inside?" Spina said, indicating the bag.

"It's not for me to say," Klimenti said. "It's the chauffeur's personal property."

"He has diplomatic immunity, no doubt."

"Of course."

"In that case he can prove it," Spina said, extending his hand to Levitin, who had his embassy identification card ready. Spina inspected it and, satisfied, handed it back. Levitin remained silent, stiffly at attention, playing the role of lowly chauffeur perfectly. It was, in fact, the occupation that was marked down on his diplomatic pass.

"*Chi e?*," a woman's voice squawked over the intercom. "Who is it?"

"*Carabinieri*," the Italian lied. "Please open the door."

"The *carabinieri*! *Madre di Dio. Non ho fatto niente*." The woman was horrified. Mother of God. I've done nothing.

"It's an emergency. Open the door immediately."

There was a long buzz and a click as the locks opened. Spina's lieutenant drew a pistol as he went in.

"I'd like you to accompany us," Spina said, indicating Klimenti and Kharkov.

The door led into a small courtyard, the flagstones worn smooth over the centuries. The stairs were narrow. Although they were whitewashed to give light the walls smelled of damp and rot. As they went up, eyes peered at them through peepholes in doors. The Roman's door was not locked. His room was a garret with the sloping roof forming part of the walls.

The Italian stopped, sniffing the air. He turned to Spina, his face pale. Klimenti caught the smell too, a warm, sickly rich aroma that made his stomach feel instantly queasy.

"*Mannaggia*," Spina cursed. Damn! He drew his pistol. Kharkov and the Italian agent went in first.

The blood was fresh and had not yet congealed although it was already darkening. It covered most of the floor. Spina and Klimenti stopped at the threshold because it was not possible to go any further without stepping into the sticky ooze. The light was on. The Roman lay sprawled face down on his bed, naked, his dark eyes turned to them, sightless now, revealing the dreadful wound.

"*Gesù Cristo!*" Spina turned around and leaned against the door. The Italian pushed past them and went outside. The blood drained from Kharkov's face. He gagged and it took a supreme effort not to join the Italian on the stairs. The smell was as thick as the ooze on the floor, suffocating him.

He had never before seen a man with his throat cut. The ugly gash, black now, went almost from ear to ear. The human body contained five liters of blood, and whoever had killed the Roman had done it so he would bleed himself empty.

"Shut the door," Spina ordered. "Get out of here."

They went down the stairs quietly, careful not to draw the same attention they had received on the way up, fleeing the warm, rich stench of blood. As they came into the lane, they gratefully sucked in lungfuls of exhaust-polluted air and spat.

"*Cazzo!*" the Italian muttered and sagged against the wall. Fuck!

Levitin regarded them with amazement and asked in Russian, "What's wrong? What's going on?"

"Later," Klimenti snapped. "I'll go with you," he told Spina, and ordered Kharkov and Levitin: "Disappear."

There was no argument. Kharkov understood the situation perfectly.

The Alfa was a high-performance car and it darted through the traffic with the swiftness of a dragonfly. Quickly they were into via Nazionale, turning off for via San Vitale and into a narrow cobbled lane that led beneath an arch into the Questura, the fortresslike headquarters of DIGOS. Spina showed his pass to a guard armed with a machine pistol, who waved them into the central courtyard.

The Questura shone with polished floors; its wood paneling was scarred, its flagstones worn. Spina took Klimenti to an unmarked office on the second floor. It contained only a desk, a telephone, and several chairs. The only paper in sight was a large pad on the desk. There was nothing else, not even a wall calendar. Spina was making sure Klimenti learned absolutely nothing about his operation.

The smell of blood was still with them, like a fog, permeating their clothing, clinging, cloying.

Spina said, "You were breaking the rules tonight, Colonel. If I want to push this, I could get you kicked straight back to Moscow." He shrugged eloquently. What else could you expect from the KGB? He was not happy about holding hands with his accustomed enemy. "If you'd kept our agreement and come to us with your information about Salvatore, he might still be alive—and of some use."

Klimenti said, "We were afraid it was a trap. We had to be sure SISDE weren't up to their old tricks, trying to make fools of us."

"I assure you, Colonel, it was nothing of the kind."

"And I assure you equally, Commissario Capo, that you can't give that guarantee, not unless SISDE have suddenly taken to revealing their hand to you personally."

Spina was caught in his own web. He could not pursue it further without virtually admitting he was a SISDE agent. He scowled. "You've agreed to cooperate, Colonel. I suggest you start."

Klimenti nodded. "On the Saturday night preceding the assassination of Comrade Lysenko, Salvatore approached two *Pravda* correspondents and told them he was willing to sell them a story about a sensational scandal in the Soviet Embassy. The approach was made in a bar and they were a little drunk. When they pressed him for more information, he refused. All he would tell them was that it involved homosexuals. He hinted at blackmail but refused to tell them any more. Unless they paid for it."

"How much?"

"Half a million dollars."

"He had nerve, this Salvatore."

"When they heard the figure, they became convinced he was just another boastful homosexual trying to give himself an exotic and glamorous image. Even so, the *Pravda* men reported the approach. If Salvatore was telling the truth, it was a pretty serious situation. Unfortunately the figure of half a million dollars was considered so ridiculous that nothing was done."

This was a lie. The KGB had conducted an internal investigation that had revealed a host of sexual infidelities among the Soviet colony in Rome, but no homosexual adventures or affairs involving Italians. In the light of this information they came to the conclusion that Salvatore had been sent by SISDE and on the next approach would relent and name a KGB agent whom the Italians wanted to discredit. It was an old tactic—smear and innuendo, sowing distrust. It was decided to leave the next move to Salvatore.

The KGB's interest had been resurrected after Morozov revealed that Tarabrin had been caught in a raven trap in Rome. Suddenly Salvatore's boastful behavior took on a different significance. The *Pravda* men had been sent to reestablish contact while Levitin and other agents checked every aspect of Salvatore's background, seeking the hand of SISDE. The *Pravda* men had offered Salvatore five thousand American dollars as goodwill, provided he gave them more information that would help them to establish that he spoke the truth. Salvatore had been too clever to fall for this trap. He was aware that once he accepted the money, the KGB would force his hand by threatening to expose him as a Soviet spy. On one hand, if he was a SISDE agent, he was playing hard to get. On the other, he was obviously confident of the value of his wares.

"And tonight?" Spina asked.

"Tonight we were going to tell him we'd agreed to his price."

It was another lie. They were going to turn Salvatore over to Fadeyev, who was at this moment waiting in the Soviet compound with several of his experts from the SPHs. Klimenti was sure they included an acupuncturist. Whoever had killed Salvatore had done him a favor.

Spina said, "The VFP knew what he was up to. They probably saw him talking to the *Pravda* men. I'm surprised they didn't kill him earlier, when they had finished using him."

Klimenti said, "It wasn't necessary. They probably convinced Salvatore that he was working for SISDE. All he knew was that he was paid to snare a Russian homosexual."

"It's possible." Spina shrugged a lot, even for an Italian.

"How'd you find out?" Klimenti asked.

"We received a telephone call informing us that the Russians were about to kidnap an Italian citizen who could help us in our investigations. She gave us Salvatore's name and address. We went there immediately."

"The caller was a woman!"

Spina nodded. "You realize what the call means."

"Salvatore was already dead—and she knew it."

"They're playing with us," Spina growled. "Treating us like we're fools."

There was a knock on the door. Spina opened it to a tall man who moved with a graceful physical arrogance Klimenti would never forget. Klimenti had known this moment was inevitable; he had not, however, imagined the circumstances.

"Hello, Colonel," Bannon said, his hard cowboy face unsmiling.

2.

Lieutenant General Radchenko and Major General Nikishov arrived in Rome the next day to represent the KGB at a historic and unprecedented conference of intelligence chiefs to coordinate the global hunt for the VFP. Also attending were top-ranking officers from the CIA, the FBI, and the counterintelligence services and police antiterrorist forces of the United Kingdom, France, West Germany, Italy, Canada, Spain, Japan, India, Israel, Egypt, Holland, Belgium, Brazil, Argentina, Mexico, Australia, South Africa, and New Zealand. The only significant absentees were the Chinese and Iranians, both of whom refused to attend. The conference and its agenda were top secret.

Klimenti got Levitin to drive him to the Excelsior Hotel in the fashionable via Veneto opposite the American Embassy. Radchenko and Nikishov were staying at the hotel, posing as members of a delegation led by Oleg A. Byzov, deputy secretary of the Central Committee's Department of Foreign Affairs. Byzov's chief was one of the ten members of the Central Committee Secretariat, which met once a week with President Gorbachev to prepare policy options for the Politburo. He was an immensely influential bureaucrat.

On the way Klimenti read a letter addressed to him at the Soviet Embassy. With pleasure he had immediately recognized the bold scrawl:

299

Dearest Papa,

I miss you and Papasha does, too. Sabotka even, would you believe? He refers to you as the Man of Mystery and, for once, he isn't being sarcastic. I have to leave them to themselves during the day but I've been staying at Shabolovoka Street, Papasha's faithful servant every night and morning, although it takes some effort—he's so independent and accustomed to looking after himself. If I'm too attentive, Sabotka gets jealous and starts sulking, but it doesn't last long—he soon finds something else to vent his emotions on, especially since you gave him that damn radio. He's so wild and Papasha's so gentle and calm.

Wouldn't it be absolutely wonderful if we were all together right now? In Rome! Seeing the sights! Wouldn't it be something to share! Papasha says it's not what you see that counts but who you see it with, the memory is in the person, not the place, and he's right, of course. So I wish we were with you, to make our memories together, you and Papasha and I (Sabotka, too), drinking wine and eating exotic pasta and sitting in the sun. Ah well, perhaps one day! I'm fine and studying hard.

Love, Nadya.

The letter was breezy and quick, pure Nadya. There was no sense of hurt or heartbreak. Was it possible she was already over Bannon? That what she had experienced was infatuation, in love with the love affair and not Bannon himself? At first, she had suffered. For a week after Bannon's departure from Moscow they had hardly seen her; when they did she was sullen and quick-tempered. When she began reappearing she was quiet, very unNadya-like, and Klimenti's father had prowled around her like a mother cat, strangely aggressive, protecting her from intrusion. Klimenti, whose anxiety for Nadya was increased by his conflicting senses of guilt and relief at having got rid of Bannon, was content to step aside. He had even been glad to leave Moscow, knowing that she was beyond Bannon's reach and in good hands. He sensed from her letter that she was looking ahead, dreaming new dreams, a good sign.

Klimenti felt an unaccustomed sense of loneliness. His training, his discipline, his trade craft—but particularly the death of his wife—had made him an insular man. It made him a little frightened to find himself without his accustomed armor. He no longer felt secure.

They passed a bookshop that prominently displayed placards featuring the black-and-white visa photograph of Leonardo—to Klimenti that would always be his name—and proclaimed in blood-red print on black, *Il Poeta Assassino*, The Killer Poet. Klimenti got Levitin to stop, and they went into the shop. Even though Klimenti did not speak or read Italian he could not resist the impulse to buy a book. He felt he owed it to Leonardo.

The book was thin and ridiculously expensive; the publishers had rushed publication, confident that sensation would carry the market. It contained an eight-page biography of Leonardo, thirty-eight poems and a half dozen pages of photographs: Leonardo as a child with his parents; as a student; on his wedding day, the bride pretty and pale-skinned but thin for an Italian girl; Leonardo and his wife with their first baby, and then photographs of the children growing up. The photographs left Klimenti with a sense of dissatisfaction. They were amateurish, and in all of them Leonardo had the face of a totally unremarkable man, a face easily lost in a crowd or quickly forgotten if met alone. Not once did he show the haunting depth of sorrow and strength that Klimenti could not forget. It was only in his visa photograph, which had all the power of a death mask, that Klimenti could feel the soul of a poet, the essence of the man. All the other living masks were limp disguises.

"Ask him how it's selling," Klimenti told Levitin.

The bookseller was an elderly man, beautifully dressed in a suit with a hand-tied bow tie, a hangover from some distant generation. He responded to Levitin's question with an energy that belied his years.

"It's only the first day. But he says he's been in the trade a long time and it's got the smell of money all over it."

The old man's hands flew as quickly as his words, flicking the air.

"He has the face of a martyr. In the city of martyrs, how can such a book not sell?"

Klimenti wished Radchenko was there to hear the bookseller's words. They would drive him crazy. The thought gave Klimenti satisfaction and he smiled, encouraging the bookseller into a fresh outpouring.

Levitin translated, "The reviews of his work have been good. But, with apologies to the dead author, that means nothing. These days, you can count the people who read poetry on your penis." Levitin laughed at the old man's colorful terminology.

"The reason it'll do well is he's a poet, an assassin, and a martyr, all in one. Such combustion! The women won't be able to resist it."

The bookseller was enjoying his subject and his audience.

"He says he has a face to torment women with its promise of agony," Levitin said, blushing at the extravagance. In Italian it sounded right. In English it sounded false and affected.

"He's a very perceptive man," Klimenti said. "A poet himself, perhaps?"

Levitin translated. His Italian was surprisingly good, and the bookseller smiled and shrugged.

"He says he wishes it were true. There's a poet inside all of us, but we strangle him at birth because we're afraid of the truth he reveals to us. You need extraordinary courage, superhuman strength, to be a poet."

The bookseller was a small man with the face of a burnt chestnut, and Klimenti was sure he saw sadness in his eyes. Klimenti was surprised, and gratified, to hear him use the name Leonardo.

"He says this one, Leonardo, was lucky. *La sua morte fu il suo poema più grande*. His death was his greatest poem."

"He's right," Klimenti said and went out into the street. The old man had told him a lot about Leonardo and he was sure it was all true. He wondered what Fadeyev would make of the old man's words; Fadeyev, who was desperate to understand Leonardo so that he could re-create him for his own foul purposes. Klimenti would never tell Fadeyev about the old man or what he had said. It would be a violation.

"He's Italian," Levitin shrugged. But he too had caught some of the old man's mood and was quiet for the rest of the journey.

Montgomery, too, had become something of a cult hero. The VFP had capitalized on his identification by releasing to the media aspects of Montgomery's background that the intelligence services had suppressed. His background and the crisis that had brought him to the attention of the VFP ideally served their propaganda because Montgomery came from the high priesthood of nuclear physicists, a believer who had recanted and condemned the faith.

At the Cavendish, the Physics Department at Cambridge University, Montgomery was an experimentalist whose thesis on low-energy nuclear interaction attracted attention. He took his master's degree and went to work at the Atomic Weapons Research Establishment at Aldermaston. After two years of working on nuclear implosion triggers, he picked up where his Cambridge thesis had left off and six years later was a world-respected expert on radiation damage in nuclear weapons and the development of special alloys to limit it.

Montgomery married an Israeli student and disappeared into the Negev Desert, where he worked in the top-secret underground nuclear weapons factory buried six stories beneath an Israel Atomic Energy Authority experimental reactor near Dimona on the Beersheba–Sodom highway, helping to produce an arsenal that made Israel the world's sixth most powerful nuclear power.

The moral crisis for Montgomery began with the Israeli invasion of Lebanon in 1982 and climaxed with the increasingly brutal Israeli repression of Palestinians. He became totally disillusioned and full of guilt at the work he had done for a nation that was being criticized increasingly in language normally reserved for white racist South Africa. Montgomery and his wife divorced and his children assumed her family name. Montgomery went to Italy where, afraid for his life, plagued by remorse, forsaken by his family, alone and lonely and without direction, he began a downward slide that culminated in a nervous breakdown and a clumsy attempt at suicide by taking an overdose of sleeping tablets. When he had disappeared a year ago, it was believed that the Hand of God, the Mossad execution squad, was responsible.

The photograph the VFP supplied showed a man who looked younger than forty-two, tanned and healthy from the Negev sun. It was a private face, intelligent and perhaps sensitive. He was strong bodied, a man who liked walking, another solitary pastime. Montgomery had none of the dramatically ravaged looks of Leonardo but they shared the same haunted quality that marked them as men apart.

When Klimenti and Levitin arrived at the Excelsior, the driveway was blocked by several cars, one of them a Zil limousine with diplomatic plates and flying the Soviet flag. The center of attention was an imposing-looking Russian, whom Klimenti recognized as Byzov. He was accompanied by a young woman, stylishly dressed and attractive enough to draw a pack of *paparazzi*, the brazen photographers who stalked via Veneto spying into the private lives of the famous and rich. They had sensitive noses for scandal, and the sight of a Soviet VIP in the company of a beautiful woman sent them into a snapping frenzy. Byzov was divorced and had a reputation with women. It was rumored that Gorbachev had told him to get a wife and settle down.

Byzov, it seemed, was still having a fling. As his companion turned to slip into the rear of the Zil, Klimenti saw her face clearly.

Zhenya Stepanov.

"That's definitely a Kremlin ration," Levitin sighed, hot with young envy.

Zhenya! With Byzov, the rake of the Kremlin. Was she really his lover? What had Levitin heard on the gossip grapevine? And then Klimenti remembered—and, to his chagrin, with relief—that Zhenya was an Italian specialist in the Foreign Affairs Department, one of their most skillful translators. She had obviously been loaned to Byzov for his mission in Rome, whatever it was. Of course, that was it. She was on official duties. It was all perfectly innocent.

Except for the fact that lowly translators on official duties did not ride in the back seats of Zil limousines with Kremlin bureaucrats. And why hadn't Byzov used someone from the embassy?

Klimenti didn't want to think about it. It was none of his business; it didn't matter. In that case, why was he so flustered?

The truth was it did matter, and he didn't like it at all.

The Zil and its escort cars slid smoothly away. The police motorcycle outriders fore and aft were tough young men who had machine pistols strapped across their chests and they turned their sirens down to a menacing growl.

"Those Zils are big enough to screw in," Levitin muttered as he parked the Lancia.

Nikishov was waiting for him in the coffee shop. He was thinner, pale from the Moscow winter and his own personal travail. He took Klimenti aside and warned him about Sabotka's most recent behavior.

"I must tell you, the Fifth Department is becoming very concerned," Nikishov said.

The Fifth Department controlled dissidents and was known disparagingly as the Thought Police.

"There've been some demonstrations against nuclear weapons and he's been hanging around. In fact, he's become quite an identity among the younger people. His status as a former *zek* has made him an instant folk hero. You know how those Moscow intellectuals idealize anyone Beria got his hooks into."

So, Sabotka was marching. At last he had found his audience. Klimenti had seen an Italian television report on a demonstration in Red Square over the weekend and he had been surprised at the number of Muscovites, several thousand at least, who had marched. There had also been big weekend disarmament marches in Czechoslovakia, Poland, and Hungary. That morning there had been reports on fresh nationalist disturbances, this time in Georgia. The caldron, long cooked by harsh repression, was bubbling now that Gorbachev had lifted the lid.

"And my father?" Knowing his loyalty to Sabotka, Klimenti was alarmed.

"He goes along but he doesn't take part. We feel—the Fifth Department believes—he's trying to keep Sabotka out of trouble. So far there've been no problems. No arrests."

Arrests. The word hung over them. *So far*.

Wanting to change the subject, Klimenti asked, "Why'd they send Byzov?"

Nikishov gave him a sharp glance. But he did not ask about Zhenya Stepanov, even though he could hardly be unaware of her inclusion in Byzov's retinue. He said, "We're having trouble with our Italian comrades and Byzov's been sent in to pull them into line."

The Partito Comunista Italiano was the biggest communist party in the West. It had 1.8 million members and controlled 30 percent of the national vote, a situation Moscow had frequently manipulated to its own advantage.

"There's been tremendous pressure among their rank and file for the Party to come out in support of the VFP," Nikishov said. "It'd be a humiliating slap in the face for the Soviet Union. Not so long ago, all Byzov would have to do is call a meeting and tell them, 'Comrades, you're hurting the Soviet Union,' and that'd be the end of it. But not anymore. The blasted VFP have stirred up such a furor the membership is in revolt, and the Italian leadership are fearful for their own necks. For once, they're more afraid of their own countrymen than of Moscow."

Nikishov shook his head dolefully. "Everything's changing," he said. "I never agreed with that bloody wall in Berlin, but since they pulled it down, everything's gone haywire. Everywhere. From one point of view, it's all quite exhilarating. But from another, it's quite terrifying."

He was a man of certainties who dreaded doubts more than fear itself. So had Lysenko and his plotters, Klimenti thought. How many more in the Soviet Union shared the same fears? He was also surprised that Nikishov, normally the most circumspect of men, had revealed himself. It was getting away from Moscow and the weight of its silence. Here, in sunlit Rome, even Russian lips were loosened. But this was only Nikishov's first day.

He needs a friend, Klimenti thought. He's lonely, too.

"I'm working with Bannon again," Klimenti reported and, seeing alarm on Nikishov's face, smiled. "It's all right. I've got no plans to kill him. This time there's no need."

"I'm glad to hear it." Nikishov laughed nervously, not completely convinced.

But it was true. When they had met in Spina's office, Klimenti was surprised to feel no hostility toward the American. The reason was simple. With Nadya safely in Moscow, Bannon was no longer a threat.

"We seem to have absolved each other," Bannon had said. "The VFP are real, after all, just as you insisted."

"Yes," Klimenti had said.

One word! That's all it had taken. One simple yet absolutely momentous word and everything between them was changed. Acceptance by both men that neither the KGB nor the CIA was involved, that the VFP were indeed their own masters, had revealed the extent to which the deep cancer of mutual malevolence had dangerously blinded the world's two most powerful espionage services. It was not that they suddenly trusted or liked each other. It was something far harder to define, an understanding that they were both willing to recognize a mutuality of interest and were prepared to subordinate other consider-ations to this one end. Even so, the adjustment was made only with difficulty. It was easier, less complicated, less dangerous—and a lot more satisfying—to fight the old familiar enemy.

"These characters have declared war," Bannon said. "Against the United States and the Soviet Union."

He had paused to emphasize his words. "Against *us*."

Klimenti nodded. "Against us."

It was a remarkable step, this fusing of identity.

Klimenti wondered if he would ever be able to tell Nikishov about it. He doubted it. They could only move so far toward each other until, like the poles on a magnet, the forces of similarity began to repel each other.

"Where's Radchenko?" he asked. "Am I to report to him separately?"

"It's not necessary," Nikishov said. "Major Kharkov's doing it personally, this very minute."

3.

Commissario Spina spoke English with a strong Midwestern American accent, which he had picked up from his brother who ran a chain of pizza restaurants in Chicago. He had the preliminary results of the post-mortem examination on Salvatore and he gave them to Klimenti and Bannon in another anonymous office, this time in the Ministry for the Interior, better known by its address, il Viminale.

"Salvatore died of massive blood loss caused by incisions to his jugular vein and *both* his carotid arteries. His larynx was also completely severed. All of them by a single incision, one slash, a clean cut, from ear to ear. A razor, probably. According to the pathologist, it would require considerable skill and unusual strength. The cut went from left to right. The pathologist is of the opinion that to deliver such a blow, the murderer needed to be behind the victim, using his body as an anchor, the victim's head pulled back to expose and stretch the throat. Like stretching a rubber band before you cut it."

"In that case the murderer was right-handed," Klimenti said.

"There's something else. They found sperm in the deceased's anus and on his buttocks, dropped there when a penis was withdrawn after ejaculation. We know Salvatore had a shower when he got up and he had no customers that afternoon. So it's almost certain that the sperm came from his killer."

"He fucked him!" Bannon swore.

"That's right. From behind. When he was finished, he reached down, grabbed Salvatore by the hair with his left hand, pulled back his head, and cut his throat with his right. The pathologist says that although he's not personally experienced such a case before, there's information that such killings are sexual, the act itself causing ejaculation. In the States they call them snuff killings."

Spina looked at his hands. He wore a wedding ring. They were unremarkable hands. Could humans really use their hands to do such things to each other?

"Something doesn't fit," Klimenti said. "In Moscow, when the VFP killed Tarabrin, it was done quickly and, if you can say such a thing about murder, humanely. Salvatore's murder, the sheer perverted brutality of it, goes against the grain."

Spina shrugged. "They sent a homosexual to kill a homosexual. Perhaps they just didn't know he was also a sadist. It's equally possible they instructed him to make it look like a homosexual revenge killing, to put us off the track."

Bannon said, "Then why the tipoff?"

For the first time Spina showed exasperation. "I don't bloody well know," he said in idiomatic English. "You tell me."

"I don't know either," Klimenti said mildly. "But a new factor's entered the equation. It's possible they've lost control of one of their killers."

Spina stared at him, his anger gone.

"We're not after a sadist," Spina said quietly. "We're after a maniac."

"It could be a real break," Bannon said grimly. "The more he kills, the more chance we've got of getting him."

Il Viminale had been chosen as the venue for the intelligence forums because it was a high-security building, well guarded and with restricted access. Even so, extra police had been posted. A gathering of the world's top antiterrorist police was a natural target, and the Italians were taking no chances. Attendance at each forum was restricted to twenty delegates, one representative from each nation. Apart from considerations of physical security, there was another factor in limiting the audience—the information being exchanged was highly sensitive and the forums had been agreed on only after the Italians had given guarantees that there would be no leaks to unofficial sources. Each delegate went through three security checks—at the main gates, in the entrance lobby, and at a checkpoint outside the briefing room.

They came with remarkable punctuality, all of them arriving within a few minutes of the appointed hour, 11 A.M., carefully estimating in advance the time it would take them to pass the security checks and take their seats. Several of them already knew each other, several were perhaps even friends, veterans of past cooperation. A number were enemies. Quite a number were using false identities. But, friend or foe, they had not come to linger or to exchange pleasantries. They had come to listen, to question, and to report back; and they sat in watchful silence, distrustful of each other and wary of being manipulated. Klimenti felt the tension as soon as he entered. So did Spina and Bannon for, without further acknowledgment, they split up, sitting apart. At the checkpoint, they had been searched for tape recorders but had been allowed to take in notebooks and writing implements. An official recording of the forum would later be delivered under seal to each embassy.

Academician Fadeyev led off the first session. He spoke in Russian and his words were translated through headsets. The delegates had been briefed on his background by their own intelligence services and they listened with respect, well aware of the pioneering nature of Fadeyev's work in the field of punitive psychiatry.

Fadeyev began by focusing on contradictions in the backgrounds of Leonardo and Montgomery when compared with the usual run of terrorists. Neither came from an oppressed class or race with a strong hate object. Neither grew up in a society undergoing serious upheaval. On the contrary, they had come from orderly middle-class backgrounds. Neither had known poverty, deprivation, extremism. Neither was young nor, it was presumed, impressionable. Neither had vague values systems. On the contrary both had highly developed reference and values systems. Both were middle aged, both had families, conditions that engendered antipathy to violence. Both were highly intelligent and resistant to conditioning. Neither of them sought refuge in group identity. On the contrary, they were loners.

"Their behavior as assassins was also unusual. They operated alone, removed in time and distance from the group psychological support so important in other terrorists. Obviously they were able to do without constant reinforcement of peer values. The last days of their lives were spent in almost total isolation, subjecting them to loneliness, which would have tested the strongest of wills."

Fadeyev spoke without a tremor of emotion. His coldness reached out into his audience.

The most obvious conclusion that could be drawn from this information, Fadeyev said, was that each of the assassins was conditioned in isolation, an extremely difficult achievement. A complicating factor was that both had to be *turned against* a deep and maturely developed antipathy to violence and, no doubt, terrorism. Their thinking had to be totally reversed, not developed along a line it was already taking, as was the case with most terrorists. It made the task immeasurably more difficult and the ultimate achievement all the greater. This would require a setting of total seclusion, most likely a private hospital with excellent facilities, and a team of brilliant psychiatrists, psychologists, neurologists, dieticians, and nurses. There was probably only one conditioning team. Such talent was not easily found, let alone won over to so deadly a task. The VFP had to be very careful in their recruitment; a wrong move, a refusal, could betray them.

Depending on the time needed—and it was unthinkable that such results could be achieved in a short time—the costs would run into millions of dollars for the four assassins so far produced.

Fadeyev believed the assassins had been recruited from within psychiatric institutions. "They knew precisely the kind of human putty they were looking for," he said. "They didn't go wandering around the streets looking for them."

The initial processing would involve a lot of failures, so it was most likely carried out in normal psychiatric institutions, *farm* clinics that could absorb the early rejects without attracting undue attention. It was probable, Fadeyev argued, that the VFP ran a worldwide chain of private clinics. "They'd need to cast a wide net," he said. "That would give them a rich harvest to choose from."

For the first time he showed emotion. He smirked, and it turned his cold human features into an animated monkey face; the smile cut grooves and wrinkles that gave him a simian quality of craftiness. How extraordinary! Was Fadeyev, when he experimented with humans, taking revenge for all the apes?

The staffs in the farm clinics would be totally unaware of their involvement. Their reports on patients would be fed into a centralized system, perhaps a computer, from which the VFP team would select suitable subjects. These would be moved under the pretense of seeking more specialized care to a clinic where more detailed testing could be done to decide the subject's suitability for the final stage of conditioning. The testing would be thorough because once they had started on more intensive conditioning, it would become riskier to abandon those subjects who did not come up to scratch. Fadeyev was sure that once the secondary culling process had been completed, the subjects were then moved into total isolation in a clinic devoted entirely to their conditioning.

The achievement was truly something to consider. Fadeyev said, "A year ago, the two assassins we know about were crushed human beings, pathetic wrecks. Yet both these abject creatures reemerged as killers who functioned effectively under great duress and then willingly submitted to a violent death. They had become terrorists of extraordinary commitment. They had in effect been re-created, reborn. And let me tell you quite frankly, gentlemen, that it was a quite miraculous transformation."

How had it been done? "We'd all like to know," Fadeyev said. "We're still discussing it." He did not say that some of the foremost experts in the world had not been able to reach agreement. Each had his own theory and none wanted to surrender it. Some, like Fadeyev, had sinister secrets to protect and were unwilling to risk them to the professional—and inquisitorial—scrutiny of their colleagues.

"For your purposes, how is not as important as *where*," Fadeyev said without apology. *How* was a dangerous secret, not for them to know.

"Are there any other questions?" Fadeyev asked fatuously, and got a laugh for there had been none. It was a mere formality. His preparations to depart the podium indicated he did not expect or welcome questions.

Bannon stood up, taking them all by surprise. The audience was composed of men accustomed to making hard decisions in very difficult fields of endeavor, but none of them had wanted to match wits with Fadeyev, and certainly not on his terms. Bannon, however, stood at ease, so languid that his posture was almost contemptuous.

"Excuse me, learned Academician," he said with a warm smile, and Fadeyev, already leaving, stopped and glared.

"*Da*," he snapped in a voice that would have discouraged almost anyone but the suicidal. "What is it?" The interpreters translated, but even their soft flat voices could not remove the sting from Fadeyev's words.

"How did the assassins get into psychiatric institutions in the first place?" Bannon asked.

"The normal way," Fadeyev said, frowning. "They asked for help."

He turned to go. But Bannon refused to be dismissed.

"But they wanted to die. We know at least two tried to kill themselves."

Fadeyev turned to confront Bannon, his face tight with anger. The American smiled guilelessly, a model of patience and good manners, and Klimenti realized there was more to Bannon than he or any of them had imagined. He had something of Radchenko's audacity but somehow managed to lace it with an easygoing, deceptive charm, which disarmed his target. Fadeyev must have come to the conclusion that Bannon was not going to be intimidated, because he answered him.

"I'm sure they all attempted suicide at some stage. But suicide quite often is a desperate cry for life." On anyone else's lips, they would have been words of compassion, but Fadeyev made them seem heartless.

It was so obvious, so straightforward, it shocked them. Leonardo and Montgomery and the two unknown assassins weren't seeking to die. They had sought help so that they could live, and the VFP had given them death.

Fadeyev stared at the audience with contempt. "Perhaps now you'll understand the magnitude of their achievement," he said.

A murmur ran through the listeners. It gave Fadeyev satisfaction to see that they did understand. He stared down at Bannon, who was still on his feet, waiting.

"*Da?*" he said again, challenging the American to continue.

"Thank you, Academician," Bannon said, completely unperturbed. "What happens to those who don't come up to scratch?"

"Who knows?" Fadeyev said. He might have said, *Who cares?* Failures weren't important.

"What would you do with them, Academician?" Bannon asked and for the first time there was a hard edge in his voice. He was no longer smiling and his eyes were cold with dislike. "Would you send them back to the institutions?"

Klimenti remembered another time at Dzerzhinsky Square, when Kharkov had asked the same question of him, and that had been his answer, *We take them back to where we found them*, and he knew now that it was a lie. He had believed it at the time but now he knew he had been deceiving himself, and Kharkov had unwittingly found the truth. *It'd be kinder to kill them*, he'd said in pity, and he was right.

Fadeyev looked down on Bannon with scorn.

"Would *you* send them back? And risk the entire operation?"

For a few pathetic human failures.

"No," Bannon said, his face set hard against himself, condemning himself before the entire audience. "I wouldn't."

Fadeyev's eyes swept slowly around the delegates. He was the only one among them who was not afraid or ashamed of the truth. Watching his cold, unfeeling face, Klimenti thought, he's not a healer, he's never been a physician. He's a killer, pure and simple. But even that wasn't right. Fadeyev was an experimentalist. That's all. Instead of mice and monkeys, he used people, and you could work a kind of morality into that. Once again, remembering all that had been attempted in East Berlin, remembering Fadeyev's simian grin, how shocking it had been, that hideous monkey face, Klimenti felt unclean.

Bannon sat down. Without another word, Fadeyev left the podium, his triumph complete.

As the delegates filed out, Spina came up to Bannon and asked, "Why'd you do it?" Klimenti stopped to listen. He, too, was curious about Bannon's motive.

"For what he's done in the SPHs." Bannon addressed the Italian but his eyes were on Klimenti. "For all the poor wretches he's got his hands on."

Klimenti saw the challenge in Bannon's eyes but did not accept it.

"God help them," Spina said, and meant it.

"God's no help at all," Bannon said flatly and walked away.

Spina said, "What he did took courage, and something more."

"A conscience," Klimenti said. "A dangerous thing."

Spina regarded him with surprise. "You felt it too?"

"I think we all did," Klimenti said. "That's why no one wants to know him."

"I don't think it worries him," Spina said and there was admiration in his voice. "I think it would have worried him more if he hadn't done what he did."

"For a professional, a conscience is a luxury." It was the truth, but the words sounded shallow even as Klimenti spoke them.

"You don't think Bannon's a professional?" Spina regarded him with surprise.

"Very professional. That's why his behavior was so out of character."

"Not out of character," Spina said. "Beneath our professionalism we are all another person. In some it's buried deeper than in others and is harder to find. But it's there, grown into us before we learned to suppress it with our professionalism. Perhaps we were seeing the other Bannon."

Spina sounded saddened by these thoughts of humanity. The Italian was perceptive, a quality to guard against.

Even so, Bannon's behavior worried Klimenti. He had not expected it of the American; it showed he was more unpredictable, more susceptible to emotional stimuli than Klimenti had believed. It made him all the more dangerous. Klimenti remembered his own crisis in Moscow and how it had led him, against all professional rationale, to set out to kill Bannon. It struck him that one day the tables might be turned and Bannon, against all reasonable sense, might come stalking him. He would succeed, of course, just as Klimenti would have succeeded but for Nikishov's intercession. Of that Klimenti had no doubt. Strangely he did not feel hostility. Instead he felt an affinity with Bannon, and this troubled him more than anything.

At 5:11 P.M. Greenwich Mean Time, a man stepped out of a crowd gathered outside a discreet house in Berkeley Square to spot the departure of the Prime Minister. He lifted high his right hand in which he grasped an electrical switch. "Fascist murderer," he screamed.

The Prime Minister's bodyguards did not hesitate. Two threw themselves on top of the Prime Minister. Another shot the assassin. Within seconds of the assassin's death, the Prime Minister was safely in the back of the awaiting Daimler and speeding away to No. 10.

The electrical device the man had waved aloft was identified as a simple battery-powered clacker switch. It was connected to eight sticks of gelignite the assassin carried around his midriff, stuck into the belt of his trousers.

When tested, the clacker exploded a detonator. It would have worked. If the assassin had not paused to shout out his hate, thus giving the bodyguard a chance to draw and fire, he would almost certainly have killed the Prime Minister and many others in the crowd. Had the assassin strapped the gelignite to his chest, it would have been exploded by the impact of the 9mm bullets that killed him. As it was, one bullet struck within an inch of a stick of gelignite.

Pressed by the media, police said they were absolutely certain the assassin was not from the VFP. How could they be so certain? A superintendent said cryptically, "He failed."

4.

Twice every day, at ten minutes past seven, morning and evening, Klimenti waited in his hotel room for the telephone to ring. He had initiated the contact by sending a message on the hotel's facsimile machine to an American communist who ran a bookshop specializing in socialist newspapers and literature and who frequently received orders from abroad for American material. The message requested that he forward an English-language edition of John Steinbeck's novel *The Grapes of Wrath*, outlined arrangements to pay for it, and was signed Simon J. Baxter—a name as American as apple pie. The name was the trigger; the message itself was meaningless and contained no hidden code. The key was in the information that was automatically included on every fax message—the time of transmission and the fax and telephone number from where it was sent, thus establishing the time and the contact point.

The bookseller had taken the message to a dead drop whose location was changed every month by a telephone call from Squirrel. He and the bookseller had never met, and the bookseller believed he was acting on behalf of the American Communist Party. He had then placed an advertisement in the Personals column of the *Washington Times*: "Simon, Come home." This alerted Squirrel, who read the column each morning, that a message awaited him.

In the morning the telephone rang and Klimenti grabbed the receiver, almost dropping it in his haste.

"*Da?*" he said automatically, a mistake. The Russian was enough to frighten Squirrel off, and desperately he sought to cover it up, "Yes," the language they used, and then he felt foolish and relieved and disappointed all at once, because an anxious female voice said in American, "Honey? Is that you, honey?"

She had the wrong room. As Klimenti put down the telephone, his hands were sweating. If it had been Squirrel, he would have blown it. *Da!* The language of Dzerzhinsky Square muscling in, taking control. Squirrel would have cut the connection immediately, without hesitation.

If you need to warn me, say something, anything, just one word, in Russian.

The truth was Klimenti had not had his mind on the job. Sitting there, waiting, he had let his mind wander. *Zhenya*. He had almost put Squirrel on the run, into deep cover, beyond reach, and all because of a young woman, a . . . *one-night stand.*

Damn! Why didn't Squirrel make the contact!

It was dangerous for Klimenti to hang around and Squirrel knew it. He had never gone down to the wire like this. If he was holding off, it was because he had to—and that was more worrying than anything. Waiting around, hanging in, was tough stuff and it took strong nerves. The longer you waited, the greater became the possibilities of disaster. Klimenti had seen men of proven courage badly mauled by the tension of waiting. He knew that the process of destabilization was insidious, hardly noticeable at first, and when you did become aware, when the butterflies grew fangs and began chewing up your guts, it was well advanced and you were in trouble. Big trouble.

Well, Klimenti was in control, the butterflies were just butterflies, not piranhas, and that's how it was going to stay. Going down in the elevator, Klimenti thought, to hell with Zhenya Stepanov and Byzov. It made him feel better.

Tonight, Klimenti told himself. Squirrel will make the contact tonight.

Levitin was waiting in the lobby with a summons from Radchenko. "It's to be in the *referentura*," he reported, visibly impressed. The *referentura* was set deep within the embassy, a cell within a cell, behind thick concrete walls and ceilings to make it impenetrable to listening devices. It was the embassy message center, containing all its cipher machines and codes. It also contained the strongrooms where top-secret documents were stored, never to be removed beyond the *referentura*. One room was set aside in which the Ambassador, the KGB *residenz*, and other staff could hold private conversations. It was the one place in all of Italy where they could be absolutely sure that the Italians and the Americans were not listening in. The *referentura* was "swept" twice a week in case treacherous staff had smuggled in bugs.

The embassy wasn't far, several blocks past Termini Stazione, the city's main railway station. It was a massive granite building that occupied most of a block fronting on via Gaeta, a narrow street in an unfashionable quarter. The *referentura* was on the second floor. Klimenti was escorted by a guard who passed him over to another guard on duty inside the *referentura*. The conference room was small and spartan with several NO SMOKING signs. There was no ventilation for the simple reason that air ducts were ideal conduits for voices. Air was circulated by a fan and by leaving the single door open when the room was not in use, an inadequate arrangement that ensured that the air was always stale and sharp with a peculiarly metallic tang.

Klimenti had to wait only a few minutes before Radchenko strode in, followed by Nikishov and Academician Fadeyev, who sniffed the air and grimaced. Radchenko scowled and said, "Bunkers stink worse," dismissing in advance any complaints. Klimenti was pleased by the Academician's discomposure.

It was only the second time Klimenti had seen Radchenko in civilian clothes and he was once again impressed by the way the removal of his military accouterments only served to emphasize the raw physical brutality of the man. With his rugged peasant features, so strong and cunning, he would make an absolutely wonderful—and absolutely ruthless—Mafia don. The Sicilians would adore him.

Fadeyev did not bother to acknowledge Klimenti or Nikishov. Klimenti was sure now that Fadeyev hated—worse, despised—his fellows. Klimenti did not know what had occurred in Fadeyev's life to warp him so venomously against his own kind, but he suspected he was a man who was mortally afraid; that was the poison in him, his terror, and this was something you could understand. Fadeyev had prospered under Stalin and in many ways that was worse than suffering, because the Boss was suspicious of all who did well out of him. He had been fond of saying that if you plucked a chicken alive it clung to your feet, and he had looked after the fat chickens personally. Terror was Stalin's whip, driving his featherless and craven brood to greater inhumanity, and Fadeyev had obviously been one of the most inspired.

"Academician, if you would." Radchenko spoke politely but the words were nonetheless an order, leaving no doubt about who was in command.

Fadeyev said, "It would be a disaster for the Soviet Union if the Americans beat us in finding out how the VFP condition their assassins. The great prize at stake is not the assassins themselves, although I admit it would be an advantage to have several specimens"—he actually smiled as he said this—"to work on. But they would be of limited value and would eventually have to be disposed of. They are, after all, ultimately expendable. That's the reason for producing them. To use them."

Fadeyev's eyes were like black opals, bright and hard. Did monkeys have black eyes?

"The great prize is the process by which the assassins are conditioned. We need to know how it's done, and to learn that, we need to get to those who do the conditioning. They have made a break-through the importance of which I cannot exaggerate. Whoever acquires this knowledge will have the means to produce the ultimate terrorist weapon, assassins who cannot be stopped."

With a feeling of revulsion, Klimenti understood Fadeyev's admiration. The VFP had succeeded where the Academician had failed. Klimenti wanted to squeeze his skinny neck. Unconsciously he stroked the scar below his mouth. Fadeyev saw it and his eyes glittered. Did he know? Fadeyev had not been in Berlin at the time but surely he was aware of the circumstances that had brought his experiments to a close, when one of the trainees he had sent them from the SPHs had gone berserk and slashed Klimenti with a knife. The poor wretch was dead; Klimenti was sure of it now, another victim to chalk against Fadeyev. Surely Fadeyev knew how the scar had been inflicted. And he was smiling. Klimenti wished he could take revenge for all the innocents.

"It is absolutely essential we learn how they do it. It would give us unlimited opportunities."

That's how Fadeyev saw it, a breakthrough in the science of human manipulation, man management, the art of turning wounded people into murderers. If Fadeyev mastered it, he would be able to produce an endless supply of self-destructing assassins—and empty the psychiatric wards at the same time. His failures in East Berlin would be forgiven. What a stupendous achievement! There'd be SPHs all over the Soviet Union, and Fadeyev would be in charge. His own private haloperidol gulag.

"You mustn't let the Americans get to them first," Fadeyev said.

Radchenko, his peasant face closed up, his peasant eyes hard with control, said, "If they do, Academician, we'll just have to snatch them back for you." He paused and added, a touch of irony, "Won't we?"

"Yes," Fadeyev said, his black eyes unwavering. "You will."

Without further ado, not even a parting glance, Fadeyev walked out. They were all glad to see him go.

Radchenko got straight down to business. "Since the VFP clinics are located in the West, since the main impetus is with the Italians, it's almost inevitable that the VFP conditioning team will end up in the hands of the Americans. They'll pay whatever price the Italians ask. So would we, but I'm afraid the Italians won't make us the offer. Our only chance is to get to the VFP conditioning teams first."

For the first time, he smiled. "And kidnap them."

Klimenti felt a sudden escalation of tension in the room. The plan to kidnap Salvatore—one man—had been fraught with risk, as the outcome showed. But a whole *hospital*, staff and patients included!

"The task before us is to achieve a maximum result using a minimum of force, in total secrecy, on hostile terrain." Radchenko looked sternly at each of them in turn. "Which is why I'm giving the responsibility for planning the operation to you two."

Despite their shock, neither Klimenti nor Nikishov exchanged glances. Both of them stared steadily at Radchenko, using him as an anchor while their minds furiously computed all the ramifications. The mission was well nigh impossible; Radchenko had as much as admitted it.

"You've decided against the *residenz*," Nikishov said coolly. Normally, the operation would have gone to the KGB agents who operated in Rome and who had the advantage of knowing the terrain. They also ran networks of Italians—union officials, police, municipal officials, federal civil servants—whose assistance could be of incalculable importance. Nikishov was demanding to know why they were being bypassed. Klimenti admired his determination.

"They're not good enough," Radchenko said. "Not for this mission. It is of the utmost importance that there be no evidence that can be traced back to us should something go wrong. Failure will be bad enough; being caught out will be a catastrophe. Not just for us, the KGB, although that alone will be hard to bear. But for Comrade Gorbachev."

Gorbachev's name fell among them like a hammer hitting an anvil, throwing sparks. Unconsciously all of them stiffened. Radchenko was prepared to kill to protect Gorbachev's life and they had no doubt that he would do no less to protect his honor.

"That's why I've come to Rome—to take charge. The ultimate responsibility—success or failure—will be mine."

Radchenko smiled wanly, surprising them. "I hope you'll appreciate that apart from the welfare of the Soviet Union, I also had very personal motives in selecting my team."

It was as close as he would ever come to paying anyone a compliment.

"Who are we using?" Klimenti asked.

"Israeli-born Arabs," Radchenko said. Since the Israeli repressions on the West Bank, there'd been no shortage of volunteers. If anything went wrong, the Israelis would be blamed.

"Who trained them?"

"The Executive Action Department."

So, Klimenti thought, they're giving us the really hard lads. The Executive Action Department was also known as Department V (as in Victor) and was the most secret unit within the KGB. It trained personnel for *mokrie dela*, "wet affairs" such as murder, kidnaping, and sabotage. They were certainly the right men for the task ahead. Even so, the Executive Action teams were considered bad news. Like all units that are called on to do dirty and desperate acts, they had their own codes of behavior and morality, most of which held normal human standards in utter contempt.

Radchenko said, "The assault team's leader is the best man we have. I chose him myself and I assure you of his total cooperation." He went to the door, opened it, and beckoned. "Come in, please."

The assault team leader came through the door and stood stiffly at attention. Even in his civilian slacks and soft leather zippered jacket, he looked the perfect soldier.

Radchenko smiled, enjoying the surprise.

It was Kharkov.

5.

The telephone rang and Squirrel said, "Today's *Herald Tribune*," and cut the connection.

He had spoken only three words but Klimenti immediately recognized the dry rustling voice. There was no time to waste. Squirrel would wait only an hour.

Klimenti was exhausted after a torrid afternoon making plans with Nikishov and then briefing Kharkov and Levitin. But his tiredness was forgotten as he took the fire stairs down to the lobby, coming out behind the *caribinieri* who was posted to watch for him at the elevators. He bought that day's *International Herald Tribune* and returned to the lobby, placing himself where he was out of the *caribinieri*'s line of sight and where he could watch the reception desk. He turned to the Personals and found the notice he was looking for: "Simon, ring 7281200." Mentally, he moved the second digit forward one digit and the fourth digit back one digit. The number was 2782100. It was a simple code, designed not to beat professional code breakers, who would see through it immediately, but to prevent crank calls.

Klimenti picked his target carefully, a young American couple going for a night out. He watched as the receptionist put their keys in their message box. The room number was 823. Klimenti gave them ten minutes and walked boldly to the elevators, his back to the *caribinieri*, knowing that he would be watching for him only among people leaving the elevators, not among those entering.

Klimenti went to the eighth floor, found room 823, and opened the door with a picklock. The couple had left a lamp burning and it was sufficient for him to direct-dial Washington, punching in the number Squirrel had sent him. It was, he knew, a public telephone somewhere in the city, a different one from the public phone Squirrel had direct-dialed the trigger call from. Squirrel would be waiting by it. The only record of Klimenti's call would be on the young couple's hotel account and, if they noticed and complained, it would be a mystery; there was no way the call could be connected with Klimenti or Squirrel. It was a perfect cutout. The signal rang six times before the connection was made.

"My friend," Squirrel said. His voice was full of warmth and concern and Klimenti felt a surge of relief. Softly he told Squirrel all that he should know. They spoke for five minutes and when Klimenti let himself out of the room after carefully removing any evidence of his presence, he felt the weight of guilt he had carried these past weeks dissolving into warm assurance that he had made the right decision.

It had not been easy, even though Klimenti was aware that the sense of alienation, which had begun with the KGB's ruthless manipulation of Nadya's affair with Bannon, was deepening. To whom did he owe his first loyalty? The KGB or Squirrel? The *apparat* that had fostered and protected him? Or to those whom he protected, his daughter and his father? Yes, Morozov too, now that he had drawn the crusty old Academician into the conspiracy—and that's what it was, a *conspiracy*. But against what?

The moment he asked this question, Klimenti knew the answer, just as he had the morning in Moscow when he set out to kill Bannon. It was a conspiracy *against the enemy*, and the enemy was clear: all the agencies charged with suppression. That included all the intelligence agencies in the world, the CIA and the KGB chief among them, and all those who worked for them, acting against their own people in the guise of protecting them, crushing them in the name of freedom. All his professional life Klimenti had been one of them. He had been an enemy of his people, of *his own family*, and when he realized this, the decision was made because blood was thicker than dialectics and love was stronger than discipline.

The traffic noise from five floors below insinuated through the windows, punctuated by the sharp blast of car horns. The sounds increased Klimenti's sense of isolation, of being removed from the human mainstream.

He sat staring at his bedside portrait of Marusya, needing her now more than ever. Of all the photographs he had, this was the one he loved best. The photographer had caught a sense of dreamy mystery; the eyes promised so much and hid much more. Marusya had an instinct for secrecy and surrendered it only with difficulty, sometimes with love, full of excitement at the sharing of herself, sometimes with loathing, hating him for stealing from her; yet all the time she had promised that a little at a time, more of her secrets would be revealed, she would give him more of herself, and that was all he wanted.

It was the strongest part of her hold over him, this promise of unrevealed mystery. And the promise had never been completely fulfilled; there were so many of her secrets he would never learn, not now.

There were some wounds that could never heal. Yet Klimenti treasured the pain, loving it.

He turned on the television and found himself watching a report on another demonstration in Red Square. The square was packed with several thousand people and they weren't just students. There were workers, ordinary citizens, men and women, young, middle-aged, and old, and they carried placards calling for disarmament. Suddenly there was a surge in the crowd and Klimenti saw the Militia moving in, wielding long batons, and the camera cut to show two Militiamen beating at a young woman who was carrying a banner Klimenti could not read. The demonstration proceeded peacefully, the report said, until some demonstrators began waving placards in support of the VFP. Then the police charged. There were several hundred arrests.

On an impulse Klimenti put a call through to his apartment in Moscow. Sabotka answered. "Klimenti, is that really you? All the way from Italy?"

"Hello, Sabotka. Is Papa there?"

"He's visiting Academician Morozov. Tell me, Klimenti, what's it like in the free world?"

Sabotka was drunk. Klimenti was disappointed he had missed his father but, on the other hand, he was pleased to think that he had become friendly with Morozov.

"Is Nadya with them?"

"Nadya! Nadya's in Czechoslovakia."

"Czechoslovakia!" What was going on?

"That's right. Since last weekend. She's gone for a skiing holiday for two weeks in the Carpathians. What's the problem?"

"There's no problem. I'm just surprised she left while her grandfather was in Moscow."

"She didn't want to go. But Sergei heard she'd been offered the holiday and he insisted."

"Offered?" It was becoming more and more perplexing.

Sabotka laughed. "She's a beautiful girl."

Sabotka was right. Nadya was perfectly capable of turning the heads of many a well-placed and influential Russian. And you certainly needed influence to have the foreign currency to pay for a holiday in Czechoslovakia. It was a good sign that she was putting Bannon behind her. Even so, Klimenti felt a twinge of disapproval. He was more prudish than he had realized, at least when Nadya was concerned. A hypocrite!

"She telephoned last night, just to make sure we're all right. Which we are, considering the whole fucking country's a prison. The only free men are the dead. I know, I buried them in the permafrost. In the Kolyma."

There was truculence in Sabotka's voice and, with alarm, Klimenti remembered the pictures he had seen on the television.

"Sabotka, what's going on?"

"We've been down in Red Square, marching," Sabotka said. "Well, me anyway. Sergei just hangs around, looking on."

So Nikishov had been correct. Klimenti felt a surge of anger. Sabotka could do what he liked. He didn't give a damn about Sabotka, as long as he didn't drag his father down with him.

"Listen, Sabotka, you keep Papa out of it, you hear? If you've got any sense, you'll keep out of it, too. Leave it to the students, the

young people. You've done your time. You know what it's like to be
a *zek*."

Sabotka said, quieter now, "We're all *zeks*. It's just that some of
the prisoners—*them, those bastards*—have more privileges. That's
all."

He was hopeless. It was totally useless trying to talk sense to him.
Angry and exasperated, Klimenti said, "Tell Papa I called."

"Of course."

There was contrition in Sabotka's voice and Klimenti immediately
felt his anger abating. The old scoundrel knew how to get around you.
In that respect he was like an old dog, uncannily sensitive to every
mood. When you thought about it, Sabotka had many of the supernat-
ural qualities normally attributed to animals. Why not? He was as much
animal as man. The Kolyma had seen to that.

Even though Klimenti had not spoken, Sabotka sensed his softening and came in, tail wagging.

"Tell me, Klimenti," he urged. "What's it like in Rome?"

"Warm."

"They say the food's very good."

"Excellent."

"And the wine?"

"Some of it."

"And their women?"

Aaaah! So there it was, the heart of it. Women were always a
touchy matter with Sabotka, who had missed out on so much.

Klimenti sighed. "Sabotka, I don't know about their women."

For a moment, silence. Then: "You're in Rome, eating their food
and drinking their wine—and you haven't even bothered to taste their
women!" Sabotka's voice rose with indignation. He could not believe
it. "They've let you off the leash, they've let you *out*—and you've done
nothing about it."

It was the truth. Klimenti had never thought about it in such terms.
"Russians are good enough for me," he said, angry with himself for
even bothering.

"It's not a matter of good enough," Sabotka shouted. "Of course
Russian women are good enough. It's a matter of wasted opportunity.
You got it, a rare thing for a Russian, and you're throwing it away. It's
a crime."

The cantankerous, horny old bastard. But he was right.

"Excuse me, Klimenti Sergeyevich, you're obviously very intelligent and you've gone far. But I think you're sometimes a stupid man."

The line went dead. The old reprobate had got in the last word. Klimenti was furious. He slammed the telephone down so hard it bounced out of its cradle and he had to pick it up and replace it. The sly, cunning, treacherous old bastard!

Zhenya!

A Russian woman in a foreign place. She was the source of his frustration, not Sabotka. Yes, Sabotka was right. She was there to be tasted. Sabotka had stripped the problem down to its most basic level, hunger; sex was food to him, bread, meat, and potatoes, to be gobbled when it was available. And he was right. Klimenti should not waste the opportunity. He should give up this monk's existence and stop fooling around and go out there and start feasting.

After all, he was a man of the world; he had taken many women to his bed without any consequent emotional upheaval. Some of them had been beautiful, some beguiling, some shameless. Some had been very nice women, some had been real bitches. But none of them had challenged Marusya. She had always outmatched them all, more beautiful, more beguiling, more shameless; nicer and a bigger bitch, too. She was more of everything, more than any of them.

More than Zhenya.

It was the first time Klimenti had coupled Marusya with any other woman and he felt guilty. He began to understand that he was afraid of Zhenya.

Klimenti felt his life was unraveling, coming apart at the seams. So much that he had accepted without question, his loyalty to the KGB, his devotion to Marusya, was being challenged. These two factors had been fundamental to his existence, governing the way he thought and acted. And now one was so dangerously honeycombed with distrust that it was quite possibly beyond recovery and the other, Marusya, the deepest wound in his psyche, was under assault.

For the first time in his life, Klimenti confronted the frightening vacuum of faith lost. He would never again be quite the same person. He saw his own hypocrisies, the strengths that had turned out to be weaknesses, but at least they had been familiar, *his*. Now, he felt himself a stranger: Who was he? Where he was going? And why? He was exploring uncharted territory—himself. He felt apprehension. Only Nadya and his father remained constant, unchanged, and they were far away.

For once, thinking of Marusya did not comfort him. He sat up most of the night, going over the plans he and Nikishov had drawn up. In the end exhaustion came to his rescue and he slept. But it was a bad night, full of troubled dreams.

6.

In the morning Klimenti went out into the noisy, fume-filled Roman day determined to nail down this mission Radchenko had given him. He was too irritable to be hungry and drank only strong black coffee for breakfast. When Kharkov and Levitin turned up, he greeted them perfunctorily and sat in the back of the Lancia, scowling at the traffic, no longer admiring the zestful confusion that resulted from everyone, including the police, breaking all the rules. Rome was a city in which even the nuns walked against the traffic lights, something which normally impressed Klimenti immensely and more than once had caused him to smile at this un-Soviet anarchy. But not today.

Klimenti had developed a liking and admiration for Kharkov, but the knowledge that the tough young major was a specialist from the Executive Action Department tempered his attitude. Had circumstances dictated that Klimenti and Nikishov were expendable, Kharkov would have been the man for the job. Kharkov, with his handsome face and winning smile and good manners. Once again Klimenti was reminded that, in this business, emotion was the ultimate betrayer. Getting to like people you worked with could be dangerous.

They joined Nikishov in the *referentura* and went over their plans. Kharkov's team of six Israeli Arabs was already in a safe house, keeping a twenty-four-hour telephone watch. An Italian agent would telephone them with the location of the VFP hospital as soon as it was

331

known to the Italians. None of them, Radchenko included, knew the identity of the agent, who had been personally recruited by the *residenz*. Although none of them said it aloud, they all understood that the agent worked for one of the Italian security services. The nature of the information he would be providing made this quite obvious.

The *residenz* was insisting on exactly the same protection for his agent that Klimenti had forged for Squirrel. Klimenti felt this was a vindication of his actions the previous night.

Two of the team posing as Palestinian Red Cross representatives were out buying two secondhand ambulances, ostensibly for shipment to the West Bank, where there was much work for the vehicles. The Italians had already made many similar deals with the Lebanese and no questions would be asked. Two other team members were hiring two big furniture moving vans and two Fiats, both the light blue color favored by the *caribinieri* for their unmarked escort cars. The last remaining squad member was to buy four ambulance drivers and four *caribinieri* uniforms. In all cases payment would be offered in cash. By nightfall the team was to be on an instant-readiness alert.

When the tip-off came, Levitin and three of the Arab Israelis disguised as ambulance officers would drive the ambulances to the scene, followed in the van and two cars by Kharkov and three Arab Israelis disguised as *caribinieri*. They would use their sirens to get there quickly. What could be more normal than ambulances and police on a mercy dash?

They were working on the basis that after locating the VFP conditioning clinic, the Italians would keep it under observation long enough—at least twenty-four hours—to photograph the entire staff coming and going, so that those off duty could be picked up at home. The Italians' normal operation was two men in a surveillance van with a video recorder and still camera. Kharkov and his "*caribinieri*" were to take them out.

Kharkov would leave two "*caribinieri*" on guard at the hospital entrance and would then join Levitin in the ambulances to lead the assault on the hospital. There were bound to be guards disguised as male nurses. Killing was to be avoided, but if it was necessary it was to be done swiftly with silenced pistols.

Klimenti said, "We can't advise you how many patients and staff there'll be. At least ten, perhaps twenty. Unfortunately the escape plan makes it impossible to use more than two ambulances, so you'll have to stack them in as best you can."

Klimenti emphasized the importance of removing all the medical records, which would be taken away in the van. They would learn as much from the records as they would from interrogating the hospital staff and patients.

"You and your *caribinieri* will have machine pistols and rocket launchers," Klimenti told Kharkov. "If you meet any opposition coming out, they must be totally obliterated before they can radio a description of the ambulances. There must be no pursuit."

Kharkov nodded grimly. "RPG7s will do the job."

Levitin went pale.

Klimenti continued, "Your men are to speak only Hebrew. No one is to be captured. No one is to surrender. There must be no evidence to incriminate the Soviet Union."

"The wounded?" Kharkov asked, knowing the answer but wanting it for the record.

"If you can't take them out, you're to shoot them."

Levitin gasped.

"That's an order," Klimenti told him quietly.

"Yes, sir," Levitin said, consciously straightening himself.

"There's no need to be embarrassed," Klimenti said. "If you can't do it, say so now."

"I can do it, sir," Levitin said, his face totally devoid of color now, and Klimenti felt sorry for him, knowing what it had cost the young man to say those dreadful words.

Nikishov went over the escape plan. On leaving the VFP hospital, the ambulances would rendezvous with two large furniture moving vans and drive straight up their lowered loading ramps. The moving vans would depart as soon as the ramps were lifted. Kharkov's team would be picked up by the cars and driven to the safe house, where they would disperse, taking different routes out of Italy.

Two paramedics in each van would keep the captives sedated in the ambulances while the moving vans drove to either Naples or Genoa, depending on the docking schedules of three Soviet cruise vessels—the *Adjara*, the *Dmitry Shostakovich*, and the *Lev Tolstoy*—which operated out of the Black Sea port of Odessa. On any given day, one of the three vessels was in one of the two Italian ports.

The captain would be alerted that a team of high-ranking Soviet doctors was coming on board. They would be led by Fadeyev. The captives would be taken to the crew's hospital ward, where Fadeyev and his men would immediately begin "treatment" while the vessel returned to Odessa. They would be flown to a Moscow SPH, where their misery would begin in earnest.

Radchenko approved their plans. "Give me a password for the Italian agent," he demanded.

"Leonardo," Klimenti replied without hesitation.

"Why Leonardo?" Nikishov regarded him quizzically and Klimenti wondered if he had betrayed himself. It was possible that Levitin had been reporting on him and they knew about his visit to the bookseller and his interest in Leonardo's success.

"Because he succeeded in a very difficult mission." It was not until he said it that Klimenti realized he was proud of Leonardo, as if he had been one of his own men.

"Yes," Radchenko said, nodding energetically to emphasize his complete agreement. "It's an omen, a good sign."

7.

Spina surprised Klimenti and Bannon by taking them to lunch at a small *ristorante* on the via Cavour, in the poorer section where it ran into the Piazzo del Cinquecento in front of the railway station. He gave them each a handsome pictorial book on Rome.

"A gift from my department," Spina said. "The director approved the expenditure."

Bannon smiled. "Commissario Capo, I hope that's the only piece of disinformation we'll hear from you."

Spina laughed, a little embarrassed but still pleased that his deception had been found out. "Who knows?" he said. "You might find time to see some of the city."

He was proud of Rome and the sentiment was genuine. He gave Klimenti a sly glance. "Other than the Campo dei Fiori."

The *ristorante* had a billboard outside announcing the daily specials. It was plain and inexpensive, hardly a showplace, but Spina made no apology. "The food is excellent," he said. "But its real advantage is that the people from il Viminale consider it beneath their dignity to come here." Spina ordered for them all: a thick bean soup, pasta with melted butter and Parmesan cheese, salad and grilled calves' liver. He was right: the food was excellent and plentiful, and they ate it with thick crusty bread. He ordered two bottles of mineral water and a bottle of Barolo.

"It's barbaric to eat without wine," Spina said, although both Klimenti and Bannon observed that he was careful to consume twice as much mineral water. Soon there grew among them the cautious and tentative camaraderie that can exist between enemies who respect each other and who find a rare occasion to meet on absolutely equal terms, recognizing themselves in their foes. It was very similar to those occasions when soldiers declared truces and went into no man's land to succor the wounded and collect the dead and discovered their common humanity.

The three agents were careful not to be demonstrative; they spoke quietly and listened attentively, exercising all the restraints expected of them; but beneath their civility each sensed an empathy that, without any other clamor to overwhelm it, enabled them to enjoy the meal and the company. Klimenti was not the least troubled by the fact that he had that morning prepared a plan to deceive and defeat both his luncheon companions. That existed in another dimension which, like the soldiers walking the killing ground in peace, was merely suspended for the moment.

In this mood, Klimenti asked Bannon where he had acquired his Russian. He spoke too well to have learned it solely at the CIA language schools and he had not been in Moscow long enough to become so fluent. It had been decisively developed before he had arrived.

"In Gary, Indiana," was the surprise reply. "From my grandmother, my mother's mother. Both my grandparents were Russian. From St. Petersburg."

"They were immigrants?" Spina asked. His brother, his uncle before that, a great-grandfather before them all, had migrated to America and prospered.

"No. My grandmother was a refugee. She fled the Soviet Union in 1927 after they killed my grandfather."

"Oh!" Spina said.

Bannon looked directly at Klimenti. "My grandfather was a Bolshevik. His trouble was he really believed Lenin meant what he said. Stalin had different ideas."

There was no accusation in Bannon's eyes. Klimenti had a feeling he wanted him to understand something that was very important to him.

He sensed that Bannon was reaching out to touch him, and he felt a shiver run up his spine.

"He died in the Lubyanka," Bannon said without emotion.

Yes, Klimenti thought, knowing why he had shivered.

Bannon said quietly, "They killed all the Bolsheviks. Eventually. My grandmother was pregnant with her first child, my mother. She got out through Finland, married a Swede who went to the United States and became a farmer. He was a good man and she loved him. But she never forgot her Bolshevik. And she never forgave his killers, not even on her deathbed."

Klimenti sat in solemn silence, seeing again the putrid concrete cell which stank of death and pain. It had been one of the killing cells, where they shot those whom they wished to disappear without a trace, to prove they had never existed. He hoped that Bannon's grandfather had not died there but out in the courtyard where he could tilt back his head and see the sky and breathe clean air.

"Let's drink to your grandfather," Klimenti said.

"A Russian and a Bolshevik," Bannon said proudly.

"A man who died for his beliefs," Spina said.

"Bannon is not a Russian name," Klimenti observed.

"No. My father was Irish."

Klimenti knew he would get only a rebuff if he probed further.

They split the lunch bill and the tip and strolled back to the Piazza del Cinquecento, where Spina left them. He was plump and smooth and yet still managed, in a very Italian way, to look tough and dangerous. They were, Klimenti thought, a very graceful people.

"Did they ever issue a death certificate for your grandfather?" Klimenti asked.

"No."

"Would you like one?"

Bannon stared at him in surprise. "Why?"

"It's something. A death certificate is the only confession a Soviet citizen gets that they killed some of his family. They don't like issuing them—but they do, if you fight, ever since Khrushchev exposed Stalin's crimes. Getting one is a small victory for the living, a gesture of respect for the dead. If your grandmother was alive, she'd understand. She was Russian."

"You can swing it?"

"Yes. It'll take time, but they kept files on all the Bolsheviks."

They. Not *we!* Did Bannon notice?

"One day the Bolsheviks will all be resurrected. Your grandfather too." Klimenti knew he spoke more in hope than in conviction but he felt it was important.

"No strings attached?"

Klimenti regarded Bannon in grave silence.

"I'm sorry," Bannon said and meant it. "His name was Dementiy Terentyevich Yeromin."

"No strings attached," Klimenti said. "I'm doing it for your grandfather. A Russian."

He walked away. He did not look back but he was sure—he could feel it—Bannon was watching him as he went.

The *referentura* had become their headquarters, but it was an unsatisfactory arrangement. Apart from its claustrophobic atmosphere and bad air—Klimenti overheard Levitin referring to it as the "Führer Bunker" and thought it an apt description—it identified them as a cell apart in the embassy framework, and nothing was more guaranteed to attract unwelcome attention.

It was a classic example of tight security defeating itself, so Klimenti made arrangements for Kharkov to report to him in a busy workers' coffee house not far away. The hum of café noise—the hiss of steam from the *espresso* machine, the clatter of crockery, the high-pitched excitement of Italian chatter—vibrated against the windows and made it impossible for even the best equipped surveillance van to pick up their conversation. They took a seat where they could watch for anyone entering with a shopping bag or satchel that might conceal a tape recorder. They spoke in Russian, their faces averted from the window. It was possible to videotape conversations and lip-read what was being said.

Doing this, exercising his tradecraft, outwitting the enemy, made Klimenti feel good; at moments such as this he truly understood how much he loved the hunt, the hunted turning on the hunter but never certain, always fearful that this was exactly what the hunter wanted, and that it was a trap. It was always the snare you didn't see that strung you upside down to be gutted at leisure. He remembered Radchenko's warning after their dinner in Stalin's roost and wondered if Spina, too, was a country boy, sensing an ambush behind his smooth Roman urbanity.

He had heard the contemptuous talk among the KGB professionals at the embassy, so he warned Kharkov, "Don't underestimate the Italians. They've been doing this a lot longer than we have."

Kharkov reported, "The purchase of the vehicles has been arranged but we must have them all thoroughly checked mechanically. We don't want them breaking down on us. The problem is, we can't force the Italians to work overnight."

Klimenti ordered, "No later than midday tomorrow." Kharkov and Levitin had done remarkably well and it was good to see they were being thorough with the vehicles. This was not the time for the whip, nor was it the time for praise. So he left a vacuum, knowing from his own experience that it would spur both Kharkov and Levitin to maintain a supreme effort without panicking them.

A blue Lancia darted to a stop outside and a beautifully uniformed *caribinieri* slipped out and walked quickly into the coffee shop. He was tall and graceful and came unerringly to their table. He saluted smartly, a model of soldierly courtesy.

"I've been asked by Commissario Capo Spina to take you to him immediately," the *caribinieri* said in good English. "It's urgent, sir."

Klimenti paid for their coffee and went across to the car. They drove with the siren blaring, flashing through the traffic, and Kharkov watched the driver covetously. You could never learn to drive like that in Moscow. To learn to drive like that, you had to grow up amid chaos.

"Where are we going?" Klimenti asked.

"Piazza del Popolo."

"Popolo?"

"*Si*. Popolo." The Italian shrugged. Why not Popolo?

The Piazza del Popolo was on the edge of one of the city's most beautiful quarters, a vast square caught beneath the steep escarpment of the Pincine Hill, which rose up to become the gardens of the Villa Borghese. It was at the apex of a triangle of fashionable streets that accommodated many of the city's most elegant buildings and most expensive merchants. It was not far from the via Condotti and the via Frattina, which fed into the Piazza di Spagna, a favorite gathering place for Romans and tourists alike, who came to wander and mingle and watch and, quite often, to mate.

Kharkov was afraid that Spina had already uncovered the VFP
clinic and that all their planning and work was undone. "They knew
exactly where to find us," Kharkov said in Russian.

"He has also told us he knew exactly where to find us," Klimenti
said. "That was a mistake. Next time we'll make sure he doesn't."

The Lancia darted past a tall office block that was guarded by
police. Among them Klimenti saw young uniformed women, wearing
bulletproof vests and carrying machine pistols. They looked tough and
determined.

"Partito Communista," the *caribinieri* said, waggling an admoni-
tory finger under his companion's nose. "*Buono. Buono.*"

"*Niente,*" the driver growled and they both laughed.

There was no sign of a Zil, but Byzov, no doubt, was inside, doing
his utmost to convince the Italian Communists to toe the Moscow line.
With Zhenya at his elbow. Klimenti quickly drove the thought away.

A huge crowd packed several blocks of the via Corso where it fed
into the Piazza del Popolo. They carried placards denouncing the
United States and the Soviet Union. Others waved aloft the Moscow
Martyrs poster. Everywhere he looked, Klimenti saw the portraits of
Leonardo and Montgomery. The most frequently displayed placards
bore what was now recognized as the VFP slogan:

> Condemn the Guilty!
> Save the Innocents!
> Disarm!

The crowd chanted it: "*Condannate i colpevoli! Salvate gli
innocenti! Disarmate!*" As far as Klimenti could see, they were
representative of the community at large, young and old, rich and poor,
male and female. The disarmament and conservation crusades cut
across class, sex, and age. Marshals with bullhorns directed them. The
roar rose up and fell away and rose up again, endlessly repeated.
Despite the noise they were orderly and good-natured. Peace was their
cause and nonviolence had become the hallmark of similar demonstrations all over the world. There had been violence only when police had
charged the crowds—in Moscow, in Rio de Janeiro, in Montgomery,
Alabama, and in Sydney, Australia—actions that were not only futile
but ultimately self-defeating, serving only to win the demonstrators
more sympathy and support.

"Anarchists," the *caribinieri* said, revealing that the attitudes of those who were charged with enforcing the law in Italy were not very different from their counterparts in the Soviet Union. Or anywhere else for that matter.

Spina was waiting in an Alfa Romeo parked in a side street on the River Tiber side of the piazza. Bannon was with him. Klimenti and Kharkov got into the rear seat.

"I'm told you know him," Spina said and passed Klimenti one of the two photographs that the KGB had released worldwide four hours after Batrakov's assassination. As always, Klimenti was caught by the astonishing beauty of the heavily lashed eyes that drove women crazy with envy, seeing them in a face marred only by its feral cruelty. Spina passed across a second photograph. It was of Big Dog. The Ferret and Big Dog were on the Most Wanted list of every police force in the world. By now their photographs had been displayed in newspapers and on television in cities, towns, and villages worldwide. Countless thousands of frustrating hours had been wasted pursuing false leads. Not once had police confirmed a definite sighting.

So Big Dog had gone back to the Ferret, loyal to the last.

"They're in Rome?" Klimenti asked.

Spina pointed. Across the street and half a block down was a small *pensione*.

"Two men, one a giant, the other small and quick. They've both grown mustaches and Tabidze's dyed his hair, but we're sure it's them. They checked in four days ago on German passports. The *pensione* manager recognized they were speaking Russian. He fought with the Italian Third Army at Stalingrad, was captured, and spent six years in a labor camp, so he knows the language well."

"That's one very suspicious old man," Bannon said.

"He's paid to be," Spina said. "We recruited him when we were after the Red Brigades. It's finally paid off."

"Are they inside now?" Klimenti asked.

Spina shook his head. "They go out every day. They don't seem to be short of money. The *pensione* offers a special rate, room, three meals a day, but they've taken just the room, with a bath and telephone, and eat out. We've got men in the hotel, across the road, in the shops next door. We'll take them when they come back."

"You've been into their rooms?"

Spina nodded. "There's just their clothes, nothing else."

"No weapons?"

"No."

Klimenti said, "Then they're carrying them. Revolvers or pistols. And Tabidze will have a knife. Perhaps two. One for throwing. One for stabbing."

"A knife?" Both Spina and Bannon were suddenly tense.

"Yes," Klimenti said. "I think we've found the man who cut Salvatore's throat."

"Jesus," Bannon said.

"He's called the Ferret," Klimenti said.

"If he killed Salvatore, then he's well named."

"He likes to kill with a knife. He's capable of doing what was done to Salvatore."

"There's nothing in his record about being a homosexual," Spina said.

"He isn't," Klimenti said. "He likes schoolgirls. He was humiliating Salvatore. For pleasure."

"*Figlio di puttana*," Spina cursed. Son of a whore.

Bannon asked, "You've got riflemen?"

"Yes. Expert marksmen."

"Then don't take chances. Order your men to shoot them in the legs the moment they can get a clean shot."

Spina stared at Bannon with new respect.

"Both legs," Bannon said. "In the knees if they're good enough."

"They're good enough."

"Only Tabidze," Klimenti said. "The big one, Big Dog, isn't a killer."

"Both of them," Bannon said, staring at Klimenti with hard eyes. Spina thought it was a challenge and he saw that the Russian sensed it, too. There was a strange stillness in the car.

Bannon said, "A man on the run, involved in an assassination, facing a tough interrogation, maybe torture, life imprisonment, is a potential killer. Why take the chance?"

He was right. Big Dog had made his choice and had to pay the price. Even so, Klimenti wished it wasn't necessary. He remembered Big Dog's uncomplaining courage when he and Zhenya had worked on him on the bathroom floor, and his hurt at Tabidze's treachery. Yet he had refused to give him up and now he was by his side again. In the whole world, Big Dog loved only two people, one of them his grandmother. And the Ferret. Big Dog would kill. Not for himself, but for Tabidze.

"You're right," he said and looked away.

Spina gave the orders over a cellular telephone. His instructions were greeted with silence.

"Acknowledge," Spina grated.

"In the knees, Commissario Capo?"

"In the knees."

"*Merda!*" Shit.

"The small one cut a man's throat. From ear to ear."

"*Pezzo di merda!*" Piece of shit.

"The moment you can get a clean shot."

"Yes, sir."

"To my knowledge, they've never shot anyone before," Spina said. "I feel sorry for them."

"You'll feel a hell of a lot sorrier if the Ferret gets to one of your men," Bannon said grimly.

"Are you armed?" Spina asked Klimenti and Kharkov.

"No, neither of us," Klimenti said.

Spina turned to the American. Bannon gave his answer by taking a revolver out of a shoulder holster and checking the load. It was a .38-caliber Smith & Wesson and Klimenti saw that Bannon loaded only five of the six chambers. It was information that could be useful one day.

"I didn't think I'd need one," Klimenti said. "Until now."

Spina shrugged. "It doesn't matter. It won't be necessary for you to do anything except confirm it's them. The big fellow should be a simple matter. But it could be difficult with Tabidze. And we have to be absolutely certain before I give the order to shoot."

Spina paused to emphasize his next words: "You realize that any hesitation on your part could be fatal. For one of my men."

"I'll recognize him," Klimenti said. "Whatever Tabidze's done to disguise himself, I'll still recognize him."

There was a harshness in his voice that caused Spina and Bannon—and even Kharkov—to look at him with interest.

"How well do you know him?" Bannon asked.

"He tried to kill me."

Kharkov was astounded, both by the information and by the fact that Klimenti had chosen to reveal it.

"With a knife?"

"It's his favorite weapon."

"He's killed his last man," Spina said. "I promise you that."

They sat in silence, watching the demonstrators. After a while, Bannon mused, "There must be close to a quarter of a million people. And this is just the beginning."

"You sound impressed," Klimenti said.

"It reminds me of the anti-Vietnam marches. Look what they grew into. Remember what they achieved."

"And Solidarity," Spina said. "Don't forget Poland and what's happened in Eastern Europe. The people mobilized, turning against authority."

"I marched in the Sixties," Bannon said. "I lost my eldest brother in Vietnam. Six days before his tour of duty was due to end."

It was a strange conversation, with the thunder of the crowd falling over them. There was a final tremendous surge of sound and then the demonstration was over and the crowd began dispersing, pouring into every available side street like a dam overflowing. Within minutes the Alfa Romeo was marooned in a sea of people.

Spina became alarmed. "This is hopeless," he cursed. But there was nothing that could be done. All around them flowed people, thousands of faces, moving slowly, shoulder to shoulder, a human crush. "A cockroach couldn't get through," Spina swore.

It was Big Dog whom Klimenti saw first. He stood head and shoulders above the crowd and he had worked his way to the opposite side of the street, the side on which the *pensione* was situated. He was thirty meters away and coming toward the Alfa, moving with the press of the crowd. Klimenti's eyes darted from face to face but he could not find Tabidze. He felt immediately uneasy, exposed, as if it were he, and not the Ferret, who was walking into a trap. Unwittingly he cast a quick glance behind, as if he expected danger to be lurking there.

"There's Big Dog," Klimenti said, pointing him out. "You can be sure he's not far from Tabidze."

Spina issued orders on the cellular phone. "The crowd makes it impossible to take them in the open. We'll take them the moment they enter the hotel. Get rid of all the staff, anyone who's there. You've got three minutes."

"Do we still shoot them, Commissario Capo?"

"As soon as they're in the lobby. In the knees."

"Yes, sir."

Big Dog was opposite the Alfa now, no more than ten meters away. Despite his height, the crowd blocked his view of the car. He had clipped his hair to a crew cut and his mustache was quite fair; he could pass for a German. In another fifty meters he would be at the hotel.

"Where's Tabidze?" Bannon cursed. "Where is the little shit?"

"He's there," Klimenti said. "Somewhere."

Klimenti's flesh goose-pimpled. He was sweating, and it was cold sweat. He remembered the hand stabbing for his crotch in the Hotel Belgrade, so fast, the Ferret showing him how easy it was with a knife. And the night he went to see Big Dog's mother, in the dark; Tabidze had cut Shileiko's throat and had almost got him, too. And now he was sweating cold sweat. Was he afraid of the Ferret?

"If Tabidze's not with him, we'll have to call it off," Spina cursed. "It's Tabidze we want most of all."

Big Dog had passed them now, his broad back to them. He was using his left arm to stop people pressing against his right shoulder. His wound still troubled him. In a few minutes he would be inside the hotel.

Spina held the telephone in his sweating hand, his frustration obvious. He had less than a minute in which to make a decision.

"Fuck it," he swore. "Where's that fucking Ferret?"

Without Big Dog to lead them to him, they would never find Tabidze.

"Fuck it," Spina swore again and lifted the telephone to call his men off.

"Wait," Klimenti said.

Big Dog had stopped against a building, letting the crowd flow around him. He stood so tall above the press that they could clearly observe his head as it turned, searching among the crowd. Klimenti sank deeper into the gloom of the car.

"He's waiting for Tabidze," Spina rejoiced. "He's waiting for the Ferret to catch up."

"Tabidze's sent him ahead to sniff the air," Bannon said. "He's using him as live bait. Just in case."

"He's a ferret, all right." Spina was calm now, sure his quarry was about to walk into his trap. "Get ready," he ordered into the telephone.

Klimenti saw Big Dog's head snap around in the same instant he heard the word, spat through the hubbub of the crowd like a jet of venom.

"Cheka!"

That's all. Just one word. Even so, he recognized the voice. He turned in the direction it came from and saw the beautiful, cruel eyes no more than two meters away, on fire with malevolence, and in the same instant they were gone. He saw a flurry and heard cries as Tabidze fought against the on-pressing stream of people, and then Big Dog was moving, too, forgetful of his wound, his shoulder down and charging, hurling people aside, coming through in a bow wave of falling bodies, using his great strength to cleave a passage through the crowd.

In the front seat Spina and Bannon were cursing and kicking at their doors, trying to get them open against the weight of the people falling back from Big Dog's onrush. Klimenti got his door partly open and squeezed out, knocking a woman over and stepping on her. Her boyfriend swore and kicked him and Klimenti put his elbow up and went through him, lifting him under the neck and over, feeling him underfoot, too. And then he was clear of the car and Big Dog saw Klimenti and stopped in shock.

"Big Dog," Klimenti shouted, reaching for him. "Big Dog."

Big Dog stood there and Klimenti clearly saw him shake his head, as if he were arguing with himself, and then he resumed his charge, scattering people. Women were screaming and men were shouting. Klimenti fell into Big Dog's wake, tripping once over a body. A hand brutally jerked him up again.

The Ferret! The thought went through him as sharply as a knife and he turned, screaming in rage and fear, striking out, and saw the astonished face of Kharkov.

"Colonel, it's me!" Kharkov shouted, throwing his shoulder forward to take Klimenti's chopping hand.

Klimenti stood there, panting and sweating and knowing the truth now; *I'm afraid of the knife.* His blow had hurt Kharkov. The young major was holding his left arm, which hung uselessly by his side, his face screwed up in pain.

Klimenti turned and went after Big Dog, aware of Kharkov stumbling behind. He heard a shot, then another. The screaming became total pandemonium as people tried to flee, to throw themselves to the ground. Big Dog picked up a woman and held her as a shield. She screamed and kicked but he held her as easily as a child would carry a doll. The shots spurred him to even greater fury and he made faster progress.

"Colonel, look out!" Kharkov shouted and Klimenti turned and saw Tabidze coming in, his left hand held high like a karate fighter and his right coming in low with the knife, striking always for the groin, wanting not just to kill but to disembowel. Kharkov lunged between them, striking for the knife with his good arm. He missed and Tabidze drove the knife in, ripping upward and across, snarling and biting as Kharkov closed in on him, grappling, the knife in his belly, refusing to let go, the knife ripping and Tabidze's fangs slashing into his throat. Then it was too much: the knife was ripping again, up and across, more than any man could take. Kharkov stumbled and Tabidze stepped back, freed from the struggle, his hand slippery with blood and losing its grip on the knife. Kharkov turned around, clutching at his belly, and Klimenti caught him as he fell. They both went down, trampled by the hysteria of the crowd recoiling from Tabidze.

Kharkov gurgled in pain, his blood pumping over Klimenti; neither of them felt the feet that trod on them. Then Bannon was over them, slashing with his revolver, driving people back and shouting. A hot blinding light hit Klimenti's face, an impact so bright he felt it was an explosion in his head. Bannon got the crowd away and the light was full on Kharkov's face, contorted in a terrible grimace, as pale and waxen as another face Klimenti remembered, the face of the corpse Morozov had used in his experiment at the Taman Guards rifle range. He knew Kharkov was dead.

"Tabidze," Klimenti whispered. "The Ferret."

"He got away," Bannon said with a curse.

Gently Bannon tried to help Klimenti, but he brushed him away and sat on the cobblestones, embracing Kharkov, whose blood was still warm, wondering about the white hot light.

8.

Klimenti came back to reality from somewhere far away. He felt an overwhelming lassitude, like a lover after an orgasm. He sat naked on his bed with a towel around his waist, coming back from where he had been, still floating and light-headed, waiting for his brain to achieve solidity again.

They had cleaned him of Kharkov's blood in a hospital, where doctors had tried to admit him for observation for shock. But he had refused, and they had stared at him without comprehension. It was some minutes before Klimenti realized he was talking to them in Russian and there was no translator; Levitin, who spoke the language with its beautiful music, was in the safe house. They had tried to give him an injection but Klimenti had knocked it away. He refused even a hot drink, fearing sedation. He had walked out, pushing aside the protesting hospital staff, until the *caribinieri* stopped him in the elevator. Spina and Bannon had arrived by then, with Nikishov and a translator, a young woman from the embassy. But he would not stay, and they had given up the argument and brought him back to the hotel.

Klimenti had asked Spina, "Have you got him?" It was a stupid question and it was a bad sign that he was asking it.

"No," the Italian had said gently and Klimenti had smiled, shocking them. They had looked quickly at his eyes, seen something wrong there too, and exchanged uneasy glances. At that moment, Klimenti could not have told them why he had smiled. He knew he had done it and he had seen they were alarmed; he knew he should not have done it. Even so, they had been unwilling to resort to force and they had let him go inside and shut the door in their faces.

In the shower, Klimenti had found some of Kharkov's blood dried and stiff around his testicles and he had felt the same stupid grin coming onto his mouth, a force within itself. This time he grasped what it meant, why he was glad they hadn't got Tabidze; because if they caught Tabidze, he wouldn't be able to kill him, and that's why he was grinning. Standing there with the hot water beating down on him, feeling Kharkov's dried blood on his crotch, Klimenti knew he was going to gut the Ferret the way the Ferret had gutted Kharkov—in, twist, rip—he was going to do it. He was smiling in anticipation of what he would see in Tabidze's eyes. He felt an almost sensual drowsiness and found himself sitting on the bed and not even remembering getting there. He wanted to stay where he was, dreaming of Tabidze's long-lashed eyes and what he was going to do to them.

Klimenti stared at the photograph of Marusya and didn't see it for a while; when he did, he saw a stranger.

He put on jeans and a shirt and turned on the television, flicking across the channels, the images bursting out at him and then disappearing in mid-squawk. Then he saw Kharkov filling the screen, his face washed with the deadly white hot light, his eyes already glazed and finished. Klimenti saw himself, cradling Kharkov's body and rocking him; his chest was wet and black with Kharkov's blood and there was blood on his face, too; he could not remember that. His head jerked around so that he was staring straight into the camera, and that shook Klimenti more than seeing Kharkov, seeing for the first time his own eyes as they flung their fear straight into the glare of the camera's lights. There was no mistaking his terror and it shocked him to see it, because he was not aware of having been afraid at that moment.

Klimenti switched the television off. He felt numb and frightened. *My eyes, my eyes, Little Mother, did you see my eyes?* What he had seen there was exactly what he had dreamed of seeing in Tabidze's eyes, what he was going to inflict into them with such pleasure.

Tabidze. Tabidze. Tabidze. The name banged into his brain like bullets.

There was a knock. Someone was at his door. Nikishov? Perhaps even Radchenko. Klimenti straightened himself, a soldier, and went to the door and opened it and forgot everything.

"Hello, Klimenti," she said with a half-shy, half-bold undecided smile.

"Zhenya!" She was standing there, wrapped in the expensive fur coat she had worn the night she came to him in the Zapo, and all he could say was *Zhenya*, so complete was his confusion. What was she doing here? How had she known where to find him? He almost asked it. For a moment he felt a fright, the strangest feeling, a hollowing in his belly.

"I saw what happened on television," she said. "It was . . ." Her words fluttered away, lost, totally inadequate. She shook her head in distress.

"Oh!"

"I was . . . worried about you."

She was pale. Her eyes were gray and he saw anxiety in them. He was very sensitive to eyes lately.

"Perhaps you don't want to see me," she said, too quickly. She was blushing now and a little flustered. In a minute her embarrassment would force her to flee and he realized that was the last thing he wanted her to do.

"Of course. Please." Klimenti stepped aside and Zhenya came through and he smelled her, and remembered; and already—just the sight of her, being so close, remembering—he felt an end to the doubts and suspicions, the turmoil that had plagued him since he had seen her with Byzov. He knew now what he wanted.

"Are you all right?"

"Yes." He was unable to say more and Zhenya saw this and bit her lip.

Klimenti reached out for her coat and she gave it to him with quick willingness, with a tight smile of gladness. He felt her warmth and suppleness and saw to his surprise that she was not dressed for going out but was wearing a simple woolen skirt and blouse and low-heeled shoes—very sensible winter clothes, wholesome and demure. He felt ashamed for all the images he had conjured of her and Byzov together. What a fraud he was!

"I've got only vodka," he said. "But it's Polish."

"It's my favorite." She tried to smile but it didn't work; she was too concerned, and he saw it and drew strength from her apprehensiveness. It made him feel good to know she was worried about him.

"Good," he said and laughed—a rather silly laugh. "Sit down. Sit down."

She sat on the edge of a lounge chair, very prim and proper. He sensed some of the vulnerability she had shown in the Zapo.

Klimenti poured two glasses of vodka and handed one to Zhenya. She sipped at it. The last time—the first time—they had drunk together was in the Belgrade and she had tossed it down in one swallow; he had thought she was a rather reckless young woman, and she had been.

"It's good to see you," he said. "Thank you for coming." Such tepid formality! He felt clumsy and stupid. "How did you know where to find me?"

Zhenya shook her head. "It's not important," she said and lowered her eyes.

He wondered at her answer, but only briefly. She was right. It wasn't important. What was important was that she had come. He felt an overwhelming sense of gratitude and gladness, knowing now how badly he needed her.

She lifted her eyes, confronting him. "I was frightened for you."

Twice before she had come to him, and he had failed her. And now she had come again. She was braver than he, ready to risk more. He had nothing to say to her that would not shame him. He stood watching her, holding his untouched vodka. What a wretch he was, a miserable fake. And she was so brave, risking herself.

"I've thought about you a lot," Klimenti said, his need greater than his fear, knowing that this time he had to commit himself.

Zhenya put the glass down and got to her feet; she stood in front of him, her hands by her side, looking up into his eyes.

"Why did you follow me that day in Moscow?" There was a husk in her voice.

"I wanted you," he said. It was out, he had said it, and it was a great relief.

He was trembling and Zhenya saw it and her eyes widened.

"And now?" she asked, a whisper raw and hoarse.

"I need you," he said and reached for her, and the moment she came to him was an end to everything. He entered her, she took him into herself, before they were undressed, hungering for each other, full of urgent heat, burning them in their fingertips as they tore at constricting clothes and on their skin and in their tongues and in their lips and inside them, the hottest of all, quaking and pulsing, expanding and contracting—a molten, living magma that grew so hot it filled them totally and blew out of them in a liquidating emptying. Their eyes were full and gentle with their new knowledge of each other.

Klimenti felt a completeness he had forgotten, and he knew he had come to the end of a long emptiness. He felt full again as he had long ago, and he lay in quiet thankfulness, her breath warm on his neck.

Soon Zhenya stirred and remembered what she had seen on the television; she trembled and wept for him, her tears salty on his mouth. She told him of her fright at seeing the television report on the early news, and then her panic. And then, as she had sat in her hotel room, not knowing what to do, there had been a knock on her door and a tall, elegant Russian, handsome, a little older than Klimenti, had told her, "Klimenti Sergeyevich is in trouble." He had driven her to the hotel and told her the room number. When she had asked his name, so she could thank him properly, he had smiled and told her, "It's not necessary. It's enough that you're going to him."

"He had a sad, lonely face," Zhenya said. "Do you know who he was?"

"Yes. A friend." Nikishov, longing for his unfaithful wife, knowing the power of love. "A better friend than I had thought."

Zhenya said, "I was so afraid you'd send me away." And he held her tighter, knowing the full measure of her courage. "Klimenti, you're a strange one," she told him, "not to know when a woman wants you."

"I was afraid, too, and I didn't have your courage," he said, and she kissed him and purred in her happiness. She was brave enough for both of them.

"I know now," he said.

She laughed. "I should hope so."

Zhenya put her hands between her legs and wet her fingers and put them in his mouth, so that he could taste their loving, and her lips and tongue came with them, her fingers in both their mouths.

"Oh, Klimenti, I love the taste of us," she gasped, and it began all again, slower this time, supple and skillful, exploring and experimenting, feasting their eyes as well as their senses, and learning from each other.

Later she went to the bathroom and he heard her singing; he hugged and muzzled a pillow with her musk on it, a happy man.

When Zhenya came back she stroked his cheek and said, "Klimenti, I have to go. They have room checks to make sure we haven't got beautiful young Italians in our beds. If I'm not back by eleven, they'll start asking a lot of ugly questions." She pulled a face. "I'm sure the woman I have to share my room with is an informer."

She saw his disappointment and laid her cheek against his. "Klimenti, I don't want to go. I want to stay with you. But I have to."

"I know. Will you come tomorrow?" The words were thick in his throat. He wanted her already.

She nodded eagerly, like a child. "I'll come earlier, so that we can have more time together."

"Would you like to go somewhere? A restaurant?"

"No," she said, kissing him. "I want to make love."

Klimenti felt absolutely beautiful. "I'm not arguing," he said.

At the door, troubled again, she said, "Klimenti, are you still afraid?"

"No," he said and she looked at him a long moment before she smiled and went out the door, shutting herself from sight. He wondered if she had known he was lying.

Klimenti lay for a long time thinking about Zhenya and what they had done and what it meant to him. With a sense of guilt and sadness he held the portrait of Marusya, knowing she no longer had the power to overwhelm Zhenya as she had all other challengers. This time he did not even want the victory to be hers; he was no longer in the thrall of her mysteries, the promise of her untold secrets.

There was a knock. *Zhenya*. She had returned, risking censure for him. He pulled on jeans and went to the door, his sadness gone. But it wasn't Zhenya. It was a young man who introduced himself as the assistant night-duty officer from the embassy. He said, "Colonel, I'm sorry to disturb you but the duty officer didn't think it was proper to use an open telephone line."

"There's a problem?" Klimenti beckoned him inside and shut the door.

"I'm not sure, sir. A man, a Russian, telephoned the embassy, demanding to talk with you, asking for your hotel address. We were immediately alarmed because no Russians outside the embassy are supposed to be aware you're in Rome. Of course, we refused and asked him to leave his name and a contact number. He wouldn't do it. Instead, he asked us to give you a message. He said when you heard it, you'd come running. It's a little embarrassing, sir, but it's up to you to be the judge."

"The message?"

" 'How's the lady with the nice tits?' "

9.

Klimenti buried himself in the shadows of the Church of San Clemente, watching the empty streets. The church wall abutted onto the side street and if anything moved out in via San Giovanni in Laterano, he would see it. Further down he could see the floodlit walls of the Colosseum, its graceful darkened arches like tiers of dead eye sockets. He listened for footsteps, the sound of an urgent car, but there was only the wind rustling a newspaper along the footpath.

There were several vehicles parked in the Laterano but none of them were vans that could be used for surveillance. Klimenti had already walked past each car to check that there was no one crouched out of sight. If he was being watched, then it had to be from a building and there was nothing he could do about that.

All cities change character in the early morning hours when they are quiet and empty, but in raucous, noisy Rome the difference was more noticeable. The people were so intimately fused into the city's character that their disappearance had the shock of an amputation. Without the human foliage to protect him, Klimenti felt exposed. He wished he had Kharkov along to watch his back.

But Kharkov was dead.

Klimenti had come half an hour before the appointed time and already forty minutes had elapsed. No one had approached. He held a 9mm Beretta beneath his leather jacket. With his back against the church he could not be taken unawares. Even so, they might come for him in a car or on a motor scooter, crossing the open ground quickly, and he intended to be ready.

Before coming he had consulted the picture book Spina had presented to him and from it he had learned that San Clemente was a twelfth-century church which had been built over a third-century church that had been partially destroyed by fire. The early Christians had built the first church on a place of pagan worship, the Temple of Mithras, the God of the Roman Legions. The temple was still there, buried eighty feet below, which is where the ground level of Rome was in the time of Christ. As far as Klimenti could discover from the guidebook, the side door was the only entrance in use. It was an ordinary door, its lock no challenge to a professional.

A voice whispered, "Psst, Colonel," and he turned to his right and saw nothing except the darker shadow of the church door. He heard it again. "Psst, Colonel." Big Dog was already inside San Clemente. He had been waiting in the doorway all the time, watching to make sure Klimenti had come alone.

Klimenti went along the wall, holding the Beretta hard against his stomach where it could not be struck or kicked from his hand, hammer back and ready to fire. Any blow would discharge the pistol; if he went down, his assailant would go with him.

Klimenti pushed the door open with his foot and when it had swung all the way back he went in quickly, stepping away from the door and going down on one knee, the pistol ready. But no blow, no shot, came. He was too professional to feel foolish; only amateurs felt silly about doing what had to be done, even when it turned out to be unnecessary. That's why amateurs died, not doing it the one time it was necessary.

Klimenti took out a flashlight but did not switch it on. He stood against the wall, adjusting his eyes, feeling rather than hearing the emptiness of the building with its fluttering shadows cast by the weak and flickering light of an oil lamp. There was no other light, and beyond the pale halo of the lamp the church was in total darkness.

"Big Dog," Klimenti whispered and his voice rustled through the darkness, losing itself.

His answer came with the tap of metal on stone. A gun barrel against a wall.

"Big Dog," he spoke louder to show impatience. Another faint glimmer of light appeared directly across the church, swaying with eerie gentleness. He switched on the flashlight and began a careful sweep. The beam illuminated a face of cruel suffering, emaciated arms outstretched in supplication, a mosaic of Christ on the Cross. Klimenti shivered. He went across to the light and saw it was another oil lamp.

Big Dog was lighting his way.

The lamp was at the entrance to a wide stone staircase that led downward. The stairs were wide and descended straight down perhaps fifteen meters. Klimenti's sneakers made no sound as he went down, acutely aware that the flashlight betrayed his every move.

It was not Big Dog he feared. It was the Ferret. Tabidze, down there in the cold blackness, heavy with the immense weight of time, thick with the density of suffering. With his knives. Tabidze, the twentieth-century pagan, waiting in the place where the worshipers of Mithras slaughtered bulls on the altar and dripped the blood onto legionnaires, swearing their oaths of fealty.

Tabidze was luring him to become a sacrifice, beneath the church that bore his own name: Clemente.

The lower church was made of Roman brick, the low roof supported by massive arched columns. Except for shadows it was empty of adornment. Klimenti felt he had stepped into an ancient tomb. This was a place built by Romans for Romans, a different people, the old Romans, long gone now. He was an intruder, just as surely as any grave robber. He went quickly, afraid that if he dallied his nerves might betray him and leave him frozen and unable to move, to go or to come, transfixed, as that figure of agony above had been.

Big Dog had placed a third oil lamp before the altar, an offering. Its light fluted and flickered upward, showing the bare marble. And, just within its illumination, a confessional. One door open. One door closed.

Big Dog waited.

Klimenti shone his flashlight onto the closed door. The light went through the lattice and he saw a vague outline that was too big to be the Ferret. Even so, Klimenti searched carefully around the empty church. His light found faded Roman murals, the eyes huge and dark and Egyptian, a lost people, but there was no sign of Tabidze.

As soon as he entered the confessional, he could feel Big Dog's body heat steaming through the lattice, the salty odor of nervousness.

Big Dog had chosen to remain out of sight to conceal whatever disguise he had adopted. Klimenti wondered how such a big man had moved through a city of short people without being noticed by those who hunted him. It was quite a feat, and an incredible risk to take under the circumstances.

He put the Beretta against the lattice where Big Dog could see it but not grab it.

"The hammer's back," Klimenti said. "A touch is all it'll take. I go, you go."

"You think I want to kill you, you must be crazy."

"Not you. The Ferret. Tabidze."

"And I'm the bait?"

"Why not, he's your *paichan*. You're his faithful servant. You do what he tells you."

"*Paichan!* You believe that?"

"You're well named, Big Dog. Both of you."

For a moment, Big Dog was quiet. Klimenti had the feeling that his remark had hurt.

"Listen, Colonel, I took a big risk trusting you, coming here. That's gotta be worth something."

"What do you want?"

"I want you to cut out this *paichan* shit."

Klimenti was astonished by his vehemence. Big Dog was one of the two most wanted men in Italy—the whole world—and he was worrying about what Klimenti thought of him. Klimenti eased down the hammer but kept the pistol in his hand. If he'd had the Beretta in the Piazza del Popolo, Kharkov would be alive.

"How's the shoulder?"

Klimenti was sure he heard a sigh of relief.

"It's OK. Sore, but it's clean and mending, thanks to that old geezer you got to stitch it up."

"He was an Academician."

"An Academician?"

"He did it for your grandfather. The men who died in the Dzerzhinsky Tractor Works."

"And he's an Academician. Shit, that's something."

There was no doubting the wonder in Big Dog's words. In the country he had grown up in, it was inconceivable that an Academician would come to help a criminal—or anyone, for that matter. The moat of privilege that kept the common herd back was too great, too jealously guarded.

"Did Tabidze send you?"

"No. If he knew what I was doing he'd kill me."

"He'll kill you anyway. One day."

Again Big Dog was silent. Then he said, "It's not his fault." And Klimenti realized that he still loved the Ferret. Tabidze might no longer be his *paichan* but he was still his childhood companion, the only person with whom Big Dog had shared his secrets, and Klimenti knew that it was useless to expect him to betray Tabidze—even to save his own skin.

"You don't know what his life's been like," Big Dog said. *"You just don't know!"*

Klimenti sat in silence, knowing he had no answer and feeling the pain and the anger and the frustration through the lattice.

Big Dog said, "Colonel, what happened today, I didn't even know it until I saw it on television. I was too busy dodging bullets."

"Tabidze didn't tell you?"

"All he said was he'd lost his knife."

"Did he tell you he killed a man a week ago? He cut his throat. But that's not all he did to him," Klimenti said and told Big Dog how Tabidze had used Salvatore.

"Shit," Big Dog breathed. The fumes coming off his sweating body were particularly rank now.

"And you still trust him?"

There was no answer.

"You can't save him, Big Dog. You can run with him but you can't save him. For a little while, maybe. But not in the end."

"I can't walk away. I can't do it."

"If you want to stay alive you have to."

"I can't leave him all alone," Big Dog said simply, and Klimenti felt the depth of his pain, this man who understood loneliness so deeply that he would sacrifice himself rather than condemn another to it. It also told him something he had not suspected: that Tabidze was vulnerable and had his fears and hurts, too. *Tabidze needed love.* It was a shock.

"There'll be no deals for Tabidze," he said harshly, frightened by this glimpse of humanity in the man he was going to kill, *wanted to kill*.

"He knows that," Big Dog said. "He's not afraid to die. He's never known that fear. I think it's the reason he can kill so easily, because he has no respect for life. Not even his own."

"Why'd you come here then?"

"I want to go home, as soon as I can get the Ferret set up someplace safe," Big Dog said. "I want you to fix it so that I can go back and look after my grandmother."

Klimenti did not know what to say.

"You're my only chance, Colonel." Big Dog was anxious now. "You've seen what it's like out there—an old woman, living alone in that rat hole. She needs someone to look after her, to make sure she's comfortable and no one's going to come around giving her trouble."

Klimenti remembered the spotlessly clean apartment in a building that stank of poverty, filled with the stolen bounty of a grandson's love; and the little old woman bent with hardship but her spirit unbroken, the softness of her horny hands and the memory she had brought him of his own mother, another wound reopened. *Little Mother*.

"You've been good to her." Big Dog's voice was insistent now, pitched with urgency. "You took her food and money, two hundred rubles, before you left Moscow."

So he knew.

"She writes," Big Dog said. "She told me. She doesn't complain but I know she's lonely and I've got to go back and look after her, like she looked after me all her life."

Klimenti had suspected that Big Dog would keep in touch. He'd asked her about it but she'd lied to him without batting an eyelid.

Klimenti said, "Lead me to Tabidze and you're on the next Aeroflot flight out of Rome."

He could feel Big Dog shaking his head.

"Just me," he said. "That's all. No one else. Just take me to where Tabidze's hiding and leave me alone with him."

"*You*, Colonel? Just you? I don't understand."

"You don't have to, Big Dog. Just take me to Tabidze. Lead me there and walk away and by tomorrow night you'll be back in Moscow with your grandmother, all forgotten and forgiven. A new record, a new start. A job even."

He was pushing too hard, but he couldn't help it. He wanted Tabidze too badly.

"Jesus, Colonel. What is it? Your voice! I never heard you like this before."

"I'm going to kill him," Klimenti said harshly and heard the sound of his own breathing in the silence that followed.

"No," Big Dog said, and they both waited in silence again. He could hear Big Dog breathing, too, in this duet of tension and nervousness.

Big Dog said, "I've got something else to offer, Colonel. Someone who can lead you to these VFP maniacs you're chasing."

No, Klimenti thought, don't give me the VFP. Give me Tabidze.

"Who?" he asked.

"Do I go back home?"

"It depends on who it is and what it leads to. You get paid on results, not promises."

The confessional rocked as Big Dog shifted his weight and Klimenti thought, he's gone, and made no move to check him although the pistol was still in his hand. He could guess what Big Dog was offering and, although it was important, he was strangely disinterested. If he stopped Big Dog now, they would never find the Ferret. He would slip away with all the skill and cunning of a wild animal. Big Dog would lead them to Tabidze. The Ferret could be invisible, but not with the lumbering Big Dog by his side.

Klimenti wondered how long it would take the Ferret to realize this and kill Big Dog.

"All right," Big Dog said. He had not fled, after all, but had merely shifted his position, thinking it out. "I want your word, Colonel. You get the man I give you, and I get to go back home."

"You trust me?"

"I'm here, aren't I?" Big Dog growled, not liking it at all.

"You have my word," Klimenti said. It was a lie and he didn't give a damn. While Tabidze was alive, until he led them to him, Big Dog would never go back to Moscow, no matter what price he paid.

"Don't let them screw this up," Big Dog said and told him about Klaus, the fat Bavarian who sold medical equipment to the Soviet Union, the man who had consigned the packing cases in which the plastic explosive had entered Moscow, who had commissioned the theft of the Zil limousine. His information was what Klimenti had expected with one important surprise. Big Dog had the addresses of Klaus's home and company.

"The Ferret followed him after their first meeting," Big Dog said. "He knows a chance at blackmail when he sniffs one. When we came over the border he was our best chance for some easy money. We were watching him, just to be sure no one else was onto him, when one day he stopped in his tracks, turned around, and walked straight up to the Ferret and told him he was *looking for him*. You wouldn't believe it. The Ferret was so angry I thought he was going to cut him right there and then."

"What did he want?"

"I wasn't allowed to hear. The Ferret didn't tell me. That's how it's always been, even when we were kids." There was a note of pride in Big Dog's voice; he valued his loyalty more than his own freedom, a real slave. The more he learned about the big man, the more Klimenti wondered at the strength of his bondage.

"All the Ferret told me was there was work for us in Rome, instant cash. American dollars and a lot of them."

"Who was the contact in Rome?"

"I don't know. That's the Ferret's job."

"What is it you do, Big Dog? What does he use you for?"

"I watch his back. I listen."

"Listen!"

"He likes to talk. He gets lonely and he likes to have someone he can . . . well, *talk* to."

"What does he talk about?"

"Like anyone else." Big Dog was offended. "What he wants to do. His dreams. Secrets."

Dreams! Secrets! The Ferret, who liked to cut throats, and worse. A dreamer, a man of intimate secrets! It was shocking. Indecent. It wasn't possible. But he knew Big Dog was not lying. It was hot in the confessional now, his own body was steaming; he was bathed in a sweat of anxiety, afraid of this knowledge of the Ferret's humanness and yet unable to resist it. He was confronted with a new and unwelcome reality. The Ferret was beginning to exert a fascination over him and Klimenti told himself to be on guard.

"He's human," Big Dog said in his offended voice, taking Klimenti's silence for scorn. "Just different, that's all."

Klimenti asked quietly, "He's afraid of being alone?"

"Isn't everyone?"

Klimenti whispered, "If you let me kill him, he'll never be lonely again."

There was no answer and Klimenti became aware of a loss of heat, a sense of emptiness beyond the lattice. Big Dog was gone. Klimenti stepped out, Beretta ready, ran to the staircase, and looked up in time to glimpse a priest moving quickly and silently into the light of the oil lamp above, the long black skirts of his soutane whispering against his legs, his broad-brimmed round hat pulled low over his ears. There was nothing to distinguish him from any of the other thousands of priests who wandered the streets of Rome, except that this priest was exceptionally big. And he carried a machine pistol. Then he was gone.

10.

By 9 A.M., a quick exchange of coded signals between the KGB staff of the Soviet embassies in Rome and Vienna had confirmed that a manufacturer of medical equipment, Arzneimittel Hersteller GmbH, indeed existed at the Industriegelaende Nord, Werkstrasse, Wien Neustadt, and that one of its salesmen, Klaus Nagel, had made seventeen trips to Moscow in the last three years. They confirmed Nagel's home address in Währingerstrasse 18, Bezirk. The Vienna KGB was ordered to begin immediate around-the-clock surveillance on Nagel.

In the *referentura* Nikishov said, "Big Dog might still be bluffing. There's a big black-market trade in medical supplies from West Germany. That might be the limit of his association with Nagel. After all, he and Tabidze are smugglers."

In the hard light of day he was a hunter again, a different person from the man who had sent Zhenya to Klimenti.

Klimenti, who had not yet had a chance to thank him, shook his head. "No, he's telling the truth."

Radchenko said, "Don't you think it's dangerous to place so much faith in the word of a criminal?"

"He was right about the Zil and the garage in Moscow," Klimenti said.

Radchenko said, "I find it hard not to be impressed, although with great reluctance, by a man who refused to sell out his comrade to gain his own safety."

"I find the whole episode rather worrying," Nikishov said coolly. He distrusted informants over whom he did not have absolute control. "You took a lot on yourself when you let him walk away."

"I would have had to kill him to stop him," Klimenti said. "And he's no good to us dead."

Klimenti had slept only a few hours. His body ached with tiredness, as if he had been beaten, and he had a thumping headache, all the symptoms of an adrenaline hangover. Radchenko, who knew a lot about combat exhaustion, watched him carefully. Klimenti seemed to be in control, but it was always difficult to be sure. It had taken a lot of nerve, risking a rendezvous with Big Dog so soon after the trauma of Kharkov's bloody killing. Radchenko knew fighters and he understood how difficult it was to maintain rationality when you had been washed with the blood of your comrades.

Klimenti said, "May I ask what arrangements are being made about Major Kharkov?"

Already he had trouble recalling his face but he knew that would come later. The faces never went away. They were with you forever. Like the faces in Berlin he could never forget, but which he could never conjure up when he wanted to. Kharkov had joined the gallery. Why were they always so young?

"His body is being flown back to Moscow this morning."

"His family?"

"His mother, a brother, two sisters. They're being brought to Moscow," Radchenko said. "He was a country boy from a village in the Urals."

As they left the *referentura*, Klimenti reflected that the expression on Radchenko's granite face had been almost kindly.

Nikishov walked quickly, and Klimenti realized he was trying to escape his gratitude. He did not want to talk about last night. But it was a debt Klimenti could not ignore, in spite of Nikishov's prickliness.

"Simis, about Zhenya Stepanov."

"It's not necessary," Nikishov said, walking more quickly.

Klimenti took his arm and brought him to a stop. "Simis, I want you to know that what you did is important to me. It was a great kindness."

Nikishov was fretful. "I shouldn't have interfered."

"Perhaps not, but both Zhenya and I are grateful that you did. Particularly me."

"I wish you happiness," Nikishov said. "As long as you let me go now."

Klimenti released his arm, smiling through his tiredness. "Don't worry, Simis. I won't tell anyone you're really a fairy godmother."

Nikishov blanched and hurried on.

Bannon and Spina were at the Ministry of the Interior. They, too, noticed how haggard Klimenti looked but made no comment, knowing that quite often sympathy openly expressed defeated its true purpose. Their shared experiences had begun to temper their relationship, and they were on guard. There had been no relaxation of security and Klimenti stood wearily as he was searched. He was glad to find a seat and sit down.

The podium was taken by a middle-aged American, Dr. Gustav Wallheimer from Columbia University, whose two widely acclaimed books, *The Politics of Terrorism: David versus Goliath* and *The Global Psychosis*, had made him an internationally recognized authority on mass motivation and manipulation. Wallheimer had remarkably pink and chubby cheeks and small but protruding rosebud lips. He was so nicely porcine—so plump, smooth fleshed and big haunched—he was a cannibal's delight. He was conservatively and expensively dressed and wore a heavy gold ring on each hand and a prohibitively expensive gold Cartier watch, all of which he flashed to his audience as he tugged at the sleeves of his jacket, an unintentionally flamboyant gesture. Wallheimer's consulting fees were so huge they could be afforded only by major corporations and the CIA.

"Gentlemen," Wallheimer said, "assassins of this caliber don't grow on trees. The difficulty in finding suitable subjects for conditioning, the need for a highly specialized and qualified staff working in total secrecy, the length of time involved, the enormous cost—all these factors militate against a plentiful supply of assassins who are willing to self-destruct. We know we are up against a highly professional organization. From this we can deduce that they would not be wasteful with such rare resources. Yet in one week they expended, they literally blew away, *four.*"

The word swept over them like a sonic boom. Wallheimer paused for breath, as if the shock of it—*four in one week*—had knocked the air out of his lungs.

"That's how you've got to think of it," Wallheimer said. "As the first *barrage*. When they're ready they'll fire the second."

Terrorism, Wallheimer continued, had become so commonplace that individual condemnation of any group of terrorists was directly related to the threat those terrorists presented to the individual, specifically and personally. If the perception of threat was strong, so was the condemnation. But if no direct threat was perceived, the level of condemnation was low, often nonexistent. Secondly, individuals were loath to condemn terrorists if their victims were seen to be deserving of the threat—in other words "guilty"—and the terrorists were perceived to be acting for a good cause—in other words, were "right." Who, except the Germans, condemned acts of terrorism against the Nazis in the Second World War, even when they resulted in the killing of innocent civilians?

The VFP obviously could not hope to produce enough self-destructing assassins to get rid of all their proclaimed targets, the nuclear hawks. There were simply too many of them. The purpose of the assassinations, therefore, was fourfold: to give dramatic focus to the VFP and its demands for nuclear disarmament by grabbing world attention; to identify a highly selective target group and denounce its members as "guilty," thereby winning public neutrality; to convince the ordinary citizens of the world that they were acting on their behalf, thereby winning acceptance; and to convince the same citizens that there was no direct risk to them, thereby winning approval. So far the VFP had been outstandingly successful in all objectives.

"It is my opinion that the level of public acceptance will grow," Wallheimer said. "The fear of nuclear annihilation, catastrophes such as the near nuclear meltdowns at Three Mile Island and Chernobyl, the Alaskan oil spill, all the associated manmade anxieties that are perceived to threaten life on the Planet Earth—the destruction of the ozone layer, the greenhouse effect, the poisoning of the oceans, the destruction of forests, the pollution of the air, acid rain—all these have created a truly global psychosis. Everywhere ordinary citizens are becoming increasingly distrustful of, and hostile toward, their governments, seeing them as ineffective or, worse, deliberately deceitful.

"This 'global psychosis' has united mankind in a way never before possible, regardless of nationality, political creed, religion, color, sex, or age. The issue is survival, our most primitive, our strongest emotion, the force that brought us successfully through millions of years of evolution. The protection and propagation of the species—a force so vital, so compelling that you don't even need language to express it, you don't have to be able to read or write to understand it.

"Now, suddenly and dramatically, in a manner we cannot ignore, all this simmering dissatisfaction has found a new champion—the Vigilantes for Peace. They are holding a match to a fuse—and that fuse is fear, distrust, hostility, a growing conviction among ordinary people that they have to fight for themselves, to rely on mass mobilization as the only safeguard of their own future.

"What the VFP have launched is not a campaign of terror. It's a crusade. Listen to their own words—*for* the innocents, *against* the guilty. A crusade in which they are seeking to isolate the two greatest world powers, the United States and the Soviet Union, to make them the focal point of global resentment. They are seeking to show the ordinary citizens of the world that they can treat the superpowers with contempt. Not with awe.

"But that's not all. By striking selectively at nuclear hawks, they are seeking to raise both presidents above their 'guilty' advisers, to make them the torch carriers of human aspirations for peace and security. They are seeking to raise a global clamor for truly inspirational leadership."

Wallheimer looked down at his audience and Klimenti was not sure what he saw in his eyes. Was it contempt? "So far, gentlemen, they have succeeded brilliantly. I must add, however, that I personally have the utmost confidence that you, the assembled representatives of the forces of repression, the guardians of the good ship Planet Earth, will do your duty and destroy the Vigilantes for Peace."

Wallheimer walked off the podium and exited by a side door without giving them another glance.

As they left the auditorium, Spina said, "So we're charged with stopping the world revolution. And this time, according to our learned professor, it's *everyone*."

Klimenti said, "He didn't wish us good fortune in our mission."

"Coming from a CIA adviser, it was very radical stuff," Spina said.

"We're a pretty radical organization," Bannon said, and neither Klimenti nor Spina could be sure whether he was serious.

As they went out into the sunlight, Spina said, "When I went home last night, there was a poster plastered on our living room wall. Do you know what it said?"

"*Condannate i colpevoli! Salvate gli innocenti! Disarmate!*" Bannon said with surprising fluency.

Spina nodded. "Then I went to the bathroom."

"*I Martiri di Mosca.*"

"My wife's reading his poetry."

"What did you do?" Klimenti asked.

"Do? What could I do? My wife, my daughter, my son, they'd all been in the Piazza del Popolo."

They walked on. "Besides, I agree," Spina said. "Who wants to be frizzled by a hundred-megaton bomb? Who wants their children to become thermonuclear negatives, their shadows scorched into some damn footpath? Who wants nuclear bombs? Who needs superpowers?"

"So what about the VFP?" Bannon asked, quiet now, his eyes intent.

Spina shrugged. "Who wants assassins?" And a few steps further on, showing the depth of his conflict: "Fortunately we've got our duty to do."

"Yeah," Bannon said somberly. "What'd you think of his poetry?"

Despite his hard leanness, his face could be marvelously expressive when he wanted it to be—watchful and distrustful, fierce and full of latent savagery, and now, deeply curious.

"You think I read his poetry?" Spina said, caught completely off guard and not sure how to answer. Klimenti thought, Bannon's right; he, too, could see what Bannon had sensed in the Italian. It wasn't only Spina's wife who had been affected by Leonardo's words.

"There's an English-language edition coming out next week," Bannon said. "I've ordered a copy."

Bannon too! The tough American, reading Leonardo! What an achievement for the poet.

"I didn't like it very much at all," Spina said. "It was rather difficult and at times quite painful to read. He was a man of agony, not happiness. But when I put the book down, I felt I had learned something of value. I felt he was *important*, not in the sense of being special, but in the sense of being a human being, like the rest of us. And I think I got this sense because he made me feel that I was important, too. Just another human being. But important at the same time." Spina shrugged, sensing unsuspected poetry in himself and embarrassed once again. "I'm not a man of words."

"I know what you're saying," Bannon said sympathetically.

One of Spina's men came hurrying up and spoke in a burst of excited Italian. Spina turned to them. "Three assassins have just killed the French President as he left the Elysée Palace."

The French President! The three agents stared at each other in disbelief. France with its pitiful Force de Frappe was one of the world's six top nuclear powers. But it was not a superpower, a target for the VFP—the French, for all their pride and posturing, were not factors in the disarmament equation. Killing the French President would make no impact at all. It was a waste of assassins, of precious assets.

"Did they self-destruct?" Klimenti asked. A surge of excitement overwhelmed his tiredness.

"No," Spina said. "Bodyguards killed two and wounded the third. He's still alive. They used machine pistols from a car."

"Then they're not the VFP," Bannon said.

Klimenti nodded in emphatic agreement. He was sure of it, too. Wallheimer, the fat American, was right. He had predicted it. A crusade.

"They've ignited a fuse," Klimenti said. "They've started a conflagration. A chain reaction of terrorism."

First the British Prime Minister. Now the French President. Where next would a terrorist strike, inspired by the spectacular success, the fearless scorn, of the VFP? No national leader could now be considered safe. Already the sirens were going, rising and falling and then revving up again, the wail of twentieth-century distress, mankind's wounded nerve shrieking its despair. The Italian security forces were rushing to protect their own leaders. In every country, on every continent, it would be the same, a tremendous diversion of security resources *away* from the hunt for the VFP, directed to the suppression of actual or suspected terrorists. How many more copycat killings would they inspire? How many terrorists groups were there?

Hundreds more.

"Every terrorist group in the world's going to jump onto their bandwagon," Bannon said. "They're all going to start cutting loose. Not a bad result, for the expenditure of four assassins."

"They saw it coming," Spina said. "Chaos! The best camouflage for terrorists to hide in."

Spina's aide begged, "Commissario Capo. Contact DIGOS. Please."

But Spina ignored him. "The legend grows," he said. For once, he forgot to shrug. "The VFP don't fail. The VFP don't get taken alive. The VFP don't get taken at all."

"We'll take them," Bannon said. "And you can bet on that, too."

He was very American, Klimenti thought. Very sure of himself. Very determined. Very brave.

"Yes," Spina said but with none of Bannon's vehemence. "You are right. In the end we will take them. But let me tell you, it had better be soon, before the legend becomes an indestructible myth. And then, no matter what happens, they win."

Spina's assistant finally succeeded in hustling him into an Alfa, which tore off, tires smoking, siren howling.

Bannon smiled wearily. "What about you, Colonel? You going to read him? Leonardo, the killer poet?"

"I doubt there'll be a Russian-language edition."

Bannon smiled. "I wouldn't bet on it either."

He walked away. What an unusual, perplexing enemy he was turning out to be, Klimenti thought.

At a newsstand, the front page of the right-wing newspaper *Il Secolo* caught his eye. Above the fold was a four-column photograph of Zhenya and Byzov, their heads close together, whispering secrets. The headline read: *"Dalla Russia con Amore."*

Klimenti didn't need much Italian to translate it.

From Russia with Love.

11.

Zhenya had said she would come early so that they could spend more time making love, and now her promise alternatively mocked and scalded Klimenti. He told himself several times he would not wait for her, but in the end he went to his hotel room, doing his best to rationalize his behavior. What did it matter to him if Zhenya was Byzov's lover? She was a beautiful girl and he would be stupid—absolutely crazy—not to take advantage of the opportunity and share her favors, without complaint or jealousy. He had no hold over her, nor she over him. She was free to do as she wished—and who was he, who had had many lovers, to judge her?

Jealousy was acid in his guts. After all the years of emptiness there had been too much emotion, too quickly. He had to shut it off, to get control. Klimenti knew he could do it.

Then there was a knock on his door and Zhenya stood there and, once again, it all fell to pieces.

"Klimenti," she said in that husky voice that made his spine shiver, her gray eyes opening to him. She stepped in and put her arms around him, not holding back, enveloping him in herself. She did this so trustingly, offering herself without hesitation and so completely that Klimenti lost himself; and she felt his hunger and murmured her delight onto his lips.

They undressed each other, caught in a lovers' thrall of touch and

372

taste—where emotions trembled exquisitely and more expressively than words—Zhenya casting him shy-sly glances. "I love you looking at me like that," she said, opening to him, and he surrendered himself in another emptying.

Afterward, exhausted, he slept in her arms, their sweat mingling and cooling, content and safe. A soft shaking awakened him. Zhenya was sitting by him on the bed, fully dressed. She had showered and wore no makeup, but her lips were full from their loving, giving her a sultry look. She smelled good and Klimenti reached for her. She held his hand down. Her face was grave.

"What is it?" he asked, afraid once more.

"This," Zhenya said and showed him the newspapers, *Il Secolo* and the *Herald Tribune*, which he had bought so that he could read about Byzov's love affair. He had read avidly, the interviews with hotel staff on the condition of Byzov's bed linen, the very personal women's toiletries in his bathroom, the breakfasts-for-two that he ordered every morning, and the fact that his translator, the beautiful Miss Zhenya Stepanov, never left his side and was the only one in Byzov's entourage who had a bed that was never slept in. Ashamed, he had thrust the newspaper in the trash basket in the bathroom.

Klimenti felt like a petty thief.

Zhenya said quietly, "You read *this*—and you could still do all we did together?"

"I threw it out," Klimenti said. "It doesn't matter."

"You thought I was Byzov's lover—and you still made love to me?"

Klimenti was silent. He did not know what to say and was afraid of making it worse.

"You didn't think it was important?" Zhenya was calm, but it was the composure of travail. She had steeled herself for this.

Klimenti said quietly, "I've no right to intrude in your life. I thought it was important that I recognize that. What else could I do but put it aside?"

"You could have asked if it was true." Zhenya made it sound so simple Klimenti flinched.

"I told you. I don't have the right."

"If it was important, you would have *claimed* the right. If it was important, you would have asked."

"It's important."

"Then why didn't you ask?"

Klimenti fell silent. If he told the truth he would condemn himself.

Zhenya said it for him. "You didn't ask, you didn't claim the right, because you believe it's true. That I'm Byzov's mistress."

Her eyes were no longer gray but smoked with anger.

"Fucking him!"

"Zhenya!"

"Is that what you think of me, Klimenti? A hot little cunt, running from you to Byzov. Doing for him what I do for you. *All of it!*"

The frankness of her language, her fearless honesty, shook him. Klimenti wanted to cry out, "No!" But he could not. It was exactly what he had thought, and she saw the truth in his face.

"You diminish me, Klimenti. But more than that, you've diminished yourself." She stood up. She seemed older, stronger, and her composure frightened him more than her words because it was more dangerous. He wished she would rant or burst into tears, claw at him, scream insults—anything except this deadly calm.

"You're not the man I thought you were." Zhenya's voice was no longer sharp with anger but quiet; she spoke in sorrow. Klimenti did not look up until he heard the door shut.

He took a shower, dressed in slacks and a turtleneck sweater, put on his soft Italian leather jacket, and went for a walk. The night was cold on his face and he welcomed it. It was not late, only twenty past nine, and the restaurants he passed were all crowded, warm, and happy places where people ate with gusto and much gesticulation, not afraid to express their enjoyment. Condensation steamed against the windows. He walked without direction, aware that he was being followed, two men in a dun-colored Opel, taking turns to go on foot; at least the car was different. He was sure they were Spina's men. It didn't matter, he didn't care; he had nowhere to lead them.

He wanted to be back in Moscow with familiar things, in his flat with his father and Nadya, Sabotka even; he wanted to feel safe. He knew this feeling but he had experienced it previously only in moments before danger, the waiting time before going in, and later when it was all over. In those moments, simple, ordinary things assumed great value, the more ordinary the better, and loved ones became especially precious, for they promised security. The need was a signal of vulnerability.

Klimenti thought about Zhenya and her dangerous composure; in that moment in his hotel room he had seen the full measure of the woman in her, and her strength filled him with admiration and pride. He had glimpsed it in Moscow and should have been warned, but his own jealous conceit had been too busy worrying about itself, too preoccupied with its own silly vanity to see the truth. Now it was too late and he accepted the judgment; it was what he deserved. He dismissed all thoughts of telephoning her, sure that it would be futile and humiliating for both of them. He felt a sense of loss but no pain, which was remarkable considering how his earlier jealousy had troubled him. He was emotionally exhausted; his ability to feel had been sucked dry. In this he was lucky, for it dulled what could have been a considerable hurt.

Klimenti heard music, the joyful burble of a clarinet, and he turned into a bar. A jazz band was playing, piano and drums and bass and trumpet and trombone, with the clarinetist doubling as a saxophonist, all going together now, wild as the music; the whole place was moving with it, feet tapping, heads bobbing, bodies swaying, the wonderful music lifting them up so that they caught the glances of strangers and smiled, *Isn't it great*, and their eyes laughed, *Just great!* Sometimes the music got so big in them it was too much to contain and they broke out and spun and jived and rocked in the cigarette smoke, unabashed, freed by the music and the people around them, yelling for more.

Klimenti got a beer and found a seat at a table, feeling at home among strangers as he let the music go to work in him, driving away his emptiness and replacing it with a quiet, reflective sadness. Marusya had loved jazz; she had adored the black musicians and the singers, their wonderful faces and sad histories, and collected all their records; he had them still, in Moscow. When she got up and danced, everyone had watched, feeling her wildness and sorrow. The music brought her back to him and he knew that he had begun to say a farewell, the beginning of a parting. Zhenya had given back Marusya and had taken her away at the same time, and what she had done had changed him. To his surprise, feeling sad in a place of such joy and abandon was quite a good feeling; sorrow, he learned, could be gentle and warm.

He did not want to lose this and when a hand touched his shoulder he did not look up, hoping they would go away, knowing they wouldn't.

"Excuse me, Colonel," a voice said in Italian-English, and Klimenti finished his drink, a gesture of resignation, before he turned to see whom Spina had sent. He recognized him immediately—the young man who had been with them when they went up the stairs and found Salvatore's body.

"So you've finally got your orders," Klimenti said and walked out to the Opel, which was parked across the street. They drove in silence for fifteen minutes and Klimenti thought it through. By the time the Opel turned into the entrance of a large villa, he had worked out the deal he was going to make.

Caribinieri guarded the gates. Police cars were parked in the driveway, along with two ambulances. With relief, Klimenti saw there were no bodies, no morgue wagons.

Levitin and his team sat on a bench in the lobby, handcuffed and guarded by *caribinieri* with machine pistols. Levitin looked unusually handsome and young in his police uniform. He was also unusually pale but otherwise undaunted.

He said in Russian, "We walked into a trap."

"Was anyone hurt?"

The Israeli Arabs looked up in surprise, recognizing Russian, and hope flared in their surly eyes.

Levitin shook his head and smiled wanly. "Only my pride."

"It's not your fault," Klimenti said. "We were set up, right from the start."

Spina came in. Bannon was with him. Neither of them said anything. Klimenti regarded the Italian with admiration, wondering how long he had been baiting this trap for the *residenz*'s mole. Finally Spina gave expression to their feelings. He shrugged.

"Did they leave anything?" Klimenti asked.

Spina shook his head. "Not even a fingerprint."

"When did they pull out?"

"There's nothing here to tell us. We're interviewing the neighbors."

"How many rooms?"

"Twelve that could have been used for patients."

"Twelve!"

Bannon said, "They knew we were coming. They know everything we do—before we do it."

"How did you find them?"

Spina said, "They're using highly specialized drugs imported from Vienna. We followed the trail."

Klimenti indicated Levitin and his men. "They'll be on tomorrow's Aeroflot flight to Moscow. If they're not, we'll leak the story about our mole. I don't think your government would survive the scandal."

Bannon laughed outright, admiring his audacity. Spina shrugged. He said, "You're probably right."

An hour later, the teleprinters in the Soviet Embassy in Rome carried a coded signal from the Soviet Embassy in Vienna. It said that at 5:52 P.M. that day, the subject of surveillance, Klaus Nagel, was killed when a radio-controlled bomb exploded in his car as he drove home from work.

The VFP had either become aware that the KGB were watching Nagel or had anticipated their interest. And foreclosed. Another lead was extinguished.

12.

In the morning the newspaper and radio stations announced the retirement because of ill health of General Giovanni Barigioni, Deputy Director of the Italian Intelligence Service, SISDI. A statement from the President's office praised the great service Barigioni had rendered his country. Several astute journalists wondered why, if Barigioni had been such a wonderful patriot, the President declined to read the statement aloud for the benefit of the microphones and cameras. They began digging but got nowhere. There were no leaks, unusual in Italian politics.

The communist newspaper, *L'Unità*, also announced that Comrade Byzov was flying back to Moscow the following day after successfully concluding his mission in Rome. *Il Secolo* claimed the credit, saying President Gorbachev had been infuriated by Byzov's love affair with his beautiful translator, Zhenya Stepanov, and reprinting its lurid revelations. The Italian Communist Party issued an angry denunciation of the newspaper, the Italian press in particular, and the Western press in general.

The *Herald Tribune* carried a paid notice: "Simon, phone home" and a seven-digit telephone number. So soon!

Klimenti left the hotel and walked until he found a public telephone. This time, the number he rang was in Rome.

In the *referentura*, Radchenko announced that he and Nikishov were taking the *residenz* to Moscow for debriefing. "Interrogating," Nikishov said flatly. "It's important we learn when and how the Italians realized Barigioni was spying for us."

"For some considerable time," Klimenti said.

"What makes you say that?" Radchenko asked.

"Commissario Capo Spina. His real job is with Italian counterintelligence. It's obvious now that he was put under cover as a DIGOS agent because the Italians saw from the outset that the hunt for the VFP was an ideal opportunity to set a trap for Barigioni."

"That's true," Nikishov said. "They knew—but they had to catch him red-handed."

Radchenko thought for a moment and then said, "You'll find there've been some changes in Moscow. Deputy Chairman Poluchkin has retired. With full honors, of course."

"Ill health?" Nikishov asked out of politeness.

"Partly," Radchenko said. "Partly a failure of faith."

"Poluchkin lost faith?" Klimenti could not restrain himself. He simply did not believe it. Poluchkin, the battle-scarred old warrior! The Sword and the Shield! He clearly saw the wounded eye bulging hideously in the ravaged face, a stern old Commissar full of German steel and loyalty.

Radchenko said, "He's an old Commissar. The Party's been his life. I don't believe he ever came to terms with the Party surrendering its monopoly on power. He also became nervous about all the trouble in the republics. He wanted to get a lot tougher and stamp down on the nationalists. He came to believe he was witnessing the dissolution of the Soviet Union."

"There was another plot?" Nikishov exclaimed.

"No. It never went that far and I am personally sure that Comrade Poluchkin would never have permitted it. However, he was part of a group that was exerting pressure for a change in policies, and Comrade Gorbachev can't permit that. There can be no going back," Radchenko said. "The Soviet Union must change or it will collapse economically. As for the nationalists, they'll be pulled into line, one way or another. It's a matter of faith. *It will be done.*"

He regarded them with his small red eyes, probing, sniffing them out. If he found weakness, a lack of faith, he would strike, ruthlessly. He was Gorbachev's man, utterly.

Klimenti was glad of it. Gorbachev needed all the Radchenkos he could muster. "Yes," he said and Nikishov, not to be outdone, nodded energetically, showing faith.

Radchenko stood up, short and pugnacious and full of strength and conviction. *Faith*. A man to admire and fear. Radchenko's parting gesture took them by surprise. He extended his thick, sausage fingers and shook their hands, crushing them.

"It was a good plan," he said. "You did well. But for Spina and Barigioni, it would have worked."

Then Radchenko was gone and the *referentura* seemed empty. A force had gone out of it.

Klimenti rode with Nikishov in an embassy car to Fiumicino Airport. He felt it was important that he be on hand to say farewell to him and was at a loss to explain why.

"Byzov's mission has been a complete failure," Nikishov said. "The Italians refused to pull their members into line. And to top it off—this ridiculous scandal!"

Strands of a late morning mist floated past them.

"Oh, Byzov's guilty of the indiscretion, all right," Nikishov went on. "But the newspapers had the wrong woman." He kept his gaze averted, a decent man who did not want to see the relief that spurted into Klimenti's eyes.

"Byzov's already personally apologized to Zhenya Stepanov. A rather courteous gesture, I thought."

"What about the photograph of them together?"

"It was taken during their conferences with the Italians. She was translating. SISDI brushed out the background and convinced the newspaper they were in a restaurant, a lovers' tête-à-tête." Nikishov shrugged. He had done the same thing himself, causing mischief at every opportunity.

At least Byzov had apologized. Klimenti had not done even that, and he understood now the full strength of Zhenya's outrage. She had wanted him to have faith—the word Radchenko had invested with such importance—to trust her. Once again he had lost her through his own cowardice. He was becoming very tired of himself.

Spina was waiting at the airport with an escort for Levitin, who had been kept in custody overnight. Levitin was dressed in a suit of his own clothes, sent around by the Soviet Embassy. There was no sign of the Israeli Arabs.

"Where are they?" Klimenti demanded. "They were part of the deal."

"They handed them over to the Israelis," Levitin said bitterly. "They sent them to their death."

"They were carrying Israeli passports," Spina said. "We sent them home."

In that case they were worse than dead. Spina glared at Klimenti and Levitin, angry that he was part of it. "Why didn't you give them the protection of Soviet citizenship? I thought you looked after your people. I thought you always got them back."

Neither Klimenti nor Levitin had a suitable reply. From the start the Israeli Arabs had been expendable and they had known it as well as anyone else.

Spina signaled the escort away and left them without another word. Levitin was pale. He put out his hand awkwardly. Klimenti shook it.

"Good luck, Colonel. I'll miss working with you."

"Thank you, Major. I'm sorry to be losing you."

"It was a good plan," Levitin said. "We could have done it."

"Yes," Klimenti said. "You would have pulled it off."

Levitin nodded, needing to convince himself. The loss of his men, the fate that awaited them, had affected him deeply; he was learning that he was not immortal or bulletproof, a hard lesson that always came as a surprise to young men.

Nikishov was sitting quietly and withdrawn. He, too, had an unhappy future to contemplate and Klimenti felt sorry for him, returning to an empty flat and the memory of an unfaithful wife.

"May I ask a favor, Simis?"

"Of course." Nikishov was surprised.

"Would you please telephone my father at my apartment and tell him everything's fine with me? He worries."

"Certainly." Color had returned to his pallid cheeks and Klimenti realized that Nikishov was pleased that he had asked. "I'll do better, I'll stop in."

"Go for dinner," Klimenti said. "He's a good cook."

"I'll see," Nikishov said, embarrassed now, as he was by all human warmth. He extended his hand and Klimenti took it. "Be careful, Klimenti," Nikishov said. "Even Poluchkin lost faith." He went quickly, before Klimenti could reply. It was a strange warning—until you thought about it and realized how true it was.

Spina was waiting. He had put his anger aside. He said, "Bannon's invited us to lunch to meet a special guest."

"Who?"

"A most interesting man. Dr. Gustav Wallheimer."

Close up, Wallheimer was even pinker. He was freshly scoured and smelled of soap and perfume, altogether a little too aromatic, Klimenti thought. The restaurant was a pleasant surprise, overlooking the noisy bustle of the Piazza Campo dei Fiori. Looking down across the square, Klimenti could see the café where he had waited with Kharkov and Levitin. Now his two aides were gone.

Wallheimer regarded Klimenti with interest. "I hadn't expected the KGB," he said with the same directness that had characterized his address at il Viminale.

"We're on the same team," Spina said, and smiled. "Well, sort of."

"Some of the time." Bannon laughed.

"In that case, these Vigilantes for Peace continue to work miracles," Wallheimer said good humoredly.

For a fat man, Wallheimer ate daintily: mussels in wine, grilled redfish, and salad. He drank mineral water. "I'm under doctor's orders to lose weight," Wallheimer sighed. "In Italy, of all places."

Once again Klimenti and Bannon were content to let Spina order for them and consequently were confronted with *lasagne*, veal in a cream sauce with mushrooms and red peppers, and a large salad. They drank a white wine. Wallheimer watched them with ill-disguised envy.

"What more do you want to know about these assassins?" he asked, rather abruptly and with bad temper, wanting to escape the torment that was spread before him.

Bannon said, "Why? How?"

"I can't tell you how. I have my own theories, of course. All of us do. None of us seem to agree, so I can honestly tell you there is no weight of opinion in favor of any theory. On the other hand, if I did know, I certainly would not tell you in the presence of the KGB. As a matter of fact, I wouldn't tell you under any circumstances."

"We understand that," Spina said.

"As to why, I take it you refer to the motivation of the assassins?"

"Yes."

"Why is it of interest? Surely your job is to hunt them down, not psychoanalyze them. That's my job."

Klimenti said, "We're hunters, doctor. A good hunter understands—intimately knows—his prey."

"It'll help you find them, to know why they're prepared to self-destruct?"

Bannon said, "It'll help us understand them. To that extent it will help us hunt them."

Wallheimer looked at them each in turn. Finally he said, "You know, gentlemen, I'm not so sure it will help. Understanding might lead to sympathy. And sympathy might lead to mercy." He turned to Klimenti. "What happens to the hunter who knows his prey so well he feels his pain?"

"You've not hunted men, have you, Doctor?"

"No, of course not." Wallheimer was a little discomfited.

Klimenti said, "A man is a prey different from all others. Few animals can kill you. A man can and most usually *will*. If you hunt him hard enough."

"So?"

Bannon said, "Mercy is your own death sentence."

Spina nodded. "No mercy."

Wallheimer looked at Klimenti. "And you, Colonel?"

"We hunt hard, Doctor. It's our job to run them to ground."

"Hmmm," Wallheimer said, thinking over their answers.

Bannon, fearing they would lose him, said, "We found their hospital. Last night, on the outskirts of the city."

Wallheimer jerked upright. "You've got them?"

"They'd evacuated. The hospital was deserted."

Wallheimer's disappointment was as great as his excitement; and Klimenti thought, he wants them as badly as Fadeyev. If Wallheimer got his hands on them, he would probably do exactly what Fadeyev would do. Despite the different personalities, despite the borders and differing political systems it served, science was empirical.

Spina said, "Our forensic scientists took the air-conditioning units in each room apart. They found dust and human hairs. Their tests identified hair from at least twenty-seven different people, eight of whom had high concentrations of bromine. They believe—they're positive—there were eight people undergoing treatment."

"Eight!"

Spina nodded. "Undergoing treatment."

Wallheimer made no attempt to hide his astonishment. "Good Lord, I thought three or four. But eight! At the same time."

"What was the word you used, Doctor? *Barrage.*"

"In these terms four is a barrage. But eight!"

Spina said: "Doctor, tell us why these people are so willing to die."

Wallheimer took his time thinking about it. All his former good humor was gone. Finally he said, "I'll tell you the little we know. The rest is deduction. Both assassins we've identified underwent psychiatric examinations, Leonardo in prison, Montgomery in a state hospital. These reveal several factors they had in common. Both were highly intelligent, highly motivated, dedicated men, burying themselves in strict and demanding disciplines—one a nuclear physicist, one a poet. Both had had extremely high self-esteem. They saw themselves as visionary, aloof from the common herd. This tended to isolate them within narrow values systems, protected by powerful egos. Often such people are intensely selfish, sacrificing everything for their work—family, friends, relaxation. Of course, they are not aware of it; they are too blinded by their commitment to see it. It is generally believed their work is their obsession. In reality the obsession is self-gratification; their work is the means through which they achieve it."

Wallheimer was sitting by the window and he paused, looking down on the square below, bellowing with life, positive and tangible.

"You'd be surprised how often people like that—intelligent, dedicated, superior—crack up. Sometimes it's quick—an earthquake, a sudden, devastating failure. More often, it's a gradual process of small defeats, dissatisfactions, the realization that it's all a waste of time, the onset of maturity forcing drastic reappraisals. Both Leonardo and Montgomery lost faith in their work and thus the whole support system for their self-esteem. The higher their self-esteem, the more devastating was its loss, the greater the morbidity. The results were genuine but unsuccessful attempts at suicide. Which is when the VFP found them. Academician Fadeyev was correct when he said he believed the VFP knew exactly what they were seeking."

"Broken geniuses?"

"Perhaps not geniuses. But men capable of obsession."

"How did they rebuild them, Doctor?"

"They offered them an obsession, a way back."

Bannon regarded him skeptically. "Disarmament as an obsession? A cause, yes. But an obsession, something to sacrifice yourself for? Surely not!"

"It's difficult to believe," Klimenti said.

Wallheimer said, "You're blinded by your own experiences, your own distrust. You're too sophisticated, too corrupted, the victims of your own systems, to deal with such a simple, honest, straightforward notion as disarmament. Which, of course, is exactly why fifty years of almost nonstop disarmament negotiations have produced practically nothing. You might not have realized it, but you three—you, Mr. Bannon, you, Commissario Capo, and you, Colonel—are exactly the kind of people the VFP are turning us against."

He spoke quietly, almost in sorrow, as if he was forgiving them their stupidity. "We need men of courage who are capable of faith and trust," Wallheimer said. "That's what the VFP are telling us, and I, for one, believe them."

"You're not on our side, Doctor?" Bannon said.

"No," Wallheimer said. "Not anymore. I can't be. I'm for humanity, the survival of the species."

"Then why are you here?"

"I told you. If I help you understand your prey, if I help you get to know them . . ." Wallheimer shrugged. "Who knows?"

"You're trying to subvert us?" Bannon laughed, but the words were harsh.

"You work it out," Wallheimer snapped, his eyes flashing with anger.

"Forgive me, Doctor," Bannon said. "But you're quite a shock."

Spina said, "But disarmament isn't the assassins' new obsession, is it, Doctor?"

Klimenti had a feeling the Italian had already guessed the answer.

"You're quite right, Commissario Capo. Disarmament is not the obsession. It's the focal point, the mission, the work object to which the assassin's energies and egos are directed during his reconstruction. In fact, the obsession is the same old one. That's why they're prepared to take such extreme measures to get it back."

He looked at each of them in turn. "The obsession, gentlemen, what drives them, is the restoration of self-esteem."

"They'll *kill* themselves to regain their self-esteem?" exclaimed Bannon, whose self-esteem was high.

Wallheimer said, "They've already experienced a despair so deep, so traumatic, that they sought death as a release. This time death will be a triumph. You must understand that martyrs are intensely selfish people. Martyrdom is seen as a sacrifice. You keep referring to it in those terms. But you're wrong. Martyrdom is an arrogant act of ultimate self-gratification."

"I understand them," Spina said, a man born in the City of Martyrs. "Now I understand his poetry."

"Thank you," Wallheimer said. "That alone has made my trip to Rome worthwhile."

Klimenti and Bannon had nothing to say.

When they went out into the noise of the piazza, Bannon said, "Doctor, there's something that Commissario Capo forgot to tell you."

Spina shrugged. He did not object.

Bannon said, "Three of the VFP assassins are women."

13.

That night Klimenti changed into casual clothes. He put the 9mm Beretta into his waistband and two extra clips into his jacket pocket, along with a black woolen seaman's cap. He left his tape recorder playing a tape he had recorded several days previously, capturing the sounds of a man moving about a hotel room, making coffee, using the toilet, rustling newspapers, writing, ordering and eating a meal. The tape ran for an hour, enough to give him a head start if the Italians—or the Soviets—were listening in. He shut the door without making a sound.

Klimenti went down the fire stairs and out through the hotel's basement into the back street. He pulled the woolen cap down over his ears and hunched up against the cold, hands in his pockets and gripping the Beretta ammunition clips in case he needed to fight. He took a bus, went several blocks, got off, caught a bus going the opposite direction, got off, walked, switched buses again. For two hours, he traveled aimlessly back and forth across the city. When he was sure he was not being followed, he took a taxi to the Olympic Stadium and wandered among the homosexual prostitutes who dallied there. Men came in cars—usually rich men in expensive cars—and took them away. A lot of other men hung around, either curious or trying to work up the nerve. The transvestites among them carried on outrageously, shrill as frightened sparrows.

Squirrel was waiting behind the wheel of a hired Opel. Sitting next to him was a transvestite, a tall, thin young man with plucked eyebrows and pouting, heavily painted lips and a blond wig.

"Thank you," Squirrel said and passed the prostitute some money. "I enjoyed the conversation."

"Is that all?" the transvestite demanded in American English, piqued that he had not been called on to pass the ultimate test of his femininity.

"I'm too old," Squirrel said gently. "But you're very beautiful. Very sexy."

"Oh, well," the transvestite said, his pride salvaged. He got out and gave a wicked smile through the open window. "I could have got it up for you."

"I'm glad that's over." Squirrel sighed. But he was also a little hurt that the transvestite had accepted his excuse so readily. "Too old" indeed!

He was, Klimenti knew, sixty-two. He was, Klimenti also knew, heterosexual.

"Hello, my friend," Klimenti said, an old greeting, much honored. He swung open the car door and climbed in, taking Squirrel's thin, dry hand in both of his own. "You came sooner than I anticipated."

Squirrel smiled and did not remove his hand. "All my life I've been doing what people expected of me. Meeting with you is always an excuse to break the mold."

"Let's go," Klimenti said.

"Gladly."

They drove for fifteen minutes, Squirrel watching the traffic, Klimenti checking to see if they were followed.

"We're clear," he said.

"Do we have time to go to a restaurant?" Squirrel asked. Each year they sat down at a table and ate and drank for several hours, a feast of celebration and renewal. It was also a discovery.

"It's too risky. I don't have a lot of time," Klimenti said and Squirrel sighed. "I look forward to our little chats," he said but he did not question Klimenti's decision.

They parked the Opel on the Tiber embankment overlooking Tiberina Island. From here Klimenti could walk to his hotel. This was one of the widest sections of the river and the water swirled with unusual speed on either side of the island's stone bulwarks, giving the impression that it was an ancient hulk pressing through the water. The silhouette of the church of San Bartolo rose up against the lights from across the river, another Christian edifice built on the ruins of pagan worship, in this case the Temple of Aesculapius, Greek god of medicine whom the Romans had borrowed to cure their ailing; they had been unrepentant thieves who took only what was useful.

Squirrel was a handsome man to whose face age had come with benevolence, deepening its character without lessening its sense of strength, conviction, and intelligence. He was an American aristocrat of impeccable New England pedigree and wealth, educated at Harvard, Cambridge, and the Sorbonne. He had chosen a career in law and, by instinct, had found his true vocation in Intelligence. His excellent education, however, had imbued him with deeply held liberal sentiments, a dangerous combination. He was not a communist, nor did he believe in communism. Yet for eleven years he had supplied the Soviet Union with information on the United States's nuclear buildup and policies, steadfastly refusing to deliver intelligence in any other area.

Seven Presidents had valued his services and with good reason. Squirrel always put the interests of his nation first, without equivocation. Even though he had supplied information to the Soviet Union, Squirrel did not consider he had betrayed his country. On the contrary, he was convinced he was acting in its best interests by keeping the United States out of a nuclear war neither it nor the Soviet Union could win. He saw it as his duty to counter the influence of dangerous elements within the United States and Soviet Union who saw eventual nuclear war as inevitable.

Squirrel had never discussed any of this with Klimenti. From the outset he had refused to present his motives or have them questioned. At first this had caused great difficulty for the KGB because it was basic that every spy had to have a motive—greed, hatred, belief, revenge—that could be used to manipulate and threaten. Eventually a careful analysis of the information Squirrel supplied and, equally important, his timing, convinced the KGB that he was acting to maintain the nuclear balance, the foundation for the doctrine of Mutually Assured Destruction.

Squirrel said, "I got what you wanted."

"I'm sorry I had to ask." Klimenti's regret was real for he was aware that he had broken a long-held discipline. They had agreed that Squirrel would not respond to requests for specific intelligence. To Squirrel that would have been *spying*. Squirrel gave them what he saw fit.

"This was different. Personal, for you," Squirrel said. "What made you suspect it?"

"Everything I've seen, learned about Bannon, tells me he's too professional to be caught out like that. It was too innocent, too naïve, even in the cold of a Moscow winter. Here, in Rome, I was able to see it—see him—in a clearer perspective." Klimenti shrugged. "The light's different. You see things differently."

"I'm sorry to tell you you're right," Squirrel said gravely. "The affair was instigated by your daughter, not by Bannon. Bannon, in fact, was ordered to break off the contact. Your daughter, however, persisted. She pursued him, raising the suspicion that she was acting on instructions from the KGB. So Bannon was instructed to play it out."

Squirrel lifted his hands in the darkness, submitting, helpless before the truth. "They were right. She was working—works—for the KGB."

In the quiet of the night, Klimenti could hear the gurgle of the river as it dashed against the island. So this was the truth. Nadya, his daughter, was a honey trap. A *vixen*, a KGB slut. No, that was unjust. If she was a slut, then they were all sluts, and once again Klimenti contradicted himself, this time with a savagery that made him tremble—it was the truth, *they were all sluts*. For the *apparat*.

"Are you all right?" Squirrel had felt the tremors.

Klimenti spoke softly, talking to the river, remembering, a caustic shame that had never left him, even after all these years. "Do you know how a boy from an obscure village, the son of a tractor mechanic, the grandson of a peasant, came to be chosen among the elite? How he was chosen to go to a special school run by the KGB? Then Moscow University? A peasant boy!"

"Don't condemn yourself, my friend," Squirrel said gently. "It's the same everywhere."

"He informed," Klimenti said. "From the age of ten. On his playmates, then his schoolmates, his teachers. Later, in university, on everyone."

"You were too young to understand what you were doing."

"Yes, when I began. *They* told me and I obeyed, a good little Komsomol. But even then I knew it was wrong because they told me not to tell my father, and that made me ashamed. But I went ahead and did it, because I was afraid, because I saw their power and wanted to be part of it. Even then, in short pants and bare feet."

"It was the same in our colleges and universities in the fifties," Squirrel said. "You had Beria, we had J. Edgar Hoover and McCarthy. When I was a young man, people informed on everyone they even remotely suspected of socialist sympathies. Their friends, colleagues, professors. The local storekeeper. It was a relief to escape to England."

"We informed on *everyone*," Klimenti said. "*Everyone* was suspect."

"Your father?"

"No. I never informed on him."

Squirrel sat quietly, watching Klimenti with sympathy. Neither he nor Klimenti was surprised by the confessional tenor of their conversation; they had shared secrets before, seeking understanding. Theirs was an unusual relationship in every respect.

"It's over, done, gone," Squirrel said softly.

No, it was still with him.

And now it had turned a full circle. Nadya had gone the same route. The only difference was that he had sought to join the elite and she, already one of them, was protecting her own position and privileges. Who was he to condemn his daughter, he, the father who had set the example? He wondered when Nikishov had recruited her. Her beauty, intelligence, and language skills made her a valuable acquisition. And he had ruined it all by attempting to kill Bannon. It must have shaken Nikishov badly because it had caused him to abandon his target.

He remembered with anger that he had believed Nadya was grieving for her lost love and had felt guilty. Now she was skiing in Czechoslovakia, and that too was in the right perspective. Was it really a holiday? Or was she again working for Nikishov, the indefatigable honey trapper, always on the lookout for someone to subvert?

Squirrel said, "Klimenti, I thought hard about giving you this information. The only reason I went ahead is because I realized you suspected it—otherwise you wouldn't have asked—and doubt is always more terrible than certainty. I also knew I couldn't lie to you."

Klimenti nodded. At that moment he did not have words of gratitude, and they were at best a poor tribute to Squirrel's courage.

"There's something else I have to tell you," Squirrel said. He paused and watched the lights on the river and before he resumed he turned to face Klimenti, a man confronting a task he was not about to enjoy. "About your wife."

"Marusya!"

"The way she died."

"Marusya was killed in Washington eleven years ago. A drunk ran her down with his car." Even now, Klimenti tasted the bitterness. "He killed himself, too."

"No, Klimenti," Squirrel said. "Your wife was killed by the CIA."

"No," Klimenti snapped. He shook his head, denying it, full of fear. "It was a drunk. I saw the body in the car." He grabbed Squirrel and shook him. "I saw the bastard's body."

Squirrel made no attempt to release Klimenti's grip. Instead he clasped Klimenti's hands, pressing them against his chest, a gesture of physical surrender, offering himself as a token of his veracity. "Please," he said. Klimenti relaxed his hold. "The body you saw was a drunk who'd died in a car accident half an hour earlier. The car that ran down your wife was driven by a professional CIA killer disguised as a policeman. As soon as he had killed your wife he dragged the dead drunk under the steering wheel, in the pretense of trying to save him."

Klimenti held Squirrel by the lapels and shook him, gently this time, losing. "No," he implored. "No."

"Klimenti, the only witness was a policeman. Remember?"

Klimenti stopped shaking Squirrel. He remembered. Marusya, broken, torn, crushed, lying in her own blood on the cold, icy street, the steam pouring like a filthy mist from the sewers. Her body had assumed an impossible posture, achievable only in death. Even so, she had been beautiful, her face composed and unmarked.

Klimenti released his grip but Squirrel still held his hands. Klimenti knew now why he was so afraid of the truth. "Why?" he croaked, mesmerized by fate, unable to escape it.

Squirrel licked his lips. His mouth was dry. He was having difficulty talking. He tried the word and it didn't come out. He cleared his throat and said it.

"Me."

"You?"

Squirrel's face was a death mask, hollowed by pain. He said, "They knew you'd recruited someone inside the CIA. Your people got careless. The NSA intercepted your exchanges with Moscow. They even got the code name, Squirrel. And you."

"They knew that! Eleven years ago!"

"Three months after I gave you my first information. But you were too careful to be caught out by surveillance. They knew it was useless trying to get you to defect." Squirrel's voice quavered. His words were accusations as much as statements, condemning Klimenti. "You were too much in love with your wife for sexual blackmail. They were desperate, Klimenti. So they killed Marusya, knowing it would force your recall to Moscow. They were hoping that in the turnover, the new agent would lead them to Squirrel."

Klimenti heard him clearly, but his brain was incapable of absorbing the reality. It was transfixed by a single overwhelming horror—he had been responsible for Marusya's death—he, Klimenti Sergeyevich, who adored her, the man she loved.

"It didn't work," Squirrel said, his voice harsh with dryness. He had run out of saliva. "I warned the KGB."

"They knew!" For eleven years, the KGB had known the truth about his wife's death. And had not told him.

Squirrel said, "They were afraid it would warp your judgment, destroy your operational effectiveness. That you'd seek revenge." He licked his lips. This was hurting him, too. "And they were right."

"Right!" The word was a distant echo, a hollow drum sound in Klimenti's head. If that was right, then what was wrong? What constituted rightness and wrongness anyhow?

"I told them not to tell you," Squirrel said, and there was despair in his voice now. He knew what this confession was going to cost him, and yet he had to finish it. "I needed you. They needed you. Without you, I could not have done what I did. My work—our work—was more important than your personal feelings. Something had to be sacrificed, Klimenti."

Squirrel was hunched down in the seat, his head on his chest, heavy with pain. "It was the only time I bypassed you, Klimenti. I had to do it. That's the way it's always been. You're a professional. You understand."

It was a plea.

Professional! All his life, Klimenti had thought it the most admirable of words, professionals the most admirable of people. The best. Now the word came to him coated with deceit. Everything he and Squirrel had done together had been protected by a lie. By his wife's murder.

"And what now?" Klimenti asked, dead-voiced, dead-spirited, dead-souled. Squirrel had been a big part of him and now there was only emptiness. "What do you expect me to feel now? Gratitude? You expect me to understand, to accept it? Not to warp my judgment? Not to seek revenge?"

"No, I don't expect that at all," Squirrel said. "But now it doesn't matter."

This time he did not have the strength to face Klimenti. "I've retired," Squirrel said. "I'm finished. Out of it. The CIA. The whole cesspool."

There was a tremor in his voice. He was very emotional.

"You're free of me, Klimenti. We're free of each other. There's no longer any need to keep the truth from you."

It was true then. Squirrel was breaking the manacles, freeing himself of the chains of the spirit that had bound them more strongly than iron shackles. Klimenti felt totally calm. Too calm, removed from reality.

"I'm going to live in Tuscany," Squirrel said. "Someplace where they don't talk about nuclear weapons."

A rich man among peasants, seeking solace. Well, Klimenti thought, he had earned it. He had never taken a cent from the KGB. He had acted out of conviction and asked nothing in return. A rare man. A good man. Noble, perhaps. Klimenti knew all this, just as he knew that he could not forgive him this one lie.

"It'd be nice if you could visit," Squirrel said. "But, of course, that's out of the question."

Unless I decide to finger you to your friends, Klimenti thought with a squirt of malice. All I'd have to do is turn up and knock on the door and give you the kiss of Judas and walk away and there'd never be any peace for you, my friend, the way there'll never be any peace for me. But it was gone instantly. He would not do it. Even now he would not—could not—betray Squirrel.

"Say something, for God's sake," Squirrel begged.

Klimenti looked across. Squirrel was distraught. "Did your Moscow team run a Russian Jew named Navachine?" Klimenti asked.

"Navachine?" Squirrel shook his head. "No. We had no one in Moscow by that name."

And that, too, was what Klimenti had suspected.

He got out of the Opel. "Goodbye," he said and walked away, not looking back.

A professional!

And then Klimenti remembered who and what he was—a man, full of frailty, nothing more, neither judge nor jury, but a fellow traveler, his feet in the same dust. He remembered what Squirrel had meant to him. He turned and went back to the Opel. Squirrel had his head down and was not aware of his approach until Klimenti was standing by the car.

Squirrel looked up, his face pale and riven with distress. Klimenti would never forget it. The pity he felt was for both of them.

"Good luck," Klimenti said, feeling lonely already.

He spent a long time walking.

Faith, he thought. Without faith, we're just mollusks slithering along in our own slime.

At the Hotel Michelangelo, the receptionist handed Klimenti an envelope that had been left in his key slot. The only address was his room number. He did not recognize the writing. Zhenya! He opened the envelope.

Inside was a lock of thick, soft hair. Zhenya's hair!

There was a crude drawing of a dog with a chain around its neck. The chain led off the page. Klimenti turned it over. There was another drawing, showing the chain continuing from the page edge to the neck of a naked woman with a pornographically exaggerated vulva. The chain continued from the woman's neck to a human figure with an enormous phallus, fully erect. The man figure had an animal head— cunning, salivating, vicious. A ferret's head! Printed Cyrillic letters said in Russian: "SAME PLACE. NOW."

14.

Big Dog was waiting inside the narthex of the church. The door opened soundlessly and Klimenti stepped inside, shutting it behind him quickly so that he would not be silhouetted by the streetlights. He stood against the wall, adjusting his eyes to the sudden dark. A blast of light hit his face, blinding him.

"Put your hands in front of your face," Big Dog said. "Where I can see them."

Klimenti held his hands in front of his eyes, palms outward. He could not see beyond the glare of light.

"Give it to me," Big Dog said. "With your left hand. Hold it in front of your face."

Klimenti took the Beretta from his waistband and did as he was instructed. Big Dog took the pistol. Immediately the flashlight went out. After the brightness the dark was complete; Klimenti could see nothing.

"Let's go," Big Dog said, taking his arm and leading him into the street, surely the biggest priest in all Christendom in his tent-sized soutane and his round hat pulled down over his eyes. Moving next to him, Klimenti felt ridiculously puny even though he sensed no threat from Big Dog. He had come to surrender himself, not to fight, and Big Dog knew it.

"You left her with Tabidze," Klimenti hissed. "With him!"

"Shut up," Big Dog growled and wrenched Klimenti along. But Klimenti sensed alarm as well as anger in his roughness.

"You saw the drawings," Klimenti accused. "And you left her with him. Alone. After what she did for you, you gutless bastard."

"I won't tell you again," Big Dog snarled. "Shut up or I'll clobber you."

He dragged Klimenti to a van with blacked-out windows and flung him in the back, where he handcuffed him to a bar behind the driver's seat. He took a roll of marker tape and wrapped it around Klimenti's head, blindfolding him but leaving his nostrils and mouth free.

Klimenti said quietly, "If he's harmed her, I'll kill you, too."

Big Dog drove in silence for a few minutes. His lack of response had nothing to do with fear. Not for himself, anyway. It was all to do with uncertainty.

Finally Big Dog said, "He's not going to damage trade goods, is he?" He was seeking assurance as much as giving it.

Klimenti sat silently, refusing to help. He wanted Big Dog unsure, fearful.

"He wants to make a deal," Big Dog said. "She's the price tag. So he's not going to hurt her. Right?"

Klimenti said nothing.

"You arsehole," Big Dog raged and drove faster, spinning the van around a corner and hurling Klimenti out of his seat.

"Goddamnit," Big Dog swore. "He promised me."

"The Ferret *promised*!" Klimenti sneered. Big Dog swore foully in Russian.

"The drawings were to frighten you, that's all," Big Dog said. "Now, shut up."

He drove violently, taking his anger out on the van. After a while he said quietly, "I didn't like it. I told him the pictures weren't necessary—the hair was enough. You'd come, anyway." And, after another pause, "He knows he's finished unless he can do a deal. I promise you, I wouldn't have let him hang onto her if I wasn't sure of that."

"You took her?"

"Fedor Yustinovich would have frightened her. I wanted to make it easy for her."

They did not speak again until the van stopped. Klimenti heard the sound of electrically operated roller doors opening and shutting. They were entering a building. Big Dog unshackled Klimenti from the bar and helped him, still handcuffed, from the van. They walked a short distance over cobblestones. Big Dog opened a door and pushed him through. The air was damp and stale and Klimenti smelled something else, heavier, lingering.

"It hurts less if you do it quickly," Big Dog said but Klimenti still gasped as he tore the blindfold tape off, taking some of his hair with it.

They were at the top of a set of steps. The walls and roof were old Roman flat bricks held together with mud-straw mortar. The roof ran parallel with the stairs, making a tunnel going downward. A single light bulb hanging from the roof cut sharply etched shadows. The tunnel caught the sound of their feet on the worn stone and shuffled it back at them. As they went under the light, their shadows flicked across the walls and overtook them and danced out from their feet, sliding up the door below. It was of heavy steel and reminded Klimenti of the door to the cell in the bowels of the Lubyanka. Seeing it, he recognized the smell; this was also a place of confinement, only infinitely older.

Big Dog paused before the door, facing Klimenti squarely. He whispered, as if he were afraid the shadows were listening, "Listen, Colonel, you've got to understand—if you don't do a deal, the girl's dead. You, too."

The stair shaft caught his words and rustled them together into a hiss. There was an imploring urgency about him.

"You'd let him kill her?" Klimenti demanded. "After what she did for you?"

Big Dog flinched. He scowled. He did not like it at all. He said harshly, "He'll only do it if you refuse to make a deal. It's up to you, Colonel. Whether she lives or dies."

This time the words came back in a rush, full of anger and torment, the emotion exaggerated by the echoes ". . . dies, dies, dies . . ."

The steel door slid open and Tabidze stood there, his beautiful eyes afire with scorn. "He speaks the truth," the Ferret said and laughed, flooding the shaft with the sounds of cruelty. There was an air vent above the door. He had heard every word.

Big Dog, feeling foolish, thrust Klimenti through the door with unnecessary force and grunted, "I was just making sure he knows the situation."

"He knows it, all right," the Ferret said, smiling at Klimenti. "That's why I'm surprised you came, Colonel."

"Where is she?" Klimenti demanded. They were in a room cut into the rock. It was about five meters wide and the walls were no more than three meters high. It was difficult to measure the length because shadows at both ends suggested it extended beyond the area lit by a single bulb in the ceiling. Horizontal slots had been cut into one wall, half a meter high, about the same deep, and a little less than two meters long. They were cut three high, like bunks spaced along the wall, and Klimenti realized that was their original purpose, sleeping holes for the early Christians who had dug the catacomb and lived here to escape persecution. The odor was the smell of ancient death.

"She's OK?" Big Dog said. He meant it as a statement of reassurance but it came out a question, loaded with doubt which did not escape Tabidze.

"You were worried about her, Anton Anisimovich?" the Ferret asked silkily, the formality a threat in itself.

Big Dog shrugged uneasily. "She's trade goods. Better left undamaged."

"See for yourself," the Ferret said and switched on a roof light that revealed more of the catacomb. There were several tables on which sat sets of weighing scales. Plastic gloves lay discarded. Against one wall were stacked cardboard cartons of glucose. Other cartons contained glassine envelopes. There was a water heater for the workers to make coffee and a small refrigerator. Empty soft drink bottles lay around. It was a factory where pure heroin smuggled in from Lebanon was mixed with glucose and packed into one-ounce sachets for street sale.

There was no sign of Zhenya. The Ferret went across to an electric winch that operated a hoist used for transferring the cartons to and from the floor above. As the hoist descended, Klimenti saw Zhenya sitting in it, her knees against her chin, her hands handcuffed behind. She was fully dressed and apparently unharmed.

"Klimenti," Zhenya cried in despair. "Oh no! No!"

Big Dog glared at the Ferret. "Why'd you do that?" he demanded.

The Ferret ignored him. "I told you he'd come," he said to Zhenya pleasantly.

"Oh, Klimenti," Zhenya sobbed. "He's going to kill you."

"It's all right, lady," Big Dog said gently. He helped Zhenya out of the hoist. "He's here to take you home. Aren't you, Colonel?"

"Yes," Klimenti said and the Ferret giggled, high and sweet, a girlish sound. He was getting excited.

Zhenya's face was full of anguish and fear. "No. He's going to kill you. He told me."

"He knows it," the Ferret giggled. "He knows it and he still came." He squealed with delight, an unnatural sound that brought goose pimples to Klimenti's flesh.

"He's kidding," Big Dog told Zhenya, shaking her gently. "Don't pay any attention. He's teasing, that's all."

"No," Zhenya sobbed. "Do something. Please."

"The Colonel's come to do a deal," Big Dog said, turning to the Ferret. "Tell her."

"The Colonel's come to do a deal," the Ferret mimicked and burst into another giggling fit. Big Dog stared at him in amazement, unsure what to believe, and then all doubts were canceled because the Ferret stopped giggling, as suddenly and as completely as if his voice had been guillotined. He stepped forward, his face contorted with venom, and he hissed into Klimenti's face.

"You've come to die, haven't you, Colonel? For this little rich bitch, this bit of cunt for the born-to-rule brigade."

Klimenti caught the stench of his breath, rancid with excitement and tension, and he went forward, manacled hands grasping for the Ferret's throat, and his fingers almost got there, touching flesh, before Big Dog jerked him away. The Ferret stepped back. There was a knife in his hand; it had come so quickly none of them had seen him unsheath it, but it was there, glinting in the light.

"No!" Zhenya screamed. "No!"

"Fuck it!" Big Dog shouted, holding Klimenti back. "What's going on? We're here to make a deal, for Christsake."

"The deal's done and he's accepted it," the Ferret whispered, his voice hoarse and low now and trembling with sexual excitement. "He stays, she goes."

"No!" Big Dog yelled. He could not believe it. In his frustration, he hurled Klimenti out of the way and into the stack of cardboard cartons. He smashed his fist onto the table, knocking over weighing scales.

"You said a deal. You said we had to do a deal, otherwise we're finished." He stood there, his huge body imploring, his hands outstretched, begging. "If you don't do a deal, we can't go home."

Klimenti scrambled to his feet. Zhenya ran to him, throwing herself at him, off balance with her hands manacled behind. Klimenti lifted his arms over her and held her against him. He could feel her trembling but she was no longer crying.

"Klimenti," she gasped. He crushed her against him, giving her his warmth and the last of his strength, rocking her gently. She shut her eyes.

"Touching," the Ferret sneered. "Very touching. The lovers' last embrace."

"No one's going to die," Big Dog said. There was an edge of desperation in his voice and another quality, as Russian as his soul: stubbornness. "We can do a deal. Tell him, Colonel."

"There's no deal for him," Klimenti said. "He killed two of our men. The only deal he's going to get is a bullet in the back of the head."

For a moment Big Dog was dumbfounded. He could not believe it. "But you came," he said. "*You came.*" And then he understood it and he stared at Klimenti and Zhenya in awe. "Jesus."

"We don't need to do deals," the Ferret said to Big Dog, no longer so sure of him now and needing to calm his fears. "With the contacts I've got, we'll be all right."

Big Dog shook his head, trying to come to grips with it. Klimenti lifted his arms from around Zhenya and took her across to Big Dog, who watched them with dull eyes.

"No," Zhenya begged when she realized what was happening. "No, Klimenti. Please."

"Look after her," Klimenti said and Big Dog nodded and said nothing. Zhenya tried to throw herself back on Klimenti but the giant put an arm around her, restraining her as gently as he could.

"No, Klimenti, please," Zhenya begged. "Let me stay with you."

"Get going," Klimenti snapped at Big Dog. His resolve was breaking.

Zhenya kicked and fought but Big Dog held her securely. Suddenly, she stopped struggling and turned to the Ferret. "Anything," she implored. "Anything you want. I'll do it. Please."

The Ferret gaped at her. He was absolutely shocked. Then rage overtook him. *"You!"* the Ferret snarled. "You think I want to fuck *you!*" He waved his hands across his body, washing himself clean of her, his face grotesque. "It's him I want to fuck," he whispered. "With this." He held up his knife. The blade glistened in the light, beautiful and terrible. The Ferret's face seemed swollen and all of them saw it and realized what it was: killing lust. His eyes were feral. Slowly, sensually, his tongue slid out and licked the gleaming blade, making love to it.

Zhenya struggled but Big Dog held her easily, hardly aware of her; his entire concentration was focused on the Ferret, whom he watched with fascination. Violently, he shook his head, seeking to clear it of doubt and fear and confusion.

Klimenti picked up a weighing scale and stepped forward, holding it with both manacled hands, ready to parry and strike. He was determined not to die easily.

The Ferret laughed, thrilled by the promise of a kill and hot for the foreplay, the game of death; how he loved it. "Oh yes," he sighed. "Oh yes."

"Get her out of here," Klimenti snarled at Big Dog. "Damn you, get her out of here."

"No!" Zhenya screamed, waking Big Dog from his trance, kicking and trying to get at the Ferret. "Stop him!"

Klimenti began circling. The Ferret had transferred his fighting knife to his left hand and reached down to his leg and arched upright in beautiful human symmetry, his body bent like a bow, arm back, poised to throw. In his hand was a flat-bladed throwing knife.

"Drop the scale," he ordered. "Or I'll take your throat out from here."

"No," Klimenti said. "You won't do it."

The Ferret tensed and flicked his arm. Klimenti did not move. No knife came. The Ferret fell smoothly back into his throwing posture. But some of his arrogance was gone. "What makes you so sure?" he sneered. "I can hit you anywhere I want."

"I know," Klimenti said. "But it's too quick a death. Too easy. And that's not how you want it, is it?"

The Ferret shook his head, his eyes gleaming.

"You want to fuck me, you'll have to come right in," Klimenti said. He reached forward, beckoning with the scale. "Come on, Ferret. Right to me. All the way."

"Stop him," Zhenya snarled at Big Dog, kicking him.

The Ferret laughed, but there was uneasiness in it now. "Slowly. I'm going to do it to you so slowly, a thousand delicious little cuts. Your lover, Colonel. Like no lover you've ever known."

He laughed again, reassured by his own promises. "But first I'll take some of the sting out of you."

"Please," Zhenya begged Big Dog. "Please."

The Ferret's arm began to curl and Klimenti knew that this time the knife was coming.

"No!" Big Dog shouted, surprising them both. They had forgotten completely about him and Zhenya. The Ferret hesitated long enough to see that Big Dog had a machine pistol aimed at him. He held Zhenya with one hand and the weapon with the other. The Ferret gaped, truly astonished.

"No," Big Dog said, quieter now. His face was set with stubbornness. He was through being pushed around. "There'll be no killing."

"Put it down!" the Ferret commanded.

Big Dog shook his head. "Throw and I'll kill you."

The Ferret was so astonished he lowered his throwing arm. "You wouldn't do it," he said. "I'm your *paichan*."

"Not anymore." There was no uncertainty in Big Dog now and the Ferret was the first to realize it.

"Big Dog, we're friends, old mates." He spoke soothingly, a master calming a frightened beast. "Ever since we were kids we've been together. I'm your only friend."

"That's right," Big Dog said. "You're my only friend."

"The only one who didn't laugh or call you names behind your back, like those other curs." The Ferret grimaced to show his hatred. "The only one who never barked, who never howled like a dog, when you passed."

"That's true," Big Dog said softly. "You're the only one who listened."

"Listen to me now," the Ferret entreated. "Trust me. Just like in the old days. I've never let you down."

Big Dog nodded and Klimenti was afraid he was once again falling under the Ferret's spell. He shouted, "He ran out on you when the bullets were flying at the Belgrade. He deserted you then and he'll do it again."

"Shut up," Big Dog said, watching the Ferret.

"Take her up top and fuck her," the Ferret said, sure he had won. "When we're finished here, we'll do whatever you like. I promise you."

"You told me, you promised, you'd do a deal," Big Dog insisted stupidly. "Otherwise I wouldn't have gotten her."

The Ferret frowned. He made a poor show of concealing his irritation. He was not accustomed to being questioned by Big Dog.

"Stop worrying. Take her up and fuck her."

"No," Big Dog said and meant it. The Ferret stiffened with anger.

"Watch him," Klimenti called. "He'll throw."

"Kill him," Zhenya begged. "Please. Kill him."

"Shut up," Big Dog snarled. But he did not take his eyes off the Ferret. "Keep out of it."

This was between him and the Ferret, his only friend. It was personal. This was a matter of love, of the soul. And the Ferret knew it.

"Anton," he said softly. "Don't do it."

"Get going." Big Dog waved the machine pistol. "I'll keep them here all night and tomorrow to give you time to get out of Italy."

"Anton," the Ferret coaxed. He was afraid. Of being alone. He was afraid of being without Big Dog, and for the first time Klimenti understood the true nature of their relationship.

"No," Big Dog said. "No more talk. Get going."

Fear worked in the Ferret and turned to rage. "Cur," he spat and threw, uncoiling so quickly neither Big Dog nor Klimenti knew what was happening until it was over. Big Dog grunted. The haft of the throwing knife protruded from his right shoulder. He dropped Zhenya and held the machine pistol with both hands.

"Shoot," Klimenti screamed. "Kill him."

The Ferret waited, as still and as deadly as a matador, his body arched with pride and defiance.

"You won't do it," he said. "I *know* you."

"You're wrong," Big Dog said, his voice steady. Blood was

flowing around the steel and soaking his clothes. "You try that again and I'll cut you in half."

The Ferret watched him, calculating. Soon Big Dog would faint from loss of blood. But how soon?

But Big Dog knew him too well. "Get going," he shouted. "Or I'll kill you."

He fired a burst into the bricks behind the Ferret. "Now!" he screamed, swinging the machine pistol onto the Ferret. "Now!"

The Ferret went, quickly and smoothly, slamming the steel door behind him.

Klimenti lunged for the machine pistol, but Big Dog shoved him off with surprising strength. It was his last burst because he sank onto the floor beside Zhenya, clutching the machine pistol to his bloody chest. He gasped and hung his head: he was crying. Numb and without expression he held out his hand, giving them the keys to the handcuffs.

Klimenti freed Zhenya and himself. She clung to him.

"He's hurt," Klimenti said. "We have to help him."

Zhenya knelt by Big Dog, who lifted his tear-stained face and tried to smile.

"Lady," he gasped. "Here we go again."

They left the knife in the shoulder; withdrawing it would only increase the flow of blood.

Big Dog said, "He only wanted to hurt me. If he'd wanted to kill me, I'd be dead."

"That's true," Klimenti said and Big Dog gave him a look of gratitude.

Zhenya had cut up her skirt to make wads for the wound.

"Lady," Big Dog said, trying to smile. "You've got nice legs too." Zhenya kissed him. He blushed with pleasure.

"I have to kill him," Klimenti said. Big Dog hung his head. Zhenya sat by him, holding his hand. When he lifted his head, Klimenti saw the pain in his eyes.

15.

Somewhere in the night a siren howled, a faraway sound, reminding Klimenti that it was the twentieth century. Here amid the ruined arches he was immersed in timelessness, and the wind carried the sighs of centuries of suffering and death. It was a place full of motionless shadows; only sounds moved here, seeping around the pitted and worn stone columns. Countless thousands had perished in this most savage of arenas, more innocents than gladiators, and more thousands of animals; the sand had been soaked with their blood. But the earth was gone now, revealing the underground cells where they had awaited death, the crumbling walls jagged like broken teeth. Once the mob had howled for gore and glory, possessed by a blood frenzy, a quarter of a million of them at a time. Now there was only one man and the whispering wind and the still shadows.

Klimenti stood unmoving in the dark of the Colosseum, listening. He had been waiting an hour; he would wait all night if necessary. He knew how to fight in the shadows and this was how you did it, with patience, in control, as still as the ruined arcades that rose around him. He had got there first and the advantage lay with him. The Ferret would be moving, a shadow among the shadows, and that would betray him, movement and sound. Klimenti was attuned to catch both.

He held the panty hose in his right fist, caressing the knots he had tied in the crotch. There were four of them carefully spaced. Zhenya, when she had taken off the garment and given it to him, had not understood the purpose and he had not told her. But Big Dog had known what he was doing and had looked away, his heart hurting more than his wounded shoulder. Even so, he had told Klimenti what he needed to know.

"It'll be quick?" he begged.

"Yes," Klimenti said. "He won't feel anything."

But he had been lying.

He did not look at his watch. To do so would have required movement; he knew the quality of the prey he hunted and even the slightest movement was capable of giving him away. Both of them, the Ferret and Control, would come early for their rendezvous, to watch and wait, not trusting the other. But Tabidze, the Ferret, was an animal of the dark and he would come earliest, sniffing the wind; Klimenti was sure of it.

If Control came first, it would change the manner of the Ferret's dying. He would be forced to use the machine pistol. Klimenti did not want this to happen. He knew exactly how he was going to do it and he wanted no one to interfere.

Control he would take care of later. Control he wanted alive.

From the dark there came a cry of insensate fury and, despite his discipline, Klimenti jerked around, the machine pistol ready. He recognized the sound. It was a cat mating, shrieking in the night. After a while it was quiet.

He waited, his muscles hurting.

Another siren wailed and Klimenti silently cursed it, for it destroyed the sensitivity of his hearing, overcoming all other sounds, the ones he needed to listen for: the scuff of soft footfalls on rock, the rustle of clothes, the hiss of breathing, almost imperceptible but there to be heard if you knew what to listen for and how to do it. The siren warbled and grew fainter, going away from him, but still loud enough to drown out everything else, and he did not hear the Ferret's approach or see him until he was two arches away, twenty meters, a flicker of movement across a patch of thinner dark, suddenly gone.

It was enough. Only the Ferret moved with such graceful fluency, an effortless slither.

The Ferret was standing in the dark, waiting and watching, and Klimenti held his breath and felt his heart pumping and was glad of the siren, because he had seen the Ferret first and now it was his ally, robbing the Ferret more than him. He opened his mouth and let the breath out; it was quieter than breathing normally.

The siren died away and the silence was so complete Klimenti heard his heart beating, hard hammer hits inside his chest.

The Ferret moved, a shadow within shadows, slipping forward across the arch, stopping at the next column. He was only ten meters away. Klimenti had trouble controlling his breathing. He was afraid the Ferret would hear the thunder of his heart. He was afraid the Ferret would sniff him out, catching the sour stink of his sweat.

For one moment of absolute terror, Klimenti was overwhelmed by a sickening heave of panic, his guts a steaming mash, and he wanted to run, to get away from the Ferret and his deadly knife. The prey was deadlier than the hunter, and he was afraid of his claws. The scar below his mouth was alive again and he felt once more the awful coldness of the cut, so cold it burned like dry ice, so sharp and quick he had not known what had happened until he felt the spurt of warm blood, and had screamed, a shriek of the same terror he felt now, his throat hot and dry and sore.

He was sure the Ferret would smell his fear.

And then the Ferret came to him, crossing the darkness between them like a cat, a ripple of eloquent grace, smooth and supple and quick. He was beside Klimenti before he sensed him and Klimenti felt rather than saw him jerk away, feeling the sudden surge of hard-muscled energy as the Ferret spun out, his knife arm drawing back to strike.

He was fast, but not fast enough because Klimenti clubbed him with the machine pistol and kicked him in the knee, going in hard with his heel. He heard the cartilage break and a grunt of pain. The Ferret's leg went from under him and he tried to counter it by throwing himself away, driving with his good leg. But once again, Klimenti was faster, going in and kicking again, breaking the knee this time. The Ferret screamed and went down, knife slicing the air in a deadly pattern of defense. Klimenti kicked him in the elbow and heard the knife fly away, clattering on the stones. He went down with his knees into the

Ferret's chest and throat, crushing off another scream, and with a vicious lunge he hooked the stocking around the Ferret's throat and crossed it, twisting and driving down with his knees, emptying out the precious last air. He drove down and twisted and choked, the Ferret thrashing beneath his weight, arching with unbelievable strength, even with one leg broken and useless, levering his good left leg, whiplashing with a last frenzy. He threw Klimenti off so that his only grip was on the stocking and Klimenti wrenched it, twisting, screwing, driving his knuckles in behind the knots, blocking off the carotid arteries until the Ferret stopped struggling; with the blood supply cut off to his brain, he had passed out.

Klimenti found the knife in the dark. It was a commando killing knife, fine-pointed for stabbing. The Ferret had added his own refinement, honing the blade to razor sharpness. He liked to cut as well.

Klimenti had not forgotten how he had killed Kharkov.

He knelt by the Ferret, waiting for him to regain consciousness. His throat was horribly swollen and blackening and Klimenti could clearly see where the four knots had bitten into the flesh. After a while, he put the knife point under the Ferret's left ear and cut into the sinew and felt him tremble. The Ferret was shamming.

"Open your eyes or I'll cut your throat," Klimenti whispered and pressed the point in deeper.

The eyelids opened and Klimenti gasped. The dark eyes that looked up at him had a quality he had never seen in them before: there was no hate, no feral rage, no vicious cunning. The eyes were soft and lustrous and moist, a woman's eyes fringed by long and delicate lashes. *A lover's eyes.* For a moment, Klimenti thought that he could not go through with it. He could not turn away from those eyes. They did not blink but gazed up at him steadily, with longing, full of entreaty.

Klimenti nodded, understanding him, telling the Ferret he knew what he wanted. The Ferret's mouth twisted into what Klimenti thought was a glimmer of a smile.

Gently, not wanting to hurt him now, he lifted the Ferret into a sitting position against the column. The Ferret grunted with pain but did not cry out or protest. Klimenti put the knife into the Ferret's hands, clasping them around the haft. The Ferret stared up at him, his eyes full of trust and knowledge. He was a child again, before the warping began. Slowly, Klimenti turned the Ferret's hands, reversing the knife until it was against his heart.

"Aaah," the Ferret sighed. His chest heaved. His hands clasped the knife in an iron grip. Klimenti would never again be able to break them free.

Klimenti thrust hard, surprised at how easily the knife went in, driving it into the Ferret's heart. For a moment life trembled through him, a last shudder of movement. And then it was gone and the eyes were dark and empty, and his head fell forward.

Klimenti stood up. The Ferret's hands still clasped the knife, buried to the hilt into his chest. He sat there, his head bowed over his hands, an attitude of prayer and contemplation.

Klimenti went deeper into the darkness. His whole body was quivering from the exertion and the loss of fear. He felt drained of strength and sat down and pulled his knees under his chin, hugging himself to stop the trembling, suddenly very cold, right through, even his heart. He sat thinking about the Ferret and the way he had died and what he had seen in his eyes, and all the time he was watching and listening, caught in a deadening calm, feeling no emotion whatsoever, neither triumph nor regret. Nothing.

Control came out of the night and knelt by the Ferret, saw what had happened and went quickly away. Klimenti saw who he was, was not surprised, and did not use the machine pistol. Instead, he followed him.

Half a block away, Spina sat in his blue Alfa Romeo, watching. He was alone but all he had to do was call up reinforcements on the radio and take them both. But he did not.

Klimenti turned, out of force of habit, checking behind. There was a movement in the car; he was sure it was Spina acknowledging his recognition. He went after Control, wondering why Spina had let them go.

Soon Klimenti realized he was not so much following as being led. Not once had Control stopped to check behind; he had not loitered, made any sudden changes of pace or direction or doubled back, all of which Klimenti would have expected him to do if he wished to protect his back. Instead he went steadily on, slowing his pace when he was well clear of the Colosseum, skirting around the Roman Forum and turning for the river. By the time they reached the Tiber they had fallen into a pattern, Klimenti thirty meters behind, walking almost in step and making no effort to conceal himself. It was early morning and in the quiet Klimenti could identify the scuffle of their footsteps falling together.

They walked past the spot where he had sat with Squirrel, retracing Klimenti's path across the Ponte Mazzini, heading into the narrower streets of Trastevere, the city's oldest quarter and site of one of the original villages. Now their footsteps echoed back from stone cobbles and brick walls. The streets became shorter and Klimenti closed the gap. Control made several turns and finally Klimenti came around a corner and found him standing halfway down the street, waiting for Klimenti to identify the house he was entering. Then Control went in and the street was empty.

Control had issued him an invitation. He had deliberately led him to what was undoubtedly a safe house. As they walked, Klimenti had considered all he knew about Control, the man and his circumstances, marveling at the way he had pulled it off in Moscow, under surveillance the whole time and yet still succeeding; only a superb professional could have done it, and an agent of that caliber did not lead you to a safe house unless he had good reason to believe—to *know*—that he was in command of the situation.

He wondered if Control, too, had seen Spina and was aware his cover was blown. From now on he was a hunted man, his usefulness ended, under a death sentence. The VFP would kill him rather than let him be taken alive. But while Control lived, he had no recourse but to kill Klimenti. The equation was simple and perfectly clear—either Control or Klimenti had to die. Yet his actions had clearly shown that he expected Klimenti to follow him into the house.

Klimenti waited at the corner, thinking it through. Finally, he understood it, the factor that gave Control the confidence to act with such audacity. Control had put his trust in Klimenti. He trusted him to understand it, knowing that once he did, he would not be able to walk away.

Klimenti went to the door and knocked. It opened almost immediately. Control had been waiting for him.

"Come in, Colonel," Bannon said, his thin cowboy face solemn and hard, and Klimenti stepped in and shut the door and saw her standing by him, small against Bannon's lean toughness, holding his hand. Her eyes were big with the shadows of pain and she was paler than he had ever known her and thinner, the withering of love and grief.

"Hello, Papa," Nadya said.

PART III

—

MOSCOW

1.

It was a warm day and the city was actually quite cheerful, waking from a long winter's sleep. Spring was a beautiful time anywhere in the world, but especially after the bitter dark of a Russian winter. On days like this, the citizens of Moscow rejoiced that they had endured and were eager to grasp all that the sun promised. It would be too soon gone and was not to be wasted. The city had hidden its winter wounds in swaths of greenery; there were many trees and parks and they blossomed with amazing swiftness.

Klimenti remembered Rome and the treeless piazzas and the shit-colored bricks and was glad he was home again. The sun beat down on his Zhiguli and he was sweating freely as he watched the Intourist parking area. An Intourist driver would pick her up at the Cosmos Hotel, where the switch had been made, and deliver her to the airport. The flight to Frankfurt left in an hour and Klimenti had come to make sure she got out. After giving it a lot of thought, he had decided that he could not come up with a better way of getting the assassins into the Soviet Union and their covers out and he had retained the system operated by Bannon. It had failed with Leonardo only because Tarabrin had been careless in his selection and the decoy had lost his nerve. But there was a big difference between Klimenti and Tarabrin, both in their professionalism and moti-vation.

Tarabrin, he thought wryly, had been drafted. Klimenti was a volunteer.

Klimenti wriggled and felt the sweat slide down his armpits, wondering how it was going with Bannon, who was now the world's most wanted man, hunted by every police force and intelligence agency on the planet, his face everywhere, even here in Moscow. He thought about the American a lot. Yesterday Nadya had put his hand on her swelling belly. She was four months pregnant.

Bannon had known that night in the safe house in Rome that he would not live to see his child born. He had led Klimenti there to take Nadya home, somewhere safe, where she and the child would not be fugitives. Klimenti had been moved by their stoicism and he realized Bannon and Nadya had been living in expectation of that moment for a long time. When the morning came, Bannon was gone. An hour later Klimenti had blown his cover. He had no choice; Spina had seen him and had done it already, anyway. It still worried Klimenti why the Italian had given Bannon the chance to go underground. Neither he nor Spina could report the other's hesitation without condemning his own. They had never discussed it. Yet every time they met, Klimenti was aware of a certainty that they had come silently to an understanding to let it rest.

Nikishov had said nothing, but Klimenti believed he knew the truth, that his plan to entrap Bannon had backfired. Nadya, of course, had lied. In her report she said simply that the decision to send her to Rome in pursuit of Bannon had been a mistake, alerting Bannon, who had not been deceived by her protestations of love. It was a relief to Klimenti to learn that Nadya was not a professional honey trap or a regular agent. She had been approached by Nikishov the morning after she had first slept with Bannon, when the relationship was still innocent and the attraction basically sexual. Nikishov had used a tried and tested ruse: he had appealed to Nadya's pride and her love for her father by saying that Bannon was an American agent, ruthlessly exploiting her to get at Klimenti. In her shame and chagrin, Nadya had wanted to break off the relationship, but Nikishov had convinced her the best way to protect Klimenti was to deceive Bannon into believing he was succeeding.

She had gone back to Bannon with smoldering anger. But hate is deep tinder, and so is love, and somewhere in the bitter Moscow winter nights, Nadya and Bannon had found truth in each other. Klimenti understood how it had happened; in fact, he had never understood his daughter more completely, or loved her more.

Since his return Klimenti had met Nikishov only twice and he had been withdrawn; Klimenti was sure he saw the telltale signs of heavy solitary drinking. Perhaps Nikishov's personal problems helped him understand Nadya's position. Perhaps Nikishov, like Klimenti, saw the relationship between Nadya and Bannon as a triumph of the human spirit over the impersonal machinations of the machine, the *apparat*.

Klimenti owed Nikishov. He would do all he could to help him.

Later, when they were back in Moscow, Nadya told him the child was her idea; she had not told Bannon what she was doing until she was pregnant. She had not cried once since the morning Bannon left. Nor had she smiled. At first her calmness had frightened Klimenti; she seemed too fatalistic, lacking a will to live, surviving only for the unborn child. He feared for her sanity, even her life, once the child was born. She had taken over Klimenti's shortwave radio and kept it tuned full time to the BBC. She was waiting for what she dreaded but knew was inevitable, news of Bannon's death, for she knew he would not be taken alive. She was holding her breath, holding down on everything, holding back her grief for that moment of final release, when she could mourn him with proper Russian wildness. The part of her that was peasant, her inheritance from Klimenti, knew instinctively what to do.

When Bannon was dead, she would breathe again. So, with sadness, Klimenti prayed for Bannon's death, the ultimate, inescapable release.

Nadya's Zapo was parked across the road, crushed down on its springs by a weight it was never meant to carry. Big Dog was slouched down in the seat, the steering wheel jammed against his chest, his head almost touching the roof. The tough little engine had almost expired getting him to the airport, struggling to reach a top speed of eighty kilometers per hour. Big Dog was guarding Klimenti's back. He was devoted to Zhenya, giving her all the loyalty he had once given the Ferret.

An Intourist Volga pulled into the parking area and the driver got out and opened the rear door. Marina, the prostitute from the Hotel Belgrade, got out, looking very Nordic in her smart Western clothes and with her hair dyed blond. She had made herself up to look older.

Even so she was a striking woman, immediately drawing glances. At last her dream was coming true; she was leaving the Soviet Union. In the West she would be free to become what she wanted and Klimenti hoped she would not become a whore again. Zhenya liked her.

By now Hilda, the woman whose identity Marina had adopted, was in the safe house, alone. She had gone there straight from the Cosmos. She was only thirty-four and almost as beautiful as Marina. She had been a nun, until she went to El Salvador and lost her faith in the Church and, for a while, in herself and her God. The Vigilantes for Peace had found her in Panama City and given her a new road to salvation.

Gorbachev needed strong men to back him more than ever before. He was increasingly being isolated as the protagonists to the left and to the right became more and more polarized. Once again, Russians were turning against each other while the Stalinists waited. . . .

Klimenti followed Marina into the airport terminal. He stood watching as she presented her passport and visa and then moved on to have her luggage checked. Marina did not turn to look back as she passed through the final checks and walked to the waiting lounge for the flight to Frankfurt. She was leaving Mother Russia without regret.

Klimenti went outside. It was so hot that Big Dog had got out of the Zapo and was leaning with his elbows on the roof, mopping himself with a handkerchief. He saw that Klimenti was leaving and squeezed back inside. Klimenti drove the Zhiguli across the outer ring road until he connected with the Minskaya Chausse. He turned southwest, leaving the city behind. It did not look so ugly or dramatic as it had that day he had driven south with Nikishov in the big black Chaika. The flat fields were showing green as the spring crops broke through. The dilapidated old *izbas* seemed more jaunty; you could differentiate the horizon, where the land ended and the sky began; the sky was blue and cloudless.

Winter's oppression had been lifted from the land and the people. Everyone, everything, felt—*was*—lighter.

Klimenti thought about Bannon again, remembering his beautiful physical arrogance, the languid threat that lurked within. Recruiting Navachine, making him believe he was working for the Israelis, and then delivering him to Nikishov, marking him out, had been brilliant as well as audacious. It had achieved exactly what Bannon wanted, setting the KGB and CIA at each other's throats. Bannon could have maintained his deception if he had not alerted the VFP conditioning clinic in Rome that Spina was onto them. It was one of those difficult responsibilities, in which Bannon's duty had overridden his personal safety. What was the fate of one man when measured against that of the eight assassins he saved? In any terms it was a good price to pay, and Bannon had paid it without hesitation. From that day Spina had become suspicious and had begun following him. He had also checked the weapons of all his marksmen in the Piazza del Popolo. None had been discharged. The shots fired that day had been Bannon's, shooting to silence Tabidze.

Bannon was a good man to have on your side. Klimenti could think of no greater tribute.

Spina, too.

Klimenti thought about Hilda. He had met her twice since her arrival four days ago. At the first meeting he had outlined the ground plan and instructed her to walk it, getting her line of sight. At the second, yesterday, he briefed her on the identity exchange.

"I know Bannon," she told him and, seeing how startled he was, she had smiled. "He told me to tell you. He also told me you'd be shocked. Not the information so much but at the breach of security."

"Is he alive?" Klimenti asked.

Hilda nodded solemnly, and Klimenti had a sudden intuition that Bannon, like Hilda, did not have long to live.

"Bannon and I were together once," Hilda said. "He told me to tell you that, too."

"You were a nun!"

"I was. But when I met Bannon in Panama City, I had stopped being a nun. I had stopped being many things I had once been. We had a lot in common. I'd been in El Salvador and lost my faith and he'd been with the Contras raiding into Nicaragua and lost his, too. We were both suffering, both orphans, lost people. For a while we saved each other."

She referred to him as Bannon. It was her way of showing her respect.

"That's where they found you?"

"Yes."

"Who?"

"No," Hilda said. "I won't talk about that."

It was strange that Klimenti didn't know who he was working for. It was also a relief. He could not betray them. He knew why he was doing it, and that was enough.

"Do you really think you can win?" he'd asked Bannon before they parted.

"Sure," the American had said, his faith strong again. "Do you know a better way?"

No, Klimenti did not know a better way. He didn't have Bannon's certainty. But he had come to believe the message: *It is just that the guilty few die, so that all the innocents may live.*

Hilda said sadly, "He was very gentle with me, the only man I knew. I'm not glad it happened but I'm not sorry either."

"You've found your faith again?"

"Yes, I've found God again. He was there all the time. It was I who got lost, not God, and I found my way back to salvation."

"If you've found your faith, why go through with this?"

Hilda took his hand. He felt like a child. "Salvation is personal. But faith is a selfish thing if you keep it just for yourself. For me, it is not enough. It was never enough. Christ knew that when He died for mankind. He showed the way."

Klimenti wondered if Wallheimer would understand.

When he left, she was praying. She would be praying now, talking to her God.

At 6:45 P.M., in another eight hours, Klimenti would help Hilda into her suit of plastic explosives and hide her and a rifle bag containing an RPG7 and two HEAT rockets in the back of a municipal works truck Big Dog was at that moment stealing. He would drive the truck to Marx Prospekt and park it on the edge of the Alexandrovsky Gardens. Workmen were laying a new drainage system and no one would notice a works truck left there overnight, particularly on a *subbotnik*, a Saturday of unpaid work, the spring cleanup when the citizens "volunteered" to scrub away the winter scourge; they were everywhere with their brooms and brushes and cans of paint.

From the rear of the truck, hidden by its tarpaulin, Hilda would have an unobstructed view of the ramp leading from the Kutafya Tower into the Kremlin.

At exactly 7:30 P.M., a Zil limousine would collect the Chairman of the KGB from his private Dzerzhinsky Square entrance below his third-floor office suite to drive him to an official dinner in the Kremlin in honor of the six new candidates whom Gorbachev had promoted to the Politburo after his recent purge; the Chairman was one of them. The Zil had the number plate MOC 001 and was easy to identify. Even so Klimenti would be sitting in a stolen Volga in Marx Prospekt and would send a signal, one bleep, on a radio to warn Hilda of the Zil's approach. She would have two minutes to kneel in the covered truck and line up the RPG7. The Zil would slow to a crawl as it went up the rampart, perfectly exposed, a clear shot. Hilda would not miss. She would have time for a second shot.

Klimenti carried a second radio. If Hilda failed to self-destruct, he would use it to detonate her suit of plastic explosives.

Klimenti drove to the village of Zhukovka on the bluffs overlooking the Moskva River. As it was Saturday, the village was crowded with well-dressed matrons who were shopping at "Khrushchev's store." Young men and women, *Sovetskiye detki*, the "Soviet kids," the children of the new rich, lounged around, eyeing each other, seeking weekend dalliances.

Klimenti went into the store and bought some Swiss chocolates for Nadya, five hundred grams of Hungarian pepper salami, a jar of Georgian olives and another of Polish dill pickles, and a bottle of Polish vodka. On second thought he also bought two bottles of Russian vodka. His father and Sabotka had moved into the dacha to look after Nadya, who lived there permanently. Nadya's love for her grandfather, always strong, had deepened with dependency, and Klimenti occasionally felt a tinge of jealousy when he saw them together. Sabotka kept out of the way and had turned out to be a natural farmer, planting every inch of available land with vegetables, scorning everything that could not be eaten. He had a passion for tomatoes; to Sabotka, they epitomized all the ripe abundance that had been denied him in the Kolyma.

The dacha belonged to Morozov, who put his foot down only when Sabotka started to dig up the Academician's rose garden. Morozov had declared "flower zones" from which Sabotka's spade was banned and checked them jealously every weekend when Klimenti and Zhenya drove him down from Moscow. With six adults in the small house, it was rather crowded but no one complained. In fact all of them secretly enjoyed the sense of family intimacy after spending the working week alone. Klimenti and Zhenya enjoyed the childish conduct of Sabotka and Morozov as they worked the garden, watching each other with distrust.

When he left the store Klimenti caught sight of Poluchkin as his bodyguard helped him from his private Volga. It was the first time he had seen the former Deputy Chairman since his return to Moscow and Klimenti was shocked at how quickly he had aged. His strong Commissar's face had collapsed on itself, concealing its awful wounds. The fires that had tormented his wounded eye seemed to have been extinguished. He used a walking stick. Without his duty to hold his tortured body together, it had begun to fall to pieces. Retirement was not a rest cure but a death sentence, and it saddened Klimenti to see him so. He was the last of a dynamic generation, the men who had saved the Soviet Union from the Nazis. And enslaved it, too, in the name of another tyrant.

Radchenko had taken Poluchkin's position as one of the KGB's six Deputy Chairmen. It was possible—indeed likely, considering Gorbachev's faith in the stumpy soldier—that by tomorrow he would be Chairman.

Klimenti continued south but did not go as far as Usovo, where it had all begun. Instead he turned off the main road and took the paved access road that led past an almost continuous settlement of dachas to the Moskva River. Morozov was influential enough to have snared a block of land fronting the forest belt that protected the river from development. The dacha had been converted from an old stone coach house and loft, onto which Morozov had added a kitchen and bathroom. It was cool in summer and warm in winter and capable of year-round use, although it was seldom occupied in winter.

Morozov was watering his budding roses, going to great pains to make sure not a drop fell on Sabotka's tomatoes. Apart from their horticultural range war, he and Sabotka got on fine. The old *zek* had begun sniffing around among the summer neighbors, seeking a willing widow or even a bored wife, and Morozov was quietly hopeful he would find a pair, one for him, too; Sabotka's obsession with sex had awakened in him a forgotten need and he was careful to pamper the former convict's prickly pride. "Hey, nephew!" he shouted, waving a bony fist in greeting. His hearing had deteriorated but he still refused to retire.

Zhenya heard him and came out of the bathroom. Her face was clean-scrubbed, and she had tied a towel into a turban and, as always, Klimenti felt a heart-kick of pleasure. She was barefooted and wearing shorts and a loose-fitting shirt, and he felt her smooth, tight skin and smelled her freshness when she came up and kissed him and took the bundles from his arms.

"Nadya's sleeping," she said. "A walk in the woods'd be nice."

Her gray eyes laughed up at him with pixyish mischief and Klimenti felt a rush of blood as he watched her take the shopping into the house. Her legs were already tanned from the sun. She was, in fact, tanned all over. When she came out she carried a quilt and gave Morozov a brazen smile. He knew what it was for, and she knew it and proudly did not give a damn. Morozov sighed wistfully as he watched them go and hoped that Sabotka would be back soon with good news. The old Academician's delight in Zhenya was surpassed only by his love for Nadya, and he had taken to inviting Zhenya to lunch every Friday in Moscow's most expensive restaurants, flaunting his importance outrageously.

"I felt her tummy," Zhenya said as they walked into the woods, hand in hand. "It's going to be a boy."

Klimenti nodded happily, content with her company.

"Women know these things," Zhenya told him cheerily, weaving her mystery around him.

They spread out the quilt and undressed each other with languid sensuality and made love in the noonday sun speckling down through the birch trees. They came here every day, shedding the restraints the crowdedness of dacha life imposed on them. Later they refreshed themselves with a plunge in the river; the water was still cold and the shock of immersion had them gasping for breath and laughing. Invigorated, they went back to the dacha, walking quickly, for they were hungry, their feet driven by thoughts of pepper salami and olives and fresh bread and vodka.

Sabotka was back from his hunting and watched them approach with ill-disguised envy. Klimenti's father had come out to enjoy the sun.

"It's a hard trial," Sabotka sighed. "The warm spring sun, a river, two beautiful young women, a full belly three times a day."

"A trial! It's your idea of paradise," Klimenti's father said and regretted it immediately, for joyful wickedness flared into Sabotka's eyes.

"Only if you're the one who's doing the screwing," Sabotka said, rubbing his hands with pleasure. It had been a good morning. "And that's a problem I think I've finally got licked."

Maybe he'd let Morozov in on it—and maybe he wouldn't. He laughed aloud at the thought of the Academician's hangdog disappointment. Damnit, how could he refuse the bony old bugger?

"Where's Nadya?" Klimenti asked as he came up to them.

"Listening to the radio," his father said. Morozov was with her. They took it in turns, especially when she was listening to the BBC.

"I'll go," Zhenya said and was on her way to the house when a wild cry came from within. Klimenti went past Zhenya at a run and burst into the house. Morozov was standing helplessly, his arms out, trying to hold Nadya, who flailed at him, fighting him off, clawing her face and drawing blood.

"No!" she moaned and then a shriek. "No!"

But her eyes held the truth and, with it, despair.

The radio had announced that in Washington, the director of the CIA was dead. The VFP had struck there first. The director liked to play an early Saturday morning round of golf, and they had got him with a high-powered rifle as he teed off on the second hole.

Nadya began keening, rocking herself, and when Klimenti went to hold her she cried out, "No!" and stepped back, tearing at herself again, ripping her shirt and clawing into her breasts.

"Leave her," Zhenya said from the door where she stood with Klimenti's father and Sabotka. It was a voice of command and the men obeyed without protest, heads down and humble before her strength. Zhenya went to Nadya, who did not resist, and Zhenya took her in her arms and began keening and rocking, her cheek against Nadya's so that their tears ran together, salting their mouths. Their cries were shrill and terrible and yet beautiful and both Klimenti and Morozov shivered as they walked out into the hot sunlight, where his father and Sabotka waited anxiously.

"The VFP released the assassin's name," Morozov said, forgetting to shout. His hands were shaking. What he had seen inside had unnerved him more than anything he had experienced in the cellars of Stalingrad.

He had self-destructed, of course.

"She'll be all right now," Klimenti's father said. His voice was trembling and Sabotka put an arm around his old comrade's shoulder and led him to a bench set against the side of the house to catch the sun. Morozov went and sat with them, three grayheads, shaken by the savagery of young grief.

Klimenti stood by the door. He was not sure what he felt more strongly, sadness or relief. At last Nadya had begun grieving, and to all things begun there was an end, and with each ending there was a new beginning.

He would tell Hilda about the director of the CIA before she went out to die. She had known it would be Bannon. He remembered her solemn eyes.

The sounds from within the dacha had become a low moan, throbbing with pain. Already the catalytic process of cleansing was beginning. Klimenti did not cower from the keening, as the others did. He rejoiced in it, proud of his two women, sure now of their power to heal themselves. All of them.

The sun was hot on his face. Klimenti felt calm and prepared, remembering the American who would give him his first grandchild.

If the child was a boy, they'd call him Harry.

ABOUT THE AUTHOR

PHILIP CORNFORD was born during a cyclone in tropical North Queensland, Australia, in 1940. He was a newspaper reporter for twenty-five years, covering stories in the United Kingdom, Canada, the United States, Europe, Southeast Asia, India, and Pakistan; and was a war correspondent in Afghanistan and Lebanon. He has sailed yachts around both Cape Horn and the Cape of Good Hope and crossed three Australian deserts in the quest for stories. Since leaving newspapers in 1982, he has written a feature film, a television mini-series, and two novels. He has three adult sons and lives in Sydney.